THE SHAPE IN THE NIGHT

Mark's thoughts were shattered when a loud roar suddenly filled the night.

The howl rapidly built to a piercing shriek and then immediately faded. It echoed in the forest for several seconds, leaving behind an uncanny stillness.

Mark's eyes darted back and forth as he tried to pinpoint the source of the sound. His grip on the hatchet tightened as he stood up, crouching defensively, and scanned the surrounding darkness. Every wavering shadow cast by the fire seemed fraught with danger as he waited for the sound to be repeated. When it was, it came with a deafening roar and a flurry of dark motion as something charged out of the forest and headed straight at him.

For a single heartbeat, Mark was paralyzed with fear. He felt more than saw the two eyes that were locked on to him. They burned with a cold, green fire. There was a heavy thumping sound of feet trampling the forest floor as the black shape rapidly closed the distance. Long arms reached out. Firelight reflected off two sets of long, curved claws . . . .

THE MOUNTAIN KING

RICK HAUTALA

LEISURE BOOKS NEW YORK CITY

To Craig Goden, Dave Hinchberger, and Steve Bissette.

A LEISURE BOOK®

June 2001

Published by

Dorchester Publishing Co., Inc.
276 Fifth Avenue
New York, NY 10001

ISBN 0-8439-4887-6

Printed in the United States of America.

THE MOUNTAIN KING

"Wolves will dig up the graves of your ancestors, and panthers will gnaw on the bones of your children. . . ."

Chapter One
Sudden Snow

"I think we're screwed!" Phil Sawyer said. His mouth was a thin, tight line above his coat collar as he looked over his shoulder at his friend, Mark Newman.

"Not quite yet," Mark replied.

They were high above the timberline on Mount Agiochook in Maine, near the New Hampshire border. It was a beautiful, brisk mid-September afternoon, but a swift storm cloud was sweeping out of the west like a raven's wing—silent and black. With rising apprehension, the two men watched as shadows rippled like a gush of dark water across the contours of the distant hills. Behind the swift-moving front was a slanting gray haze of precipitation.

"If that's just rain, we're only going to get a little wet," Mark said.

"What do you mean *if?*" Phil asked. There was a tremor in his voice as he wiped sweat from his forehead with the back of his hand. "I'm sweating my *ass* off. It can't be cold enough up here to snow, can it?"

Mark shook his head and squinted as he watched the fast-approaching shadow spread over the valley below. Within a matter of minutes, the blue sky had turned soot gray.

"Wouldn't be all that unusual. 'Specially this time of year," he said, sniffing the rapidly chilling air. " 'N it sure as hell looks like a snow squall to me."

Phil's eyes widened as they shifted back and forth between his friend and the onrushing storm.

"What the hell can we do? Where can we go?" He was fighting hard to keep his voice steady. "Shit! If we were down the trail a bit, under the trees—"

"Yeah, we might just get wet," Mark finished for him. "This high up, though, it more than likely's gonna be snow."

"Enough to screw us?" Phil asked, glancing around the bare, rock-strewn slope. The summit, perhaps a mile away, looked like a dark, carved stone pyramid against the fast-moving clouds. The wind gusted with a sharp, knife-edge chill.

Phil was an inexperienced hiker, and it was obvious to Mark that he had no idea what to do in an emergency. As far as Phil was concerned, this was supposed to be nothing more than a pleasant, late summer three-day hike through Grafton Notch, heading northwest from Hilton, Maine, to Gorham, New Hampshire, along twenty-four miles of the Appalachian Trail. It had never crossed his mind that it might snow this early—not in September.

"I think we're just gonna have to hunker down and wait it out," Mark said. He pointed to the right, where the slope seemed to drop off. "There's a ravine over there that'll give us some shelter."

Shrugging his shoulders to settle his backpack, he started across the steep rock face with Phil close at his heels. The air went suddenly still, hushed with expectancy as the sunlight darkened. Every tone of color, every detail on the mountainside shifted as though seen through dark sunglasses. When the two men were less than halfway to where Mark was taking them, a low, mournful sound almost like a bestial cry filled the air.

"What the hell?" Phil shouted, stopping in his tracks and looking behind them.

"Just the wind," Mark said, smiling grimly.

"No fuckin' way," Phil said, narrowing his eyes and staring back at the way they had come. He clenched his gloved hands into fists and crouched as though preparing for an attack.

"You've heard too many of those stories about this place being haunted," Mark said with a laugh as he indicated the summit with a waving gesture. "Come on. If we don't find some shelter soon, we're gonna get slammed!"

The stormy darkness closed around them like an enfolding blanket, but there was no silence beneath that blanket. Shrill whistling noises rose higher as the wind sliced over the rocks. Then came a loud roaring sound as the clouds unloaded and snow and ice began to pelt the mountaintop.

"Hurry up!" Mark said, having to shout to be heard above the shrieking wind.

Strong, fitful gusts slammed the two men from all directions. Pellets of ice rattled around them like a hail of bullets. Within seconds, their view of the summit was lost as the mountainside became glazed with a coating of ice that made even the most carefully placed step treacherous.

"I told you!" Phil shouted. "We're *screwed!*"

Snuggled down inside the collar of his jacket, Mark barely heard what his companion had said.

"We just gotta make it to the ravine," Mark replied, waving his arm encouragingly.

Both men crouched low to prevent the strong blasts of wind from knocking them off their feet and sweeping them away. Skittering like overgrown rock crabs, they forged ahead in the direction Mark had indicated. The wind-driven snow thickened until neither one of them could see more than a few feet in any direction.

"Stay close!" Mark shouted. "I don't want to lose you!"

"I don't either."

Glancing over his shoulder, Mark saw Phil struggling along behind him, no more than a slouch-shouldered, gray blur inside the snowy maelstrom. He cursed himself for not thinking and acting more decisively. They hadn't planned on any rock climbing, so they had brought along no climbing ropes. At the first sign of bad weather, he knew he should have taken the time to tie themselves together using a tent rope or something.

But it was too late now.

Any delay before they found shelter from the cutting wind and snow might prove dangerous, possibly fatal. Waving his arm encouragingly, Mark forged ahead, keeping a watchful eye out for any hazards that might suddenly appear out of the storm.

"It can't be much further now!" he shouted.

His face and hands were numb from the cold. His feet kept slipping out from under him as the ice coating on the rocks grew thicker and slicker. Up ahead, through the twisting sheets of snow, he finally saw a dark gash in the landscape.

It had to be the ravine he was looking for.

Trusting that Phil was right behind him and could see where he went, he scrambled on all fours over to the edge of the opening. Satisfied that this would at least keep them out of the direct arctic onslaught of wind and snow, he slid down into the little bit of shelter the steep drop-off afforded. He could barely hear the scrambling sounds Phil made as he followed him down into the narrow gorge.

"Hey, some fun, huh?" Mark said, smiling as he turned to look at his friend.

What he saw was a mask of misery, despair, and worry. Phil's face was raw and red; his eyes were watering from the stinging cold and wind. Phil tried to say something, but his teeth were chattering so badly, whatever he was trying to say was lost.

"What do you say we open up the tent and cover ourselves?" Mark said.

Even though he was wearing gloves, his hands were nearly frozen. His fingers fumbled to untie the carrying case. Thankfully, the wind didn't reach its icy fingers down into the ravine where they crouched; so although it seemed like long minutes, it was really only a matter of seconds before they flapped open the tangle of blue nylon and pulled it over them like a huge, puffy comforter. In an instant, near total darkness embraced them, and the shrill whistle of the wind lessened.

"All right," Mark said. "We're fine for now."

Both men were panting heavily as they supported the tent with their hands to give themselves a bit of breathing space. "You hanging in there?"

For a moment, there was no response from Phil; then he sighed deeply and said, "Yeah—I guess so."

Buffeted by occasional gusts of wind, the chilled tent material shifted and crinkled. It sounded like a blazing fire all around them, but it offered only a fraction of the heat a fire would. A cold, dark, stony silence enveloped the two men as tightly as the storm that embraced the mountain's summit.

"How—how l-l-long do you t-t-think this will l-l-last?" Phil asked through chattering teeth.

Mark shook his head. "No idea. Can't imagine it'll last very long. These things tend to blow themselves out pretty fast. The weather forecast said it was going to be nice all weekend."

"Wh—what if w-w-we have to s-s-stay up-p-p here like this all n-n-night?"

"We'll just have to wait and see," Mark said.

He was shivering too, but he didn't want to let it show because of how obviously unnerved Phil was. Besides, he could already feel a change in temperature beneath the tent from their trapped body heat. He was confident they would weather this just fine.

For several minutes, both men were silent as they listened to the wind shrieking all around them. Neither could deny that—at times—it sounded more like a wild animal, bellowing its rage at the storm-tossed sky. The tent flapped like a gigantic flag in a hurricane wind as ice and snow pelted against it like a shower of stones.

"Well, aren't you *glad* we decided to go for a hike this weekend?" Mark asked.

A deep, hissing sigh was Phil's first response; then he whispered, "Shit, man, this is making me wish I had never even moved to Maine."

A sudden gust of wind jostled the tent, almost pulling it away. The men clutched the tent's edges and held them down until the breeze lessened. Then they settled back against the hard rocks, grateful, at least, that they were out of the direct wind.

"Yeah, that's right," Mark said. "You're not even from around here, so you probably haven't heard the stories about this place."

"Stories? What kind of stories?"

"About the mountain being haunted."

"Yeah—sure," Phil said, sniffing with laughter. "I'll just bet . . ."

He started to laugh louder, but then he fell silent when, from far off, they once again heard a low, moaning howl. It rose gradually, warbling higher and higher until it suddenly cut off as though swept away by the wind. Although neither man said it out loud, they both thought it sounded much more like a howling animal than the wind. Mark could feel the spike of Phil's fear like a tangible entity inside the tent.

"That sound—" Phil said, "tha—that's just the wind, right? Just blowing over the rocks, echoing like in a cave or something . . ."

"Of course it is," Mark replied.

In truth, the sound had tingled a nerve inside him, too. He had lived in this area his whole life and had been to the top of Mount Agiochook an uncountable number of times. In all those times, he could remember hearing a sound like that only once before, and that had been on a humid August night with no wind whatsoever. He couldn't stop himself from adding, "Unless, of course, it's the ghost that supposedly haunts the top of the mountain."

Chapter Two
The Zipper

"Wh—what ghost?" Phil asked, unable to disguise the winding tightness in his throat.

"Ahh—I'm just pulling your leg," Mark replied as he shifted uneasily on the cold rocks, trying to get comfortable. He wished to hell the storm would just pass by so they could get out from under the tent and see how bad their situation was. "You know how it is with places like this. There are dozens—probably hundreds of stories about campers getting lost and disappearing up here on the mountain. Hell, every summer at least one or two people get lost out here. Usually out-of-staters. And there are always reports of people seeing and hearing things."

"Hearing things . . . You mean like that noise we heard a while ago?"

Mark shrugged, making the tent material crinkle.

"Yeah—well, hell, there are Indian stories about

this mountain that go all the way back to before the white man came. Even the name of it—Mount Agiochook—means something like 'dwelling place of the Great Spirit' or something like that. They say the Indians never dared to come up here because they thought the summit was haunted by the spirits of their dead warriors. The *evil* ones, of course. And something called the—the *Pomoola*, some sort of demon or devil, is supposed to live up here."

Mark sniffed with laughter.

"You know how it is with these things," he went on. "Just myths and rumors. Never any real accurate descriptions or authenticated sightings of . . . *whatever* the hell they think might be up here."

The two men were silent for a few moments as they hunkered down in the close darkness and listened to the wind howling all around them. They were both tensed, waiting for that particularly mournful sound to be repeated, but they heard nothing except the wind and the harsh hiss of snow and ice, blowing over the tent and rocks.

"Sounds like it might be easing up," Mark said after a while. The tent was trapping their body heat a bit too well. Sweat glistened like spring dew on his face and ran down his neck.

"Think we ought to give it a shot?" Phil asked. He wasn't even trying to disguise the nervous tremor in his voice.

In answer, Mark lifted one corner of the tent and looked up out of the ravine. The last traces of the storm were skimming away to the east like windblown tatters of black cloth. The men shook the coating of ice and snow off the rumpled tent, then stood up and stretched their cramped arms and legs. From the west, slanting afternoon sunlight glanced off the fresh coating of ice. The sloping plane of rocks leading up to the summit looked like it was made of pure crystal.

"I guess *this* is why they call them the White Mountains, huh?" Phil said.

"Beautiful, isn't it?" Mark replied, inhaling deeply and squinting as he surveyed the area. "But you know, as beautiful as it is, you have to respect wilderness like this. A storm like the one that just passed would have killed less experienced hikers."

"Less *lucky* hikers, you mean!" Phil said, forcing a chuckle. "You keep forgetting that, until I moved here from New York last year, I spent most of my life in the city."

"More's the pity," Mark said, clucking his tongue as he began folding up the tent and stuffing it into its carrying bag. "Well, I may make a mountain man out of you yet, but I think conquering Mount Agiochook is going to have to wait for another weekend. Maybe next spring. What do you say?"

"Sounds reasonable to me."

"Yeah, we probably ought to head back down to the tree line before dark."

Once their gear was packed and ready, they started out with Mark in the lead. As beautiful as their surroundings were, the going was extremely tough and slow. Both of them kept slipping and sliding, too many times to count. Luckily, neither one of them got seriously hurt. All the while, though, Mark was dreading what he knew was ahead. The trail this high up on the mountain wasn't much of a problem, even with the ice-coated rocks and fitful gusts of wind that trailed after the storm. But they were on the eastern slope, and Mark knew they were going to have to cross the narrow ledge called The Zipper. The name was pure hikers' gallows humor for the sound a careless hiker would make if he went over the edge and slid down the sheer rock face drop of almost fifty feet.

Zip-p-p and you're gone!

They had crossed The Zipper on the way up. Now they would have to cross again on their way down. If the cliff edge was covered with ice, that was absolutely going to be the most difficult part of their descent.

But they didn't have a choice.

They didn't have the equipment necessary to camp above the timberline, and there was no alternate route around The Zipper unless they swung far around the summit and connected with the Round Top Trail on the western side.

Mark was going to stop and mention his concerns to Phil, but then he decided not to give him anything more to worry about—at least not until the time came. They hiked on, mostly in silence.

"Do you think, once we get back down, we maybe should forget about the whole thing?" Phil asked. He was several paces behind Mark, but his voice echoed clearly from the rocks around them.

Mark was still dwelling on how they would get past The Zipper, so he didn't answer right away. He was racking his brain, trying to think of another way off this damned mountain.

"Let's just get down from here first," he replied without looking back. "Then we'll see what makes the most sense."

"Oh, Jesus!" Phil said as soon as the narrow ledge came into view. "I forgot about this place."

Several feet from where the trail funneled down to

the ledge, Mark drew to a halt and glanced back at his friend. "You aren't intimidated by it, are you?"

Phil smiled thinly as he studied the narrow shelf of rock they would have to cross. Altogether it was more than forty feet to the next wide-open area; at its worst, the ledge was no more than six inches wide for a stretch of more than twenty feet. A fresh coating of ice reflected sunlight that hurt the eyes if they stared at it very long.

"And to answer your next question—" Mark said. "No. There's no other way around it, not unless we want to backtrack for a couple of miles."

"Shit!"

Both men pondered their situation in silence for a moment. Then Phil said, "Do you think the heat of the sun might melt it?"

Mark shook his head. "Not today. Can't be more than a couple of hours of sunlight left. Besides, we're on the eastern side of the mountain. Sunlight won't be hitting this ledge until tomorrow morning."

"*Shit!* And *shit* again!" Phil said. Then, sucking in a deep breath, he added, "Well, if we're gonna do it, let's do it and get it the hell over with. You want me to go first?"

Mark nodded agreement, figuring he would be of more help if he was behind Phil. In truth, he knew if either one of them went over the edge, there wouldn't be much the other could do. Hell, in the next few minutes, they *both* might find out for themselves exactly what sound a hiker made while sliding straight down The Zipper.

"Be careful now, and remember one thing," Mark said.

"Yeah—what's that?"

"If you *do* fall, try and look over to your right. You'll get one hell of a great view on your way down."

"You're a real laugh riot, you know that?" Phil said.

He sucked in and held his breath, and then, keeping his face turned toward the rock wall, started inching his way out onto the ledge. The wind was strong, spinning up little tornado funnels of snow and ice. With every step he took, his feet almost slipped out from under him, but he pressed himself hard against the rock wall and kept pushing forward.

"How's it going?" Mark asked, careful not to sound too uptight.

"It's a real bitch!"

"Well, you're doing just fine. You're already more than halfway past the narrowest part. Just keep close to that rock, and you've got it made."

With less than six feet to go, Mark's worry for Phil began to subside as his worry for himself began to rise. Then, in an instant, it all changed. Like a vision from a nightmare, Mark saw Phil's left foot slip to one side. The sudden shift of weight threw him off balance. Paralyzed by a sizzling jolt of fear, Mark watched as his friend swung around. His hands clawed viciously for something to grab on to, and he snagged a small outcropping of rock, but it gave him only a moment's reprieve. His gloved fingers couldn't hold. They let go, and with a single trailing shout, Phil disappeared over the edge.

"Jesus! No! Phil!"

Mark's voice as well as Phil's fading scream echoed from the surrounding mountains, but what resonated most in Mark's ears was the harsh *zip-p-p-ping* sound Phil's body made as he slid down the ice-slick cliff side. In the echoing silence that followed, Mark stared at the empty ledge, momentarily incapable of believing that his friend was gone . . . just like that.

Mark edged as close to the brink as he dared to go and looked down, but the slanting rocks blocked his view of the base of the cliff. Cupping his hands to his mouth, he shouted, "Yo! Phil! Phil! Can you hear me?"

No response from below. There was just the hollow moaning of the wind as it gusted around him.

Mark knew there was a broad expanse of sloping rock ledge below The Zipper that ended with an even bigger drop-off that had been dubbed "Katherine's Leap." There was a story from the 1800s about a young girl who, despondent about a failed love affair, climbed up there and leapt to her death on the rocks below. The only way down to the base of The Zipper was from the bottom. Short of falling down there himself, Mark had the challenge of getting safely across The Zipper before he could climb down to check on Phil. And there was no guarantee he could make it, but he knew he had to if only so he could find out what had happened to Phil.

Bracing himself, Mark started edging out onto the narrow rock shelf. His feet kept threatening to slip out from under him, but he choked back his fear and moved steadily toward the other side. When he was halfway across, he twisted around and looked down to see if he could catch a glimpse of Phil. He wasn't prepared at all for what he saw.

Thirty feet straight down, almost lost in the gray swirl of blowing and drifting snow, he saw a dark, crumpled form that had to be Phil. He wasn't moving. Mark was about to call out to him when he saw something else—an indistinct shape that moved across the rock ledge toward the base of the cliff. Out on the exposed cliff above Katherine's Leap, the wind was strong. It swept the newly fallen snow high into the air. At first, Mark thought he was imagining this, that what he saw was nothing more than a shadow created by the windblown snow; but then he saw that the shadow had substance, and it was moving straight across the rock-strewn ledge toward his dead or seriously injured friend. Mark almost lost his balance as he craned his head around to watch.

"Jesus, no! No way!" he said as his view of the thing became clearer.

For a panicked instant, he thought it might be a bear, coming to attack Phil. Then he saw that whatever it was, it sure as hell wasn't any bear. It walked erect, swinging its long, thick arms at its side like a lumbering human being.

Was this another hiker? Someone who had seen Phil fall and was coming to help?

Mark sucked in a breath and was about to call out, but then he froze.

No, this wasn't a human being . . . not unless it was someone dressed up in animal skins. The creature moved over the icy rocks with a surefootedness that no human hiker could ever have achieved. Even through the swirling snow, it looked large, at least six feet tall by Mark's estimate. He only caught glimpses of it, but he noted that it was dark-skinned with a sloping forehead and backward-pointing skull. It walked with a shambling gait that reminded Mark of the way apes move.

Swiftly and silently, the creature came over to the foot of the cliff where Phil lay. It leaned over him as though inspecting him and then, with a quick, sure motion, lifted Phil's limp body and swung him over its shoulder. The creature glanced back and forth, sniffing the air as though sensing danger. Then it let loose a loud, echoing howl that sounded uncannily like the mournful wailing sound Mark and Phil had heard earlier. Moving with a swift, effortless stride, as though Phil's added weight meant absolutely nothing to it, the creature shambled away and was soon lost in the blinding haze of blowing snow.

"No! No *fucking* way!" Mark whispered. He shook his head as if that would help his numbed brain accept what he had just seen. His pulse was slamming like a hammer in his neck, and his entire body was trembling. He had to have imagined it all!

After staring awhile in dazed disbelief down at the foot of the cliff where his friend should still be, he braced himself and finished making his way across The Zipper. But even after he was on relatively solid ground, he couldn't stop trembling.

He knew he had to move fast. If he didn't get down off this mountain before nightfall, he would die of exposure . . . or worse! He might end up another victim of whatever the hell that creature was that had just carried Phil away!

Chapter Three

Two-timer

"I dunno . . . I just don't like doing it like this, you know?"

"Don't worry. It's not *your* problem."

"Bull*shit* it's not my problem! If your husband ever finds out I was here, he'll make *sure* it's my problem, all right!"

"Yeah, sure, but he'll never find out. Come on, Dennis! Jesus! . . . Sit your butt down! Relax a little, will you? God, you make me nervous when you pace like that!"

"I'm sorry, okay? I—I just *can't* relax!"

"How about a beer, then? Maybe that'll help you unwind . . . unless you want a little of . . . *this*."

Even with her hands cupped over her ears, Sandy Newman wasn't able to cut out the voices that drifted up to her bedroom from the living room. She took a deep breath and closed her eyes tightly as she cringed beneath her bed covers, trying her hardest not to think about what was going on downstairs. Of course, knowing Polly, her stepmother, as she did, it wasn't all that hard for Sandy to imagine what was happening.

"*God damn you! God damn you both!*" Sandy whispered in the darkness underneath her bedcovers.

It was a little past nine o'clock on Saturday night, but Sandy had gone to bed early because she hadn't been feeling all that well. Her stepmother had accused her of faking being sick so she could miss school on Monday, but that wasn't true at all. Sandy's senior year at high school had started just a few weeks ago and, so far, was going great. She was actively looking forward to finishing off her high school years with straight A's so she could get into her first-choice college, either Bates or William and Mary.

No, she really *had* been feeling lousy for the past three days, and right now, more than anything else, all she wanted to do was sleep.

But the voices coming from downstairs—and what she imagined Polly meant when she said Dennis might want some of *this*—were keeping sleep at bay.

"I'm telling you to forget about it, all right?"

"Yeah, but I—"

"Come on. Sit down on the couch next to me. Let me give you a back rub."

"I don't *want* any goddamned back rub!"

"Then how about a *front* rub?"

"Jesus Christ, Polly, will you cut it out? Shee-it! It's one thing to fool around a little back at my place, but

I—I don't know . . . I mean, you really want to do it right here, right now?"

"You got any better ideas?"

"I dunno. I mean, in your own home—in *Mark's* home? Key-rist! It—it just doesn't feel right."

"Hey, let *me* feel it. I'll tell you if it *feels* right or not." Polly let loose a low, malevolent laugh.

Their voices were as clear as if the two of them were standing right there in Sandy's bedroom beside her. Sandy closed her eyes and focused on the shimmering darkness behind her eyelids, trying to shut out the voices. She desperately wanted to clear her mind, but there were just too many questions.

Like *why* was her stepmother acting like such a . . . such a *slut? Why* had her father ever married her in the first place? Had she always been like this, or was this something new?

As much as Sandy hated the word *slut*, it seemed to fit Polly perfectly.

This certainly wasn't the first time Sandy had suspected her stepmother of fooling around.

Oh, no.

She had seen the way she and Dennis Cross, the man who was downstairs with her now, acted whenever they met around town. Dennis worked at the Mobil station on the corner of Main Street and Salmon Road. Yeah, good old Dennis. All-around gas jockey and married woman's stud. Just last week, when Sandy and Polly had driven in to the Mobil station to get some gas, Sandy had wondered why both Polly and Dennis had chuckled so hard when he asked if she wanted him to check her oil.

While Dennis might not be as handsome as he seemed to think he was, he wasn't exactly ugly, either; but how could her stepmother cheat on her father like this? How could she stand to be touched by those callused, work-stained hands? Had he even tried to clean the oily black rings from under his fingernails before coming over tonight?

Other *why* questions filled Sandy's mind.

Like: *Why* couldn't her father see what was going on? He certainly wasn't stupid, but he had taken off for a weekend hike with his friend from work as if everything at home was just peachy-keen. Could he *really* be totally blind to it all? Or was he pretending that he didn't see it . . . for whatever reason? Maybe he did know about it and had simply given up. After all, two failed marriages wasn't much of a confidence builder.

And why, Sandy thought, *why* did she feel so nervous, so tormented about telling her father about all of this?

She knew she should. She knew she *had* to, but doubts and worries and concerns filled her. How would her dad react? Would he even believe her? They'd had more than their fair share of conversations about how he thought Sandy wasn't giving Polly a fair break. He objected to the way Sandy treated his new wife with such cool, aloof distaste—at best.

But what did he expect?

Sandy's *real* mother had left home when Sandy was only ten years old, and in all that time she had never called her or visited her. She might as well be dead, as far as Sandy was concerned. Maybe she was. Either way, it was the kind of loss she knew she would never get over. Things weren't supposed to happen that way. And no matter what her father thought about his first failed marriage, Sandy wondered how he could ever expect her to accept, much less like, someone like Polly.

And thinking of Polly, how would *she* react if—no, not *if—when* Sandy told her father what she knew?

Would she deny it all? Would she make up some half-assed excuses? Would she break down in tears and say she was so-o-o sorry and promise never to do anything like that ever again?

Or would she try to get even with Sandy? Maybe she'd have Dennis or someone else hurt her.

Sandy found herself wishing—*praying* that her father would come home tonight—right now!—unannounced so he'd catch Polly and Dennis screwing around in the living room. That sure would make things easier. Then he'd *have* to deal with it!

Once again, the discussion downstairs drew her attention.

"Don't worry about her, all right? She's asleep."

"Yeah, but what if she can hear us?"

"She's asleep, I tell you. . . . She went to bed early, saying she was sick. And even if she isn't asleep, so what? What's she going to do, huh?"

"Maybe tell her father . . . or maybe he'll find out for himself."

Yes! Please, yes, God! Sandy thought, clenching her fist desperately.

"Christ, how many times do I have to tell you this? Mark isn't going to be home until tomorrow night. He's going to call me when he and Phil—"

"Phil Sawyer, right?"

"Yeah. When he and Phil get out of the woods and find a phone booth somewhere near Gorham, New Hampshire. I have to drive out there to get him, I suppose, if Sandy's sick. So just forget about Mark, all right? He's a good thirty miles away from here. Come on—"

Sandy's heart pulsed heavily in her neck, almost choking her when she distinctly heard the rustle of clothing and the rasping sound of a zipper being opened.

"You like this . . . don't you?"

"Ummm."

"Well, then . . . come on. Get the rest of those clothes off and show me a little appreciation, why don't you?"

Sandy took a deep breath, held it a few seconds, and then let it out in a slow, rattling hiss.

"You'll be sorry . . ." she whispered to the close darkness under her bedcovers. "Just you wait! You're gonnabe*real*sorry,you—youtwo-timinglittle . . . *slut!*"

Chapter Four

Down Off the Mountain

Flames rose like slick, orange tongues high into the night sky, but the glow of the campfire could only reach so far; beyond the sphere of light, the night curled around Mark like a dark, threatening beast. The air was numbingly cold as he sat with his back to the blaze, his every sense tuned to the brooding silence of the surrounding forest. Every vagrant breeze, every snapping branch drew his attention. It was well past midnight, but he knew sleep wouldn't come as he watched and waited with his camping hatchet clutched tightly in his right hand, a cold cup of coffee in his left.

"This is ridiculous . . . absolutely fucking *ridiculous!*" he muttered, but he didn't dare drop his guard even for an instant. Danger was a palpable presence, hovering all around him.

During the torturous hike down the mountain,

Mark had seriously begun to doubt what he had seen. The creature *couldn't* have been what he had thought it was! Other than moose and bears, there simply weren't any animals that big in Maine. And none of them, not even bears, wandered that high above the tree line. It was totally insane to think there might be something like a mountain gorilla or whatever on Agiochook! What he had seen must have been something else, something distorted by the snow and the glare off the ice.

Or his panic.

In all likelihood, it probably had been another hiker, coming to Phil's rescue. Or else it had been Phil himself. Maybe that dark shape at the base of the cliff had been Phil's discarded backpack, and the shambling figure had been Phil, hobbling off to find his own way off the mountain.

But no matter what he thought, Mark couldn't deny the sense of danger he felt pressing in on him from all sides. In a deep, primordial way, he sensed that he was being stalked. From all the years he had spent hiking, hunting, and camping in the Maine and New Hampshire woods, this was the first time in his life that the forest had actually held the threat of genuine, deadly menace.

"But it *couldn't* have been what I thought it was," he whispered. "No fucking *way!*"

His eyes darted to one side, following the faint crackling of leaves from somewhere deep in the darkness.

I was just freaking out a little . . . because Phil fell off the cliff . . . I probably imagined the whole damned thing! he thought, even though it felt a lot like he was trying to convince himself.

But whatever the case, Phil was in all likelihood still up there on the mountain, maybe still crumpled at the base of The Zipper, either dead or seriously hurt. Mark had been so intent on getting down off the mountain before dark that he hadn't gone down to check. Now that he had time to think about it, he knew he still wasn't thinking clearly, that he was letting his imagination get carried away.

And worst of all, he couldn't decide what to do next.

Should he continue down off the mountain so he could go find help? Or should he head back up and do whatever he could to find and help his injured friend, even if it cost him his life? Maybe Phil had staggered away from the cliff and was now lost on the mountaintop.

Mark's thoughts were shattered when a loud roar suddenly filled the night.

"*Jesus Christ!*" he shouted as he leapt to his feet.

The howl rapidly built to a piercing shriek and then immediately faded. It echoed in the forest for several seconds, leaving behind an uncanny stillness.

Mark's eyes darted back and forth as he tried to pinpoint the source of the sound. His grip on the hatchet tightened as he stood up, crouching defensively, and scanned the surrounding darkness. Every wavering shadow cast by the fire seemed fraught with danger as he waited for the sound to be repeated. When it was, it came with a deafening roar and a flurry of dark motion as something charged out of the forest and headed straight at him.

For a single heartbeat, Mark was paralyzed with fear. He felt more than saw the two eyes that were locked onto him. They burned with a cold, green fire.

There was a heavy thumping sound of feet trampling the forest floor as the black shape rapidly closed the distance. Long arms reached out. Firelight reflected off two sets of long, curved claws. An instant before it was too late, Mark ducked to one side as he swung out wildly with the hatchet.

The blade connected with . . . something.

The shock of contact almost tore the hatchet from his hand as a loud howl of pain and anger filled the night, so close his ears began to ring.

The figure streaked across the open fire-lit space like a midnight freight train and then disappeared into the inky gloom of the forest. A thin haze of yellow dust from the forest floor swirled in its passing, the only visible indication that *something* had actually gone by. Silence dropped like a blanket over the forest, broken only by the raw gasping of Mark's breathing as he crouched defensively and scanned the shrouded forest.

"*Come on! Come on, you son-of-a-bitch!*" he yelled.

His insides were trembling wildly as he shook the hatchet above his head.

"*Come back here and fight me!*"

He paused and listened, but could hear only the thundering rush of his pulse in his ears. The night was cold and silent, but it still seemed laden with danger. Mark stood rooted to the spot, his body tensed as he waited for another attack. Already his exhaustion and the sharp bolt of fear were giving this encounter the eerie dissociation of a bad dream, like it hadn't really happened. Shuddering wildly, he ran his hand across his face.

"Jesus! Gotta get a grip . . . Gotta get a grip," he muttered as he shifted back and forth, straining to catch sight or sound of whatever had just tried to kill him.

Nothing but impenetrable silence filled the forest.

After a while, Mark relaxed his guard a little and sat back down at his campfire to watch and wait. He knew he would be inviting another attack if he started traveling before morning, so he piled more wood onto the fire and let the blaze reach high into the night sky.

Hours later, just as the first hint of dawn tinged the eastern sky, he packed up his few supplies and started out on the trail again, his hatchet in hand. He was determined, now, to get back to town and report the incident. After that, he would return to the mountain to search for his friend. Only this time, he was going to come well armed.

All day, Mark hiked through the forest, keeping to the blazed trail that was the shortest route out. His progress was aggravatingly slow because he was tensed, expecting to be attacked at every turn. Shortly after noontime, nearly faint with exhaustion, he paused for a quick lunch at the crossing of the Bull branch of Sunday River. He was still more than five miles from the nearest road, and from there he had no idea how long it would take to walk or hitch a ride back to Hilton.

The day grew steadily warmer. He wanted desperately to rest but didn't want to chance getting too comfortable and falling asleep. He was surprised that all day he hadn't encountered any other hikers. Perhaps the bad weather yesterday had discouraged any plans anyone might have had for a weekend hike up Agiochook. The rushing roar of the Bull River masked all other sounds, so he ate hurriedly and then continued his trek, knowing that he had to get out of the woods before dark.

Although he never saw or heard anything to indicate that he was being pursued, he still couldn't shake the persistent feeling that *something* was tracking him. Worn down by exhaustion, he began to imagine that he was being pursued by Phil's ghost, which was hungry for revenge for leaving him dead back at the base of The Zipper. The bright, sunlit forest held dark, menacing shadows that seemed to coil as they waited to spring out at him. The pleasant songs of birds and the soft hiss of the wind in the pines overhead were grating, like fingernails being raked across a chalkboard. Even the blue vault of the sky seemed somehow dull and lowering, as if it wanted to press him down into the cold, dark earth.

Mark was nearly delirious when, just before dark, he staggered out of the woods onto Route 26. With the sun setting behind him, he guessed home was in the opposite direction, so after taking a quick swig of water from his canteen and adjusting the backpack on his shoulders, he started down the road, heading east. He was anxious to meet the first car or truck going in his direction, but there was never much traffic on a road like this, so he walked on as darkness spread from the woods like an ink stain over the road. Dazed from fatigue, Mark didn't even hear the semi bearing down on him until a blast from the air horn shattered the night.

"*Chrtst!*" he shouted as he wheeled around on one foot and snapped up his thumb. There was a loud gasp of air brakes and the soft, tearing sound of tires skidding on asphalt as the truck downshifted and slowed to a stop. Mustering a last burst of effort,

Mark walked up to the sixteen-wheeler as the passenger's door swung open. He heaved his backpack off and clambered up into the cab.

"Thanks for stoppin'," he said breathlessly.

The driver looked at him with a curious expression. "Thought I'd better. I wouldn't want to read in the newspaper how the next truck passin' by turned you into street pizza."

In his exhaustion, Mark missed the joke as he settled back against the seat and took a deep, shuddering breath.

"If you don't mind me sayin', you look like shit warmed over," the truck driver said.

Mark rolled his head and stared blankly at him as he nodded. "Umm. You wouldn't by any chance be heading to Hilton, would you?"

The driver stepped down hard on the accelerator and revved the engine. The truck growled like an angry beast in the night, and Mark couldn't help but remember the howl that thing had made when it had attacked him the night before.

"I'll be passing through," the driver said. He popped the gear shift into first and stepped on the accelerator. The truck lurched forward.

Mark didn't respond. His head was thrown back against the seat, and he was already sound asleep.

Chapter Five

Back Home

"Before I drive you home, I'd like to take you over to the hospital, if you don't mind."

Guy LaBrea, Hilton's police chief, was frowning as he watched Mark, who was sitting in his office, shivering as he sipped at a cup of coffee. It was his second cup within fifteen minutes. Guy didn't like the way Mark's eyes were so red-rimmed and runny. His skin looked sallow, almost sickly; and from what Mark had just finished telling him, Guy wasn't so sure Mark was thinking all that straight, either. "Not packing a full seabag," as he liked to say.

"I don't need to go to the hospital," Mark said, his voice soft but firm as he fought to maintain a rational tone. "All I need is a hot shower, maybe a bowl of soup, and a good night's sleep and I'll be fine."

Guy almost said something but remained silent.

"What I want you to do is get a search party organized to go up there and find Phil."

"Sure, sure I will. I'll get on the phone and do just that . . . just as soon as I haul your ass into the emergency room so the doctor can check you out."

Mark shook his head angrily.

"For Christ's sake, Guy! For all we know, Phil's still up there, either dead or unconscious at the base of The Zipper. If *you* don't do something about it, then I sure as shit will!"

"No need to get all wound up, okay?" Guy said. "Truth to tell, I don't see how Phil could've lasted the night up there—not with how cold it's been getting lately."

"Christ! What are you talking about?" Mark shouted, but then he checked himself, sat back, and forced himself to relax. Then, against his will, he started snickering softly to himself. "Oh, I get it. You don't believe me, do you?"

"Well, I think you maybe—"

"Are delirious, right? Maybe a little out of my mind or something, is that it?"

"Not at all."

Mark set his coffee cup down carefully on the desk beside him, fighting hard to keep his hand from trembling.

"Well you've got it wrong, Guy! *Dead* wrong!" He clenched his hands into fists and pounded them in frustration against his legs. "I *know* what I saw, all right? I know it!"

"Yeah. You say you saw Bigfoot."

"Jesus Christ, Guy! I don't know what the hell it was! I just know I saw this . . . this *thing* that had no right being there. It sure as shit looked like some kind of bear or ape or something, but . . . but—fuck! I don't know . . ."

Guy let loose a small laugh that fueled Mark's anger.

"You won't think it's so fucking funny after you send someone out there and find Phil's body, now, will you?"

"No, no," Guy said, suddenly sobering up. "It's not that at all. It's just—for a second there, I had this image of Bigfoot, you know, hitchhiking from Oregon to Maine."

"Jesus *Christ!* This is Phil Sawyer we're talking about!"

"I know, I know," Guy replied. "Look, Mark. As soon as you agree to let me take you into the emergency room for a quick checkup, then I'll get on the horn to the Forestry Department and—"

"*No!* I want you to do it *now!*"

Guy sat back and rubbed his hands down the side of his face. "Christ, it's dark as shit now. We can't get someone up there till morning, anyway."

"I don't give a shit! Don't they have helicopters with searchlights or something?"

Guy nodded. "Well, yeah—I suppose they do, but still, I don't know if I—"

"Forget what I said about what I saw or what I *think* I saw, all right? Just report a missing hiker and get those Forestry assholes out there so they can earn their pay this week!"

"Yeah—well," Guy said, "they earn their pay as it is, I suspect. Hell, just last July they *more* than earned their pay when they spent nearly the whole month looking for those two hikers from New Jersey that went missing. Remember that?"

"Shit, yes. I was out there beating the brush a few

days, myself. But this is *Phil* we're talking about! This is the guy I work with at the mill day in and day out!"

"Okay, okay," Guy said, reaching for the phone. "I'll give Fred Gibbons a buzz."

Guy held the receiver tightly while he looked up the number, then punched the buttons. While he was waiting for someone to answer, he added under his breath, "And right after that, I'm taking you down to the hospital . . . even if I have to cuff you to get you there."

"All right . . . all right! I'll go!"

Mark stayed where he was while Guy made the call. He was thankful that Guy omitted any mention of the "huge, dark, furry shape" he had seen. Then, once he was assured that a group of rangers would organize a search and go out first thing in the morning, he followed Guy out to the cruiser for the short drive to the hospital. He thanked Guy and told him he didn't expect him to wait while the doctor checked him over. Once the brief examination was completed, Mark got dressed and walked out into the lobby. He intended to phone home for Polly or Sandy to come and pick him up, but he saw Guy sitting there, waiting for him.

"I told you you didn't have to wait for me."

"Hey!" Guy said with a shrug. "What are friends for? So, did you get a clean bill of health?"

"Just what I told you. Dr. Blaine said all I needed was some rest."

"Cruiser's waiting."

"Let me give Polly a quick call, let her know I'm on my way home."

After phoning home, Mark and Guy walked back out to the police cruiser. They spoke very little on the short drive out to Mark's house on Cole Hill Road.

Mark still seriously doubted how much—if anything—of what he had seen up on Mount Agiochook had been real. The glaring, antiseptic reality of the hospital had reduced the threat of that large, shadowy figure until it seemed to have no place whatsoever in the real world. Still, Mark couldn't shake the gnawing worry that his eyes *hadn't* been playing tricks on him, that he *had* seen—something. But how could it have been real?

If his fatigue and fear hadn't weakened him to the point of hallucination, that meant there really might be something—something *dangerous* up there on Agiochook!

"What the fuck is Dennis Cross's car doing in your driveway?"

Guy's voice broke into Mark's reverie. He shook his head and looked up as Guy slowed down in front of Mark's house. The cruiser's headlights swept like a probing searchlight across the front of the house and the red Mustang parked there.

"Goddamn! That son-of-a- . . ."

Guy took a deep breath and held it as he pulled to a stop at the bottom of the driveway and killed the engine. Mark already had his door open and was halfway up the driveway, moving with a speed that bespoke his anger. Someone was sitting in the car. Mark knew it had to be Dennis because he was so damned fussy about his '83 Mustang he would never let anyone else drive it. He grabbed the car door handle and flung the door wide open, ready to drag the man out onto the lawn if he had to. Guy hustled up the walkway a few steps behind him, his hand on his service revolver just in case things got out of hand.

"Hey!" Mark shouted, leaning his head into the car. "What the fuck do you think you're doing here?"

"Ahh, I was—I was just on my way to work. Third shift for the next few weeks at the mill, you know?" Dennis stammered. He gripped the steering wheel tightly with both hands as if he didn't dare let go of it. "My—uh, my damned car started acting funny on me, so I pulled in to see if I could borrow some tools to fix it."

Mark scowled as he studied Dennis, trying to read if there was anything else beneath the stupid-ass grin he was wearing.

"So, you got it fixed now?" Mark asked.

Dennis nodded. "Yeah—yeah. Just blew a spark plug is all. Put a new one in, no sweat."

"Your hands don't look like someone who's been working on a car."

"No, well, your—ah, wife let me wash up after I was done," Dennis said. His voice had a slight tremor to it that made Mark suspicious, but he forgot all about Dennis Cross as he slammed the car door shut, turned, and went up the side stairs to the kitchen door. He hardly noticed as Dennis started up his car, backed out onto the road, and drove away.

"Hey! Polly! I'm home!" Mark shouted as he strode into the kitchen. A moment later, Guy appeared in the doorway with Mark's backpack in hand.

For a moment, there was nothing but silence. Then from somewhere inside the house a voice called out, "Mark? Is that you?"

Scuffing footsteps approached. Polly walked briskly into the kitchen but then stopped short, her eyes widening with surprise when she saw Police Chief LaBrea standing there beside her husband.

"Oh, Mark!" Polly said. "You don't know how worried I've been, wondering when you were going to call. I've been waiting all afternoon for you to call from New Hampshire." Frowning, she stared back and forth between the two men. "Is something the matter?" She looked past them, out the window toward the driveway.

Mark frowned deeply, then hiked his thumb toward the kitchen window. "Dennis Cross was just leaving when we drove up."

"Yeah, he—uh, he stopped by on his way to work. God, Mark! I was worried sick when you didn't call this afternoon. Guy. Why are you here? Has there been any trouble?"

Mark sighed heavily as the accumulated fatigue of an entire night without sleep dropped onto him like a hammer. His legs suddenly felt unable to support him. He nodded slowly. "Yeah—Phil got hurt up on the mountain yesterday."

"Jesus, is he all right?"

Mark shook his head. "No. I don't know. He got lost. I don't know where he is."

"Oh, my God!" Polly said, taking a backward step and leaning against the counter for support. Mark thought her reaction seemed just a bit exaggerated, but he didn't say anything. He was ready to collapse, and all he could think about was how incredibly nice a hot shower and then bed were going to feel. He was about to thank Guy and excuse himself when the kitchen door burst open, and Sandy walked into the kitchen. Her jacket was draped over her arm, and her book bag was slung over one shoulder. She stood in the doorway a moment, panting heavily. Sweat darkened the ringlets of hair above her forehead.

"Hello there, beautiful," Mark said, moving over to her and giving her a big hug. "Who you running from?"

"Huh? Oh, no—no one," Sandy said. "I saw the cop car out front and sort of panicked, I guess."

Her eyes danced from side to side as she looked at her father's face close up. Her lower lip was trembling as she opened her mouth as if to say something else, but words wouldn't come.

"Hey, are you okay?" Mark asked, sudden concern darkening his brow.

Sandy bit her lower lip and nodded once, quickly. "Yeah. Sure. I was going to . . . I was just heading back from Karen's house, and I . . . Dad, we have to talk."

"Not right now, sugar-babe," Mark said, letting his shoulders drop wearily. "I've got to get some shut-eye before I fall apart."

He took a shuddering breath and let his head drop. His eyelids felt as though heavy weights had been suspended from them. Dark, swirling waves were crashing inside his head, tugging at him, threatening to pull him under even as he stood there, staring blankly at his daughter.

"Now if you'll excuse me," he said. His voice was no more than a whisper. "I'd better get upstairs. See you in the morning, all right?" He started out of the kitchen, then stopped and looked back at Guy. "Oh, and thanks for the help."

"No sweat," Guy replied as he carefully placed the backpack down on the floor.

"Let me know when you hear from Gibbons, all right?" Mark said as he walked into the hallway toward the stairs. His feet dragged heavily on the floor.

"I swear to God, if you don't follow up on this, I'm gonna go back up there myself and find him."

"You just get some rest for now," Guy said. "We can talk about it in the morning."

"You bet the Christ I will!"

Chapter Six

Night Sweat

Mark awoke with a cry and found himself sitting up in bed with his hands clutched like claws in front of his face. His eyes were wide open, and his gaze frantically darted around the darkened room, seeking something to anchor onto. A thin line of silver moonlight that edged the window shade drew his attention.

"Huh? What is it?"

Polly's sleepy voice drifted to him from the darkness like a soft, feathery touch.

"—you awright?"

Mark's throat felt scorched. He couldn't take a deep enough breath to speak. Cold sweat bathed his face and neck, making him shiver violently. Although he realized—now—that he was wide awake in his bedroom at home, the nightmare he had just wrenched himself out of still clung to his awareness and wouldn't let go. He sighed heavily and closed his eyes, trying to shut off the terrifying flood of images that filled his mind, but that only made them worse; they swept across his mind's eye like a fast-moving storm cloud. . . .

Phil Sawyer was dead at the bottom of a cliff that telescoped dizzily in and out. The friction of his rapid slide down the cliff had ripped off most of his clothes, so his battered, nearly naked body lay on the rocks spread-eagled, half buried in a snowdrift. His skin was nearly as white as the snow that covered him. His empty, sightless eyes, glassy with dead, black centers, stared up at a twisting, steel-gray sky. A tight grimace exposed large, flat teeth.

Somehow, Mark found himself hovering high above the scene, circling like a hunting hawk as he watched a dark, monstrous black shape resolve from the gloom that surrounded Phil. There was a brief impression that the creature had simply materialized out of the smooth stone side of the cliff, large and powerful, with rounded, thick-muscled shoulders that were covered with a thick mat of dark fur. It looked almost as if one of the many granite boulders on the mountainside had suddenly sprung to life.

Mark stared down from an incredible height at the creature. His throat was paralyzed. He was unable to scream or make even the tiniest of sounds as he watched, horrified, as the creature raised the dead man from the ground and, supporting him from behind, placed its huge, clawed fingers on either side of the dead man's bare chest. Then the creature—whatever it was—began to bend Phil backwards, continuing to apply steady pressure until ribs started to crack. Splintering bones sounded like a string of exploding firecrackers as Phil's torso was split open like a plump, ripe fruit. Uttering low growls of pure bestial pleasure, the creature stuck one hand into the gaping hole in Phil's body and fished around until it yanked free a fistful of dripping red guts. With a deep sigh that sounded almost sexual in its release, the creature stuffed the steaming gobs of organs into its mouth and began to chew noisily. Thick, bloody chunks of tangled meat fell to the ground with a sickening wet sound.

Then Mark's perspective in the dream suddenly shifted.

With steadily mounting terror, he watched as he started spiraling downward, closer . . . ever closer to this horrible scene. He felt a dark, sickening rush of vertigo. After a moment, the creature sensed him and, snorting viciously, looked up at him. When it saw him, a wide smile spread across its gore-stained face. Mark was falling with steadily increasing velocity. His arms flapped helplessly as he stared down into eyes that burned with a cold, animal fury . . . and intelligence. The creature raised its arms as though to catch him, but just before he fell into the creature's waiting embrace, Mark's terror—at last—became too sharp, too keen to bottle up inside. He found the strength to scream, and he woke up just as he realized the creature's blood-streaked face was that of Dennis Cross.

"Yeah," Mark said, gasping. "Yeah, I—I'm all right."

He swept the blankets aside and swung his feet to the floor. A chill danced up the backs of his legs to his shoulder blades. Every breath he took came in a raw, watery gasp. His pulse was pounding heavily in his ears, throbbing as if someone had a hold on his neck and was squeezing.

"It was just a . . . just a dream."

"Umm," Polly said. She rolled over and pulled the blankets up over her head.

Mark took a deep breath to steady himself, but the cold rush of fear, and the impression that he was still falling, plummeting downward, gripped him as he looked around the darkened room. He wanted to get up and go into the bathroom for a drink of water, but he was afraid that his legs wouldn't be strong enough to support him. Every muscle in his body was wire-tight and trembling. He shifted forward as if to stand, but then dropped back down on the edge of the bed. Pressing both hands hard against the sides of his face, he breathed into his cupped hands and listened to the thin rattle.

"Stop it! Jesus Christ! Just stop it!"

But even his own voice, rasping in the dark, set his nerves on edge. Dream images mingled in his mind with memories of what had really happened up there on the mountain until he was no longer sure exactly what he had seen.

Could there *really* be some kind of creature up there? Something like a Bigfoot or whatever?

It seemed impossible . . . a figment of his over-stressed imagination. He knew rationally that there could be no such thing, but if that wasn't the case, what in the hell *had* he seen? How could he verify what he had experienced?

The only sure thing was his conviction that his friend, Phil Sawyer, *must* be dead by now up there on Agiochook.

"Polly . . . can we . . . talk?"

Polly's only answer was the steady rhythm of her breathing as she slept . . . or feigned sleeping, Mark thought with a warm flush of anger.

He wanted to nudge her to wakefulness, but another wave of black terror washed over him, paralyzing him. His chest ached, his heart thudded against his ribs. He was burning to take just one deep breath, but couldn't. The night closed around him, pressing in from all sides with a steadily rising pressure. His hammering pulse throbbed in his throat so hard he thought he might choke.

"Polly!"

His voice sounded strained and oddly distant to his ears, and that only increased his rising panic.

"Oh, *shit!—Jesus!—Shit! . . . Polly!*"

"Ummm . . . wha—?"

"Polly, I . . ."

Before he could say anything more, he twisted around and reached for her, practically lunging at her in the dark.

"Mark! For Christ's sake! I was sound asleep!"

"Polly, I'm really freaking out!" he blurted, his voice nearly breaking on every syllable. "I—I've got to talk to you!"

There was a rustle of sheets as Polly rolled over to face him. Unseen in the dark, her hand reached out, touched his sweat-slick shoulder, and began to rub in small circles.

"You feel cold as death."

Mark shifted his position so he could wrap his arms around her, clinging to her with a desperate strength that made him tremble. He was close to tears but fought them back.

"No, it's just that . . . after what happened . . . up there on the mountain . . . it was so . . . so . . ."

He took a shuddering breath.

"I've never been that scared before in my life!"

"I know, I know," Polly whispered, her mouth so close to his ear he could feel the warmth of her breath. "It must have been terrible. I was worried, too, waiting all day for you to call."

Mark held her tightly and buried his face in the crook of her neck. Unable to hold back any longer, he let the warm tears flood from his eyes. His shoulders shook as deep sobs racked his body.

"It's late, honey," Polly whispered as her hand continued to make lazy circles on his sweat-filmed back. "And I'm beat. Can this wait till morning? . . . Huh?"

Mark tried to answer, but the cold, lifeless fingers he felt wrapped around his throat were tightening. Waves of panic swept through him, each one stronger than the last. Spiraling circles of light flashed across his vision, blinding him as he tried to sink down into the warmth of his wife's embrace.

But as much as he tried to feel safe and secure, he also sensed the vast distance that separated them. Perhaps it was just from the stress of what he had been through over the past few days. Perhaps it was the residue of his dream and the horrible monster he had created using Dennis Cross's face. Or maybe it was the surge of suspicion he had felt when he had seen Dennis's car in his driveway, a suspicion that he had felt before but had tried his best to block out and deny.

Or maybe it was something else entirely.

All he knew right now was that, even in the arms of his wife, he felt as lonely and lost as an abandoned child. He knew that neither Polly nor anyone else would ever be able to fill the deep, hollow hurt inside him.

"No, I . . . I . . ." he said, but then his voice trailed off as he rolled away from Polly. Her hand dropped to the mattress, and almost instantly her breathing resumed the deep, steady rhythm of sleep.

A stinging loneliness filled Mark. Tears streamed from his eyes and soaked into his pillow. After a moment, he closed his eyes and prayed to relax, but he couldn't get rid of the thought that, like Phil, he had been crippled and left for dead at the top of a rocky, windswept mountain. Through his seemingly bottomless misery, he had only one clear thought, one faint spark that held his attention as he lay there trembling in the dark.

I have to do something about it!

Even if it's as little a thing as going to visit Phil's wife tomorrow morning, or as big as packing up a week's worth of supplies and heading up to the mountain and staying there until I find him, I *have* to do *something!*

Chapter Seven
Mutilations

The night was clear and cold. A fingernail slip of moon rode high in the western sky, lining the distant jagged edge of the White Mountains with faint silver. Dusty stars sprinkled the sky like powder on blue velvet as a brisk wind shifted across the land from the north, bringing with it the promise of approaching winter.

Within the silent shadows of the woods that bounded Josh O'Connell's seventy-five-acre farm, a large shadow moved with surprisingly fluid ease along a hidden forest trail. It made almost no sound other than a near constant sniffing as it tested the wind. The creature stealthily approached the edge of the forest and looked out across the open field toward O'Connell's barn and farmhouse. Faint moonlight edged everything with silvery lines which, to the creature's light-sensitive eyes, fairly vibrated with purple energy.

The creature cringed back into the brush as it stared across the wide expanse of open ground. Having lived its entire life high up on the bare, rocky slopes of the mountains to the north, it was not afraid of open spaces. It felt comfortable being exposed to the wide arc of sky. But here in the lowlands, it sensed danger, and it knew caution.

After two days of following the trail of the hairless, two-legged creature it was pursuing, the creature was hungry. Hot animal smells wafted on the night breeze to its sensitive nostrils and stirred the beast's hunger until it became a burning craving in the pit of its belly.

Somewhere back on the trail, just as dark was falling, it had lost the scent of the small creature it had been tracking. After leaving a clear trail the whole way down the mountain and into the forest, the tracks of the small creature had suddenly disappeared on the wide strip of trail that was as hard and unyielding as the mountaintop that was the beast's domain. The small creature's sickly, sour scent, spiced with fear, had been lost beneath the stinging stench of heavy smoke. The creature had no knowledge what fear was, but it knew fire and smoke well enough to respect and avoid it.

Not having paused to eat for two days and nights, it was now nearly starving. The hollow gnawing in its stomach had replaced everything else in the creature's mind, and the smells drifting across the field meant only one thing—food . . . hot-blooded, raw, red meat!

After watching silently for a long time and sensing no immediate danger, the creature finally left its hiding place and shambled noiselessly across the open field, all the while sniffing the air for danger. From far off, it heard the sound of a dog barking; but the more immediate, the more demanding sound was the soft lowing of the cows inside the barn. As the heated animal smells got steadily stronger, a red haze filled the creature's brain until, by the time it reached the back of the barn, it was nearly crazed with bloodlust.

With a single thundering roar, the creature reared back on its hind legs and smashed both fists against the weathered side of the barn. The impact smashed the gray planks inward like they were made of balsa wood. In an instant, the night was filled with the sounds of panic-stricken animals as the creature burst through the splintered wood and roared its challenge. It smelled as much as saw the terrified cows as they stomped and bellowed frantically in their stalls. Raising its clawed hands high above its head, the beast charged the nearest animal—a year-old calf. The creature smashed through the flimsy wooden barrier and, with one mighty swipe of its claws, laid open the calf's flank and belly.

The calf bleated, wild with pain as it staggered and fell, and its guts dropped in a wet heap onto the straw-covered floor. The calf tried to get up to run, but its feet got tangled in the uncoiling ropes of its own intestines, and it fell. Lurching to one side as its thin front legs folded up, it rolled over onto its side, all the while bleating in terror.

Leaning forward, the creature picked up the steaming pile of organs with both hands and stuffed them into its mouth. The red haze clouding its vision began to clear as stringy meat, barely chewed, slid down its throat. Hot blood streamed from the corners of the beast's wide mouth as it lifted the dead calf from the ground and thrust its face into the bloody gash. It made sickening slurping sounds as it feasted on the tender flesh and internal organs.

Inside the house, asleep on the couch with an empty beer can in one hand and the television remote control in the other, Josh O'Connell came instantly alert when he heard the sudden uproar coming from the barn. Leaping to his feet, he ran into the back entryway, grabbed his high-powered flashlight and twelve-gauge shotgun from the closet, and charged out into the night. The chilled night air made him shiver as with brisk, steady strides, he crossed the dooryard and entered the barn by the side door. The cone of light from his flashlight weaved and danced around the barn, illuminating the rising cloud of yellow dust and hay chaff that hung suspended in the air, looking like thick, sulfurous smoke.

"Just what the fuck's going on out here?" Josh shouted.

Bracing the flashlight between his arm and chest, he checked to make sure the shotgun was loaded. He clicked off the safety and, holding the shotgun in one hand, the flashlight in the other, swept the area back and forth. His eyes blinked rapidly as he tried to pierce the cloud of dust that obscured the stalls at the far end of the barn. The cacophony of terrified animal sounds filled the barn, hurting his ears, but below that, Josh heard something else—a low, grumbling, snorting sound that reminded him of what a pig sounds like when it's slopping down.

At first, all Josh knew was that *something* was going on here. His first thought was that some kids might have tried to sneak into his barn to play a practical joke, maybe do a bit of cow-tipping, but the joke had backfired. When he finally saw the massive dark figure squatting in the calf's stall at the far corner of the barn, his resolve suddenly wavered.

"Jumped-up Jesus H. Christ!"

In spite of the chilly night, sweat broke out like dew across Josh's forehead. The shotgun felt suddenly heavy and useless in his hand. The flashlight beam wavered as he pointed it at the dark shape, unable to believe what he was seeing. A large, dark-furred animal, looking for all the world like a huge bear, was crouching in the stall, holding the limp carcass of one of last year's calves up to its mouth and munching on it like it was an ear of corn. From beneath low-hanging eyebrows, eyes glistened green in the glow of light as they stared back at him.

Josh's heart gave a quick, hard double thump in his chest as an icy ball of fear filled his stomach. A corner of his mind was telling him that this was completely crazy, that he had to be imagining this, but then the creature pulled its face away from its bloody feast and, snarling, let the carcass slide from its grip to the floor. Every muscle in Josh's body was frozen. The pressure in his bladder grew intolerable.

"What the fucking *fuck?*"

The creature skinned back its upper lip, exposing a row of long, bloodstained teeth as it made a sharp, high barking sound. A chunk of cow flesh hanging from one corner of its mouth fell onto its blood-smeared chest.

Josh almost dropped his flashlight as a wave of dizziness swept through him. The sudden fear of being anywhere near this beast filled him with a desire to race back to the house, but he was rooted to the spot, unable to turn and run. He couldn't take his eyes off the creature, not even for a second. With mounting terror, he watched as the beast slowly stood up to its full height. With a blubbering snort, it spread its arms wide. Even within the spacious area of the barn, it looked huge—at least seven feet tall.

"No . . . no," Josh whispered as he took a quick step backward toward the door. His hands were aching from the tight grips he maintained on the flashlight and shotgun. He was trying to calculate how fast he could run—and how fast this beast might be able to run—if he made a break for it, but his leg muscles wouldn't obey the commands of his brain. At last, though, he remembered the shotgun in his hand.

"Whatever the fuck you are," Josh said, getting a slight grip on the situation, "you've done et your last cow of *mine!*"

He raised the shotgun slowly so as not to spook the beast; then, squinting down the barrel, he squeezed the trigger.

The blast of the shotgun slammed like a sledgehammer through the tumult in the barn to be followed immediately by a howl of pain and outrage. The animal's left shoulder jerked backward as a thick splotch of blood spurted like a splash of ink into the air.

Josh almost dropped the flashlight as he crouched down and fumbled to pump another shell into the chamber. His body was trembling uncontrollably. He was afraid that he had already pissed his pants, but he was determined to fight and not run unless it was absolutely necessary. To his amazement, the wounded animal didn't charge. Instead, it looked down at its wounded shoulder, grunted softly, almost pitifully as it touched the wound, and then wheeled around and bolted out through the hole it had made in the back of the barn.

Knowing that the creature was wounded and no doubt dangerous, Josh waited until he was sure it was gone before he cautiously approached the dead calf's stall. His stomach did a sour flip when he saw what was left of the calf. Broken ribs surrounded by tangled shreds of bloody meat glistened wetly in the glow of the flashlight. The floor of the stall was slick with dark, fresh blood. The calf's eyes were wide open and glistening like wet marbles that stared sightlessly up at the dark corners of the barn ceiling.

Choking back a rush of vomit, Josh stepped over the calf's carcass and outside through the opening in the barn wall. For a moment or two, he saw nothing as he swept the field with the beam of his flashlight. Then, far out across the field, down by the woods that lined the south creek, he saw a black silhouette moving silently toward the trees. Whatever it was, it walked with a curious, off-balance gait. Josh hoped that he had wounded the creature seriously, perhaps fatally. The night wind carried a faint echo of the animal's pained howl.

"Yeah, God *damn* yah! That'll teach yah, yah *bas*-*turd!*"

But Josh felt no desire to go after the animal.

Let it die in the forest, alone and in pain, he thought. Without even aiming, he cracked off another shot in the general direction the animal had taken, but by then the creature—whatever the hell it was—had disappeared into the forest. The echo of the shotgun blast rolled down into the valley and faded away.

The cows in the barn were still terrified, stomping

and bellowing in their stalls, but those sounds soon faded, too.

Once the peace of night had settled back down over the farm, Josh decided to leave everything just as it was. He ran as fast as he could back up to the house, intent on reporting this to the police immediately.

Chapter Eight
Delays

Mark was scheduled to start two weeks of night-shift work at the paper mill on Monday, but as soon as he was out of bed around noontime, he called Sam Barker, his department supervisor, to tell him what had happened over the weekend. Mark left out any mention of the "creature" he had seen—or *thought* he had seen—carry Phil off, but he insisted that Sam could contact the hospital emergency room for corroboration of his story. Sam told him it wasn't necessary and mentioned that since yesterday afternoon he had heard about Phil being missing from at least six other people. He told Mark not to worry, that he could take the whole week off if he needed to. Mark thanked him and hung up.

Even after nearly twelve hours of sleep, however, Mark still didn't feel all that rested. His sleep had been so haunted by twisted fragments of what had happened up on the mountain that everything had taken on disorientingly surreal overtones. Doubts and strange imaginings were so mixed up with fact that he was no longer sure what was or wasn't real. All he knew for sure was that one of his closest friends was missing and presumed dead somewhere on Mount Agiochook.

Sandy had left for school hours ago, and Polly was off to work at the hairdressers in town by the time Mark, wearing only a T-shirt and underpants, lumbered down the stairs and into the kitchen. He sighed heavily as he ran his hands over his face, trying to focus on something simple, like scrambling a couple of eggs or getting a pot of coffee started. But his mind was totally preoccupied with wondering what had happened to Phil, and what Guy LaBrea and the other authorities were planning to do about it. He wasn't even aware that he had taken a carton of orange juice from the refrigerator and a glass from the cupboard, and had started to pour juice, overflowing the glass until the splattering sound of liquid hitting the floor drew his attention.

"Ahh, *shit!*"

He grabbed a handful of paper towels and started sopping up the mess, but by then, the mere thought of anything—juice or eggs or coffee—hitting his stomach filled him with a squeezing nausea. Swearing under his breath, he threw the wet, wadded-up paper towels into the trash. Staring ahead blankly, he emptied the glass of juice down the sink.

"*Damn* it all! God *damn* it all! I've got to *do* something," he whispered as he began pacing back and forth across the kitchen floor. His bare feet squeaked every time he turned on the slick linoleum. "I can't just hang around the house all week, waiting for something to *happen*!"

Pale sunlight angled through the kitchen window, glinting like white fire off the faucet and sink. Mark paused in his pacing, leaned over the sink, and looked out at the sunny afternoon. The world looked fresh and clean, rejuvenated. The maple trees in the front yard had already started to turn color. A hushed peacefulness had settled over the street.

It seemed odd, almost impossible that just two days ago it had been snowing up on the mountain. Mark shivered with the memory of how cold it had been up there. His shoulders hunched up as he remembered the stinging pellets of ice and snow—his and Phil's desperate scramble across ice-slick rocks—huddling for protection under the spread-open tent—the low, whistling howl of the storm wind—and that deeper, rumbling growl that had been . . .

—been *what?*

That creature?

Mark clenched both hands into fists but stopped himself from punching anything. Instead, he sucked in a deep breath, closed his eyes, and just stood there, trembling as he fought to regain control. Worrying and getting angry wasn't going to solve a goddamned thing—least of all what to do about finding out what had happened to Phil.

Mark turned on the faucet and ran the water until it was lukewarm, then splashed several handfuls of water onto his face. It stung his eyes. Sputtering, he grabbed a dishtowel and dried his face, rubbing so vigorously that he took off at least a couple of layers of skin. Agitation swelled up inside him like thick, black poison, making his stomach do sour little flips.

At last, convinced that he had to do something right *now*, he looked up the number for the police station in the phone book and picked up the kitchen phone to dial. On the third ring, the dispatcher answered and immediately put him through to Chief LaBrea.

"Hey, Mark . . . I was just about to give you a call."

"Anything happening yet?"

After an uncomfortable pause, Guy answered, "Well, no. Nothing about Phil, anyway. Haven't really had a chance. I tell you, I've been busier than a three-balled bull in heat. Last night 'round nine o'clock, a semi jackknifed out on 26. Then, a little after midnight, just as we were getting that mess cleaned up, we got a call from Josh O'Connell out by your way, on Spruce Mountain Road. He was all worked up with some harebrained story about how a bear or some damned thing got into his barn and killed one of his prize calves."

"A bear . . . ?" Mark said, mostly to himself.

"Hell, Josh was going on and on about how he took a couple of shots at this—this *thing*. He thinks he wounded it, but it ran off, he says; and get this, on two legs, he says, like it was some kind of bear or ape or something."

"You know," Mark said, "O'Connell's farm borders the National Forest."

Mark knew that, at least as the crow flies, Josh's farm wasn't more than a couple of miles from where he had been camping the night before, when that creature had attacked him. He decided not to remind Guy of his own harebrained story.

"Yeah, well, I went out there and checked it out," LaBrea went on. "There certainly was a lot of blood, and there were some rather unusual looking tracks out behind in the pasture; but to tell you the truth, I suspect Josh has been hitting the sauce again, ever since his old lady up and left him—again. I'll bet he's just digging up that crazy-assed werewolf scare they had over there in Cooper Falls—what was it? Some fifteen years ago."

Mark decided to let Josh O'Connell and his problems slide for now and asked, "So when do you think you can get a search party organized?" He used a clipped, businesslike tone of voice to help keep some of his more unnerving thoughts at bay. He realized that he should show at least a modicum of concern for how hard LaBrea had been working, but he was already feeling defensive, suspecting that there would be a long bureaucratic delay before anything was done about trying to find out what had happened to Phil.

"First thing this morning, I put a call in to Fred Gibbons at the Forestry Department," LaBrea said. "I—Hold on. Let me check my messages. Nope. He hasn't called back yet. I'll give him a follow-up call."

"Is there anything I can do?"

LaBrea snorted with laughter and replied, "Yeah, you could get the town council to increase my damned budget so I could hire me a few more officers. I can't do shit with the manpower I have."

"If it would help, I could drive over and talk to Gibbons myself," Mark said.

"I don't see where that would do any—"

"It sure as hell would if it got some men out there on the mountain in an hour or so," Mark snapped. He tried to block out the corner of his mind that was whispering that, even if Phil had survived the fall down The Zipper, and even if he had been able to last through two nights of below-freezing temperatures up there on the bare mountain, he probably wasn't going to last much longer, not without food and water.

"I was going to say I don't see where that would do any *harm*," LaBrea said softly. "Look, Mark, I know you're really upset about what happened up there, but God's honest truth, *you* know and *I* know that you can't take it personally. It was an accident, all right?"

"Yeah, but I—"

"I know that cliff. I've been up there, and the only thing you would have accomplished if you had tried to get down there to help him would've been to get yourself killed, too."

Mark took a steadying breath and said softly, "We don't know for sure that he's dead."

"But the odds are—"

"Yeah, I know what the odds are, but I've got a gut feeling that Phil isn't dead. Look, I—I'm not sure what the hell I saw, okay, but it looked to me like someone picked him up and carried him off. And if that someone is helping him, maybe brought him down a different trail, if we go back up there we might find some tracks or something that'll help us figure out where the hell he is."

There was a brief silence at the other end of the line; then LaBrea said, "Tell you what. Why don't you drive on out and talk to Gibbons. You know where the department station is, right?"

"Sure."

"Okay. Maybe, if you're feeling up to it, Gibbons can get a couple of guys to go up there with you."

The thought of going back up on Agiochook so soon sent a chill through Mark. After the ordeal of getting off the mountain alone and fending off—whatever it was that had attacked him at his campfire—he wasn't so sure he had the strength or desire to go hiking. But LaBrea's suggestion sent a clear message that he didn't have the time or the manpower right now to get things going himself.

"Uh, yeah. Sure," Mark said. "As soon as I get something to eat, I'll drive over there. In the meantime, if you talk to Gibbons, fill him in on what's happening."

"No problem there," LaBrea replied. "Right now I'm going to head home and grab a bit of shut-eye myself. I'll talk to you later."

"Sure thing. Thanks, Guy."

With that, Mark hung up. He knew by the cold emptiness in his stomach that he should eat something, but he was too nerved up. His stomach felt like a clenched fist. He ran upstairs, took a quick shower, threw on some fresh clothes, and went out to his Jeep. Half an hour later, he was sitting in Gibbons' office, trying his best to explain why, if it was already too late today, the Forestry Department had to have a search party organized and ready to go up Agiochook first thing in the morning.

Chapter Nine

The Search Begins

Before dawn the next day, Mark drove his Jeep out to the base of the Wheaton Trail to meet Wally Doyle and John Sykes, two rangers from the State Forestry Department who were going to climb Mount Agiochook with him. Due to the heavy overcast, there was no true dawn that morning; the sky simply lightened from black to battleship gray. Before the Forestry Department launched a massive—and expensive—wide-sweep search for the missing man, Gibbons had opted to send a few men up to spend a day or two searching the area around The Zipper. Then, if they came up empty-handed, a more detailed search party would head out.

Because the weather might turn bad, or some other unforeseen situation might arise, all three men were packing heavy clothing and enough food and equipment for five days and four nights. Also, Mark was carrying a medical kit and extra rations, in case they found Phil alive. Doyle and Sykes each carried small radios with which they could call for an evacuation helicopter, in case they did find Phil's body. Although Mark tried to keep the thought at bay, finding Phil's body was the most likely event.

The hike up the mountain was exhausting but uneventful. The sky remained cloudy, and a raw, knife-edge wind drove at them out of the north. Throughout the day and especially at night, when they camped just below the tree line at the base of the summit, Mark found himself wishing he had brought along a gun. There had never been any clear indication that they were being tracked or followed, but after thinking about the "creature" that had attacked Josh O'Connell's cows and how close that was to where he had been attacked by some kind of creature, Mark almost expected another encounter like the one he'd had a few nights ago.

Although they lived in neighboring towns, Mark didn't know either of the two rangers personally; but the situation didn't exactly lend itself to friendly conversation, not when it seemed more than likely that they were here to retrieve his friend's body. After supper on the first night, with darkness pressing in on them from the surrounding forest, Mark stood by the campfire and whittled on the maple branch he'd been using all day as a walking stick. Thin curls of bark dropped into the flames and sputtered.

"Carving anything special there on your walking stick?" Wally asked. He held a fresh cup of coffee up to his mouth with both hands, and blew over the top to cool it.

"Not really," Mark said, shrugging and unable to think of anything more to say.

"I used to have one helluva great walking stick," Wally went on. "An old Penobscot Indian from up 'round Millinocket carved it for me. Had a big bear's face carved on the top. Looked like a Christless war club. I used it for ten, maybe fifteen years before I lost it. Hiking up Mount Katahdin one time, I dropped it off a cliff like a damned fool."

"Too bad," Mark said softly. He held himself back from mentioning that the only thing he had ever lost over the side of a cliff was one of his best friends.

Raising the stick to his eye like a rifle, Mark sighted down the long, smooth shaft. After a few more passes with his Swiss Army knife, he gripped the top end tightly and shook it to check its heft. Satisfied, he cleaned the knife blade on his pants leg, folded up the blade, and slipped it into his pocket, then knelt by the fire to warm his hands. Although Mark never went hiking without a walking stick, this particular one, he feared, might have to serve a different purpose; he wanted to have something close at hand that he could use as a weapon—what Wally would call a "Christless war club"—in case the creature that had attacked him before was still lurking in the area. He was tempted to tell the rangers his fear that they might be in more danger than they realized, but he let it drop, not wanting to sound like a nervous, greenhorn fool in front of the rangers.

"Hard to believe it's only nine o'clock," Sykes said suddenly. He was the younger of the two rangers, no more than twenty-five years old, Mark guessed.

"Gets dark early now," Wally said without looking up as he sipped his coffee noisily.

"Cold, too," Mark said.

"Yeah, but at least we don't have any Christless mosquitoes chewing our asses," Wally said.

Trying his best to sound casual, Mark stretched and said, "Yeah, well, I guess I'll settle down for the night. We want to get started as soon as the sun's up, right?"

"Sure thing," Wally said. "I heard John volunteer to get up and fix us breakfast in the morning, ain't that right, John?"

"Uhh—yeah, sure," Sykes said, knowing that in the pecking order of this small group, he was what Wally kept calling the "littlest pecker."

"G'night then," Mark said.

He walked over to his tent and zipped open the flaps. Feeling a bit foolish still holding on to the walking stick, he climbed inside, undressed quickly, and slid into his sleeping bag.

But sleep wouldn't come.

For several hours, he just lay there, watching the soft glow of the campfire flickering on the tent walls and listening to the muffled conversation of the two rangers outside. Their words eventually blended with the night sounds around them, and then, the next thing Mark knew, the forest was alive with the raucous songs of morning birds. Grunting softly, he rolled out of his sleeping bag and crawled to the front of the tent. In the dim gray light of dawn, Sykes was kneeling in front of the campfire, feeding the flames some dried branches to get the blaze going again. His misted breath hung around his neck like a silver scarf.

"Mornin'," Mark said softly, his teeth chattering. He didn't like disturbing the hushed serenity of the forest. He was a bit amazed—and relieved—that he had slept so soundly and that there had been no problems during the night.

He fished around until he found his clothes, zipped opened the tent flap, and crawled out into the chilly dawn. The first thing he did was wander over behind some trees and take a piss.

The campsite was still shrouded in shadow, but the first slanting rays of the morning sun lit up the snow-covered mountain peak like a fiery cone. Mark helped Sykes get breakfast going, and by the time the food was ready, Doyle had roused himself and made an appearance.

The three men ate in silence. Their agreed upon plan was to leave this campsite set up as a base camp. It was no more than an hour's climb to The Zipper. From there they could begin their search for Phil. After breakfast, they cleaned their eating utensils, stowed their food high up in the branches to discourage squirrels and other scavengers, and draped their sleeping bags over branches to air out.

Then they headed out.

Mark was tingling with expectation as he gripped his hiking stick and followed the two rangers up the steep, rocky incline. Most of last weekend's snow had melted, but in sheltered areas large patches still glistened with a dull blue glow. The morning air was surprisingly cold out in the open. All three men snuggled into the collars of their down jackets.

They moved off the marked trail and made a beeline for the base of The Zipper. As much as the terrain allowed, they walked side by side in order to cover as wide a swath as possible leading up to the cliff edge. Sheer ice made the going a bit difficult in places, but by pushing hard, they made it to the cliff in a little under an hour.

"This is the place, huh?" Doyle asked as they stood at the bottom edge of the cliff and looked up. Still shrouded in shadow, The Zipper looked like a long, wide slippery-slide made of red granite.

Mark nodded silently as they all looked around.

"See anything?" Doyle asked.

Mark shivered as he stared up the steep incline, remembering how helpless and terrified he had felt the instant he realized his friend had gone over the edge. Now, after being scoured by wind and weather for even only a few days, there was absolutely no trace of their passing. The dark spot Mark had seen at the foot of the cliff, what could have been either Phil or his abandoned backpack, was gone. No tracks were visible in the remaining patches of snow below.

"Well, let's have ourselves a look around," Doyle said simply.

They quickly spread out around the base of the cliff and started examining the area carefully. Wally found what looked like one small splotch of dried blood on the rocks at the base, but that was all. Between the sheltering rocks, drifted snow was six inches to a foot deep, but there was no indication that anyone had broken the smooth surface.

The three men fanned out wide, keeping within calling distance as they searched the side of the mountain for even the slightest trace of the missing man. After more than an hour of fruitless searching, Doyle called them back together.

Mark, who was the furthest away on the steep downside of the mountain, was about to start back when he caught sight of something in the snow between two rocks. He whistled shrilly and waved for the two rangers to join him.

"What's this look like?" he asked, pointing to the wide, rounded depression in the snow.

"A footprint," Doyle said simply, kneeling down and studying the print carefully.

"Yeah, and a pretty goddamned *big* one, at that," Mark said. He found it difficult to contain a rush of excitement. He wanted to mention the large creature he had seen, but didn't want either of the men to think he was crazy or something.

"You know, it snowed for the first time this year last weekend when my friend and I were up here, so this print *has* to have been made since Saturday." He regarded the track a moment, then added, "And I'd guess that wasn't made with a hiking boot, either."

The print did, in fact, look as if it had been made by a bare foot. At the front, there were five rounded indentations that could very well have been made by toes.

"It's human, no doubt about that," Doyle said. "But you know, especially this time of season and this high up where the weather changes so drastically, any impression in fresh snow is going to melt and refreeze dozens of times. I think that's what makes this look so big. It expands every time it does that."

He measured it against the flat of his hand. Even with his fingers spread wide, he couldn't span the width of the print.

"Naw," Doyle said, standing up and shaking his head authoritatively. "This wasn't made by no Christless bare foot."

Unconvinced, Mark shook his head as he stared

blankly at the impression. He took a deep breath and said, "Well, at least we know what direction to head."

Keeping several paces apart, all three men started moving in the direction the single footprint indicated, but after spending the rest of the day searching the rough terrain, they still came up empty. Other than the small splotch of blood on the cliff side, and that single footprint, there was no other indication that Phil or anyone else had been up here recently.

As the sun started to set in the western sky, they reluctantly headed back down the slope to their campsite and a supper of beans and brown bread.

"You know what I think?" Sykes said once they were settled around the campfire after supper.

Doyle cocked an eyebrow at his partner as if surprised that he would offer an opinion.

"I think that, come next summer, or maybe in a year or two, a couple of hikers are gonna come across a pile of bleached bones." He looked squarely at Mark. "And *then* we'll know what happened to your buddy!"

For a flashing instant, Mark wanted to slug the man, but he let the rush of anger pass, opting instead for silence. After an uncomfortable hour or so sitting around the campfire, the conversation limited mostly between the two rangers, Mark went to his tent to sleep.

Like last night, he found it difficult to sleep, but eventually he drifted off. He awoke some hours later from a dream.

He had been standing at the top of The Zipper, looking down into a thick cushion of pure white snow. Blinding white. His fear had steadily mounted as he watched the snow begin to churn as though it were alive. First two hands, thin and blackened with frostbite, reached up out of the snow; then a face broke through the surface. Mark stared in horror as the pale, gaunt face of Phil Sawyer looked up at him, his eyes sparkling with fiery anger. Phil furiously dug himself out of the deep pile of snow and then, once he was free, started to scuttle up the steep incline of the cliff. He moved like a huge spider.

"You left me here—"

Phil's voice rasped through black lips, cracked and bleeding.

"You left me here to die! . . . So I've come back for you!"

Mark awoke to find himself sitting straight up, his eyes wide open, his face slick with sweat, and his breath burning like a hot coal in the center of his chest. Both hands were clapped across his mouth, forcing back the scream that was threatening to burst out of him.

Chapter Ten

Promotion

"Hey, I've got some good news for you."

Mark was slumped in a cushioned chair in the employees' lounge with his feet up and his eyes closed. An untasted cup of coffee had gone stone-cold on the table beside him. He roused himself the instant he heard the voice of Sam Barker, his department supervisor.

"Uh—yeah," he said, vigorously rubbing his face with the flats of his hands. "Sorry 'bout that. I was—umm—"

"You were sleeping on the job," Sam said, his voice sounding flat. Only the faint trace of a smile told Mark that his boss was ribbing him.

"Yeah, well, I have been kinda stressed out lately . . . 'specially these last few days."

Sam hooked a chair by the rungs with his foot and dragged it over so he could sit down beside him. Folding his beefy arms across his chest, he sighed heavily and leaned back.

"Can't say as I blame you," he said. "Everyone I know is pretty damned upset 'bout what happened to Phil. He was a good worker and more than that—a good friend. By the way, how's the search going? You hear any news?"

Mark shrugged weakly, wishing to hell his mind would clear; but fatigue and worry over the past week had worn his resistance down.

"The rangers and I came down off the mountain day before yesterday 'cause of the weather. We . . . didn't find anything."

Sam grunted and frowned.

"They lost a day or two because of the weather, but I'd guess right now, between the men the Forestry Department and the police have put out, there's got to be better than fifty men up there."

"Think they'll find him?"

Again, Mark shrugged and shook his head.

"I hate to say it," Sam went on, "but I don't see how anyone could last up there this long without supplies, not with how the weather's been lately."

"No, I don't suppose," Mark replied distantly.

"Well, I'll tell you this much," Sam said as he leaned forward, staring earnestly at Mark. "I know you've been grinding yourself pretty hard about it. You went back up there looking for him, and Phil's wife told me how you've been over to see her, offering her support."

"It's the least I could do."

"Yeah, but you know, you can't let something like this take over your life."

"It's not taking over my—"

Sam cut him off with a quick wave of his hand; then he pointed a finger at him as though scolding him. "Lookie here! When I told you to take the week off, I meant it." He stared harshly at Mark for a moment. "You're not doing me or anyone else any good, dragging your ass around like this. Christ, the way you look, I'd say you sure as hell need some time off."

Mark took a deep breath but found that he had nothing to say.

"Now if I have to, I can get the company doctor to enforce what I'm telling you. And you know I will. But I'd rather see you cooperate with me, all right? Go on home and get some sleep—I mean some real sleep, not just dozing for fifteen minutes during your break. You have to forget about what happened up there. Let the authorities take it from here on out."

"Yeah, but I can't forget," Mark said so softly under his breath he wasn't even sure if Sam heard him.

Sam shifted his weight forward and stood up. Looking down at Mark, he said, "Oh, and there's one more thing. I want you to report to my office at seven-thirty sharp on Monday morning. I want to go over with you some of your new responsibilities as shift supervisor."

"What—?"

"You heard me right," Sam snapped. "You're getting a promotion. Staring first thing Monday morning, you're first-shift supervisor in the department." Satisfied by Mark's surprised reaction, Sam snorted with laughter. "No more third shifts for you, bud. Who knows? Maybe it'll improve your sex life."

Mark stood up and fumbled to shake his supervisor's hand as he sputtered his appreciation. Still unable to believe what he had heard, he watched as Sam left the room; then he went over to the sink and dumped out his cold coffee. Just as he was leaving the lounge, a group of workers entered. They were chatting and laughing together, but as soon as Dan Jenkins, a young man who worked with Mark in the paper coating division, saw Mark, he stopped short and nailed him with an angry stare. Catching the instant tension, the other workers all fell silent and drifted over to the coffee machine. Folding his arms across his chest and standing in the doorway, Dan watched with narrowed eyes as Mark approached.

"Well, well, well," Dan said, "I just heard you're gonna be big-time boss now."

Frowning, Mark said, "Oh, yeah? Where'd you hear that?"

Dan smirked and shook his head. "The scuttlebutt. 'Course, I figured it was bound to happen . . . I mean, now that Phil's out of the way."

A red flash of anger filled Mark. He clenched both fists and took a threatening step forward, but Dan didn't back down.

"And what exactly is *that* supposed to mean?" Mark said, his voice low and trembling.

"You know damned right well what it's supposed to mean," Dan said, straightening his shoulders and looking more than ready to fight. "It's supposed to mean that I think you knew all along that Phil was going to get that promotion over you, even though he's only been with the company a little more than a year."

"You don't know shit, you little fuck—"

"And I think it means you might have had something to do with Phil not making it back from the mountain—"

"Get the fuck out of my way!" Mark said.

He was coiled and ready to fight, but he checked himself, knowing that he had to back off. This wasn't the way to handle something like this.

"And I ain't the only one around town who's got half an idea that you might have even pushed Phil off that cliff 'cause you were pissed about him getting that job over you."

"You're full of shit, Jenkins."

Dan smiled a gap-toothed grin but still wouldn't move out of the doorway. Over by the coffee machine, his friends had all stopped talking and were watching tensely.

"So now that Phil's dead, of course it makes sense that you'd get his job."

Mark's fists were trembling as he squared off against the man in front of him. His pulse slammed heavily in his neck, and a loud roaring filled his ears. He could barely hear himself speak when he said, "Would you please excuse me?" He pushed past Dan and stepped out into the corridor.

Only seconds ago, he had been thinking he'd go out to his car, drive home, and head straight to bed. But now, he didn't hesitate as he strode down the corridor toward Sam's office. He walked right past Sam's secretary and opened the door, interrupting Sam, who was leaning back in his chair, talking on the telephone.

Sam glanced up at Mark, a look of surprise on his face.

"Hey, don't bother to knock or anything," he said as he hung up the phone. When he registered the anger in Mark's expression, he frowned and asked, "What can I do for you?"

"Is it true what I heard?" Mark snapped, fighting back the urge to shout. He walked up to Sam but checked himself from slamming both fists on the desk.

"Is *what* true?" Sam asked, a slight tremor registering in his voice.

"That Phil was going to get the supervisor's job?"

Sam's face flushed. He looked down at his hands for a moment before speaking. Then, nailing Mark with a cold, steady stare, he said, "Yeah. It's true."

Mark's mouth dropped open, but the only sound that came out was a strangled gasp.

"I know, I know you've been gunning for that slot for quite some time, Mark, but—well . . . you know, Phil had the college degree and the training from that last job he had at that mill in upstate New York. Looking at who was most qualified, I had to choose—"

"Who's most *qualified?* Jesus Christ, Sam! I've been with National Paper since high school—since *before* high school! I know this place inside and out, and I know every damned one of the people working in that division."

"I know all that," Sam said mildly, "but when I have a slot to fill, I have to fill it with the best man I can find."

"And I was second choice—after Phil!"

Running his teeth over his lower lip, Sam nodded silently.

"Well then, I guess you can have it!"

"What do you mean?"

"I mean you can fill that goddamned position with your number *three* choice. Get it? I quit!"

"Now hold on there a minute, Mark. Don't go off half-cocked."

Sam rose from his chair but didn't come around the desk after he read the level of Mark's anger in his expression.

"Hold on, *nothing!*" Mark yelled. "That's it! I've had it! I quit!"

"Don't you think you're being a bit hasty?" Sam said.

"Hasty? Jesus Christ! I'll show you hasty!"

He shook his clenched fists and again had to struggle not to slam Sam's desk—or Sam.

"I'll tell you what I'm going to do. First thing tomorrow morning, I'm going back up there on Agiochook, and I'm going to stay up there until I find out *exactly* what happened to Phil. You got that?"

"Yeah, sure. I got that," Sam said. "Look, Mark, you know, it wasn't like I was trying to do you any favors by giving you that promotion. I honestly felt that you were the most qualified person for the job."

"After Phil Sawyer! Look, Sam, I don't need any favors from you, all right?" He turned and started to leave, but then turned back. "No, wait a minute. There is one last thing you can do for me."

"Sure. Anything."

"You can put the lie to any rumors you might hear about how I pushed Phil off the cliff because he was going to get that promotion over me, okay? Until this afternoon, I had no idea what was going on behind my back."

"Absolutely. Look, Mark, I think you should—"

"That's it! You can send my last paycheck to the house," Mark said. Heaving a deep sigh, he hitched his thumb toward the view outside Sam's office window. Across the mill yard, in the late afternoon haze, he could see the distant purple slopes of the White Mountains, almost lost in a cloudy haze.

"I'm going up there," he said, his voice low, not much more than a growl. "And I'm not coming down until I find Phil Sawyer!"

Chapter Eleven

Heading Out

"Do you really have to bring a gun?" Sandy asked.

Mark glanced at his daughter as he grabbed his favorite deer hunting rifle, a Remington 30.06 700 BDL, from the gun rack in the Jeep's rear window.

"Well, you never know," he said, smiling grimly as he stepped out of the Jeep and patted his jacket pocket to make sure the extra box of ammunition was still there.

It was a little past six o'clock in the morning. Already the day was warm, a promising start to a beautiful Indian summer weekend. Sandy had gotten up before dawn to drive her father out to the base of the Round Top Trail. This was the longest of five major trails leading up to the summit of Mount Agiochook. Mark had decided to take it, rather than the Wheaton Trail or any of the other trails, because there was less of a chance that he would encounter any of the rangers who were still out searching for Phil. After all, hunting season was more than a month away, and he didn't want to be seen carrying a rifle in the woods, especially the White Mountain National Forest.

"I have no idea what I might be up against," Mark said, looking suddenly serious. Other than the initial report to LaBrea, he hadn't mentioned to anyone the creature's attack on his campsite or seeing Phil carried off by—whatever that thing had been. "If I have to stay out here for a while, I may even end up having to hunt for my own food."

Sandy knew enough about hunting and hiking so her father didn't need to mention some of the other dangers he might encounter.

"But you won't forget to meet me here in three days with more supplies, right?" he asked.

"Sure thing," Sandy said. She watched silently as her father dragged his carefully packed backpack out onto the ground and gave it a cursory inspection.

"I'm sure I'll need more food, clothes, and maybe bullets."

He glanced over his shoulder at the thin ribbon of brown trail that led up the gently rising slope and into the forest. From here, he couldn't see the mountain peak that was his goal, but that didn't matter. This wasn't a hike to make it to the summit and then come back down. He might be up there for several days, maybe even a week or more, combing the area as thoroughly as he could.

A shiver raced through him as he stared at the gloomy shadows still as thick as ink beneath the heavy pine boughs and thick brush. It was warm down here, but he knew that the closer he got to the summit, the colder it would get. Sucking in a deep breath, he hoisted his backpack and shrugged his arms into the shoulder straps. After adjusting the frame so it rode comfortably on his back, he turned to Sandy.

"So what is it?" he asked. His voice was low and tempered as he held eye contact with her.

"What's *what?*"

"You're keeping something from me."

Sandy looked at him, surprised.

"You don't think I can tell? Come on, babe—tell me what's the matter."

Sandy shrugged and rubbed her arms as though fighting off a rush of chills. "No . . . I . . . nothing's the matter."

Liar! she accused herself.

She knew exactly what was wrong!

Ever since last weekend, she had wanted to tell her father about the weekend visit Polly had with Dennis while he was away. She wasn't any fool. She knew damned well what was going on between her stepmother and Dennis, but how was she supposed to tell her father? Blurt it right out?

Uh, Dad . . . there's something I've been meaning to tell you . . . you know, last week, when you were off hiking, your wife was screwing the guy who works at the Mobil station . . . and I'm pretty sure this wasn't the first time, either.

No, that wouldn't do at all!

She had waited all week, wanting to tell him, but the opportunity to broach the subject had just never presented itself. Either Polly was around, or he was off to work, or she was at school. Throughout the week, she had been gearing herself up to deal with it this weekend, and then yesterday afternoon, her father had come home from work early and announced that he had quit his job and was going up into the mountains until he found his missing friend.

How could she lay something like this on him now, knowing the kind of pressure he was already under?

Mark placed his hand lovingly on Sandy's shoulder. "Well, if there is something bothering you, you know you can talk to me about it any time, right?"

Sandy was silent for a moment, so Mark shook her shoulder.

"I said *right?*"

"Yeah . . . sure!"

Sandy squirmed out from under his grip.

"And if it's—you know, a woman thing or whatever, something you think you can't talk about with a man—even your father—you should try to talk to Polly about it."

Oh, yeah! Sure! Sandy thought, hoping to heaven her face didn't reveal what she was thinking.

"I—well, I guess I'm just—you know, I'm kinda worried about everything," she finally managed to say.

Mark bit his lower lip and nodded. "Yeah." He sniffed with suppressed laughter that didn't have a trace of humor. "It *does* seem like the shit's been hitting the fan a lot lately, doesn't it?"

Over the years, her father had been on her case about using foul language, so Sandy was mildly surprised that he would say something like that to her. It made her feel sad for him and think all the more about the pressure he must be under right now. Inside her chest was nothing but a cold hollow.

"Stop worrying, all right?" Mark said.

Again, he gripped her shoulder and gave her a bracing shake.

"I was practically born and raised in the woods.

Hell, I know how to take care of myself out here better than I do in town."

"I know, I know, but I—"

"But *nothing*. You're going over to Karen Bishop's for an overnight tonight, right? So just enjoy your weekend. Drink a lot of Diet Pepsi and stay up all night talking about boys and listening to music or whatever, okay? Just make sure you're out here with that stuff I need on Monday afternoon as soon after school as you can get here."

"Don't sweat it. I won't let you down," Sandy said.

"I know you won't."

But I already have! Sandy thought bitterly. She felt herself close to tears and had to struggle not to start crying and blurt out what she really had to say. But she watched silently as her father turned and started up the trail. In his right hand, he held a long maple walking stick which he swung forward with every other step. His rifle was slung across his back, bouncing in time with his steps. Just before he disappeared into the foliage, he turned around and waved to her. Sandy's heart skipped a beat when she saw a stray sunbeam glint off his rifle barrel, making it flash like cold fire. She cringed, waiting to hear the sharp report of the rifle, but no sound came.

Seconds later, her father was gone, leaving her alone beside the Jeep with a silent emptiness as she wondered if she would ever see him alive again.

Chapter Twelve

Little Red Corvette

"Looks like I killed the last one," Dennis said as he crushed the empty beer can and tossed it onto the floor where it landed with the five others he had already finished off this evening.

It was a little past eleven o'clock on Saturday night.

Dennis was slouched on the couch with one arm draped around Polly's shoulder as he held her tightly against him. They were watching an X-rated videotape they had rented, but it wasn't holding his attention. He was too drunk to concentrate on much besides the slow, steady massage Polly was giving his crotch through his pants. He sighed heavily and considered trying to get things going again, but they had been at it all afternoon, ever since Sandy had left for the overnight at her friend's house.

"Kinda unbelievable, though, ain't it? The way things worked out again for the weekend?"

Polly grunted softly, not even looking up at him. He couldn't tell if she was more focused on the movie or his crotch.

"I mean, after last weekend, when good ole Mark caught me red-handed." Dennis sniffed and shook his head. "Shee-it! I thought for sure he was gonna clean my pipes."

"I'll clean your pipes for you," Polly whispered as she tugged at the tab of his zipper.

"No, no, I—uhh . . . I can't right now."

"Oh, what's the matter?" she cooed. "Did we wear out Little Willie? Is he all tuckered out?"

"No, it's not that. It's just I—uh, I'm still kinda thirsty is all."

Polly sighed and shifted a little bit away from him. "Well, by the looks of it, you've cleaned me out of beer. How about some wine?"

"Naw! Wine's for women and fags," Dennis said, chuckling softly at his overused joke. "Maybe I'll zip on out to Nicely's and pick up another six-pack."

"You didn't bring your car, remember?" Polly said. "In case you've forgotten, we're trying to be at least a little bit discreet."

"Discreet? Oh, yeah, discreet," Dennis said, shifting uneasily on the couch. He considered trying to get things started again, but he knew he was too drunk and too used up to make it. No juice left in the tank.

No, right now all he wanted—all he *needed* was another beer or two before crashing for the night. He wasn't going to be able to get it up again at least until morning.

"Maybe you could lemme drive Mark's 'Vette," Dennis said, suddenly brightening.

Mark had a vintage 1965 red Corvette stored in his garage, but he hardly ever took it out on the street. Just about everyone else in Hilton admired it, some with envy, but Dennis coveted it possibly even more than he coveted Mark's wife.

"And maybe *you* could take a flying fuck at the moon," Polly replied tonelessly.

"Aww, come on!" Dennis said, letting his hand slide down to Polly's breast and giving her a gentle squeeze. "Here you've been taking advantage of me all night, practically raping me, and you won't even let me have a little fun."

Polly looked up at him, frowning. "You didn't mean that the way it sounded, I hope."

"Course I didn't, but the store's only half a mile down the road," Dennis said, pressing the point. "Who the hell's gonna care or even notice at this hour?"

"I am," Polly said tightly. She grabbed him by the wrist and removed his hand from her breast. "And as drunk as you are, if you wrapped that car around a telephone pole or something, I think Mark might notice, too."

"Shit, I can drive just fine like this."

"The hell you can!"

Polly shifted forward to sit rigidly on the edge of the couch.

"If you're so friggin' desperate for some beer, you could walk to the store!"

Dennis snorted and shook his head. "We could both go. Get a little fresh air 'n all. Might even revive me, if you know what I mean."

Polly didn't reply. She focused her attention on the television instead.

"Well, then," Dennis said, standing up slowly and with great effort. "I guess I'll have to go all by my lonesome."

He buttoned up his shirt, adjusted his pants, patted his wallet in his hip pocket, and then headed out into the kitchen.

"Be back in ten or fifteen."

"I'll be waiting," Polly called out.

Her gaze was fixed firmly on the TV; she didn't bother to turn and wave to him as he walked out into the kitchen. He was just about to go outside when the Corvette key ring, hanging on a hook by the door, caught his attention. Without any deliberation or hesitation, he snatched it up and stepped out into the crisp, cold night.

"What the fuck," he muttered.

The only problem he could foresee was getting the garage door up without alerting Polly. Once he started up the car, he could haul ass and be gone before she even got to the front door. Of course, there'd be hell to pay once he got back, so maybe he should make it worth his bother and take an extra-long spin around the block—maybe even head out to Route 26 and see just how fast this baby could go.

"Probably faster than Markie-boy'd ever dare goose it," he whispered as he lurched down the walkway toward the door on the side of the garage. His plan was to get the car started, then open the garage door from the inside, hop into the car, and wheel on out of there as fast as he could.

As he was reaching for the doorknob, though, something—a faint snorting sound from behind him—

caught his attention. He turned and peered into the backyard but could see nothing in the darkness. The small expanse of lawn was backed by trees that stood out like thick, black lace against the starry sky. A chilly wind blew into his face, making him shiver and wish he had grabbed his jacket. Shaking his head to clear his mind, and figuring it had just been the wind or something, he turned and opened the garage door. He was just about to enter the darkened garage when he heard or sensed something moving behind him. As the heavy thump of running feet filled his ears, he spun around just in time to see the quick motion of—something—black against the dark wall of the trees. A large, lumbering dark shape was charging straight at him from the backyard.

"What the fuck—"

Before he could say anything more, the shape was on him.

It towered above him, outlined against the night sky like a mountain. Two large arms materialized from the bulk and swung at him from both sides, catching him up in a crushing embrace.

Jesus, God! Help! . . . Help me! Dennis thought, but he couldn't make the tiniest of sounds.

Powerful arms applied steady pressure, crushing him in their embrace. Dennis heard his pulse filling his ears with thunderous beats as whoever—or *whatever*—this thing was started squeezing him tighter and tighter.

Help me! . . . Polly! . . . Please! . . . Help me!

Dennis tried to resist the pressure that was bending him steadily backward, but his arms were pinned uselessly to his sides. A loud snapping sound was accompanied by a bright, white jolt of pain that slammed through his body like lightning. Dennis let out a short, feeble shout as the thing let go of him, and he crumpled to the ground. His back was broken, and several ribs had been crushed to pulp. He was lost in an explosion of pain.

No! . . . Please! Dennis thought, but he couldn't take a deep enough breath to make a sound. His body was so racked with pain it still felt as though the creature had him in its powerful embrace.

The dark figure crouched low, twisted to one side, and then spun around quickly with its huge, flat hand extended. The impact was terrific, like a stick of dynamite going off inside Dennis's head. Bright swirling lights spun across his vision, and searing flames of pain filled him as the side of his face caved in. Before the instant of pain passed, the creature's other hand slammed into his stomach and lifted him clear off the ground as sharp claws dug through his shirt and into his belly.

Sitting in the living room with the TV up loud, Polly barely heard the commotion outside. Her first thought was that Dennis was too drunk even to get outside the door, so she ignored it. But when she heard him shout, she leapt off the couch and ran into the kitchen. She slapped on the outside light and looked out the window over the sink. Beside the garage, she saw a blur of motion as a large, dark shape darted away from the garage and into the backyard. For a moment, she thought it was Dennis, but then she saw him sprawled on the walkway in front of the garage door.

"Goddamn clumsy oaf!" she muttered, thinking he had fallen down the steps and hurt himself. If she had to call for an ambulance, it was going to be just a little bit awkward, explaining how a drunk man who wasn't her husband had fallen down and hurt himself in her yard this late at night.

Polly raced outside, intending to help him, but when she was halfway down the walkway, she stopped dead in her tracks.

"Dennis . . . Are you all right?"

Halfway to him, she leaned forward, not quite daring to come any closer.

He wasn't moving. He was lying on his back, staring up at the night sky with a glazed, unblinking stare. The dark stain spreading across the ground underneath his stomach looked almost like—

"Oh, *Jesus!*"

A thick, sour taste bubbled up from Polly's stomach into her throat when she realized that she was looking at a long coil of Dennis' intestines. Her legs suddenly went all rubbery and were barely able to support her. She gagged once and covered her mouth with her hand in an attempt to hold back the sudden rush of sour vomit.

She called to him again, feebly, but Dennis still didn't move. The dark stain beneath him—which could only be blood—continued to spread. Moving ever so slowly, Polly approached the body, her breath catching painfully in her throat. Once she was close enough, she saw the keys to Mark's Corvette, clutched in Dennis' lifeless hand. Whimpering, she forced herself to bend down and take them from him. Then she spun around on her heel and raced back into the house.

She was nearly numb with shock and fear, and her hands were trembling uncontrollably as she dialed the police station. She blurted out what had happened, and the night dispatcher assured her that Chief LaBrea and a patrolman would be over within minutes.

Before the police arrived, Polly hung the Corvette keys back up on the wall, then took a shot of whiskey in hopes that it would calm her down enough so she could think up a logical explanation to give the cops as to why Dennis Cross was outside her house this late at night.

Maybe . . . just maybe, if she could make Guy LaBrea believe it, she would be able to make Mark believe it, too, when he heard about what had happened.

Chapter Thirteen

Pickup Point

Sandy came home from Karen Bishop's house early Sunday morning as soon as she heard about what had happened at her house late Saturday night. Polly was understandably distraught, even if Dennis *hadn't* been her boyfriend; but Sandy didn't believe for a second the line her stepmother had given both her and the police, that Dennis had borrowed some tools from Mark a few days ago and had been returning them late at night, trying to sneak them into the garage, apparently, so he wouldn't disturb whoever was home. All day and night Sunday, and then throughout the next day at school, Sandy felt increasingly anxious about meeting her father at their appointed spot that afternoon. She knew for certain now that, no matter what else, she *had* to tell him *everything*.

As soon as she got home from school, without even checking to see if Polly was home or not, Sandy got the bullets from the closet where her father stored them, hurriedly packed up the food and other supplies he had told her to get, and then jumped into the Jeep and took off. Tension was coiling in her stomach like sour acid as she followed Route 26 out of town toward Newry and the start of the Round Top Trail.

There weren't many houses once she got outside of Newry—just a few scattered farmhouses. After a while, the wide fields, tinged now with autumn colors, gave way to thick forest. Tall, dark pine trees closed down around the Jeep as the tarred road ended and a washboard dirt road began. The Jeep bounced and chattered over the bumps in the road, spiking Sandy's nervousness. Several times she was swept up by waves of panic, thinking that she must have taken the wrong road, or worrying that something had happened to her father, but—at last—she saw the sign up ahead that marked the beginning of the Round Top Trail. With a fantail of dust swirling in her wake, she pulled into the small parking area and stopped the Jeep.

For several seconds, Sandy just sat there, clutching the steering wheel and listening to the Jeep's engine click as it cooled down. Hazy sunlight shifted with a dull lemon flicker through the overladen branches overhead. She scanned the surrounding woods, trying to pierce the wall of dark greens and browns, but saw only the heavy sway of branches. A blue jay cried out and flew away. A red squirrel scurried across the solitary picnic table and up a tree.

There was no one around.

Come on, Dad! Where the heck are you?

She opened the Jeep window and listened to the high hissing of wind in the pines. It sounded lonely and cold, and she tried to imagine how lonely it must be up there on the mountain. She wished she didn't feel so apprehensive, but she knew there was no avoiding it. If her father didn't show, she'd be worried sick about him; if he did show, she was going to have to tell him about what had happened.

Either way, she didn't like what was going to happen.

A flicker of motion off to her right caught her attention. She turned and saw her father, waving and calling out to her as he came down the trail. He was carrying a walking stick in one hand and had an empty backpack slung over his shoulders. Gritting her teeth, Sandy got out of the Jeep and ran to meet him.

"Hey, how's it going, babe?" Mark asked, smiling through three days' growth of beard. "Got the stuff I wanted?"

Sandy almost automatically replied that everything was just fine but then simply shrugged.

Mark immediately picked up that something was wrong. "Hey, what's the matter?"

"There's been some trouble . . . back home," Sandy said. She was already close to tears. "Dennis Cross is . . . dead."

"What?"

"Someone killed him . . . in our backyard."

"Our yard?"

Sandy nodded and forced herself to continue, knowing that she had to spill it all right now or else she'd never find the courage to say it all. "The police aren't sure, but they think it might have been a bear that's been reported in the area."

"A bear?" Mark said, letting his voice trail away.

While Sandy hurriedly told him everything she knew about the grisly incident, about Polly's affair with Dennis, and—worst of all—that the police were now looking for him, her father listened with steadily mounting dismay and concern, and then anger registering on his face.

"—but only for questioning," she finished.

She wished she didn't feel like a traitor or murderer for hurting her father like this. His pain was obvious from his tight, squinting expression and the firm set of his jaw.

"Somehow I'm not surprised . . . about Polly and Dennis, I mean," he said finally. He blinked his eyes rapidly to keep the tears from forming. "I guess I just don't have a way with women, huh? First I scare away your mother, and now—now I'm not even able to hang on to Polly. *Shit!*"

He kicked up a clot of sod with the toe of his boot and gripped his hiking stick so tightly the knuckles on both hands turned white. Sandy looked at him, wanting more than anything in the world to cry and hug him, to let him comfort her and tell her everything was going to be all right, but she couldn't move.

"So anyway . . . how's it going for you out here?" Sandy asked, once she gained a bit of control. She studied him and added, "You know, I think you might look good with a beard."

Mark scraped the stubble on his cheeks and forced a smile.

"Umm—yeah. Well, to tell you the truth, I'm not having any luck. I haven't found any tracks or anything. I've set up camp a couple of miles up the trail, just across the east branch of the river. About halfway to the top." He paused a moment and looked thoughtfully back up the trail. "I suppose I'm going to have to move my camp now. In case the police come looking for me."

Sandy shifted nervously from one foot to the other. "Umm, Dad. I hate to sound—you know, suspicious or anything, but you didn't—you know, you didn't do it, did you?"

"Do what? You mean kill Dennis Cross? Come on, Sandy, don't be ridiculous!"

Sandy shrugged. "Well, I mean, I didn't think so, but I thought—you know, if you had found out about them before now, you might have lost your temper, you know, and . . . and done something."

Mark snorted with laughter. "Yeah, well, I won't *have* to do anything about Dennis now, will I? Someone else has taken care of that for me."

Sandy bit her lower lip and nodded, unable to look at the pain in her father's eyes.

"You didn't happen to tell anyone you were meeting me out here, did you?"

Sandy shook her head tightly.

"Good," Mark said.

He covered his mouth with his hand and considered for a moment.

"Look, I know the right thing to do would be to come down off the mountain right now and go and talk to the police. Guy would believe I had nothing to do with it, but I dunno." He shook his head solemnly. "I just can't do that right now. I'm going to stay up there until I find out what the hell happened to my friend. If the cops think I might have had something to do with what happened to Dennis . . . well, then, they're just going to have to come up here and find me if they want to talk to me."

"That's what I'm afraid of," Sandy said, her face

creased with worry. "What if they *do* come up here looking for you?"

"Then we'll have all that many more men who can help me look for Phil."

Sandy tried to say something but was at a loss for words.

"Look, let's get the supplies from the Jeep so I can get back up there, okay? It'll be good to have some fresh food for supper tonight."

Sandy smiled weakly and said, "I packed a few surprises for you, too."

"That's great, babe. You know, I'll be needing more food and clothes in another couple of days. Another sweatshirt or two might come in handy, too. It's been pretty cold up there at night. Think you can meet me out here again, say, on Thursday?"

Sandy shook her head. "Cheerleading tryouts are this Thursday, but I could skip them."

"No, let's make it Wednesday, then. C'mon, let's get that stuff loaded up so you can get back home before dark. I—uh—it'd probably be best if you didn't let Polly or anyone else know you told me what's been going on."

"Don't worry about that."

It didn't take long for Mark to fill up his empty backpack with the food and clean clothes. Sandy had carefully wrapped up a half pound of hamburger and had included two un-asked-for bottles of beer, which Mark planned to have for supper that night.

Once he was ready to head back up the trail, Mark gave his daughter a long, strong hug. After a quick exchange of goodbye kisses, he turned and started back up the trail, disappearing silently into the tangle of dark green shadows.

As soon as he was out of sight, Sandy had the disorienting feeling that he had never really been there. She felt suddenly lost and lonely as she stood beside the Jeep and stared at where he had gone. She told herself that it was foolish, but she feared that she might never see him again. Tears blurred her vision as she got back into the Jeep, started it up, and drove away.

As soon as the Jeep disappeared around the corner, another figure strode out of the woods where it had been hiding. It was tall and wide-shouldered, and covered with a smooth mat of brown fur. Its left shoulder was marred by a raw wound that had started to scab over. Dried black blood matted the creature's fur.

In spite of its huge bulk, the creature moved with silent grace as it came over to where the Jeep had been parked. A cold, animal intelligence burned in its eyes as it scanned the area for danger. With a low, soft grunt, it sniffed the air as it looked back and forth between the trail where Mark had gone and down the road where Sandy had gone. Its thick, black lips curled back in a snarl. Then, with a bellowing snort, it took off into the woods, moving silently through the shadowed forest as it ran parallel to the road where dust from the Jeep's passing still swirled in the late afternoon sunshine.

Chapter Fourteen

Manhunt

"Look, I don't want to have to keep repeating this, but this isn't some kind of vigilante committee or anything, okay? And it sure as hell ain't no goddamned manhunt."

Guy LaBrea was standing behind his desk, speaking loud enough to be heard above the murmur of the thirty or more men who were crowded into his small office. It was just past six o'clock in the morning. Outside the office window, the sky was slowly blending from pale gray to blue.

" 'Least as of right now, neither Mark Newman nor anybody else has been charged with anything in connection with the death of Dennis Cross, so I think it's best if we all just simmer down."

"How come?" someone at the back of the room yelled.

LaBrea looked up and saw Dan Jenkins staring earnestly at him. Ever since Saturday night, as soon as he had heard that his best friend and drinking buddy had been killed, Dan had been calling the police station, pressing LaBrea for answers as to what had happened. His question now was followed by scattered grunts and murmurs of approval.

"Why?" LaBrea said. "Because although some of you might not agree with me—" he nailed Dan with a harsh look, hoping to keep him quiet "—we haven't clearly established any motive in the situation. *That's* why! State police evidence technicians have been working on this case all weekend, so let's let them do their job, all right?"

"How about what happened out at Josh's?" someone else called out. "Ain't there a connection?"

Guy shrugged and shook his head.

"Look, I ain't in on the investigation. It's out of my hands. The only reason I called you guys in here at this ungodly hour is because I need you for . . . well, for two things. First, I want to try and locate Mark Newman so the staties can question him. Second, and more important, I got a call from the Forestry Department, asking us to assist them in their search for Phil Sawyer."

"Shit, we ain't never gonna find Phil," someone said.

" 'Least not alive," another man offered.

After a brief burst of confused comments, Dan Jenkins spoke out loud enough to be heard above everyone else. "Come on, Guy! Don't you think these two things might be a little more closely related than you're letting on?" He narrowed his gaze as he looked at the police chief.

"What the hell are you getting at?" LaBrea asked, frowning.

"Well . . ." Dan turned and scanned the crowd now that he had their attention. "I ain't about to start tellin' tales out of school, but I know for a fact—a lot of you guys who work at the mill know it, too—that Phil Sawyer was going to get promoted to shift supervisor, and Mark Newman thought *he* deserved the job. Am I right?"

Several men grunted their agreement.

"And—" Dan went on, shrugging and rubbing his hands together nervously. "Well, there's been some talk 'round town about how Mark's old lady Polly's been sleeping around, and that Dennis was kinda keeping the bed warm, if yah catch my drift."

Nervous laughter rippled through the room.

"I think if you're looking for a motive," he went on, "the fact that Dennis was shagging Mark's wife might appear motive enough for him to do what he done to Dennis."

"Hold it right there, Dan," LaBrea said, nailing Jenkins with an angry look. "Mark Newman's not on trial here for *anything*. You got that? And I hope to hell I don't need to remind you that here in America, a man's innocent until he's proven guilty. Now, the sun's up, and we've got a job to do—"

"But did you see him?" Dan shouted, trembling as he scanned the crowded room again, looking for sympathetic faces. "Did any of you guys *see* what Dennis looked like after he was through with him?"

"That's enough, Dan," LaBrea said, purposely lowering his voice to keep tempers from flaring any more.

"Most of you were at Dennis's funeral yesterday,"

Dan continued. "Closed casket! A *closed* fucking casket! You know why? Do *any* of you know why—?"

"I *said* that's *enough!*"

"Because he was ripped to shit, that's why! His stomach had been torn open, and his guts pulled out. That's what *I* heard. Come on, Frank . . . and Eddie—you guys've all heard the same things I've been hearing. Back me up on this. *Whoever* went to work on Dennis with that knife or axe or whatever really did a hell of a number on him."

"I've known Mark Newman a lot of years, and I'll tell you one thing—he ain't the kind of man who'd do something like that—to anyone, no matter what the reason."

All heads turned and looked at Sam Barker, who was standing in the far corner of the room. A few other men nodded their agreement.

"He's worked in my department a lot of years. Now, you can spread rumors all day about what his wife might or might not have been doing, and about him not getting this promotion he might've thought he deserved, but all of you men here—especially you guys who work at the mill—you know Mark, and you can't tell me you think he could kill someone in cold blood!"

"Well, *someone* did it!" Dan shouted, his face flushing red with anger. "Who else had a better reason?"

"That's not for any of us to decide," LaBrea said as he slammed his fist onto his desk. "You're way out of line here, Jenkins! I knew Dennis Cross, too. I can't very well say he was a close friend of mine, but believe me—no one wants to get to the bottom of this more than I do."

"Okay, then why don't you bring one of those hot-shot state investigators in here to tell us what the fuck's going on? Let's hear what they've found out and what they're thinking, huh? We've got a right to know. This happened in *our* town—to a friend of ours!"

LaBrea shook his head.

"And why don't you tell us why Dennis's funeral had to be closed casket? What happened to him? You went out there that night. You saw what happened to him!"

"Yeah, I did," LaBrea said mildly, trying his best to maintain control over this increasingly volatile situation. The memory of how horribly mutilated Dennis Cross's body had been sent a wave of nausea racing through him.

"So why are you covering up for Newman?"

A chorus of loud approval wafted through the crowd like a breeze fanning sparks into a blaze.

"Yeah, what the hell happened out there?"

"We've got a right to know!"

"If Newman didn't do it, then who did?"

Glancing at Barker for support, LaBrea hushed the crowd with an angry wave of his hand. "I'm not covering up for anybody! Look, we're not judge and jury here, all right? Most of you know something pretty similar happened to some of Josh O'Connell's cows."

"Maybe he done that to set up, like, an alibi or something," someone offered.

"All I can say is, the staties are working on it. What we have to do is a single, simple job—to assist in a search party for two men—one who's missing, and one who's wanted for questioning. And that's *all!* As of right now, there are no suspects in the case. I don't want anyone thinking this is some kind of manhunt, that we're out to bring anyone to justice."

"Just tell us—" Dan started to say.

"I've heard all I want to hear from you, Jenkins! We've got a big piece of forest to cover, and I'm gonna need a lot of help out there today, but I can make *damned* sure *you* don't go."

He scanned the crowd while he pointed angrily at Dan.

"You'll all find out what we know when there are some solid answers. We're not holding anything back from you for any reason." He glanced over his shoulder at the clock on the wall. "It's almost six-thirty. Gibbons should be here in a few minutes. He'll do a breakdown of the search areas we have to cover before we head out. We've even got a state helicopter for a couple of days. Oh—just one more thing. I don't want any of you fellas bringing any rifles out into the woods."

A loud chorus of disapproval filled the room. The scattered catcalls and jeers didn't abate for a while, and LaBrea had to shout to be heard.

"You heard me! No guns. With tempers heated up the way they are, I don't want anyone taking any potshots at anyone."

"Now wait just a damned minute—"

It was Barney Reynolds speaking. LaBrea let the old man have the floor if only to keep Dan Jenkins shut up.

"I can appreciate you not wanting to let the cat out of the bag, so to speak, about your investigation," Barney said. "I mean—hell, whether it was Mark or someone else, *somebody* did a number on Dennis

Cross. But you can't tell me you want us up there on Agiochook without protection."

"Protection from what?" LaBrea asked, instantly regretting that he left Barney an opening to continue.

"Why, from whatever the hell's up there on the mountain," Barney said. "Lots of you younguns might not recall some of the things that've happened around here over the years. But you all have heard about what happened out to Josh O'Connell's a few nights ago. . . ."

"Let's not trot that out again, Barney," LaBrea said. "As far as I could tell, it looked like a bear or a wolf got into his barn and killed a calf."

Barney smirked and shook his head. "To my way of thinking, there's a damn sight bit of difference between a bear's tracks and a wolf's tracks. 'N anyway, I just don't see how you 'spect us to go off into the woods and not be able to defend ourselves if we have to. What if there's a bear or something out there that's plumb loco?"

"Yeah," Dan added, "or a killer who's already killed one person."

"One?" Barney said, cackling. "I'm talkin' 'bout *dozens* of people . . . maybe hundreds over the years. We ain't gotta worry none about Mark Newman. We gotta worry about whatever else might be up there . . . the same thing that killed one o' Josh's prized calves a few nights ago. You fellas seem to be forgetting 'bout those two hikers who disappeared last July up on Agiochook, 'n all the other hikers who've gone missing 'round these parts over the years. Now, I ain't saying this thing—whatever the hell it is—got all the way into town here and did the same thing to Dennis—though I reckon that ain't impossible—but there's *something* up there, a creature of some kind that's probably been in this neck of the woods a lot longer than any of us . . . prob'ly since long before the white man came. If you listen to some of them Indian tales about—"

"We don't really have time for this," LaBrea said. "Gibbons will be here in a few minutes. I'll tell you all this much—if I find out *any* of you went out there armed today, I'll slap your ass with a fine and do everything I can to make sure you do a little time in the accommodations we have downstairs here. Can I make myself any clearer?"

There was a murmur of assent from the men in the room, but it didn't sound at all convincing. LaBrea was positive at least a few of them would bring their deer-hunting rifles or shotguns along with them . . . especially now that Barney had raised the specter of some kind of murderous creature in the woods. Before LaBrea could say anything more, Fred Gibbons, accompanied by a team of rangers, knocked on the door and entered the office. It took nearly half an hour to divide up the search areas and assign them to teams, each to be led by a forest ranger. Once that was done, more than thirty men from Hilton and a dozen state forest rangers took off into the White Mountain National Forest to find Mark Newman and—hopefully—to discover what had happened to Phil Sawyer.

Chapter Fifteen

Pursued

"What was that?"

"What was what?"

"That sound . . . I just heard something—a click or something."

"Maybe it was your brain knocking against the inside of your skull."

"No, seriously."

For several seconds, there was nothing but silence on the mountaintop; then came the clump and scuff of heavy boots on stone. The wind whistled in brief gusts that curled like cold fingers over the rocks and carried the voices down under the rock overhang where Mark was hiding. It was a damned good thing he had seen these men first and had found such good cover. He gripped his rifle tightly in his hands, cursing himself for bolting it. That was the sound that had alerted one of them, but Mark knew he had to be ready to defend himself if he needed to.

The sound of footsteps came closer. Then, off to the right, a thin, blue shadow stretched out over the down slope like a long, distorted, pointing finger. From his hiding place, Mark watched the shadow shift first to one side, then to the other as the person above walked back and forth. He knew the man was scanning the area, waiting for the sound to be repeated. As far as he could tell, there were only two of them, but he couldn't be sure. They might be just a couple of hikers, but they might also be part of the search party out looking for Phil. More than likely, though, after what Sandy had told him yesterday, they might be two of any number of men sent up to Agiochook by the police to find and bring him in for questioning about the murder of Dennis Cross.

"Probably just a rock falling or something," one of them said.

"Maybe, but it sounded like—I dunno—like something else."

"Go check it out yourself. You wanna climb down there on that narrow ledge, be my guest if you're so damned curious."

"No, *you* go and take a look! I ain't no fucking mountain goat!"

"Well, I ain't, neither."

Mark could almost place one of the voices, but not quite.

He ached with curiosity to look up over the edge of the rock and see who it was. If this was someone he knew from town, maybe someone from work, he probably should reveal himself. He could ask them what was going on in town. For all he knew, they might have found Dennis Cross's killer, and Phil might have already been found. Not willing to chance it, though, he pressed his back against the cold stone, clinging to the shadows as he breathed shallowly and waited for the two men to move along.

"This whole thing is a real pain in the ass, you know that? How much further do we have to go, anyway?"

No, Mark thought, *they don't sound anything like weekday hikers.*

There came a faint rustle of paper, and Mark realized they were checking a trail map.

"Looks to me like the Twin Brooks Trail's just over that ridge over there."

And they don't know much about this mountain, either. Twin Brooks Trail was a good three miles off.

"We're supposed to meet up with Foster's team at the fork around three o'clock, right?"

"Uh-huh. Gibbons said he wanted all of us off the mountain by dark."

The other person said something, but they were moving away, so Mark didn't quite catch it. He stayed where he was, motionless for a long time, listening as the eerie silence, broken only by fitful gusts of wind whistling over the rocks, settled back over the mountain.

Before long, the chilly air started to penetrate his down-filled jacket and clothes. His body shook, and his teeth were chattering. He desperately wanted to leave his hiding place, if only to get out into the sunlight and move around a bit to warm himself up. But then, just as he was starting to ease out onto the ledge, he heard something else. At first, it was so low he thought it might be his pulse, thumping in his ears. But it got steadily louder, and he recognized the chopping *whack-whack* of helicopter blades off in the distance.

"Ahh, *shit!*"

If there was a helicopter out, then this probably wasn't just a routine search for a missing man. Clutching his rifle, Mark eased himself up to the edge of the overhang and scanned the sky. The cloudless, bright blue stung his eyes, making him squint. At first he couldn't see it, but then, far off to his left, he made out the dark grasshopper-shape, silhouetted against the afternoon sky. It was moving at an oblique angle across the southern flank of the mountain. The sound of the rotors got steadily louder as it skimmed close to the contour of the mountain.

No doubt about it, there was *some* kind of serious search effort going on. Maybe the police and forest rangers had mounted it to find Phil; but Mark knew, if there was a warrant out for his arrest, there might be dozens of men out looking for him. It was just a matter of time before someone spotted him . . . or stumbled onto him, as those two men almost had.

"God *damn* it!"

Sunlight glinted off the helicopter's side as it swung gracefully around and started heading straight toward him. Mark cringed back into the shadow of the overhang, fighting the thought that they had already seen him and were now honing in on him. Off and on all day, he'd had the uncanny sensation that he was being watched by someone who remained unseen. Now it was easy to imagine a man up there in the helicopter, scanning the mountainside with high-powered binoculars while he radioed in directions to the men on the ground. All he needed to complete the mental picture was a couple of shotgun-totting rednecks being dragged along by a pack of bloodhounds, howling and straining at their leashes as they closed in on him from all sides.

Mark glanced over his shoulder to make sure no one else was around. It wouldn't do to let someone use the covering sound of the chopper to sneak up on him from behind. Satisfied that he was alone, he squatted close to the ground, peeking out from his hiding place just enough so he could keep an eye on the approaching helicopter. It was still flying straight toward where he was hiding.

"Come on, fly by—fly by—*fly by!*" he started to chant.

He ducked back under the rock when the rushing sound overhead grew deafeningly loud. A bulbous shadow swept across the rocks like a moving puddle of dark water. Mark didn't dare peek out at the helicopter, but he could easily imagine that it had stopped and was hovering right above him as dozens of armed men—maybe a SWAT team from Boston—swarmed down over the rocky slope toward him.

This is crazy, hiding like this! Absolutely insane! he thought. *It's not like I'm some kind of outlaw!*

But Mark's instinct to keep out of sight was overpowering. A deep, primitive instinct warned him that he would be in serious danger if the men in the helicopter spotted him. He shifted his feet up underneath him and scuttled forward, ready to duck back and hide or stand and run if anyone was close by. Peeking up over the rock, he clearly saw the markings on the gray metal side of the helicopter:

MAINE STATE POLICE

"Jesus *Christ!*" he muttered. "It *is* a fucking manhunt!"

He ducked back under cover as the whirling blades roared overhead, less than a hundred feet above him. The whooshing sound echoed from the rocky mountainside, and then the sound Dopplered as the helicopter made a slow, lazy turn and headed northwest. Within seconds, it disappeared behind the coned peak of the mountain.

"Too damned close for comfort," Mark whispered.

He brushed rock grit from his gloves and heaved a deep sigh as he sat down on his heels. A sheen of cold sweat sprinkled his forehead.

Is this how it's going to be? he wondered.

He sure as hell wasn't going to get anything accomplished if he had to hide under a rocky overhang all day, with a helicopter buzzing like an angry hornet around his head.

How many men are up here?

From what he'd overheard those two say, there might be a lot.

And who are they looking for—Phil or me?

Anger and frustration choked Mark. He had covered most of the southern and eastern flanks of Agiochook above the tree line yesterday; he had planned to cover the steeper, more treacherous western and northern sides today and tomorrow. So far he hadn't found even the slightest indication of a trail left by Phil; but if this search party was looking for him instead of his friend, he would have to alter his plans. He might have to wait here until dark before moving, and unless there was enough moonlight to see by, hiking down after dark was going to be a very dangerous proposition.

For now, though, he had a full canteen and a few trail snacks in the day bag slung over his shoulder. And he had his rifle, and plenty of ammunition if he needed it, but—*damn it!*—hiding here wasn't going to get him anywhere!

Mark sat back against the cold rock, his legs stretched out in front of him. There was nothing to do except wait until sunset, when the man said the officials wanted everyone off the mountain. But he couldn't stop wondering what those men were doing out here—and how long they would be doing it. His plans were completely screwed up, but at least right now, he had *plenty* of time to think about what to do next.

Chapter Sixteen

Attack

For the past two days, Sandy had been in a state of sustained, absolute panic. She had watched the TV news reports, read all the newspaper articles, talked to and overheard people talking downtown, and fretted about what was going to happen to her father. Although the police hadn't officially charged him with the murder of Dennis Cross, she didn't see how they could do otherwise. It was just a matter of time, now that the investigators had finished their careful examination of the area where Dennis had been killed. Of course, the police hadn't told her the results of their work; but as far as Sandy could tell, her father was in a heap of trouble.

Polly was no help at all to Sandy. Their relationship had always been strained, at best. Under this new pressure, it broke completely. They continued to live in the same house, but most of the time they both acted as if the other one wasn't even there. They ate their meals separately and didn't even bother to speak to each other when they chanced to meet. Polly had declined to go to Dennis's funeral, and went off to work every day as if everything was just fine . . . as if Dennis's horrible death in her own backyard had been no more serious than a flat tire. She spent quite a bit of time down at the police station, no doubt being questioned about that night, Sandy assumed; but just like the police, Polly wasn't telling her a thing about what was going on.

That left Sandy in a complete vacuum, wondering if her father was even still alive up there on the mountain.

Throughout the school day on Wednesday, Sandy felt agitated and tense. Her social studies teacher, Mr. Ives, talked to her after class, expressing his concern that the tension of everything was taking too great a toll on her. She insisted that she was bearing up quite well, considering the circumstances, and that she didn't want to miss any school if only to keep her mind occupied with something else. The truth was, she didn't even dare to talk about how bad she was feeling with her best friend, Karen Bishop, because she was afraid she might let something slip about how she had arranged a meeting place with her father. Although the cheerleading tryouts were tomorrow, and she knew she should stay for practice, she took the early bus home right after school.

Polly wasn't home; she was either at work or down at the police station again. Of course she couldn't have been bothered to leave a note. Just as well. Sandy hurriedly packed the food, clothes, and ammunition her father wanted, got into the Jeep, and headed up Route 26 to the Round Top Trail.

The drive up Route 26 was almost intolerable. Sandy was tempted to nudge the Jeep over the 45 mph speed limit, but she didn't want to be pulled over by a cop and have to explain where she was going in such a hurry with food supplies and rifle ammunition. By the time she got to the base of the Round Top Trail, the sun had shifted behind a bank of clouds. The forest was cast into a dark green, gloomy silence.

She pulled to a stop in the same place she had stopped the time before. Leaning over the steering wheel, she stared intently up at the trail, looking for the first indication that her father was on his way down. She was running a little late and had been hoping he would already be here.

"Come on, Dad! Jesus Christ! Where the hell are you?"

She drummed her fingertips on the dashboard in a frantic beat. The tall trees seemed to lean inward, pressing around her like a steadily tightening fist. Gusts of wind hit the side of the Jeep and whistled through the narrow slit of open window.

Sandy kept glancing back and forth between her watch and the trail. Seconds stretched into minutes, and still there was no sign of her father.

What if they've already found him and taken him off to jail? she wondered.

Or what if he's had an accident, fallen down and hurt himself?

He had told her the nights had been really cold up there. *What if he was sick, or had frozen to death?*

"Come on, Dad! Where the hell *are* you?"

The chilled air penetrated the Jeep, so she started up the engine and turned on the heater. But even with hot air blasting into her face, she shivered as she stared up at the dark green forest.

What the hell was happening up there?

"Jesus *Christ*, Dad! Don't do this to me! Don't *do* this!"

She revved the Jeep's engine, letting it whine like an overheating drill. Finally, unable to stand the winding tension any longer, she pressed her fist down hard on the horn. At first, she gave it just a few quick beeps; then she leaned on it with her elbow and kept it blaring for as long as her nerves could stand it.

What if one of Dennis Cross's friends has shot him?

What if they chased him and he fell off a cliff and broke both legs?

What if some wild animal attacked him and ripped him to pieces, like what happened to Dennis?

Sandy's body was trembling as she double-checked her seat belt, slammed the gear shift into reverse, and backed out of her parking spot. The tires splattered dirt against the underside of the Jeep's chassis, sounding like hail on a tin roof. Sandy wheeled the Jeep around and drove out onto the dirt road. All the while, her elbow was pressed down on the horn as she jockeyed the steering wheel back and forth to stay on the road.

Tears filled her eyes, and she kept up a steady pattern of long and short beeps on the horn as she drove down the dirt road until it abruptly ended. There wasn't enough room for her to turn around, so, looking over her shoulder, she backed up to the parking area again, turned around, and started down the road in the other direction. If her father was anywhere nearby, he'd have to hear the horn and know that she was waiting for him.

The tires skidded in the loose dirt as she raced a few hundred yards down the road, turned around, and came back to the parking area. Then she stopped again and stared up at the trail. When she still didn't see any sign of activity, she laid down hard on the horn again, letting it wail for a good two or three minutes.

"Where the hell are you?" she shouted as hot tears gushed from her eyes. "If you don't show up soon, I'm going to lose it completely, I swear to God I will!"

At that instant, something slammed into the side of the Jeep on the passenger's side, hitting it hard enough to rock the Jeep back and forth on its suspension.

Sandy's head banged against her window. Gasping for breath, she looked to her right and saw a face flattened against the window on the passenger's side. Foamy saliva and steaming breath smeared the glass, distorting her view, so in the first jolt of terror, all she could see was some kind of animal. Dark, glowing eyes framed by a furry face and shadowed by a sloping brow stared in at her with fierce anger. The creature's thick, black lips peeled back to expose a row of long, white teeth. Through the glass, Sandy could hear the creature roar loudly as it swung its arm back and slammed it against the Jeep door.

The impact was astounding. The metal of the door folded in like a tin can. Paralyzed by fear, Sandy sat there watching the beast, absolutely unable to react.

Again, the creature cocked back one arm and slammed a clenched fist against the Jeep. This time it hit the window like a sledgehammer. Broken glass exploded inward and hit Sandy's face like a blast of shotgun pellets. Sharp edges of glass stung her face and arms, and she screamed so loud and high her voice broke until the only sound coming out was a thin, wheezing whistle. With an angry snort, the creature reached in through the broken window, its huge, flat hand clawing frantically at the car seat, slicing the seat cover and removing huge chunks of the foam stuffing.

At that instant, Sandy's instinct for survival kicked in. She jerked the gear shift into reverse and stepped down hard on the accelerator. Dirt spewed from underneath its tires as the Jeep lunged backward with enough momentum to throw the creature clear. The huge, furry shape tumbled over several times and then lay still on the ground, its arms and legs splayed wide.

Sandy wiped her face with the back of her arm. Numbed by shock and surprise, she stared at the thin smear of blood, only distantly aware that it was *her* blood. When she looked back at the creature, she couldn't believe what she was seeing when it raised its head and, looking dazed and angry, got up slowly. Staring at her, it let loose a wild roar as it pounded its chest.

Whimpering softly under her breath, Sandy did a quick turnaround. The Jeep heaved to one side, skidding dangerously before righting itself and speeding out of the parking area. In its wake, it left a thin blue haze of exhaust.

Sandy was barely able to maintain control of the vehicle as she drove down the dirt road, weaving dangerously from side to side. She furiously wiped the tears and blood from her face, unable to believe that any of this was really happening. Her breath was a ball of fire in the center of her chest as she focused straight ahead on the winding road.

It had to have been a bear or something, she tried to convince herself. It couldn't have been what it had looked like! . . . But what the hell *had* it looked like?

She sure as hell knew that there weren't any apes in the forest, but that was what she had seen. It had looked as big as King Kong. If she needed any corroborating evidence, all she had to do was look at the smashed window and the dented passenger's door.

And those eyes! That creature had glared at her with a cruel animal intelligence!

Even under the best of circumstances, the road from the Round Top Trail to Route 26 was curvy and treacherous. Nearly blind with panic and tears, Sandy was driving much faster than was safe. Her hands ached from the tight grip she had on the steering wheel as she struggled to keep the careening Jeep on the road.

Even so, she wasn't ready for the hairpin turn.

It came up on her before she knew it. With a high, shrill scream, she jerked the steering wheel hard to the right, but it was already too late. The front right tire went over the soft shoulder of the road, and before she could recover, the Jeep roared down over the steep embankment and slammed into a stand of pine trees. Metal and glass exploded everywhere. Her seat belt kept her from flying through the windshield, but her head slammed—hard—against the steering wheel. The darkness behind her eyes erupted with spinning white stars, and then the darkness sucked her down. . . .

* * *

Seconds . . . minutes . . . hours later, Sandy came to.

As soon as she opened her eyes, a stinging jolt of pain gripped her entire body. She looked up and saw the trees and cloudy sky spinning overhead in a wild smear of green and gray. She drifted far away from herself and seemed to be detached from her body as she looked down at herself, suspended over the dashboard, hanging from her seat belt like a torn rag doll.

Waves of blackness crashed inside her head, getting steadily stronger and threatening to suck her back under as she weakly raised her head and looked out of the Jeep. She wasn't even sure which window she was facing. All around her, the forest was silent except for the distant sound of birdsong. The loudest sound was her own breathing—deep and raspy, sounding as if her head were encased in a deep sea diver's helmet.

The darkness inside her head roared louder.

The last thing she remembered before surrendering to that blackness was staring in horror as what looked like dozens of hulking, shadowy figures appeared from out of the forest and started moving slowly toward her wrecked Jeep.

Chapter Seventeen

Blood Spoor

What the hell's going on?

In the distance, Mark could hear the blaring of an automobile horn, echoing through the dense forest.

Maybe it's Sandy. It must be Sandy!

He glanced at his watch and realized how late he was, but there was nothing he could have done about it. He had been delayed because of having to avoid several of the search parties that seemed to be swarming all over the mountain. Sandy must have been waiting too long and was getting impatient.

No matter what the situation might be, Mark was still quite a way up the trail and knew he couldn't get down there fast enough.

Unslinging his rifle and gripping it tightly, he started running down the trail, no longer even trying to conceal himself from anyone who might be looking for him. His boots skidded and scuffed on the hard-packed trail, and it took a great deal of effort not to lose his footing or gain too much speed on the steep down slope.

"Hold on! I'm coming, Sandy!" he shouted, knowing—if it was her—there was no way she could hear him from this far away. The horn—and it definitely sounded like the Jeep's horn—continued to blast.

Then—suddenly—it cut off.

Oh, shit!

Mark was running so fast everything around him was a dark green blur except for the slick dirt trail under his feet. His breath came hot and fast, burning in his throat. Wind whistled in his ears, blocking out every other sound until he heard a vehicle's engine roaring loudly. He redoubled his efforts and considered dropping his rifle so he could run even faster, but if there was trouble, he might need it.

The thin trail stretched out in front of him, seemingly endless as it wound through the thick pine trees that crowded all around.

The noise from down at the trail head got steadily louder. Mark bolted his rifle, chambering a bullet, and snapped off the safety when he heard what sounded like the shattering of glass and the harsh scraping sound of tires peeling out in the dirt.

"*Sandy!*" he shouted, waving one arm wildly above his head as he broke out of the woods just in time to see the Jeep zip out of sight around the bend in the road. A thin haze of blue exhaust hovered in the air like fog.

It was Sandy, and she must have been in some kind of trouble.

It didn't take Mark long to find out what it was.

With a thundering roar, the creature sprang at him

from the trail side. Mark spun around and dropped into a defensive crouch as he brought the rifle to bear on the creature, but it was coming at him too fast for him to get a shot off. In a blur of brown fur and flashing claws, the creature slammed into Mark, knocking him off his feet. His forefinger involuntarily squeezed the trigger, and the rifle went off with an ear-splitting *crack* when he hit the ground. The recoil knocked the rifle from his hands. A split second later, a wide, flat paw swatted at him, just missing his face as it whistled past his ear. The creature's momentum carried it a good twenty feet past him before it stopped and wheeled around.

Mark's mind was paralyzed with fear as he scrambled backward, reaching for his rifle. He got it and stood up. His hands fumbled to chamber another round as the creature came at him again, its eyes blazing with fury as it raised its arms high above its head.

"Jesus *Christ!*" Mark yelled, unable to believe what he was seeing.

He instantly recognized the creature as the same thing he had seen on the mountain the day Phil had fallen off The Zipper. Although he hadn't gotten a clear view of it then or later that night, when it had attacked him at his campfire, it sure as hell was the same thing. Since coming down off the mountain, Mark had tried to deny what he thought he had seen; but now, in the bright glare of sunlight, this creature was *real*. Terrifyingly real! There was no way it could be a figment of his imagination!

But these fragmentary thoughts filled his mind in a confused rush; his only clear thought was that he had to get at least one clean shot off. As the creature charged him again, bellowing like an enraged bull,

Mark couldn't stop his hands from shaking enough to chamber the bullet. At the last instant, out of sheer desperation, he cocked the rifle back onto his shoulder like a baseball bat, crouched and timed his swing, and then, grunting viciously, swung it around in a swift arc just as the creature came within range.

The impact sent an electric jolt up his arms to his shoulders and neck. Accompanying the loud *crack* that sounded as if the rifle stock broke was an ear-splitting howl of pain. Mark ducked to one side as the creature staggered past him, its legs wobbling like those of a prizefighter who had just been nailed with a solid haymaker.

"*There, God damn yah!*" Mark shouted, his voice ragged and broken. "How'd you like *that?*"

Mark was panting heavily as he watched the creature, obviously stunned, turn and glare at him. Less than thirty feet separated them, and Mark now had the time to look at what he was facing. The sight froze his heart. Although the beast looked an awful lot like a huge ape, it also had a certain bearish appearance. Thick, brown fur—slouched shoulders—large head with sloping eyebrows—long, massive arms that had huge, clawed paws. Its eyes glistened with mingled pain and anger as it peeled back its thick lips and snarled, displaying an array of long, sharp teeth. Its left shoulder drooped down, the fur matted with the fresh flow of blood.

"*Come on! Come on, you ugly son-of-a-bitch!*" Mark yelled.

He braced his feet and readied himself for another charge. Holding his rifle back over his shoulder, he took a few threatening steps forward.

The creature regarded him with a hateful glare and

then started backing away from him, uttering a low, guttural grunt that sounded almost like a word. Mark sneered, almost laughing out loud as he lowered the rifle, bolted it, and raised it to his shoulder.

"So, you know what this is, do you?" he said, drawing a steady, careful bead on the animal. "Well, then, come on, motherfucker! Eat shit and *die!*"

The creature raised its arm high above its head, leaned its head back, and let loose a terrifying roar. The sound was deafening. A cold, hard knot tightened inside Mark's stomach, freezing him for a moment. Then, before he could react, before he could think to squeeze the trigger, the creature darted into the dense brush and disappeared in an instant. Mark pulled the trigger, and the rifle went off, kicking back hard against his shoulder, but he knew he had missed.

The beast was gone!

"Shit! Fuck!" he shouted as he slammed another round into the chamber and started off after the creature. He was confident, now, that he had hurt it, and it wasn't going to fight back . . . not unless it was cornered. When he got to where the creature had been standing, he looked down at the ground and saw a thick splotch of fresh blood.

"God damn! I hurt you more than I thought," Mark muttered as he stared into the eerily silent woods where the creature had disappeared like a shadow. The trail of crushed and broken brush was obvious, easy enough to follow, but better than that was the trail of blood. Mark knew he could keep on this trail even if it went up above the tree line, if that was where the creature was headed. And something deep inside him told him that was exactly where it was going. The wound was bleeding much more than it should have been. Maybe that one hit with the rifle butt had done the damage, but more likely, Mark thought, he might have reopened an old wound.

Either way, it didn't matter.

The creature was hurt and running back to its lair, wherever that may be, and Mark was going to hunt it down and kill it if only because now he was positive that this . . . this *thing*, whatever the hell it was, had been responsible for the death of his friend.

"But, Jesus Christ . . . what about Sandy?" Mark whispered as his gaze shifted back to the dirt road where the dust had long since settled.

It was late afternoon. That must have been her, driving off in such a hurry. She must have seen the creature, too—maybe it had even attacked her first; but Mark told himself that she couldn't have been seriously hurt. She had gotten away, driving like a bat out of hell.

So she must be all right!

He quickly scanned the area, studying the fresh tire tracks scuffed in the dirt, trying to figure out from them exactly what had happened. The sprinkling of broken glass on the ground convinced him that the creature had attacked the vehicle.

But she got away, he kept telling himself. *I saw her driving away!*

So he could put aside any worries about Sandy's safety and concentrate instead on tracking the creature back to its lair. The blood spoor was going to be easy enough to follow. The only problem he saw was if he ran into any more of those men who were out here looking for him.

Chapter Eighteen
Dark Walk

Like dark, rolling waves beating against the shore, consciousness came back in stages, and with it came the awareness of burning pain and the deeper ache of bruised and twisted muscles and bones. One particularly bright spot of pain was centered in Sandy's head. She raised her hand to her left temple and felt something sticky and crusty that was matting down her hair. Her eyes flickered open, and she held her hand up close to her eyes but could see only gauzy grayness. Groaning deeply, she let her eyes drift shut again, content that, if she was dying—or already dead—at least she was going to go without a struggle.

But she wasn't dead, and she didn't die.

After fading in and out of awareness several times, she became aware of cold air circulating around her. Her disoriented mind turned the air into icy water, and she dreamed that she was swimming in Moosehead Lake, where she and her parents used to vacation before the divorce. . . . She had dived down deep and now, tangled in the reeds, she was struggling to push herself off the cold, slimy bottom of the lake. She could feel the slick, greasy water weeds and slime underfoot, and the swirling water, tugging her downward.

". . . *Ahh* . . ."

The sound was distant. It echoed as though whoever had spoken was shouting to her from deep inside a cavern. It reverberated like a long roll of thunder that hurt her ears as it got louder, but it also brought her closer to awareness. Her arms and legs began to thrash like those of a swimmer who has lost the strength but not the will to live.

". . . Where . . ."

Stop shouting at me!

". . . am . . ."

I told you, you don't have to shout like that!

". . . I? . . ."

If you don't stop shouting, I'll have to leave!

"Where would I go?"

Although it was broken and weak, this time she recognized her own voice. It resonated with a cheap, tinny echo in her ears.

"What the . . . what the hell *happened?*"

She opened her eyes to narrow slits and saw all around her a darkness as rich and deep as black velvet. A vague memory of driving off the road returned. For several panicked heartbeats, Sandy thought that she was indeed dead or that she had been struck blind; but then, through the spiderweb crack in the windshield, she saw the jagged line of dark trees against the dusty brightness of the night sky. The skyline was at an impossible angle, but after a while she realized that she was still in the Jeep, which was lying on its side. She was rolled over to one side and hanging from her seat belt.

For a moment, she lay still, trying desperately to collect her thoughts, wondering how long she had been unconscious in the wreck. It was too dark to see the dial of her wristwatch. For all she knew, it could be after midnight. Every bone and muscle in her body felt sprained or broken; she was unable to move, but—finally—she determined that she had to get herself out of the wreck.

The cold night air made her shiver as she fumbled in the dark for the seat belt release. She tried to click it, but her weight was holding the latch fast, trapping her. She banged on it and jiggled it furiously, but it wouldn't give. Panting heavily, her body racked with pain, she managed to wiggle herself free of the restraining strap and swing her legs down. She had lost one of her shoes in the crash, so she stepped barefooted onto a pile of broken glass. A stinging cut made her cry out. Balancing on one foot, she felt around on the Jeep floor until she found the missing shoe and slipped it on.

She thought her arm would break before she could push the driver's door open, but she managed to swing it open and clamber up out of the overturned Jeep. In the darkness, she couldn't make out any details of where she was. All she knew for certain was that the Jeep was a twisted mess of metal, lying at the bottom of a deep gully. Whimpering under her breath, Sandy skittered up the steep slope and back onto the road. Once there, she bent over, put both hands on her knees, and took several deep, gulping breaths of the night air, hoping it would help control her panic.

The silent woods pressed in on her from all sides like huge, enfolding arms. Ahead of her and behind, the narrow dirt road was little more than an indistinct gray blur that was soon lost in the surrounding dark in either direction.

A tingling jolt of fear shot through her as she considered what she should do next.

She was confused and disoriented.

How far was it back to town?

Should she start walking?

Or would it be better to wait until morning, if only to make sure she started off in the right direction?

What if she ended up back at the Round Top Trail head?

And what if that horrible monster was still back there, waiting for her?

Or—worse!

What if it was nearby?

As if to justify her rising fear, just then a mournful howl drifted to her out of the darkness. It started out low, but quickly built to a rising, wavering yelp that was immediately answered by another howl, this one sounding much closer. Sandy had been camping enough times with her father to know that these were either foxes or coyotes, but the first question that popped into her mind was: What are they hunting?

"Okay, okay," she said, speaking out loud to bolster her courage. "Don't get panicky! . . . Gotta stay calm. . . . Think things through, here."

As soon as another chorus of howling began, she decided that the first thing she needed was a weapon. Too bad her father hadn't left one of his hunting rifles on the gun rack in the Jeep. She wouldn't have felt half as vulnerable if she had a loaded gun. Somewhere in the wreckage was a whole box of bullets, but what good would they do her? Right now, even a decent stick or club would feel good.

She skidded back down the embankment to the Jeep, reached up into the cab, and felt for the knob to turn on the headlights. She hadn't really expected the lights to work, so she squealed with surprise when the flood of bright light illuminated the gully and the thick wall of brush and pine trees.

Moving around to the front of the Jeep, Sandy rolled back her sleeve, amazed to see that it was well past eleven o'clock—almost eleven-thirty.

Would Polly be at all upset that she hadn't come home from school yet?

Would she be concerned or relieved that she was out this late on a school night?

Would she even bother to call the police?

Or would she simply assume that she was staying overnight with one of her friends?

Sandy couldn't stop the bitter thought that, if Dennis Cross were still alive, Polly would no doubt take the opportunity of having an empty house to do a little bit of cheating.

"Two-timing little *slut*!" she muttered.

She scrambled into the brush and searched around until she found a long pine branch that would serve her purposes. She broke off one end to make a four-foot length, then trimmed off the remaining branches with her foot. Satisfied that she now had a serviceable walking stick which—if she needed it—could double as a weapon, she went back up to the road, prepared to start walking.

After giving herself a quick check-over and finding no serious injuries, other than the slice on the bottom of her foot that hurt with every step she took, she started out. She knew the Jeep was a total loss anyway, so she didn't care if she left the headlights on. At least they would illuminate the first hundred feet or so of her hike. She tried to whistle a carefree tune, but her lips were too dry to produce a sound, so before long she gave up.

As soon as the diffuse glow of the headlights was lost around a curve in the road, darkness closed around her with an almost audible rush. Sandy immediately wished she had decided to stay with the Jeep until morning. She could have made herself as comfortable as possible inside the overturned vehicle and waited out the night. But already it seemed just as easy to forge on ahead as it did to return. The howling foxes or coyotes or whatever sounded more distant now, a little less threatening. She actually began to feel a slight measure of confidence buoy her as she focused on the dull glow of the road ahead, determined to make it home before dawn.

She had no idea how far she had walked when a sound in the woods off to her right drew her attention. She stopped short in her tracks, her body tensed. The hairs at the back of her neck prickled as she strained to hear the sound again. She tried to convince herself that it had been nothing more than a raccoon or a rabbit or some other harmless creature, but the heavy snapping of a branch underfoot had sounded like it had been made by something big.

Now the woods were silent . . . too silent.

Shouldn't there be birds singing, or crickets and

frogs? she wondered. The only sound was the hissing of the wind high in the pines.

"It's nothing," she said aloud, trying to shore up her flagging courage, but her voice sounded frail, pitifully small in the engulfing darkness.

Sandy tried to swallow the hard lump that was growing in her throat, but it wouldn't go down. All she could imagine was that a pack of wolves or a black bear or something much worse was out looking for something sweet and tasty to eat. Her pulse began to race with a high, fast throbbing in her ears.

Calm down! Just calm the Christ down! she told herself, but it did no good. Suddenly, it seemed as though all the woods around her were filled with glowing, green eyes that watched her, stalking her . . . just waiting to pounce.

Uttering a low, little cry, Sandy clenched her fists and began to jog. Within seconds, the jog turned into a full-blown run. Her feet slapped hard against the dirt road, and the wind whistled in her ears, blocking out every other sound. She tried to convince herself that she just had to get a move on, cover some ground so she wouldn't be wandering around on this deserted dirt road all night, but the panic that was building up inside her only got worse. Before long, she was convinced that there was indeed someone—or something—following close behind her, just waiting for the opportunity to strike. She increased her pace until she was running full-tilt down the road. She was so lost in her flight that she didn't notice the group of men ahead of her on the road until one of them, hearing her footsteps, turned and yelled, *"What the hell is that?"*

Sandy drew to an abrupt stop, but even before the

echo of the man's shout had faded, there came a flash of light followed by an explosion. Something buzzed past Sandy's ear like a hornet. Panting viciously, Sandy dropped to the ground and shouted, "Hey! Hold it! Don't shoot!"

"What the—? Who the hell is it?" a man shouted.

"What're you doing out here this time of night?" someone else said.

Sandy tried to answer, but her stomach suddenly squeezed, and hot vomit shot out of her mouth and nose. Bracing her hands on her knees, she leaned forward as wave after wave of nausea gripped her, wringing her out like a damp washcloth. A flashlight beam snapped on and swung around until it found her.

"I'll be a son-of-a-bitch!" one of the men said as they started back up the road toward her. "Is that you, Sandy? It's me, Tim Farrell."

"Tim—" Sandy said, still choking on vomit. Her throat was burning with a horrible aftertaste, and her knees threatened to collapse as she stood up as the men grouped around her. She could see now that there were three of them.

"I was just—" That was all she could say before another wave of dry heaves gripped her stomach.

"I know what you was," Tim said as he placed his arm around her shoulder and held her. "You was just about to get yourself killed. I'll bet you came out here looking for your daddy, like we did, didn't you?"

Sandy could only see a vague silhouette of Tim's face as he supported her, but she felt immense relief, knowing that she was safe with one of her father's hunting buddies.

"Me and a couple of the boys from the mill didn't like some of the attitudes we've been hearing 'round town," Tim went on. " 'Specially at that meeting at the police station this morning, so we came out here ourselves to look for your father, too. We was hoping to hell we'd find him before some trigger-happy asshole—pardon the expression—found him first."

"Speaking of trigger-happy assholes . . ." one of the other men said. Sandy recognized the voice of Willis Franklin, another one of her father's friends. "Umm—sorry 'bout shooting like that. I guess I was kinda spooked."

"Damn good thing you're such a piss-poor shot, too, Willis," Tim said. "Come on, Sandy. We're a bit late getting off the mountain ourselves." He sniffed with laughter. "I'm parked a mile or so down the road here. I guess we're all in this together, huh?"

"I guess so," Sandy said weakly.

"Well, don't you worry. We'll get you home in no time."

Chapter Nineteen

Hunkering Down

Just as Mark suspected it would, the trail of blood led across the east branch of the river and up above the timberline toward the rock-strewn, almost inaccessible cliffs on the western side of Mount Agiochook. Behind him, the afternoon sun was slanting down to the horizon, edging the distant blue mountains in New Hampshire with a harsh line of orange fire. Long, gray shadows stretched out in front of him as he clambered over rocks and scaled sheer cliffs, all the while searching for the telltale splotches of red. He was amazed that, wounded as it was, the creature could cover such rugged terrain so easily. No wonder, when it wasn't hurt, it could appear and disappear so fast. This thing seemed to have the agility of a mountain goat and the endurance of a bear.

After almost four hours of tracking, Mark still didn't seem to be gaining any ground on it. The blood spoor was lessening, but for it to have lasted this long, he knew it had to be a serious wound. Fewer and smaller splotches appeared further and further apart. A few times, Mark lost the trail entirely and had to swing around in a wide arc until he picked it up again. With night approaching fast, he was afraid that he would lose track of the creature for good. It hadn't helped matters that, several times throughout the afternoon, he had lost precious time hiding as the state police helicopter buzzed by overhead, or small groups of men passed by. At least so far he hadn't seen any bloodhounds!

As he tracked the creature, Mark couldn't stop wondering exactly what this thing was. He had encountered the beast three times so far but had only gotten one good look at it, this afternoon. But even after the encounter today, as horribly real as it had been, he couldn't quite accept or process what he had seen. The creature seemed more illusory than real, like something out of a horrible nightmare.

Ever since he was a little boy, he had spent a lot of time hunting and hiking in the forest. In all that time, he had never encountered anything *like* this. Of course, like most people, he had heard the stories about the Himalayan *yeti*, the Pacific Northwest's *Sasquatch*, as well as the local Indian legends about creatures such as the *Pomoola*, *Hobomock*, and *Wendigo*. In fact, Mark remembered how, on the day Phil and he had been hiking, he had teased Phil with stories about how the Indians had thought the summit of Agiochook was haunted, but he had always dismissed those stories as just that—stories.

Until now, that is.

Now he wasn't so sure.

Whatever that thing was, as impossible as it seemed, it had definitely looked and moved more like a huge ape than a bear. Mark recalled the thick, cloying animal stench as it had rushed past him and knocked him down. It had almost killed him with that powerful swipe of its paw, and by the looks and sounds of things at the base of the trail, it had also attacked Sandy or whomever had been out there.

So Mark had to accept that he was dealing with something real . . . something he had injured when he slugged it with his rifle . . . something that was bleeding profusely from an old shoulder wound which, he assumed, he had reopened.

And that meant one thing—it was something that he could kill!

Still, no matter what he thought, he couldn't quite accept what he had seen. It was crazy! Downright impossible! Several times during the afternoon, he had started laughing to himself just at the idea that there was a Bigfoot living in the Maine mountains.

How could that be?

How could anything like that live up here in the mountains all these years without ever being seen or photographed or captured?

No, this idea just plain didn't fit in with the practical, everyday experiences Mark had in the forest while growing up.

It simply didn't make sense.

But last weekend at The Zipper, *something* had shambled across the cliff side and slung Phil Sawyer over its shoulder

. . . and *something* had attacked him that night in his camp

. . . and now he was tracking *something* that was

wounded and bleeding. No matter what else, Mark was determined to find out what it was and where it lived.

And then, if only to make himself feel better because it had killed his friend and tried to kill him, he was going to kill it!

"But not today," Mark muttered as he glanced over his shoulder at the lowering sun. Thick shadows of night were already filling the valley below. The wind blew cold and lonely up the flank of the mountain and into his face, promising another night of below-freezing temperatures.

As best he could tell, the trail led over a jumble of boulders, some the size of small houses, and up a nearly flat cliff side. Mark knew it would be dangerous, possibly suicidal, to continue stalking the creature much longer today. His campsite was a couple of miles down the slope. If he had wanted to eat something other than a handful or two of trail mix and sleep in a warm sleeping bag tonight, he should have started down the mountain before now.

It was already too late.

Mark scanned the vicinity for someplace to hunker down for the night. At the very least, he had to find something out of the wind. Up ahead, in the jumble of rocks, he saw a shallow cave where one large, flat rock had fallen on top of several others. There was enough shelter so he could at least stay dry if it rained tonight. Scrambling across the rocky slope, still watchful for any search parties, he entered the shallow cave.

Sighing heavily, he swung his day pack and rifle off his shoulder and sat with his back against the cold stone as he faced the cave opening. The shelter was cramped; sleeping was not going to be comfortable, but he contented himself with the thought that, if he didn't sleep well, at least he would be awake early enough to get started before dawn.

Outside the cave mouth, the sky rapidly darkened from deep purple to black. Mark bolted the rifle and rested it across his lap as he fished a bag of trail mix out of his day pack, tore it open, and started to eat. The heavy crunching sound and lack of taste reminded him more of gravel than food. He washed his meager meal down with several swallows of water from his canteen, but he went easy on his water supply, knowing that he would be above the timberline all day tomorrow.

As night closed down around the mountain, the sky filled with a dazzling display of stars. Mark shivered and pulled his collar up tightly around his neck as he stared out at their sparkling splendor. It never ceased to amaze him how different the stars looked when he was alone, deep in the wilderness. It made him feel infinitesimally small, totally insignificant in the great scheme of things; but at the same time it also gave him a feeling of immense power, of grandeur. He could easily understand why the Indians had considered Agiochook a holy mountain. Other than Mount Katahdin, far to the north, it was about as close as you could get to heaven in all of Maine.

There wasn't enough room in the cave to lie down flat, so after his meal, Mark settled back and tried to doze sitting up with his weapon at the ready.

Throughout the night, his sleep was thin and disturbed. Sometime during the night, he suddenly jolted awake, convinced that he had heard or sensed something moving around outside the cave—the soft scuffing of padded feet on stone.

As he sat there in the dark, listening tensely, he eased the safety off his rifle and leaned forward to look out at the rocky slope. A strong wash of moonlight lit the scene with a powdery blue glow. Shadows as dark and thick as puddles of ink dotted the uneven terrain. He more than half expected to see members of a search party go by, but the mountain was absolutely silent, deserted.

He was about to attribute the faint sound to something he had dreamed, or a noise he had made shifting against the rock wall of the cave; but just as he was about to relax his guard, it came again, this time accompanied by a muffled snuffing sound. Every nerve in Mark's body started tingling when he saw a large shadow, cast by the wash of moonlight behind it, slide out across the rocks in front of his hiding spot.

There was someone—or something—out there, right on top of the rock . . . directly above his head!

Mark held his breath and waited, listening as the sniffing sound grew steadily louder. The image of a dog or wolf came to mind, but something warned Mark that this was much more serious. Whatever it was up there, it had definitely picked up his scent and had come to investigate. If it was a wild animal, Mark knew he could scare it off with a sudden noise. But if it *wasn't* an animal . . . if it was that creature he had been chasing all afternoon . . .

Moving as quietly as he could, Mark shifted his legs up underneath himself and got ready to move if he had to. He raised his rifle slowly, letting his forefinger rest lightly on the trigger. He watched the shadow shift back and forth, and he tried his best to make out what it was, but the slanting moonlight and the rocky terrain lengthened and distorted it. He kept trying to convince himself that he *wasn't* looking at a large, human-shaped figure with long, powerful arms and a thick-muscled body. He kept trying not to think that this thing had used the cover of darkness to sneak up on him from behind.

As Mark moved forward, preparing to stick his head out of the cave so he could catch a glimpse of whatever was up there, his foot bumped against his canteen. The instant the metal clicked ever so softly against the rock, the shadow above him pulled back and disappeared. Swearing softly under his breath, Mark propelled himself out of the cave, stood up, turned around quickly, and raised his rifle to his shoulder as he scanned the area.

The mountainside was almost as bright as daylight with the strong moonlight, and it didn't take Mark long to fix on the large figure scrambling over the rocks away from him. It was moving up the slope silently and swiftly, like the shadow of a passing cloud. On pure reflex, Mark raised his rifle, took aim, and squeezed the trigger. The flash and sound of the shot split the night and echoed with a long, rolling boom, like thunder. In the wink of an eye, the shadow was lost in the confusion of shadows cast by the rocks. Mark quickly bolted his rifle and cracked off another shot just for good measure, but he knew it was futile.

"Shit!" he yelled, his voice echoing from the rocky mountainside in a long roll, like a chorus of shouts.

Once again, the mountainside was deserted. Only the wind moved, like cold, dark water between the jagged boulders. Off in the distance, Mark saw a large cliff that glowed eerily blue with reflected moonlight.

He knew its name: Katherine's Leap, and high above it was the slanting, smooth face of The Zipper.

For a fleeting instant, Mark thought he saw a blur of motion halfway up the sheer rock wall of Katherine's Leap, but before he could focus on it, it was gone. It could have been nothing more than the shadow of a cloud, passing in front of the moon, but it also might have been the creature, although it was remarkable, almost impossible, Mark thought, for it to have covered that much ground so fast, especially if it was wounded.

Mark knew he would have to make Katherine's Leap his first goal in the morning. It was in the same general direction he had been heading, anyway. There were no trails or chiseled handholds up the side of the cliff. Very few people bothered to climb the cliff because it was more easily accessible from the top. But Mark figured if that thing could scale that rock wall, wounded as it was, then come morning, he would find a way to get up there, too.

Satisfied that the creature was gone and that he was no longer in danger—at least for now—he eased back into his shelter and tried to get as comfortable as possible. But for the rest of the night there would be little if any sleep for him. After reloading his rifle, he sat with it across his lap, content, as he waited for the sky to lighten with the dawn, to watch the slow, steady progress of the stars as they wheeled around overhead.

Chapter Twenty

The Wreckage

"Please, Mr. LaBrea! You have to call off the search for my father!"

It was early Thursday morning. Guy LaBrea was sitting at his desk when Sandy Newman burst into his office. He couldn't hide his surprise when he saw the wadded bandage taped to her forehead.

"Hold on a minute, now. Tell me what happened to you."

Sandy grimaced and said, "It's a long story, but first of all, you have to contact all those men you have out there in the woods and tell them to stop looking for my father." She sucked in a deep breath. "I *know* he didn't kill Dennis Cross."

LaBrea stood up and casually waved Sandy over to the empty chair beside his desk. She approached it cautiously, then sat down stiffly and leaned forward with both of her hands clenched into fists in her lap.

LaBrea noticed that she limped as she walked. He sat back down, trying to appear casual as he waited for her to start talking.

"I went out to Round Top Trail yesterday afternoon," Sandy began, her voice high and trembling. "And I saw—I think I saw what might have killed Dennis . . . maybe even Phil Sawyer, too."

"*What* killed them?" LaBrea said, arching one eyebrow. "You don't mean *who*, do you?"

Sandy bit her lower lip and shook her head as she inhaled sharply. "No. I know you're not gonna believe me, but there's a . . . there's some kind of monster out there in the forest. It attacked me yesterday afternoon."

"Is that how you got hurt?"

Sandy winced as she touched the edge of the bandage on her forehead. "It's nothing serious. Just a couple of little cuts."

"I noticed you were limping, too," LaBrea said. His mouth was set in a firm line as he regarded her, but his eyes were earnest and sympathetic when he said, "So tell me everything."

Trying to clear her mind so she could begin, Sandy took another shuddering breath, but the memory of what had happened out at the trail head still gripped her with a tightening tension.

"I—well, I know it's probably against the law, but I've been helping my father—bringing him supplies."

"Hold it right there!" LaBrea said. He slapped his hand down hard on his desk. The sudden sound made Sandy jump. "I hope you understand that, as of right now anyway, no one's charged your father with any crime of any kind, all right?"

Sandy nodded tightly.

"I know, but there are men up there looking for him. And some of them want to kill him."

"No one's gonna go killing anyone, understand? Now go on. Tell me what happened yesterday."

"Well—" Sandy said. She looked at him earnestly, wishing she felt she could trust him entirely, but she couldn't dispel the suspicion that he was trying to set her up to reveal where her father was hiding.

"Right after school yesterday, I went out to drop off some stuff for him—some clothes, food, and—uh, bullets—out at Round Top Trail. I waited around for a while, but my dad never showed up, so I—I guess I started to get pretty worried, you know? Because of all the people who were out there looking for him, and I guess I—well, I panicked a little, thinking he might have been hurt or—or something, you know? When I couldn't take it any more, I started driving back and forth, honking my horn, hoping he'd hear it and hurry up."

"But he didn't show."

Sandy shook her head. "No . . . but *something* did. This—this gigantic animal came out of the woods and attacked the Jeep."

"Animal . . . you mean like a bear?"

"Yeah, but it seemed much bigger than a bear, and it didn't really look like a bear. It was—I don't know what it was. I've never seen anything like it."

"But you're *sure* it wasn't a bear?" LaBrea said. "I'm not doubting you, but you know how in a situation like that, you might not see what's really happening. Your imagination can exaggerate things."

Sandy shook her head firmly. "No, I know it wasn't a bear. I mean, I was scared and everything, but I saw it, and it didn't look at all like a bear. It had a face that was—I know this sounds crazy, but it really looked almost human. It broke the window on the Jeep and—and tried to grab me—"

Her voice cut off with a sharp intake of breath.

"Hey now, take it easy, all right?" LaBrea said. "Would you like something to drink? A soda or glass of water or something?"

"Umm. Water would be fine."

When LaBrea got up from his desk and walked out into the hallway, Sandy closed her eyes and tried to focus her thoughts. He returned a few seconds later with a paper cup full of water. Sandy took a sip, shivered, then cleared her throat and went on with her story. In a halting voice, she described to the police chief everything that had happened, at least as clearly as she could recall. LaBrea listened patiently, interrupting her only a few times to ask her to clarify some detail.

"But none of the men you met—Willis or Tim or Frank—none of them mentioned seeing your wrecked Jeep back there on the road?"

Sandy shrugged. "No. Maybe it was too dark when they passed by, or maybe it's too far down in the gully for them to have seen it. I don't know."

"What do you say you and I take a little drive out to Round Top Trail and have a look around?" LaBrea said. "If we put together what you've just said with some of the confusing evidence the investigators found out at your house and that complaint I got from a local farmer last weekend—well . . ." He scratched his chin thoughtfully. "I'm just not sure."

"Wha—what do you mean?"

"Come on. Let's take a ride. We can talk in the cruiser on the way there."

But they didn't do much talking as they drove out of town and up Route 26 and into the forest. For her part, Sandy still felt suspicious of LaBrea, even though he seemed to be genuinely trying to help her. One thing that concerned her, though, was that he hadn't done anything to call off the search parties that, she assumed, would be out again today, looking for her father. And she would have felt a whole lot more comfortable if he hadn't had his service revolver holstered at his side. What if he was bringing her out here hoping she'd lead him straight to her father?

"It can't be far now," Sandy said once they turned onto the dirt road where a sign read: "Round Top Trail—3 miles."

Although the sun was shining brightly, and the police cruiser's heater was working, Sandy shivered as they drove down the narrow corridor of tall pine trees and thick brush that lined the roadside. Whenever she looked out her window, she imagined huge, hulking shadows slinking behind cover before she could focus on them. In broad daylight, the events of yesterday now seemed strangely remote, almost as if they were someone else's memories . . . or a dream she'd had.

"I think it's just up ahead here," she said, sitting forward on the seat and straining against the shoulder strap. "It was dark, so I'm not exactly sure where I went off the road. I know it was on one of the hairpin turns. It will be up here on the left—Yeah! There it is!"

LaBrea stopped along the side of the road, and they both got out of the car as the dust swirling in their wake slowly settled.

"Whew!" LaBrea said, wiping his forehead with the back of his arm as he stood on the roadside and looked down at the wreckage. "When you go off the road, you *really* go off the road. You're lucky you weren't killed."

Sandy gave him a twisted smile but said nothing. She watched as LaBrea scrambled down the rocky embankment and approached the Jeep, which was lying on its side in the scrub brush.

"Well, I'll tell you one thing for sure; this baby's totaled." LaBrea walked around to the front of the Jeep and, bending over, looked at the underside of the vehicle. Twisted metal and broken glass were strewn everywhere.

"What window did you say this creature of yours broke?"

"On the passenger's side."

LaBrea nodded, then after pushing against the Jeep to make sure it wouldn't turn over on him, he climbed up onto the topside, opened the driver's door, and lowered himself inside. As soon as he was out of sight, Sandy felt a wave of nervousness. Shivering, she cast a worried glance all around, fully expecting to see the shadows in the woods thicken and take on form and start closing in on her.

"Wha—what are you looking for?" she called out, fighting down the tremor in her voice. She wanted only to hear LaBrea's voice so she could get rid of the notion that she was all alone out here.

For a moment, LaBrea didn't reply; then he said something, but his voice was indistinct, as though he were speaking to her from the bottom of a deep well.

"I can't hear you," Sandy called out as she cast another worried glance over her shoulder. She felt totally vulnerable, and was convinced that there was someone hiding in the shadows, watching her.

LaBrea's head popped up from inside the Jeep. "I said, it sure does look as though *something* funny happened here."

"It wasn't funny to me."

"No, I mean—look at this!"

Raising his hand above his head, LaBrea showed her something, but Sandy was too far away to see clearly what it was. She started down the slope as LaBrea clambered out of the Jeep and jumped down to the ground.

"Looks to me like—well, whatever this thing you say you saw was, it scraped off a fair-sized piece of itself when it punched out your window."

Sandy looked at the clump of brown fur LaBrea was holding in his hand. They were both silent for several seconds, neither one knowing quite what to say. Finally, Sandy cleared her throat and said softly, "So—now do you believe me?"

LaBrea squinted as he looked at her for a moment in silence; then he said, "Well, it sure as hell looks like you were telling the truth about this."

He regarded the piece of fur in his hand a moment longer, then said, "I don't know what the hell it is or what's going on here, but I think you might be right." He looked for a moment at the woods surrounding them. "There might be something out there that's responsible for what's been happening. Let me get on the radio and see if I can cancel those search parties . . . just so no one gets hurt up there today."

Chapter Twenty-one

Katherine's Leap

Night seeped out of the sky like a dark stain fading slowly to gunmetal gray. Mark roused himself from the light doze he had slipped into, stretched his arms out in front of him, and groaned as he rubbed his eyes. A stiffening chill clung to nearly every bone and muscle as he slid out onto the rock in front of his shelter and stood up, stretching to his full height.

The sun had not yet risen from behind the mountain, so everything around him was still locked within the gloom of night. A vagrant wind stirred the air with a numbing touch of winter. From far down the mountainside, Mark could hear the distant songs of morning birds in the forest. Tilting his head back, he sucked in a deep lungful of the frigid air and held it for a moment. Under ordinary circumstances, he would have appreciated the early morning stillness, the calm, the serenity; but today a sense of caution made him grip his rifle tightly as he swung around and let his gaze shift up the steep slope of Katherine's Leap.

A rumbling deep in his stomach reminded him that what he really wanted was, if not the comforts of home, at least a hearty breakfast around a roaring campfire. But his campsite was a couple of miles away, and he was heading up to Katherine's Leap on the west side of Agiochook. A handful of trail mix and a few swallows of stale water were going to have to suffice before he started.

The incident last night stirred in his memory as he looked up at the summit, steel-gray and foreboding in the predawn darkness. It was easy enough to think that he had imagined it all. How could anything cover that much ground in so short a time and make it halfway up the cliff side before disappearing? Whenever he was in the wilderness, Mark felt an almost surreal aspect to it, especially when he was out alone, but he also knew his mind well enough not to doubt the reality of what he had seen. He was definitely tracking something . . . something that didn't fit very well into his conception of what should be out here.

"And today, God damn it, I'm gonna find out what," he said, watching his words appear as streamers of mist that instantly blew away in the cold morning air.

He took one last swallow of water, relieved himself against a boulder, then shouldered his day pack and rifle and started out as the first traces of morning light trimmed the edge of Agiochook's summit with white fire.

It took him quite a while to work the morning stiffness out of his joints and muscles. Climbing in the shadow of the mountain, out of the warming rays of the sun, didn't help any. He realized that the hunger, thirst, and exhaustion of the past few days were starting to take their toll on him. The experienced outdoorsman in him warned him that, no matter what else happened today, he would have to come down off the mountain soon, probably today. It didn't matter what he had sworn to himself or to anyone else; there was no sense jeopardizing his own life on what, with each passing day, was proving to be an increasingly futile—and dangerous—mission.

Mark tried to head straight toward Katherine's Leap, but large rocks and deep chasms impeded his progress, making the going much tougher than he had expected. For all the times he had climbed Agiochook in his life, he had never taken the western approach. He didn't see any more traces of the faint blood trail, but that didn't matter; he didn't want to waste any more precious time searching for the trail when Katherine's Leap was his immediate goal. He was thankful that, at least so far, he hadn't encountered any more search parties. Maybe they had realized how futile their efforts were, too.

After an hour of climbing, Mark was starting to feel drained, both physically and mentally. Katherine's Leap looked about as far away as it had been when he started. Looking back, he was surprised and angry at how little ground he had actually covered.

"But I've covered it all with a goddamned fine-tooth comb," he said to himself as he stared ahead at the cliff.

It wasn't until a little after nine o'clock that he was finally standing at the foot of Katherine's Leap. The cliff was at least seventy-five feet high, almost straight up, and nearly twice that distance long. Above it in the powder blue sky were faint traces of fast-moving clouds, fanning out like long, smoky fingers from the east.

At least from where he stood, the sheer rock wall looked absolutely unclimbable without ropes and pitons. No matter how far Mark ranged in either direction looking for any sign of blood, he didn't see any traces. If the creature had, in fact, come this way, it must have veered off in one direction or the other.

But which?

Unless it had—somehow—found enough toe- and handholds to go straight up the cliff, as he thought he had seen it do last night.

But how was that possible?

Either way, Mark saw no point in going up the hard way. The top ledge of Katherine's Leap was a wide, sloping stretch of rock below The Zipper. A steep but much easier climb down from there would get him to the same place—that is, if he wanted to take most of the day to hike around the side of the mountain to the eastern approach.

In all likelihood, that creature didn't go up there, Mark thought as he scanned the cliff side back and forth. Other than a few narrow overhangs and slanting rock shelves, the cliff, still cast in the shadow of the mountain, looked like smooth, red granite, worn to a flat gloss from centuries of harsh weather and numerous landslides, which had deposited tons of rock and rubble at its base.

Maybe, Mark thought, last night the darkness and moonlight had played tricks on his eyes. Maybe he hadn't actually seen the creature climbing up this cliff until it disappeared, halfway up. It made a lot more sense that it had taken some other route around the base of the cliff to . . . to wherever it lived.

But something told Mark that just wasn't so.

He walked back and forth among the jumble of stones at the base of the cliff, all the while looking up and searching for some place where he might find enough handholds to climb up. He had to keep looking down to watch his footing, and that was when he noticed the thin strip of bright orange cloth sticking out from underneath one of the large boulders. His breath caught in his chest as he bent down to inspect it. A shudder passed through him when he saw that it was the shoulder strap of a backpack.

"Oh, Jesus," Mark whispered. He knew that Phil had been carrying a brand-new Day-Glo orange backpack the day he had fallen off The Zipper. Mark had teased him about it when they had started out.

Mark bent down and pulled on the strap, not too surprised when it didn't slide out from beneath the rock. Leaning back, he pulled all the harder, but the strap was pinned down so tightly it barely moved from side to side. Bracing his feet on the rock, he leaned back and tugged for all he was worth, and still the strap wouldn't pull free.

"What the Christ!" he muttered as he put his rifle down, got onto his hands and knees, and leaned close to inspect the shoulder strap more carefully. It sure as hell looked brand-new. Of course, there was no way of knowing for certain if this was Phil's or not, but whoever owned it and however it had come to be under this rock, it obviously hadn't been here for very long. The nylon shell was still pliable and bright, not faded and brittle. Mark was certain the rest of the backpack was trapped beneath the rock, too; that was why he couldn't pull it free. His problem was, the rock was too big for him to move by himself.

A dry lump formed in his throat when he wondered, *What if the pack's not the only thing under here?*

What if, after falling off The Zipper, Phil had fallen off Katherine's Leap, starting an avalanche that had completely covered him. . . .

What if his crushed, lifeless body is buried right here underneath this boulder?

Nearly frantic with apprehension, Mark began to tug viciously on the strap, grunting and swearing under his breath. His pulse was thumping heavily in his neck, and sweat broke out on his forehead in spite of the cold. Still, no amount of effort would free it.

Suddenly he froze.

A cold prickling sensation at the base of his neck made him turn around quickly and look up. His hand reached out and closed over the stock of his rifle, and he raised the gun to his shoulder as he scanned the cliff and sky above him. It was late in the morning, and the sun still wasn't shining on this side of the mountain, but he'd had the distinct impression that a shadow had passed over him. He shivered as he looked around for something that could have caused that, but as far as he could see, the mountainside was deserted.

"Fuck it," he whispered.

He stood up, still surveying the area, unable to rid himself of the sensation that he was being watched.

After a moment, he put the rifle down within easy reach, wiped his sweaty palms on his pant legs, and geared himself up to move the boulder. Keeping a watchful eye all around, he placed his hands against the rock, braced his feet, and then, grunting loudly, began to push. At first, the boulder barely budged, but as he steadily applied and released pressure, he got it to start rocking back and forth. It made a loud grinding sound that sounded like a giant chewing. Sweat ran down his face as he clenched his teeth and built up a steady rhythm, back and forth, until he sensed the moment was right. Then, with a loud, belly-deep grunt, he heaved with every bit of strength he had. The rock teetered for a moment and then, with a slow, grinding crunch, rolled over and came to rest against another, larger stone.

Mark's pulse was throbbing in his neck as he looked down and saw—not just Phil's bright orange backpack, but also a tangle of shredded red cloth. His hands were trembling as he picked it up, shook it out, and held it up to inspect it. After a moment, he realized what it was—or used to be. Not so long ago, it had been a bright red, down-filled jacket from L. L. Bean's . . . exactly like the one Phil had been wearing on the day he disappeared. It was torn to ribbons, and the down fill removed. Mark picked up the flattened backpack, not at all surprised to find that it, too, had been ripped open and emptied.

"What the *hell!*" Mark muttered.

How the hell had Phil's jacket and backpack come to be underneath this rock?

Phil certainly wouldn't have put them here. No matter how seriously he had been hurt from his fall down The Zipper, he would have kept his jacket to protect himself from the cold nights. And both backpack and jacket looked as though they had been purposely sliced open in order to destroy them. Although they might have been tossed down here and then buried beneath a rock slide, it looked as though they had been carefully placed here, hidden beneath this boulder. Phil certainly wouldn't have done that; but if he hadn't, who had?

Who would have stuffed these things under a rock that would have taken a lot of effort to move?

And why?

Mark was pondering all of this when—again—some primitive instinct warned him of imminent danger. As he reached for his rifle, he looked up and saw a dark mass blocking out the sky above him. In a paralyzing instant, he realized that something was falling down the side of the cliff, heading straight at him. He swore aloud as he dodged to one side and raised his rifle to aim.

But it was too late.

Before he could squeeze the trigger, the snarling creature slammed into Mark with the impact of a falling boulder.

Chapter Twenty-two

Packing Up

This is no time to be sentimental, Polly thought as she rummaged through her closet, sorting through her wardrobe. She selected barely one garment in five and tossed them over her shoulder onto her bed where two suitcases lay open like the maws of hungry fish.

She had called in sick to work at the beauty parlor that morning and planned to be packed up, in her car, and several hundred miles away from Hilton, Maine, by the time she was due back to work on Saturday afternoon. She wasn't quite sure where she would go—maybe Florida, where her widowed mother lived. If she went to Florida, she wouldn't need any heavy clothes. Or maybe she'd head out west, possibly all the way to California. She told herself not to worry about it. She had done spur-of-the-moment things like this all her life, figuring out what to do as she went. She always knew she'd land on her feet, like a cat, no matter how far she fell.

Right now, all she knew was that she wanted to get as far away from Maine as she possibly could.

She wasn't entirely sure why she was so desperate to leave. It wasn't just the sudden brutality of Dennis's death that bothered her, although she knew she would never forget the bloody horror of what had happened to her lover. And it wasn't just the inevitable fact that Mark would find out about her affair with Dennis—if he didn't already know. She had a pretty good idea that blabbermouth Sandy must have told him all about her guest last weekend. And it wasn't just that she felt in danger because the police still had no suspects—much less anyone in custody—for Dennis's murder. Her guess, which she had told the police time after time when they interrogated her, was that Dennis must have owed someone money from a poker game or something and hadn't been able to pay. She hinted—but never came right out and said it—that she thought Dennis might have been involved in some drug trafficking, too.

But what prompted her to run now was much deeper than any of that.

Maybe the root cause was what had driven her to the affairs she'd had with Dennis and those four or five other men following her marriage to Mark six years ago. She told herself that she had given their marriage an honest chance, that she had wanted it to work; but for the past few years, she couldn't ignore the feeling that, every time Mark made love to her, he was thinking about someone else—about his first wife, who had left him eight years ago.

"And—like always—that makes me number two," Polly said angrily as she went over to the bed, hurriedly folded the clothes, and stuffed them into one of the suitcases. When one was full, she held the top down with her weight, snapped the locks, and then started piling the rest of the clothes along with her toiletries and some other items into the other. She worked feverishly, grimly, not even caring that she would be leaving behind most of her personal belongings. As long as she had her charge cards—which, thankfully, were in her own name—and the large bundle of twenty-dollar bills she had been saving for the past several months, she was sure she would do just fine in another town, another state.

Just as she was closing the second suitcase, she heard a car pull up outside the house. Darting to the bedroom window, she looked out and saw that a town police cruiser was in the driveway. She ducked back and peeked around the edge of the curtain to watch as Guy LaBrea and Sandy got out of the cruiser and started toward the house.

"*Shit!*" Polly muttered.

She grabbed both suitcases and slid them under the bed, taking a moment to readjust the bed ruffle. Then, after a quick check in the mirror, she forced a smile onto her face as she started downstairs just as she heard the kitchen door open and slam shut.

"Polly? You home?" Sandy called out as she walked through the kitchen and into the hallway.

"Right here," Polly said. "There's no need to yell."

She congratulated herself for maintaining the usual edge of bitchiness in her voice, knowing that Sandy would instantly suspect something if she spoke to her in any other way.

"Oh, Chief LaBrea," Polly said, feigning surprise when she saw him. "I—I hope . . . There hasn't been any trouble, has there?"

For a moment, both LaBrea and Sandy said nothing; then LaBrea cleared his throat and said, "Well, actually, there has been a bit of a problem—"

"I totaled the Jeep," Sandy finished for him.

"What?" Polly shouted.

Her first reaction, which she tried to mask, was mild disappointment that they didn't tell her Mark had been hurt or killed.

At least it wasn't my car! she thought, but she was glad she had the presence of mind to look both angry and concerned.

"You weren't hurt, were you?"

"Just a couple of bumps and bruises," Sandy said, touching the padded bandage on her forehead. "The Jeep's a complete wreck, though."

"She went off the road out on Route 26, up past Newry."

"What in God's name were you doing out there?" Polly asked.

"Just . . . just out for a ride," Sandy replied. "I've been really worried about my dad, and I—I just had to clear my head out, what with everything that's been happening lately."

Polly said nothing as she shifted her gaze from Sandy to LaBrea.

"I have to fill out an accident report so you can start processing your insurance claim," he said. "I wonder if it'd be too much of a bother for you to come down to the police station with us."

"Oh, yes—sure," Polly said. "For a moment there, I was . . . worried." Her hand fluttered like a nervous bird against her chest. "I thought—you know, that you might have found out something more about—you know, who killed . . . Dennis."

"I'm afraid not," LaBrea said.

"To tell you the truth, I don't think I'll ever feel completely comfortable until whoever did it is safe behind bars."

"I'm sure the state police are doing their best," LaBrea said, sliding a glance over at Sandy.

Polly thought there seemed to be something fishy going on here, as if the two of them were hiding something from her, but she dismissed it, thinking only of her unfinished packing upstairs and how badly she wanted to get on the road. After an awkward moment when no one said anything, she checked her watch and said, "Well, I'm due at work in an hour or so, but I suppose I could meet you down at the station. Give me five minutes to put on some makeup." She still would have enough time to finish packing, load the car, and be on the road after filling out the necessary police forms.

"No need for you to drive," LaBrea said. "I can drive you down. The cruiser's blocking your car, anyway. The forms will only take a few minutes. I can drop you off at work."

Polly hesitated, but only for a moment. She wondered why LaBrea hadn't brought the forms out to the house, but realized it wouldn't look good if she asked.

"Okay," she said brightly. "Let me run upstairs and freshen up a bit. I'll be right back."

She went quickly up to her bedroom and dialed the beauty parlor. When Marilyn answered, she explained that she was feeling much better and would be able to make it to work after all. Marilyn protested, telling her that she didn't have to push herself; she could have the afternoon off if she still wasn't feeling up to snuff, but Polly insisted that she'd be there within the hour and hung up. Grabbing her purse from her dresser, she went back downstairs.

No one said a word as the three of them walked out to the cruiser. LaBrea started up the car, backed out of the driveway, and headed for town. He and Sandy were silent for most of the drive, and that gave Polly plenty of time to wonder when she was going to get another chance to leave.

Damn! If only I'd left ten minutes sooner!

Chapter Twenty-three

". . . Help us . . ."

Sudden darkness engulfed Mark.

Then, within that darkness, there came an explosion of spiraling white-hot stars and trailing comets accompanied by a searing jolt of pain.

Something hit him hard and slammed him down against the rocks. His head hit the ground with a resounding *thump*. A flashing instant later, a huge, claw-tipped hand swiped down at him, missing his face by less than an inch but catching the front of his jacket and ripping it wide open. He was only distantly aware of the jangling metallic sounds the bullets made as they spilled from his torn pocket. They scattered like dice across the uneven ground and disappeared down into the cracks between the stones.

Mark experienced no clear thoughts, only pain and confusion, and then a vague sense of relief when he realized that the crushing weight had only grazed him.

Surprised that he hadn't been squashed flat on the rocks, he took a deep breath and held it as he propelled himself backward, scrambling over the rocks in an awkward crablike crawl. His arms and legs were flailing wildly, but somehow he managed to keep hold of his rifle. Reacting on pure reflex, he raised it and fired as the huge form loomed above him like a massive tower that was about to collapse on top of him.

The instant the rifle boomed and kicked back in his hands, the creature let out an ear-splitting howl that echoed from the cliff side and blended with the hornetlike zing of the bullet as it ricocheted off the rocks. To Mark's ears, it sounded as if not just one but dozens of creatures were shrieking inside his head, but the sound snapped him back to sharper awareness.

He flopped back on the rocky ground as his shocked brain finally registered the pain of the impact. His vision was blurred, and there was a loud rushing sound in his ears, like a blast of hurricane winds. All around him, the world was a wild carousel of sunlit blues and smeared swirls of darkness that threatened to suck him down into unconsciousness. He tried to stand up, but his body felt all rubbery and goofy, and wouldn't do what he wanted it to do. He caught only a fleeting glimpse of motion as the beast spun around on one foot like a trained circus bear, and then disappeared behind one of the large boulders.

In an instant, a muffled silence settled around Mark.

"Come on!" Mark shouted, lying back on his elbows and panting heavily as he stared wide-eyed all around him. "Where the fuck'd you go?"

He was sitting up with his legs splayed wide in front

of him and listening to the rolling echo of his voice as it faded in the distance. His body was trembling with pain and surprise. He shook his head to clear it, but that did little good. The only clear thought he had was to bolt his rifle and be ready for another attack if it came. He aimed at the spot where the beast had disappeared, and he waited, his breath coming in fast, burning gulps.

"Jesus Christ," he whispered, unable to stop the violent trembling inside him. His stomach felt like jelly. "Come on! Where the fuck are you?"

He was still completely disoriented by the sudden attack, but he couldn't stop wondering what the hell this thing was, and how it could have attacked him so swiftly, without warning, and then disappeared so completely.

But the mountainside was quiet except for the distant, whistling wind. Mark started to wonder if he had imagined what had just happened, but then, off to his left, moving away from him, he caught a shifting of darkness within the deep shadows cast by the boulders. He turned quickly and aimed, but before he could fire, the motion was gone like a passing shadow. His grip wasn't at all steady, and the bead of the rifle kept wavering back and forth as he squinted, trying to catch some trace of activity.

"Come on! Come on out, you son-of-a-bitch!"

His first impulse was to get up and pursue the creature—whatever the hell it was—but then he thought better of it. Skittering on his hands and feet, he backed up until his back was pressed against one of the larger rocks. His muscles were tensed, ready to react instantly. It took a conscious effort to slow down his rapid breathing, but at least he felt a little bit secure, knowing that he couldn't be attacked from behind. Crouching on one knee, he glanced around, concentrating on calming down while he waited. He strained to see or hear any indication that the creature was still in the vicinity, but the silence remained unbroken.

Had he killed it with his first shot?

Was it lying just behind that rock, wounded . . . possibly bleeding to death?

Or, even at such close range, had he missed it, and right now it was circling around behind him or retreating higher up the mountain to lay ambush for him someplace else?

Mark patted his jacket pocket to convince himself that all of his ammunition had spilled out of his torn jacket pocket. Only one shell remained. With trembling hands, he slipped the bullet into the breech and bolted it home. By his reckoning, he had shot only once since reloading this morning. That meant, with this one new bullet, he had five shots left.

Five shots!

He had a supply of ammunition back at his campsite, but he couldn't waste the time to go back and get it. Not now. There was no going back until he made *sure* this son-of-a-bitch was dead, whatever it was.

Every nerve in his body was stretched to its limit as he waited for the creature to reveal itself. As much as he wanted to believe that he had killed it with one shot, he was fairly certain that his shot had missed. The creature had roared in anger and surprise, not in pain. That meant it was still out there, somewhere in the rocks, waiting . . . just waiting.

Ever so slowly, keeping his guard up, Mark stood

up. His legs threatened to collapse underneath him, but he clutched his rifle for support and scanned the area back and forth, poised for another attack. Shadows clung to the spaces between the boulders. Every dark crevasse beneath every boulder fairly vibrated with dark menace. He imagined twisted animal shapes with bright, glowing eyes staring back at him. He forced himself to breathe slowly, cautioning himself not to jump and shoot at every shadow. He had only five shots remaining. If the first one hadn't done the job, then one of these was going to have to do it.

Daylight slowly swept into the valley, and the coned shadow cast by the mountain shortened as the sun passed slowly around the mountaintop toward the west. Mark shivered as he moved step by cautious step, edging his way to the rock behind which the creature had disappeared. He scanned the ground, searching for a telltale splotch of fresh blood on the rocks, but saw nothing. The lichen-covered rocks were smooth and undisturbed.

"Come on," he whispered. "Where the Christ are you? I know you're—"

His voice caught in his throat when he saw something large and dark, sprawled face-down on the rocks several feet downslope. At first, he thought it was just another shadow cast by a rock, but then he made out its shape.

"God damn! Yes!"

Raising the rifle to his shoulder and keeping it fixed on the figure, he came out around the rock so he could get a better view of the thing without getting much closer, just in case the creature was playing possum. Its arms and legs were flung out wide, conforming to the rough contours of the rocks.

It was motionless.

There wasn't even a hint of movement of the huge ribcage, but Mark stared at it for a long time, thoroughly expecting the thing to roll over suddenly and jump at him as soon he got within reach.

Keeping his rifle aimed straight at the back of the creature's head, he approached to within twenty feet. Staring at it, he felt an odd mixture of relief and puzzlement. At first, it did indeed look like a huge, brown bear. Its thickly muscled shoulders and short, powerful-looking legs were covered with a thick mat of coarse brown fur with darker hairs creating a distinct black zigzag pattern. The back of its head was bullet-shaped with thick slabs of muscle bulging at the base of its short neck. Both hands were visible; they were wide and flat, and had long, curled fingers tipped with yellowed claws.

"You faking it? Huh? You son-of-a-bitch?" Mark whispered as he took another few steps closer.

He stopped again, about ten feet away. Bracing the rifle against his shoulder, he aimed at the lower left side of the creature's rib cage and gently squeezed the trigger until the rifle cracked.

The booming echo rolled down the slope. A puff of dust popped into the air as a thumb-sized hole appeared in the creature's side. The body jolted with the impact of the bullet, but no blood gushed from the wound.

"Awright, you motherfucker! You're dead as shit," Mark said, unable to control the deep tremor in his voice. He chambered another bullet, aimed at the creature's head, and fired again. Fur and skull fragments exploded into the air as the blast of the rifle echoed from the hillside.

"I guess that about evens the score, huh?"

Mark slung the rifle over his shoulder and walked boldly up to the dead creature.

He couldn't stop staring at it, astounded by its size and how almost human it looked. As he bent down close to inspect it, his nostrils were assailed by a thick, cloying animal smell that reminded him of a cow barn. He prodded one outstretched hand with the tip of his rifle, amazed at the obvious formidable strength of the clawed hand. Something like this could easily gut a cow or horse, not to mention a man, with a single swipe. This had to be what had ransacked Josh O'Connell's barn and killed Dennis outside his house.

Using his rifle for leverage, Mark rolled the creature over onto its back until it was stopped by an outcropping of rock. The creature's blank, unfocused gaze caught and riveted him. Even in death, the thing's eyes glistened with an almost human intelligence. The pupils were dilated, looking like large, wet, black marbles. The creature's thick lips were peeled back in a death rictus that made it look like it was still snarling. Its mouth was lined with a row of sharp teeth that looked like they could bite a baseball bat in half with one easy snap.

"So what the hell are you, huh?" Mark said, addressing the carcass. "Are you a Bigfoot or what?"

As he stood there staring at the dead beast, he suddenly realized that something was wrong. It took him a moment to realize what it was, but then he saw that the left shoulder of the creature wasn't wounded. The creature didn't have the gaping wound he was sure he had seen when it had attacked him yesterday! Although a lot of what had happened was just a confused memory, he knew for damned sure that the creature's left shoulder had been bleeding, badly, either from an old wound he had reopened when he hit it or a fresh one from the damage he had done when he hit it with the butt of his rifle. That wound had made the bloody trail he had followed up to the base of Katherine's Leap.

"What the fuck's going on here?" Mark whispered.

With some effort, he rolled the creature over onto its other side and inspected the right shoulder, but that side wasn't wounded, either.

Just then, a loud *click-click-click* drew Mark's attention. He turned around quickly, just in time to see a small rock hit the ground at the base of the cliff several feet behind him. Cocking his rifle, he dropped into a protective crouch and stared up at the top of Katherine's Leap.

Jesus! This isn't the one I was tracking, Mark thought with a numbing flood of panic as he looked over his shoulder at the dead creature.

There's more of them!

A knot of fear settled in his stomach when he realized that he had just wasted two shots.

Of course, it made sense. He was a damned fool not to have realized it before now. If one of these creatures could exist up here, then there would have to be others. How else could they continue to survive?

"So how many are there?" Mark whispered as he scanned the cliff side to see who—or what—could have caused that rock to fall. Aiming his rifle up at the spot where he thought the rock had come from, he waited silently for some sign that there was another creature nearby.

Keeping a watchful eye all around, he moved slowly along the base of the cliff until he was back at the spot where he had found Phil's things. When he looked up and carefully scanned the face of the cliff, he saw a protruding ledge which he hadn't noticed before. Now, with the early afternoon sunlight glancing off it, it looked quite large.

Could the creature have been hiding up there before it attacked him?

Maybe there was a cave up there. It didn't look it from down below, but Mark was suddenly convinced that he had to climb up to that ledge and find out.

As he was staring up at the spot, a voice so faint he thought at first he was imagining it called out to him. It sounded infinitely distant, almost like it was from another world.

Mark shivered as he listened to it echo with an odd reverberation from the cliff side, slicing through the eerie silence of the mountain.

". . . Help . . . Help us . . . They're gone for now . . . Help us! . . . Please? . . ."

Chapter Twenty-four

Moving Out

From now on, the police are going to be watching every move I make! Polly thought bitterly.

She was sitting at her kitchen table, staring blankly out the window at the evening sky. Deep shadows stretched across the lawn and driveway. It had taken no more than half an hour to fill out the accident report at the police station, but the whole time Polly suspected LaBrea was using the accident as an excuse to get her down to the station for more questioning about Dennis's death. Apparently, though, the police no longer suspected that she might have been responsible.

In any event, the delay had totally screwed up her plans to be on the road by noontime. LaBrea had dropped her off at work, and there was nothing she could do to avoid it without it looking suspicious. She had stayed at work until five o'clock, and now, after she finished packing and loading everything into the car, she had been sitting here in the kitchen, chain-smoking cigarettes and sipping on a cup of coffee as she watched evening descend. She couldn't stop wondering how it would look if she just up and took off right now.

"Do I even *care* how it looks?" she asked herself.

Her voice was a raw rasp as pale cigarette smoke drifted from her mouth. Of course, the police had asked her to "stick around town" until they solved the case . . . but then again, she told herself, they hadn't *insisted* that she stay in Hilton. As long as no charges were pressed, she was free to go wherever she *wanted* to go, and—Christ on a cross!—did she ever want to go!

It didn't really surprise her that she felt so little remorse about Dennis's death. They had been lovers for several months, but she had never felt anything even remotely approaching love for him. Dennis had been good for one thing and one thing only.

Sex.

Like a grieving widow, Polly knew she would have to wait a respectable amount of time before trying to find someone else to satisfy those physical needs Mark no longer filled for her, not that he ever had.

She was pretty sure Mark already knew about her affair with Dennis—and maybe with those other men, too. Sandy had no doubt blabbed all about it to him; but even if she hadn't, Mark would have to be both blind and stupid not to put it all together. In a small town like Hilton, talk got around pretty fast, so she and Mark would no doubt be heading for divorce court sooner or later, probably as soon as he was back from his crazy-assed search up on the mountain for his missing friend.

The idea of going through another divorce didn't really bother Polly, either. This would be her third. She laughed, thinking how she was almost getting used to it. Besides, there was no love lost between them, as they say. Perhaps naively, she had simply been hoping to get out of town without any more mess.

Yeah, that was the problem.

The mess of Dennis's death . . . and the mess of Mark's inevitable discovery of her affair.

But grieving for Dennis or worrying about Mark wasn't going to help her solve her immediate concerns about what to do right *now!*

The car was packed. The gas tank was full. She should get the hell moving, but something . . . something was holding her back. She didn't think it was anything like a sense of responsibility or loyalty. Those ideals, like love, had left her marriage long ago . . . if they had ever been there in the first place.

A flicker of motion outside the window drew her attention. She looked up to see Sandy walking up the driveway toward the back steps. Polly crushed out her cigarette and quickly primped her hair as Sandy's footsteps thumped on the stairs. The doorknob clicked, and the door swung open.

Sandy snapped on the overhead light as she entered the kitchen. She looked startled when she saw Polly sitting at the table.

"The house is dark," Sandy said shakily as she draped her jacket over the back of a chair. "I didn't think you were home."

For a lengthening moment, the two women glared

silently at each other. Polly sensed that if either one of them had spoken what was truly on her mind, the words would have been fast, bitter, and cutting. She took a deep breath and forced a thin smile onto her face as she stood up and walked over to the sink to dump out what was left of her cold coffee.

Sandy cleared her throat. "Uh, thanks . . . you know, for coming down there to help me out today." Her voice was soft as she stood beside the table, letting her fingertips brush lightly against the tabletop.

Polly looked straight at her and frowned. "Your father's going to be pretty upset when he finds out what happened to the Jeep. Next to his 'Vette, that was his favorite car to drive, you know?"

"Yeah. I know."

"You're darned lucky you weren't killed, too," Polly said.

Polly's face flushed as a twinge of anger rose up inside her. All she could think was how much Sandy hated her and how much she hated Sandy right back. In a way, it was rather sad how they had never given each other a fair chance. But it was certainly too late now. This rotten stepdaughter relationship was just one more reason why she should get the hell out while she still could.

"I know," Sandy said, even softer. She brought her hand up to the wad of bandage on her forehead and touched it gingerly.

"What were you doing out there, anyway? Weren't you supposed to be in school?"

For an instant, Sandy considered telling her the truth, but she knew that she couldn't trust Polly in the least, so with a slight shake of her head, she simply shrugged and said, "Oh, I was just out for a drive after school . . . I needed some time to think."

Polly sniffed as though grimly amused. "Well, I suppose now you can start thinking about ways to help pay for the Jeep."

"Oh, I'm sure the insurance money will cover that—most of it, anyway."

Polly shook her head and almost said something but remained silent, waiting for Sandy either to continue or leave the room. The tension between them fairly crackled.

"Actually," Sandy said, fighting the tight tremor in her voice, "I was starting to think about what I'd do until my father gets back."

"And just what do you mean by that?"

Sandy stared at Polly as a hot current of anger raced through her like fire. Her hands curled into tight fists, and her legs suddenly felt all rubbery. The air in the kitchen was suddenly too hot, almost impossible to breathe.

"I mean that—that I've been thinking I might stay at someone else's house," she said, "at least until my father comes home."

"You don't say?"

"Actually, I—I already asked Karen Bishop's parents about it, and they said I could stay with them until then because—because—" She swallowed hard, but the hot lump in her throat wouldn't disappear. "Because the truth is, I can't *stand* living here . . . under the same roof with you!"

Polly took a threatening step toward her, then drew back.

"Now, Sandy, come on. I know things have been

just—just horrible for you lately. I can understand that you're under a lot of—"

"Don't even *talk* to me, okay?" Sandy screamed as the anger bubbling inside her suddenly exploded. She shook her fists wildly in front of her face as a hot wash of tears spilled from her eyes, blurring her vision. "I don't even want to hear your voice! When I just think about—about what you—what you *did* to my father, I—I—"

Her voice choked off with a strangled click.

"Yes?" Polly said, taking another step closer to her. "You *what?*"

Sandy sucked in a deep breath and held it, then let it out slowly, but the pounding pressure inside her head wouldn't ease up. For a horrified instant, she clearly imagined what she would do to Polly if she had a knife or an axe or a gun in her hands. She had heard how mutilated Dennis Cross' body had been, and she found herself wishing that whatever that thing was that had attacked her out at Round Top Trail, it would find its way to Polly and rip her to pieces.

"I—I'm going upstairs to pack," she said in a low, controlled voice. "Mr. Bishop said he'd come by to pick me up before supper."

With that, she squared her shoulders and walked boldly into the hallway and up the stairs to her bedroom.

"Wait just a minute there! You can't—" Polly said, but then she cut herself off. Anger seethed inside her, but she held it in check. There was no sense letting Sandy know anything she thought or felt. Over the years, ever since she was a little girl, living in a home with a drunk for a mother and worse for a father,

Polly had learned that it didn't pay—*ever*—to let *anyone* know what she was *really* feeling.

Heaving a deep sigh, she leaned back against the counter and listened to the muffled sounds of activity coming from upstairs. She wanted more than anything to shout up to Sandy that she'd be more than happy to help her pack, and drive her over to the Bishops' herself. She was just about to do that when something—nothing more than an indistinct blur—shifted past the darkened kitchen window.

A sudden jolt of nervousness snapped through Polly as she went over to the window and looked outside. Night had closed down around the house, cut only by the glow of a distant streetlight. The kitchen light glazed the glass with a soft, yellow reflection, making it impossible for her to see much more than the outline of the driveway and the dark block of the adjoining garage.

What if he's out there now? she thought with a sudden rush of fear. *What if the person who killed Dennis is after me now?*

Sweat broke out on her forehead. Her breathing came fast and light as she glanced over at the telephone, wondering if she should call the police and ask them to come by and check things out. It might be nothing at all, maybe just her own reflection shifting across the glass . . . but what if it *was* something?

What if she was next on someone's list?

From upstairs, she could hear Sandy stomping back and forth across her bedroom floor as she packed whatever she was getting for the night.

"Sandy . . . ?" Polly called out, surprised at how strange her voice sounded. Of course, she knew, even if Sandy could hear her, she would ignore her.

She shifted away from the window, thinking it best not to alert whoever was out there that she suspected they were there. She crossed the floor to the phone and was reaching for it when another thought struck her.

What if it's the police?

What if, ever since the night Dennis was killed, she had been under surveillance?

What if she still was their prime suspect, and they were watching her twenty-four hours a day to see if she did anything to give herself away?

"Oh, shit," Polly whispered.

She moved back to the sink, making a conscious effort to appear nonchalant to anyone who might be watching from outside. She busied herself with the dishes for a moment, then walked out of the kitchen and into the living room, turning off the kitchen light behind her. She plunked herself down on the couch and clicked on the TV with the remote control, but her mind was so filled with wondering who—if anyone—was sneaking around outside her house, that she was unable to concentrate on the show.

A few minutes later, the glow of headlights washed across the living room wall as a car pulled into the driveway. Sandy had obviously been watching for it, and she came running down the stairs, carrying an overstuffed night bag. Without a word or even a glance at Polly, she went out the front door before Mr. Bishop had a chance to get out of his car and come up to the door.

Polly jumped when Sandy slammed the front door shut behind her. She went over to the window and watched the car back out of the driveway and pull away. As soon as it was gone, she ran to the door and locked it. Moving quickly, she went through the rest of the house, checking the locks on all the windows and the back door. But even after all that was done, she didn't feel safe.

Not at all.

She imagined that there were dully glowing eyes glaring at her from out of the darkness through every window. She wished she knew something about guns so she could load one of Mark's rifles—just in case—but she didn't, so even though it was much too early to go to bed, she went upstairs and shut herself in her bedroom.

Chapter Twenty-five
Into the Cave

Before Mark could get a fix on the voice calling for help, it stopped, fading away like a vagrant breeze. He was fairly certain that it had sounded from up above, but there was no way he could be sure. As soon as the mountainside was silent again, he wondered if he had heard anything at all . . . or if he had, if it was Phil or some other lost hiker. Was he imagining things, or could someone be trapped somewhere underneath any of these boulders?

Mark called out several times, but his echo was the only answer. Maybe the stress and excitement of his encounter with the beast was making him imagine things.

Maybe he was starting to lose it.

But of one thing he was positive: there *was* some kind of creature, a creature unlike anything he had ever seen or heard of in the wild before, and it was

lying dead on the rocks at the base of Katherine's Leap. And from what he could figure, it was *not* the same creature he had been stalking since yesterday afternoon. He was positive that one had a serious wound in the left shoulder. The only wounds on this one were the entry and exit points of the three bullets he had just fired, and none of them had been in the beast's shoulder.

At first, Mark couldn't see how he was going to scale the sheer cliff to get up onto the overhanging ledge. And until he got up there, there was no telling how wide or narrow it was.

Once again, as he had earlier that morning, he started walking back and forth at the base of the cliff, carefully examining the steep sides. Whatever else had happened, the creature had definitely attacked him from above. That had to mean, if there was a way down, there was a way up.

The bright sky hurt his eyes as he looked up at the side of the cliff. The sun was just skimming over the angled surface of the rock. Even the tiniest bump made a shadow several inches long. With the light angled like this, Mark noticed for the first time many grooves and notches in the side of the cliff which hadn't appeared when the rock was shrouded in shadow. They looked as if they might even provide enough of a handhold to climb, but there sure as hell was not going to be an easy way up . . . not without ropes and climbing equipment.

Although it would be much more time-consuming, Mark knew he could hike around to the east side of the mountain and then scale down The Zipper to the top of Katherine's Leap. He could mark the location below with the remains of Phil's backpack so it would be easy enough to find from above.

But the voice he had heard—if it had been there at all—had sounded desperate and in pain. Mark didn't want to waste most of the day climbing around to the more accessible side of Agiochook.

No. One way or another, he had to scale this rock wall now.

His frustration rose steadily as he studied the narrow overhang on the cliff. Like the rest of the cliff, it was basically featureless, but the sunlight was angled just right so it illuminated a narrow channel, what mountain climbers called a chimney, running straight up to the top of Katherine's Leap. The chimney passed within a foot or so of the right edge of the overhang. Inside the funnel of the chimney, the rock looked like it was worn much smoother than the rest of the cliff side.

"Bingo," Mark said softly.

He realized that the erosion could be the result of the weather and rock slides, but something told him it was more than that.

Maybe it had been worn smooth by the creatures climbing up and down it countless times over the years.

Maybe this was how the creatures got up and down the cliff. Last night in the moonlight, he thought he had seen the beast climbing up Katherine's Leap before it disappeared halfway up. If it hadn't been an illusion, this must be where it had gone.

Slinging his rifle over his shoulder, Mark settled his day pack on his shoulders, and then braced his hands and feet along the inside of the shallow indentation.

By applying steady outward pressure with both arms and legs, he was able to shinny up the steep cliff.

His progress was frustratingly slow. It didn't take long for the muscles in his arms, legs, and back to start burning with exhaustion. It seemed to take forever to get even ten feet off the ground. He kept glancing up at the shelf of rock above him, but struggle as he might to inch himself upward, it seemed to be getting no closer.

But that wasn't his major concern. Nagging at his mind was the thought that if there was another one of those creatures up there and it attacked him now, he would be helpless, unable even to unsling his rifle before the thing was on top of him.

In spite of the chilly mountain air, sweat broke out on his brow and ran down into his eyes. He repeatedly tried to wipe his eyes on his shoulder, but that only smeared the moisture and made it worse.

He was making his way closer to the overhanging rock, inch by painful inch, but all he could think was, even if another one of the creatures didn't attack right now, every boost higher was only going to make the landing all that much more painful if he lost his footing and fell.

By the time he was halfway up to the overhang, about forty feet above the ground, the muscles in his shoulders and back were knotted with pain. Every time he slid his feet up, grit would make them slide out from under him, and he would have to press back all the harder against the rock to keep from falling. His breath came in short, painful gulps. Every inhalation was like fire in his lungs. He tried not to look down at the rocks and imagine himself lying there, helpless with his legs or back broken as dozens of creatures closed in on him from all sides.

Waves of pain racked his body. His arms and legs throbbed with every movement, but he could see that he was getting steadily closer to the overhang. His rifle kept banging against the cliff. Every time he leaned back against the rock, the bolt action would dig into his back just above his kidney; but it was too late to shift its position now.

He *had* to get up to the ledge.

Once he was there he could worry about what to do next.

Grunting and swearing under his breath, he hiked himself upward until—thank God!—the overhang was only a few feet above him, almost within reach. As soon as it was eye level, he wished to hell he dared to make a grab for it, if only to relieve the pressure and pain in his body, but he knew it wasn't time. Not yet. His feet had to be level with the overhang before he could chance making a grab like that.

It was just a matter of time . . . and effort.

He kept pushing himself up until the ledge was level with his shoulders, then his hips, then his knees, and—finally—his feet. His arm and leg muscles were trembling violently from the strain. Convinced that he couldn't hang on another second, he held his breath, shot one foot out onto the ledge and, at the same instant, pushed himself away from the cliff side.

For a sickening instant, he felt himself suspended in the air, but then he landed, hard, and rolled onto the rocky shelf. After a few tumbles, he came to rest on his back. Lying there, looking up at the sky, he let out an exhausted sigh. For several seconds he just lay there until his hammering pulse gradually began to slow. Finally, he found the strength to sit up, wipe the sweat from his face, and check out where he was.

The cliff was no more than eight feet wide and fifteen to twenty feet long. Bright sunlight washed the rock with a lemon glow and stretched his shadow out over the edge and down along the slanting cliff face. As he looked down, Mark experienced a moment of vertigo. Far below he could see the small, bright specks that were Phil's backpack and jacket. A light breeze was blowing up the side of the cliff, straight into his face. It swirled around him like frigid water. The muscle tremors in his shoulders still hadn't stopped, but he knew he had to inspect every inch of this ledge before he could drop his guard. And then he wanted to rest a while before deciding how he was going to get either all the way up to the top of Katherine's Leap or back down.

He walked to the other side of the overhang and couldn't repress a grunt of surprise when he saw that one large chunk of rock was angled outward, and behind it there was a narrow, triangular opening that looked like it led into a cave.

Stepping back and studying it for a moment, Mark realized that the opening was located just right so it would be difficult if not impossible to see from the ground except—maybe—from an extreme angle. As far as he knew, no one had ever reported a cave on the ledge halfway down Katherine's Leap. The cave mouth was easily wide enough to admit his body. In fact, it was large enough so that the creature could have squeezed through it.

Is this where these things live?

He unslung his rifle, bolted it, and took a few cautious steps forward. Then he crouched down on one knee and aimed into the opening. After clearing his throat, he called out, "Hey! Anyone there?"

His voice echoed weirdly from inside the stony fissure. He could tell by the odd reverberation that this was not just a shallow niche in the cliff; there was a fairly large space inside.

His hands tightened on the rifle stock as he aimed into the darkness and waited. After a few heartbeats, the distant, echoing voice came again, rustling like dead leaves in the gutter.

"They're gone now. Please . . . help us. Hurry."

Mark swallowed with difficulty and was unable to reply for a moment. Remembering that he had a flashlight in his day pack, he quickly unzipped the bag, took out the flashlight, clicked it on, and shined it into the opening. Dumbfounded and wondering what the hell was going on, he inched forward and stuck his head into the cool, moist darkness.

"Who—? . . . Who are you?" Mark called in a ragged whisper.

"You have to hurry . . . they might come back soon."

The voice reverberated in the darkness.

Mark swept the flashlight beam back and forth along the angled stone walls. The rasping sound of his breath was oddly magnified as he inched further into the cool darkness, keeping his rifle braced in one hand, his flashlight in the other.

He found himself in a narrow passageway that angled back into the mountain about twenty feet before it curved sharply to the left. The interior walls met at a peak about fifteen feet above his head. A track along the middle of the floor had buffed the stone to a dull gloss. Small stones and other debris, including large piles of wood, littered both sides of the entrance.

Mark hesitated, wondering if it was possible that this might, in fact, be another one of the creatures calling to him. Had they learned how to mimic human speech, and were luring him into a trap?

"Who are you?" he called out, forcing strength into his voice which he didn't really feel.

"Mark . . . ? Jesus Christ, man! Is that really you?" called the voice, which now sounded vaguely familiar. "For Christ's sake, it's me . . . Phil. Please . . . hurry!"

"Jesus Christ," Mark whispered.

He started forward at a brisk walk, following the twisting cavern back into the bowels of Mount Agiochook. Rough angles of rock made numerous niches and ledges deep inside the cave's recesses, but the major route was clearly marked by the scuff marks on the floor. Mark had the impression that feet had worn the stone smooth over the years—over centuries, perhaps. The cave twisted to the left, then opened up into a roughly triangular chamber. For a minute or two, Mark surveyed the area, but he saw no one there. A choking, rotten smell tainted the air, almost making him gag. He wondered if his ears had been playing tricks on him, if he was imagining all of this, but then the voice—now sounding exactly like Phil Sawyer's voice—called to him again.

"Where are you, Mark? Are you still outside?"

"No," Mark replied. "I—I'm in some kind of chamber."

"Keep coming. We're all the way in back here."

The echoing voice sounded as if it were coming from ten different directions at once. Mark swept the flashlight beam from the uneven floor into dozens of narrow nooks and crannies in the walls. On the right side of the far wall, he noticed a narrow passage. Crossing the floor quickly, he scrambled through the narrow passage and came out into an even larger space.

"What the hell—?" he said. No matter what he had been expecting, he wasn't ready for what he saw.

The cave opened up into a gigantic interior chamber that looked to be at least a couple of hundred feet square. The ceiling was a good fifty or sixty feet above him, shrouded with dense shadows which his flashlight couldn't push aside. The floor was littered with large boulders that looked as if they had been purposely rearranged. Several flat stone were covered with piles of dried leaves, moss, and worn fur pelts.

At the far end of the chamber, in front of a narrow shelf of rock, was a crudely made corral of thick timbers lashed together with dried-out vines. Through the slats, Mark saw a large mounded stack. As he passed his flashlight beam over it, he realized that it was a pile of animal carcasses. The smell of rotting flesh was nauseating, but he was too amazed even to retch.

"*Jesus!*" Mark shouted when something moved behind the stack of carcasses. A hand—a human hand rose up and beckoned to him.

Stunned and amazed, Mark started moving closer, walking like an automaton, unable to believe that his flashlight was shining straight into the face of his friend Phil Sawyer. Sitting beside him, their backs against the cave wall, were two other people, a man and a woman. All three of them were tied up with thick, knotted vines wrapped around their knees.

Phil squinted as he tried to look up at Mark, but

the light was too bright. His face was smeared with grime, and his clothes were torn and dirty. His hair was an oily mat plastered against his forehead. His lips were pale and cracked, and his eyes reflected a frightened glaze as he forced a wide, crazy-looking smile.

"Jesus Christ, man!" Phil said. "What the fuck took you so long?"

Chapter Twenty-six
Escape Plans

"I just—I can't believe you're still alive!" Mark said as he screwed the top off his canteen and handed it to Phil, who slurped a mouthful of water and then licked his lips greedily.

"How long has it been?" Phil asked, his voice a low rasp.

"A little less than a week. It's—uh, Thursday," Mark said, having to think a moment. "Watch it with that water. It's all I've got until I can get you out of here."

"Christ, Thursday?"

Phil closed his eyes a moment and rocked his head from side to side.

"I've only been here five days? Jesus, it feels like it's been more than that . . . a couple of weeks, at least."

"I just can't believe you're still alive!" Mark repeated.

He glanced at the other people, then offered each of them a sip of water, which they swallowed. Both of them looked much worse off than Phil.

Turning back to his friend, Mark examined the vines binding his legs. They were dried, and had been twisted together so tightly that even with his hands free, Phil would never have been able to loosen the knots. It would take a knife to cut through them. Other than that, though, Phil seemed to be in fairly good health, considering the circumstances. Mark took out his Swiss Army knife and began sawing through the crude rope.

"They're clever, I'll grant them that," Phil said. He suddenly winced and shifted to one side.

"Did I cut you?"

Phil gritted his teeth and shook his head.

"No, it's my . . . legs—I'm afraid they're both broken. From the fall off that cliff. But these bastards would have done it to me, anyway. I'm all right, though. Check out those other two first."

Mark went back to the man and woman who sat on the floor, their backs slumped against the stone wall. Their faces were gaunt with hunger and dehydration. Their skin had a pale, almost translucent quality to it, and they both smelled as if they had been sitting in their own filth for weeks. Lice and other bugs crawled in their hair and over their ragged clothes. The man's beard hung halfway down to his chest. The woman regarded Mark with eyes completely devoid of human expression, as if she didn't even recognize him as another human being.

Mark shined the light on her to inspect her injuries. There was a serious gash on the left side of her face that had started to heal but was festering. The skin around the wound was an angry red. The woman kept licking her lips and trying to speak, but the only sound she could make was a low croaking in the back of her throat. It sounded almost like laughter. It took Mark a moment to realize that, like Phil, both the man and woman's legs had been broken.

"It's all right . . . it's all right," Mark whispered as he tilted the woman's head back and let a bit more water trickle down into her mouth. "I'm going to get all of us out of here."

The woman swallowed, then made a noise that sounded almost like the words *thank you.*

Mark then gave the man another drink.

"She's not doing very well," the man said in a voice that cracked on every other word.

"Who are you?" Mark asked. "How long have you been here?"

The man's eyes fluttered a moment as though he were lost in thought, searching his memory for something that was far, far away . . . almost irretrievable.

"Phil said it was September when he came here. Is that true?"

Mark nodded. "Yeah, today's September—um, eleventh, I think."

The man nodded again and took a deep breath that sounded as if it were tearing his throat apart.

"My name's Jack—Jack Russell, and this is my girlfriend, Mary Fecteau. We're from New Jersey. We—we were hiking on Agiochook last summer—the Fourth of July weekend."

"Jesus! You're the two hikers who disappeared last summer," Mark said, sitting back on his heels in amazement. "Half the county turned out to look for you. Do you mean to tell me you've been here all this time, just sitting here in the dark?"

"Oh, no," the man said. "These—these creatures—I don't know what the hell they are, but they're intelligent. They know how to make fire, so sometimes there's been a campfire with enough light to see by."

The woman started moaning as she rolled her head from side to side. A thick yellow foam dripped from the corners of her mouth. Mark couldn't tell if she was just trying to relieve the itching of the lice on her scalp or having some kind of seizure.

Jack nodded stiffly. "Two of them . . . these creatures, they attacked us on the slope just before we got to the summit. They—they—" He tried to finish but couldn't stop himself from crying out loud. Agonized sobs racked his body, making him shudder.

"Hey, take it easy, now, Jack," Mark said, placing a hand gently on his shoulder. "Don't worry. Everything's gonna be fine."

"They—the bastards broke our legs and have kept us tied up like this ever since. Neither one of us can feel our legs anymore. We've been here so long, I know damned well the bones have healed all wrong. They feed us from time to time. That!"

He sneered as he indicated the pile of rotting animal carcasses with an angry hand gesture.

"Every now and then—there's no way of knowing how long—one of them will bring in a fresh kill. Usually it's a deer or something. They eat what they want, then throw us the scraps. About all we've had to drink is animal blood. A couple of times they've carried us out to the ledge where rainwater collects in a shallow depression in the rock, but I—I never imagined I could bring myself to eat raw flesh or gnaw marrow out of bones just to stay alive, and for what?"

His eyes went wide, and his body began to tremble. "Stay alive for what? So they can torment us like this? I have no idea why they're keeping us alive!"

Mark didn't know what to say, although, judging by the elaborate fence the creatures had constructed, his first impression was that they were treating these people like cattle. Maybe they were their stock of winter food, or if these creatures were intelligent enough, maybe the humans were being saved for some kind of primitive ritual or something.

"I'm sorry," Jack said, once he had calmed down a bit. "It's just that—Christ, you can see we're not doing very well. Tell me, how's Mary doing? Do you think she . . . you know?"

"Who can say?" Mark replied, shrugging sympathetically. He directed his flashlight beam back at the entrance leading to the cave mouth. "I'm no doctor, but I do know we have to get the hell out of here."

"How are you going to manage that?" Phil asked. He slapped his useless legs. "I'm sorry, but I'm not gonna be much help."

"First tell me what I'm up against," Mark said. "How many are there? Have you noticed any pattern to their activities?"

Phil shrugged. "I'm not precisely sure of their numbers. It's hard to distinguish them, but I'm pretty sure there are only six of them."

"Yeah," Jack said. "There's six by my reckoning, too."

"Three females, I know that," Phil said, "and at least three males—two older and one young one."

"What the hell are they?" Mark asked.

"I have no idea what they are," Phil said, "but I agree with Jack. They're intelligent as hell, no doubt about it. I don't know. My guess is they might be some kind of human throwback or something, you know? Like maybe a tribe of Neanderthals or something that—somehow—have survived into the twentieth century without being discovered."

"How can that be?" Mark asked, shaking his head in amazement.

"You got a better idea?" Phil snapped.

"No." Mark shifted uncomfortably and glanced back at the cave opening, "but it just doesn't seem possible. I mean, they can't have been up here all this time and never be discovered."

"Maybe they *have*. Maybe that's why there's all those rumors and legends about this mountain being haunted. Remember? You were telling me about that Indian monster. What was it called? *Pomoola?* Christ, since I've been here, I've had plenty of time to think about how there could be all sorts of superstitions about these things."

"Yeah . . . maybe," Mark said, scratching his chin. "It just doesn't seem possible that they could have remained undiscovered for all these years. Is it possible they've been here even as far back as prehistoric times?"

Phil shrugged. "Beats the shit out of me."

"But you say they can make fire," Mark went on. "And it's obvious, from the way they've constructed this fence and tied all of you up, that they know what they're doing. Obviously they can make plans and execute those plans. That would take some level of intelligence and communication between them. They had to drag all this timber quite a ways up the mountain, and I saw a stack of what must be firewood out in the front chamber. Do they have any kind of language?"

"Nothing I can understand," Phil said.

"Me neither," Jack added. He was leaning back against the stone with his eyes closed, as if the glow of the flashlight was too painful. "They howl and grunt all the time. I don't know if it's actually language, but they sure as hell seem to communicate, at least amongst themselves."

"So where are they now?" Mark asked, glancing over at Jack. "Do they leave you alone like this often?"

Phil shook his head. "This is the first time since I've been here that they've all left at the same time."

Mark glanced at Jack, who was nodding with his eyes still closed as though he was now used to darkness and wanted to keep it that way. "First time since we've been here, too," he said wearily. "They've never all been gone at the same time before."

"So what do you think they're doing?"

Phil regarded Mark for a moment, then said softly, "I think they're looking for you."

"What—?"

Phil shrugged. "Ever since I've been here, especially after last night, they've been taking a real keen interest in me. Jack's even commented on how they spend a lot more time with me, knocking me around and grunting at me, obviously trying to communicate *something* to me. And they're always sniffing me, too, like—I don't know, like bloodhounds, trying to pick up a scent or something."

"And last night—when that one male that was wounded came back to the cave," Jack said softly. "I think he died during the night. I heard some pretty awful sounds coming from the outer chamber. Who knows? Maybe they're all out giving him a funeral or something."

"That must have been the one I wounded yesterday when it attacked me down at the trail head," Mark said. "I hit him in the shoulder with my rifle, and he was bleeding pretty bad."

Jack shook his head. "He got that wound a couple of days ago. Looks to me like he got shot."

Mark hooked his thumb over his shoulder toward the cave opening. "Well, then, that means there's two of 'em dead, because I shot another one down at the base of this cliff."

"We heard the shots," Phil said. "That's when we started calling to you. That was the one who had stayed behind to guard us. He must have heard you coming and went to get you. We heard three rifle shots. When you didn't answer me, I figured you either didn't hear me or else the bastard had gotten you."

"Well," Mark said, glancing quickly at his watch, "it's getting late. If I don't get you out of here soon, it's going to be dark before I can get you off the mountain."

"I don't mean to be a bummer, Mark, but how the hell are you gonna get three people who can't even walk out of here?"

As if proof were needed, Phil struggled for a moment to stand, then sagged back down, exhausted.

"We can tie some of these vines together, and I can lower you down, one by one."

"With four or five of these things still out there?" Jack said.

"Shit, you're right," Mark said. "I only have three bullets left."

The three men were silent for a lengthening moment. Mark kept glancing over at Mary, who looked as though, now that rescue was so imminent, she had lost what little grip she had on reality. Her head was thrown back, hanging to one side. Her eyes were staring unblinkingly up at the rocky ceiling.

"Then I'm going to have to go down the mountain and get help," Mark said. "I can have a dozen or more men back here with rifles, ropes, medical supplies, and anything else we might need. It was a full moon last night. If I can convince the authorities, maybe we can land a helicopter up here on the ledge above and lower some men down."

Before they could discuss the relative merits of this plan any further, a loud, keening wail sounded from outside the cave. It rose to a high-pitched note that warbled up and down like a frantic siren. The tunnel throat of the cave reverberated with the eerie sound. The woman didn't respond at all, but the three men turned and looked in horror at the cave entrance.

"*Shit!*" Mark muttered. "They must have found the one I killed."

Chapter Twenty-seven

Breaking In

The night was alive with cricket song. A just-past-full moon was riding high in the sky, casting a cold silver light over the yard. Sandy was standing in the dappled shadow of a maple tree at the foot of the driveway. She shivered as she pulled her jacket collar tightly around her neck and looked up at the house.

All the lights were off. Polly must have gone to bed.

Good! she thought, her hands clenching into fists.

Moving swiftly and silently, Sandy cut across the front lawn and up the back stairs to the kitchen door. She knew what she was doing was foolish, but in her hurry to get out of the house earlier that afternoon, she had forgotten to pick up her school books. Now, a little before midnight, she had come back to get them.

She probably should have called earlier and told Polly that she was coming by, but she couldn't stand the thought of hearing Polly's voice, much less seeing her. So once the Bishops had settled down for the night, she had snuck out of the house, intent on getting what she needed for school the next day. With luck, she'd be back at the Bishops' within an hour, and no one would even know that she had been gone.

Her hand trembled as she grabbed the doorknob and turned it. The doorknob jiggled a little, then stopped. She twisted it back and forth again a few times.

"Damn it!" she whispered, her breath a small cloud that quickly dissipated in the night.

Scooching down and ignoring her fear of spiders and other unseen dangers that might be lurking, she fished around under the edge of the stoop until she found the spare key that hung there on a nail. She quickly fitted the key into the lock, turned the knob, and opened the door, being careful to swing the door slowly so the hinges wouldn't squeak. Knowing she'd be right back out, she left the key sticking out of the lock.

The house was silent and dark. Not wanting—or daring—to turn on any lights, she felt her way around the kitchen like a blind person. She hissed with disappointment when she realized that her backpack wasn't by the laundry where she usually dropped it when she got home.

Why am I even doing this? she wondered. *What the hell am I afraid of? This is my own damned house!*

She walked across the kitchen floor on tiptoes, grimacing every time a floorboard creaked. She was racking her brain, trying to think where her backpack might be. She had no idea. Things had been so confusing lately, and she had been so shaken up by the accident with the Jeep, she was surprised she could even remember how to tie her own sneakers. Knowing her luck, Polly had probably taken the backpack upstairs and thrown it into her bedroom.

The bright glow of moonlight from outside made the interior of the house all the darker as Sandy finished her hasty search of the kitchen and then moved into the hallway. She checked beside the coatrack and inside the front hall closet but still didn't find what she was looking for. Finally, after not finding it in the living room or dining room, she was convinced that she had to go upstairs and check her bedroom.

She paused at the foot of the stairs, her hand resting lightly on the polished banister as she looked up at the top landing. Her breath came light and fast. A sheen of sweat had broken out on her forehead. It was going to be one hell of a challenge to get up there and back without waking up Polly.

This is absolutely crazy! she told herself.

She knew she should just walk right up there, bold as can be, and get what she wanted. Maybe she should even *try* to wake up Polly and have a little talk with her. Maybe she should even go so far as to apologize to her for the things she'd said. At the very least, she shouldn't be acting like a criminal in her own goddamned house!

But she didn't dare turn on the hall light before starting up the stairs. She tiptoed up the stairs, wincing at every step that creaked beneath her weight. Even the tiniest noise sounded as loud as gunfire, but she told herself that everything was magnified in the dark, that Polly was sleeping soundly and wouldn't hear a thing.

And so what if she does?

The upstairs lights were off. Once Sandy got to the top of the stairs, she couldn't resist peeking into Polly's bedroom before going down to her own room. She opened the door ever so slowly and saw her stepmother, an indistinct, gray lump underneath her bed covers. Holding her breath, Sandy watched for a moment, then moved as quickly and as silently as she could down to her own bedroom.

A soft wash of moonlight was shining through the curtains, illuminating her bed and a small square of the floor. She glanced around the room, letting her eyes adjust to the darkness.

There it was!

Her backpack was slung over the back of the chair by her desk, right where she had left it, she now recalled. She went over and picked it up, then shrugged her arms into the straps, being careful not to swing the pack around in case something inside might make a noise or fall out. Once the pack was positioned comfortably over her shoulders, she went quickly back down the hallway to the stairs.

Just as she was passing Polly's bedroom door, her stepmother moaned in her sleep and rolled over, muttering something that Sandy couldn't quite make out. Sandy froze, her hand poised above the banister. Her heart fluttered in her chest as she waited several seconds, praying that Polly wouldn't wake up and see her there. The steady hammering of her pulse in her ears sped up, and an aching pressure started to build inside her bladder.

Go on! Just get the hell out of here! she commanded herself, telling herself that Polly might be half-asleep and not even remember their argument; she might think Sandy was just getting up to go to the bathroom. But she didn't dare to move . . . not yet.

But it doesn't matter! This is my house, too, so just get moving!

She lowered her foot down onto the first step. Dizzying waves of tension threatened to knock her over as she forced herself, ever so slowly, to take each step one at a time and not start running. Her backpack felt like it was loaded with bricks as it bounced painfully against her kidneys, reminding her of how badly she had to go to the bathroom.

She hardly dared to breathe until she reached the bottom step and was heading back into the kitchen. Shaking all over, she opened the kitchen door and stepped out into the night. Then, for the first time since she had entered the house, she took a deep breath, letting her lungs expand to their limit. The night air surrounded her like a cold blanket, making her shiver, but all she could feel was relief that she was out of there.

She quietly eased the kitchen door shut and turned the key in the lock to relock it. She resisted the sudden impulse to shout for joy as she jumped off the steps down to the driveway. Glancing upward, she was relieved to see that no lights had come on in the house. Polly was still sleeping peacefully.

At least the two-timing little slut is alone tonight, Sandy thought bitterly.

The flat stretch of lawn in the backyard glowed eerily in the moonlight. The distant fringe of trees shifted as a light breeze wafted their leaves. Inky shadows clung to the eaves of the house and along the side of the garage. Sandy was too elated with her success to notice that one of the shadows close to the garage shifted as she bent down and felt up under the stairs to replace the hidden key. Just as she was straightening up, though, some primitive sense warned her of imminent danger. She stood up and was just turning around when a huge, dark shape loomed above her, blocking out the night sky.

A tiny squeak escaped from her throat, but her throat closed off as two powerful hands shot out of the darkness and grabbed her, pinning her arms to her sides. She tried to resist but couldn't as thick, muscled arms spun her around, wrapped around her chest, and started to squeeze with a steady, unrelenting pressure.

No! No! her mind screamed.

She couldn't make the slightest sound. The arms forced the air out of her lungs. Bright, trailing spirals of light filled her vision as the crushing strength increased. Her head felt hot and heavy, and was throbbing with pressure. She had the brief impression that she was floating, flying away when she felt herself being lifted off the ground. Her feet kicked wildly, making her think of a frantic swimmer who was trying her best to stay afloat.

This can't be happening! . . . This can't be happening!

The night suddenly erupted as trailing red and yellow bursts of light shot across her vision. She could hear nothing but the heavy drumbeat of her pulse, slamming in her ears as her body was shaken back and forth, first one way, then the other. The powerful hands locked together across her chest and pulled inward, crunching her rib cage and collapsing her lungs.

Then other sounds filled Sandy's head.

First came a rapid series of *pops* that sounded like a string of firecrackers exploding in the distance. Then a searing jolt of pain accompanied by a single, loud *crack* close to her ears, sounding like an old board that had snapped beneath an enormous weight. Bright, intense pain roared like a hurricane inside her head, billowing in flashes of searing white heat.

Sandy never realized that her backbone had snapped in half. Thankfully, she was unconscious by then.

Chapter Twenty-eight

Bloody Feast

The beastly howl was still echoing through the cave when Mark sprang into action. After checking to make sure there was a bullet in the rifle chamber, he hurriedly glanced around, looking for someplace to hide. His first thought was to crawl underneath the pile of animal carcasses inside the corral, but the thought of lying there, buried under all that rotting meat with maggots and grubs crawling around, nauseated him.

Huge rocks were strewn around on the cave floor, any one of which Mark could have hidden behind, but he had no idea where these creatures might go once they entered their cave. If Phil and Jack's count was accurate, and there were four or five of the creatures left, he didn't have enough bullets to kill them all, even if he could take out each one with a single shot. And if he kept his flashlight off so he wouldn't reveal himself, how was he even going to see?

He had to do something, fast.

Sweeping the flashlight beam around, he noticed at the back of the cave a shelf of rock about ten feet above the cave floor with a jumble of rocks below it. He quickly decided that it would be the best place to hide, at least until he could think of something else. Even if the creatures found him there, he'd be able to defend himself better, being above their heads with his back against a solid rock wall.

Another wailing cry sounded from outside the cave, this time much louder and getting closer. However many creatures there were, they were returning to the cave. After a moment, Mark heard a low grunting sound and the heavy shuffling of padded feet on stone.

"Don't worry," he whispered to Phil, clapping him on the shoulder. "I'll get all of us out of here, I promise."

Before either of the crippled men could reply, Mark leapt over the corral railing and ran to the back of the cave. Getting up onto the shelf of rock wasn't as easy as it had looked, but once he was settled up there, he realized the place was perfect. No more than six feet wide, it slanted back about eight or ten feet. The back of the enclosure was solid rock, as if this place had purposely been chiseled out of the rock. He felt some comfort knowing that nothing was going to be able to sneak up on him from behind.

As the sounds of shuffling feet and angry snarls rang louder in the cave, Mark switched off his flashlight and flattened himself against the rock. As soon as it was pitch dark, he started worrying that the creatures might have extraordinary eyesight in the dark, or that they might pick up his scent. He had to hope that they needed at least a glimmer of light to see, and that the stench of rotting flesh filling the cave would mask his scent.

The next several minutes were sheer terror for him as he lay there waiting, surrounded by total darkness, his face pressed against the cold, gritty stone. The sounds made by the creatures grew steadily louder until Mark was positive they were inside the cave chamber. He could hear heavy breathing and the shifting of bodies back and forth across the rock floor.

As he lay there, clutching his rifle, Mark had to admit that, although at first the noises they made could have been taken for nothing more than wild animal grunts and snorts, they did seem to have a pattern. The creatures could be communicating. He was reminded of a tape he had heard of the "songs" of humpback whales. These creatures' voices, like those of the whales, seemed to repeat in definite patterns that very well could be relating simple information.

They sounded almost sad—especially one voice, Mark thought, listening to their high, keening wails and abrupt, grunting snorts. He couldn't help but think they might be grieving for the one he killed outside the cave.

But Mark didn't feel the slightest trace of pity or regret. These creatures had done far worse than *kill* human beings. By the way things looked in the cave, this wasn't the first time they had captured and tortured humans. Mark remembered all the instances he had heard about over the years of hikers and campers disappearing on or around Agiochook. The presence of these creatures would go a long way in explaining some of those disappearances. He shuddered, thinking what he might find if he carefully inspected the pile of remains.

But why are they doing it now?

Are Phil and these other two campers part of the food supply? Are they fresh meat "on the hoof," stockpiled for the coming winter?

Or is there some other explanation?

Are the creatures keeping human captives as some kind of pet, or are they being held for . . . for some other purpose?

These and other unnerving questions filled Mark's mind as he waited in the total darkness, listening to the creatures grumble and snort as they moved around in the pitch-dark cave.

How can they move around without bumping into rocks and walls? Mark wondered.

Can they see in the dark?

What if they already knew where he was hiding and—right now—they were shifting silently toward him in the darkness?

Mark concentrated his attention on relaxing, on slowing his breathing and pushing aside such thoughts. The cave echoed with low, rhythmic whimpers that reminded him of the sound a hurt dog would make.

Was it possible one of these creatures was actually crying?

Why don't they light a fire? It must be already dark outside. Have they come in to settle down for the night? How many are there? Should he risk turning on his flashlight, locating them, and then shooting—at least until he ran out of bullets? Or would that only end up getting him and the other hikers killed? Although all three captives were physically and, in the case of Mary, mentally damaged, at least they all were still alive . . .

. . . so far.

Although it made absolutely no difference, Mark closed his eyes and rested his head against the rock, focusing his attention on his hearing as he listened to try to determine if the creatures knew he was there. He realized that he was going to have to wait for one of two things—either all of the creatures were going to leave the cave again, or else one of them would start a fire, and he would be able to see exactly what he was up against.

Either way, it was going to be one hell of a long wait.

Some time later—he had no way of knowing how long—Mark awoke from the fitful sleep into which he had drifted.

Something was happening in the cave.

The creatures had all settled down, apparently to sleep, but now they were awakened by a loud screech from outside the cave. In an instant, the cave echoed with a chorus of loud, yapping cries that echoed weirdly in the cave's recesses.

Mark eased himself forward until he felt the edge of the rock and looked out into total darkness. He heard a heavy thump, as though one of them had fallen down or dropped something onto the floor. Their cries rose louder, sounding like rabid wolves, howling at the moon.

"Hey! What the hell's going on over there?" someone yelled.

The suddenness of a human voice startled Mark, but then he realized that it was Phil, calling out, no doubt, just to reassure Mark. The desire to call back to his friend was intense, but Mark knew it would be fatal.

The darkness suddenly exploded with a shower of yellow sparks accompanied by a loud rasping sound. The burst of light, as brief and as weak as it was, stung Mark's eyes like a splash of cold water. He ducked back down behind the rock edge and closed his eyes, waiting for the trailing afterimages of comets to disappear as he listened to the commotion of heavy bodies shifting about in the darkness. The quick rasping sound was repeated several times, and even with his eyes closed, Mark could see faint flashes of light, like lightning rippling in the distance.

When he finally dared to open his eyes and look again, he saw what was going on. One of the creatures was leaning over a small pile of leaves and twigs, scraping two large stones together to produce sparks. The creature kept working at it until enough sparks had landed, and a small fire began to smolder. Then the creature leaned forward and, puffing gently, blew on the sparks until a thin curl of smoke rose from the faintly glowing bed of tinder. Before long, small tongues of flame crackled on the kindling, lighting up the creature's face.

He looks like a goddamned deranged biker from hell, Mark thought as he studied the low, overhanging brow and the furry face that framed dark, deep-set eyes . . . eyes that glowed with an uncanny intelligence. If he hadn't known it before, Mark knew right then that he wasn't simply up against a pack of wild animals. These things were intelligent. They had the power of fire.

The creature continued to blow gently, and the flames rose higher, illuminating the cave with a soft, glowing globe of yellow light. The snap of recognition hit Mark hard, like a vision from a bad dream come to life when he saw that the creature starting the fire was the one that had attacked him yesterday. The fur on its left shoulder was stripped away, exposing a patch of raw flesh that was caked and matted with dried blood. Four other creatures stood nearby, watching the fire-maker.

Mark's pulse raced as he looked around at the shadowy forms lurking in the cave. With the flames underlighting them, they looked like gigantic nightmare creatures, but he saw their expressive faces that looked—he almost didn't allow himself the thought—almost *human!*

Projected onto the cave walls by the firelight, their shadows were impossibly huge and distorted. After his eyes adjusted to the brightness, Mark noticed a small shape sprawled on the floor. It took him a moment to realize that it was a human being, lying face-down on the cave floor. One of the creatures was crouching beside it, grunting as it poked and prodded the motionless figure with its forefinger.

Another captive! Mark thought. *Another human being to add to their collection!*

The fire grew steadily brighter as the creature who had lit it fed it pieces of wood. Mark realized that this new captive was a young woman. After staring at her a moment, he realized with a sickening drop in his stomach that there was something familiar about her. He stared at the girl's long, dark hair, spilling like an ink stain onto the rock floor. His heart literally stopped beating for several seconds when the creature rolled her over onto her back, and he saw who it was.

Oh, my God! Oh, Jesus!

Flashing red rage swept through Mark like a brushfire. His hands squeezed his rifle so hard his arms began to hurt right up to his neck. It was a miracle that he didn't scream out loud, leap down from his hiding place and, in an insane frenzy, attack all of the creatures, blasting at them with his rifle until he ran out of ammunition, and then flailing at them with the butt of the rifle until either he or they were dead.

But he was paralyzed with shock, frozen into inaction.

A fierce trembling gripped his body as he watched the creature lift Sandy's limp body from the floor.

Is she already dead? Mark wondered in a frantic flood of fear. Hot tears stung his eyes.

He had no idea what to wish for, whether to hope that Sandy was already dead and past any pain, or merely unconscious from the fear and pain of what had happened to her. Her arms and legs dangled loosely, and her back bent back unnaturally far as the creature turned back and forth facing the others as though displaying a trophy. All of them uttered low sounds as though pleased with this new acquisition.

Mark almost screamed aloud when Sandy's eyes fluttered open, reflecting the firelight with a glazed, distant pain. Her head lolled back and forth, but he could see her squint with unbearable pain at every motion. She looked dazed, as though caught in the grip of a vivid nightmare.

Using low grunts and snarls, the creatures seemed to address the one holding Sandy as he strutted back and forth across the cave floor. Then one of them stepped forward and grabbed Sandy's arm. With a snorting grunt, the creature pulled back while the one holding tightly onto Sandy's arm twisted away. The cave echoed a loud snap. Sandy's brief scream of pain was cut off by the raw, wet, ripping sound as her arm was pulled out of its socket.

Leaning its head back and staring at the shadowed ceiling of the cave, the creature holding Sandy let loose a loud, keening shriek. The other creature swung Sandy's severed arm over its head like a flail, gibbering with what sounded like pure animal glee. Then the one holding her body, obviously caught up in the frenzy, wrapped one arm around Sandy's neck, braced her body against his side, and with a quick jerk and snap of his body, broke her neck. A thick, bubbly sound came from Sandy's throat as her body went limp. Her eyes instantly glazed over in death and stared sightlessly ahead. They seemed to fix squarely on Mark where he lay, hidden on the ledge.

You bastards! You bloodythirsty, rotten, motherfucking bastards! Mark thought.

He wanted to jump up and scream his rage and misery, but heavy pressure was closing off his throat. He wished he could close his eyes and forget everything he had just seen, but he couldn't. Numb with terror, he had to watch as the creatures fell upon his daughter and with their horrible clawed hands, ripped off her clothes and raked the flesh away from her bones in large chunks which they stuffed into their mouths. Loud smacking sounds filled the cave as all five creatures feasted on the raw, human flesh.

Mark was numb to everything as he silently watched the horrible scene being enacted below him. He huddled on the rock ledge, sobbing and shivering. His only daughter had been killed right in front of his eyes, mutilated, and was being eaten by these bloodthirsty beasts!

You bastards! You'll pay for this! You'll all pay!

He watched in stunned horror as three of the creatures grabbed Sandy's other arm and two legs and pulled away from each other. Her limbs were torn free with the sounds of cracking bones and horrible tearing noises as her body split open. Dark blood gushed everywhere, splattering the creatures' bodies, driving them into a ferocious frenzy. Internal organs dropped to the cave floor with juicy, slapping sounds, only to be snatched up and shoved into hungry maws. One of the beasts smashed Sandy's head repeatedly against the cave floor until it split open like a ripe coconut. Then, sitting back on its haunches, the creature scooped out and feasted on the pale jelly of her brains, smacking its lips with horrible satisfaction. The cave walls reverberated with the creatures' hideous shrieks that now sounded all too much like bestial laughter. The horrible scene went on unabated until there was nothing left of Sandy except cracked bones and tangles of pink, stringy flesh.

Once the five creatures finished their grisly meal, two of them scooped up all that remained of Sandy, including her smashed skull, and casually tossed the pieces onto the pile of animal carcasses inside the corral beside the other captives. For a while the creatures squatted on their haunches, burping and grunting with satisfaction, but before long they all settled down to sleep.

Mark had lost all sense of time as he watched in horror from his hiding place. The firelight faded to an angry red glow. At some point, he closed his eyes and blocked his ears, but he knew he could never forget the sounds of the gruesome, brutal feast. Racked and shaken with tears of rage and grief, he slid down the angled rock until he came to rest against the cold stone wall. Long after the feast was over and the cave had descended into darkness and silence, his mind echoed with the last, agonized scream his daughter had made before she died.

Chapter Twenty-nine

Vow

Something moved inside the cave, bringing Mark to instant alertness.

The dim afterglow of the campfire illuminated the cave. Mark had no way of knowing whether it was day or night. What he remembered of the events of last night seemed now like fragments from some horrible nightmare, but the cold knot in his stomach and the stinging memory of Sandy's final, terrified scream convinced him that he had imagined nothing.

Sandy was dead.

Mark's mind raged and ached; his heart beat with a cold, steady knocking against his ribs, convincing him that it had been all too horribly real.

The cave was in near total darkness as the creatures, sleeping on piles of leaves and moss piled up in the corners, began to stir. One of them—Mark couldn't distinguish which one; he saw only that this one didn't have a wounded left shoulder—went over to the fire, piled on a few pieces of wood, and blew on the coals until flames erupted in a snapping blaze.

Mark watched as the creature shuffled about the cave, bending over and sniffing the other sleeping creatures until they, too, began to stir. He tried to focus on what he had to do today to get Phil and the others out of here alive, but his mind kept drawing a blank. All he could think was, Sandy was dead! Tortured and mutilated! No amount of anger or grief or *anything* would bring her back.

She was gone, and he had been helpless to stop it.

Hunkering down on the rock ledge, Mark watched silently as the creatures roused themselves. One of them picked up a long bone from the cave floor, sniffed it, and then splintered it on a rock and ran one finger along the inside to scoop out the fresh marrow. Mark's body went cold with the thought that this was Sandy's leg bone. He slid his rifle up, fighting the almost overpowering urge to take aim and shoot the creature, but he held his fire, knowing that he and Phil and the other lost hikers wouldn't survive the creatures' wrath.

Mark glanced over at the corral but couldn't see the captives clearly. They were three dark shapes, slouching against the cave wall. He had three bullets left. Perhaps the merciful thing to do would be to use them to end Phil's, Jack's, and Mary's misery. Then the creatures could finish him off in a frenzy, and it would be over with. What was the sense of living, now that Sandy—his only child—was dead?

He had nothing to look forward to.

When—and if—he got out of here, life at home was never going to be the same. Better yet, why not end it all right now with a single shot to his head and let the others fend for themselves?

Why the fuck not?

He fingered the trigger and, closing his eyes a moment, visualized raising the rifle to his head, pressing the cold metal barrel against his temple, and squeezing the trigger.

It would all be over in an instant.

Why not do it and be done with the pain and suffering? Sandy's death was going to leave a vacuum in his life that would never be filled.

Why not end it all now, with one clean shot?

He honestly wanted to do it, but then he thought that if he died now, it would leave these things still alive. Sandy's death would go unavenged, and that meant next year more hikers would disappear and end up here in this cave with their legs broken, waiting to die.

No, Mark decided as he opened his eyes and glared at the creatures as they shuffled around the cave. He imagined himself kneeling over the mangled corpse of his daughter as he vowed that those creatures were going to have to die!

He was going to wipe out *all* of them!

After a breakfast of raw meat from the pile of carcasses inside the corral, four of the five creatures departed from the cave, leaving behind one—the one with the wounded shoulder—to tend the fire and guard the captives.

Mark waited a long time, mentally counting the minutes until he was sure the creatures were far enough away from the cave before making his move. A gunshot echoing from inside the cave would certainly bring them all back. While he waited, Mark studied the one remaining creature and actually found himself thinking of it in almost human terms. It was the creature's eyes and expressions that struck him as most human, but even its movements and actions as it settled with its back against the cave wall seemed intelligent beyond what little experience he'd had observing monkeys and gorillas in a zoo.

"She's dead, you know!" someone shouted.

The sudden voice echoed like a gunshot off the cave walls. The guarding creature roused itself, glared over at the corral, and snorted viciously.

"She's dead! Mary died last night!"

It was Phil's voice, ringing out strong and clear, no doubt to let Mark know that he, at least, was still holding out.

"She couldn't take it anymore, you lousy son-of-a-bitch!" Phil yelled, his voice starting to edge up into hysteria. "She couldn't take it anymore. *None of us can take it anymore!*"

The creature shifted to its feet and started over toward the captives. As soon as its back was to him, Mark raised himself into a crouch. He supported his arm on one knee and drew a careful bead on the back of the creature's head, carefully tracking the creature's movements. Holding his breath for a second, he was just about to squeeze the trigger when he remembered that he didn't have enough bullets. If he used one now, it might well prove to be the one he would need later. One on one, he just might have a chance.

Keeping as quiet as possible, he slid down from the ledge and, resting his rifle back behind his shoulder, dashed across the cave floor toward the creature. As soon as Phil saw what Mark was doing, he started yelling again, hoping to mask the sound of his friend's approach and draw the creature's attention.

"*Are we next?*" Phil hollered. "*Is that it? Which one of us is going to be supper tonight, huh? Tell me that!*"

The creature grunted angrily, keeping his eyes on Phil as Mark rapidly closed the gap between them. At the very last instant, the beast sensed approaching danger. Letting loose a wild roar, it spun around just as Mark swung the rifle around in a wide arc.

"You motherfucking bastard!"

The butt of the rifle smashed the side of the creature's head with an impact that shattered the skull and blew a red spray of blood into the air. Without another sound, the creature spun around in its tracks, took a couple of wobbly steps backward, and then dropped to the ground. Its body twitched for a second or two, and then lay still.

"Awright! One for the good guys!" Phil shouted hoarsely.

Mark straddled the creature's corpse and then, shouting with every hit, slammed his rifle butt into the creature's face enough times to turn it into a bloody pulp. He was lost in a whirlwind of finally being able to release his rage. Sweat dripped from his face, and his whole body was trembling when he finally realized that there was nothing recognizable left of the creature's head. Stepping back, he let the rifle drop from his hands.

"Well, he sure as shit ain't going anywhere," Phil said.

Mark was panting heavily as he smiled grimly over at his friend. Then he quickly vaulted the fence and went over to where Mary lay.

"Did you mean what you said, Phil? Is she really—"

He stopped himself short when he saw that Mary was slumped against the rock, her head tilted back and her mouth wide open. Her unblinking eyes were glazed over as though she were staring far into the distance.

"Shit!" Mark whispered.

Tears formed in his eyes, but he knew the cold, hollow grief that filled him was for Sandy, not Mary. He knelt beside the woman, gently closed her eyes, and composed her stiffening hands in her lap.

"I—I'm awfully sorry," he said, turning to Jack. His voice was little more than a tattered gasp.

"I don't think she could have lived with the pain anymore," Jack said, sounding barely able to speak himself. "She—I think she just gave up—after seeing what they did to that girl—last night," Jack said,

"That was my . . . daughter," Mark said, surprised that he could speak at all.

After a moment, Jack closed his eyes and said, "I—I'm awfully sorry." Fat tears, which he didn't even try to wipe away, streaked the thick grime on his face.

Trembling inside, Mark stood up and brushed his hands on his legs as he looked at Phil.

"Jesus, Mark!" Phil said, lowering his gaze to the floor. "I'm sorry. I—I didn't even recognize her."

Mark forced himself to look over at the stinking pile of offal, knowing that, mixed in somewhere with the rotting flesh of deer and other animals were the last human remains of his daughter. He was shaking, nearly blind with grief as he walked over toward the pile. The smell of death and rotting flesh assailed his nostrils, making him gag. He saw, resting on its left cheek amongst the stripped bones, decaying flesh, and rotting pelts, his daughter's ruined head. Framed by her dark hair, her smashed face was chalky white and streaked with splashes of dried blood. Her eyes were wide open, staring, as though a photographic flash had caught her by surprise. The raw, red stump of her neck ended with a short length of spine protruding from the base. The sight of it twisted Mark's stomach. He fell to his knees and dry-heaved.

"Mark! Listen to me, Mark," Phil called out.

"There's—there's—nothing—you can—say," Mark whispered as he doubled over, clenching his arms over his stomach, and fought against the waves of sour acid that were bubbling up out of him.

"Come on, Mark! Don't look at it! You—you have to remember her for who she was, not . . . not like *that!*"

"I swear to Christ," Mark said. His fists were clenched and shaking, and his voice was low and thrumming as he straightened up. Tears were pouring from his eyes, but he wiped them on his sleeve as he looked up into the dark recesses of the cave ceiling and listened to the vibrating echo of his voice as it rose louder and louder. "You know—"

". . . *know* . . ." his voice echoed.

"I think they did it—"

". . . *did it* . . ."

"out of revenge."

". . . *revenge* . . ."

"Come on, Mark. You're talking crazy now," Phil said.

"No, I really think so. I think all along they've been hunting me, maybe ever since that day you fell off The Zipper. I think they tracked me back to my house. I think one of them, maybe the one that was looking for me, killed Dennis Cross, thinking it was me. And I think—I think they went back down there and took Sandy out of pure spite because they hadn't found me."

"I don't blame you for freaking out, all right?" Phil said. "But don't you think you're giving them a little too much credit? If they had been—"

"I don't *care* what you think, so just shut the fuck up! It doesn't fucking matter! Sandy's *dead*, and I swear to God—" He shook his clenched fists wildly over his head. "I swear on the bones of my *daughter* that I'm going to hunt down every last one of these bastards—whatever the hell they are—and I'm going to kill them all, with my bare hands if I have to!"

Turning to Phil, he lowered his voice and said, "I gave my word that I'd come up here and not leave until I found you, and I've done that. But once I get you and Jack and—" his voice choked off, and he had to force himself to continue "—and come back for Mary and what's left of Sandy, I promise you I'm not going to rest until I see every one of these bastards dead!"

A shiver rippled through him when his last word echoed hollowly from the ceiling of the cave—

"... *dead!* ..."

Chapter Thirty

"He ain't heavy . . ."

"Can't you just hike back to town and come back with some help?" Jack asked. His voice was high and edged with tension.

Mark looked at him and shook his head. "Look, I don't particularly like the choices, either, but just what the hell do you think these creatures will do to you once they come back and find another one of them has been killed?"

"Good point," Jack said, running one hand down the side of his face.

"First things first," Mark said as he fed a few more sticks into the fire. "I have to get you guys out of here—someplace safe."

"Oh, yeah?" Phil said, snorting with laughter as he slapped his useless legs. "And just how do you propose to do that?"

Mark started pacing back and forth across the cave

floor while he pondered the situation. He knew he couldn't leave both men here while he went down the mountain to get help. Even if he left them his rifle, they wouldn't stand a chance without enough bullets to finish off the four surviving beasts. And that was assuming there were only four more. For all they knew, there might be dozens of these things living in other caves on the mountain or spread throughout the forest.

But Mark was convinced that he had to get at least one man down off the mountain now, carrying him all the way if he had to. Even if there was someplace for them to hide outside the cave, the creatures obviously had a keen sense of smell and would eventually track them down. He felt uncomfortable admitting it, even to himself, but his first loyalty was to Phil. If he was taking anyone, he would take Phil. Jack was much worse off and needed more help, but that also meant he might not survive the hike down. Besides, Mark didn't have much water or food to leave behind for both of them, so it was tantamount to consigning them to death to leave them behind in the cave.

"How about up on the ledge, where I was hiding last night?" Mark said, glancing at Jack. "If I can get you up there, and take Phil with me, they may think we *all* got away."

Jack stared back at him with a glazed, defeated expression, as if he could clearly read Mark's loyalty to Phil and saw that his chances of surviving this ordeal were the least of anyone's.

"Yeah—I suppose so," he finally said through cracked lips. "It—it doesn't really matter now, I guess, . . . now that Mary's—"

"Don't you go giving up now," Mark said with a

forcefulness in his voice he didn't really feel. The memory of Sandy's horrible death was still too fresh, too painful in his mind. He clapped Jack on the shoulder and gave him a bracing shake.

"I don't think you're in any condition to handle the trip down. Let me get Phil back to town, and then I'll get back here with some armed men and clean these bastards out. That's as long as you can hang on. Hiding up there on that ledge is gonna be your best bet."

"Without a weapon?"

Mark considered offering Jack his rifle, or maybe his Swiss Army knife, but he knew that would be foolish. If the creatures found him, he wouldn't be able to fend them off. It was going to be challenge enough getting down off the mountain while there was still enough daylight even without these creatures chasing after them. Out in the open, he and Phil were going to have to protect themselves if they were attacked.

"Look, I'm sorry," Mark said, "but there's nothing else I can think of right now."

"And what if you don't make it back?" Jack asked, his voice trembling wildly now. "What if—"

"Don't worry. I'll make it back. I promise," Mark said even as dark doubt filled his mind. "For the past few days, dozens of men have been out here on the mountain, searching for me." He wished now that he had seen even a single searcher yesterday. Had the police given up the search for both him and Phil?

Jack considered a moment, then nodded and sighed. "Yeah—I guess so," he said, not sounding at all convinced.

Mark hurriedly cut the vines binding Jack's legs. He was surprised by how light the man was when he picked him up and carried him over to the bottom of the ledge. Using his jacket as a sling, he hoisted Jack up into the niche, then took the longest, strongest piece of wood he could find from the pile of firewood and gave it to him.

"Use this if you have to," Mark said.

From the cold gleam in Jack's eye, he knew they both understood that this was a futile gesture, but Jack smiled his thanks.

"Here's my canteen and some food," Mark said, handing Jack his day pack. He wished he could think of something reassuring to say, but nothing came to mind so, hoping he hadn't just signed Jack's death warrant, he left him there.

"We're gonna need this to get down the cliff side," he said as he knelt down beside Mary's corpse and cut the vines holding her legs together. He gathered up all of the discarded rope, tied the ends together, wound it up in a thick coil, and slung it over his shoulder. Then he went over to Phil.

"It's going to hurt like a bitch when I pick you up," he said, turning around so Phil could get on him, piggyback style.

"You don't know the meaning of the word *pain*," Phil replied as he hiked himself up onto his friend's back.

Once in position, Phil wrapped one arm around Mark's neck and settled into place. Mark gave him the rifle to carry and warned him that if there was danger, he was going to have to drop him so he could use the rifle.

" 'S long as you don't break my legs," Phil said with a forced chuckle.

"Glad to see you haven't lost your sense of humor.

I wish to hell you could have lost a few more pounds before we tried this, though," Mark said. Already he was puffing as he started toward the cave opening. He knew he was crazy even to be trying this, but it was the best—it was the *only* plan he could come up with.

"He ain't heavy, he's my brother," Phil said with another hearty laugh; then he was silent as Mark made his way through the main chamber and negotiated the narrow passageway, following the faint yellow circle of his flashlight back to the cave opening. They had just made their way through the outer chamber when a voice, echoing in the darkness behind them, called out.

"Hey, Mark! Mark!"

"Yeah," Mark shouted, already feeling winded from the effort.

"I don't think I like this idea," Jack shouted. His voice was wound high with tension.

"Don't worry. Just stay down and be quiet!"

"No. Please. Don't leave me here! Come back! Please!"

Mark hesitated a moment. His knees were buckling beneath the weight of his friend as he turned and looked back into the dark maw of the cave.

"Please—?" Jack shouted. "I—I know I won't be able to stand it here alone. I don't want them to find me. They'll kill me! They'll rip me to shreds, just like they did—did to—"

His voice choked off abruptly, and Mark was thankful that he hadn't said Sandy's name out loud.

Taking a deep breath, Mark called back. "Just hang in there. I'll be back here to get you within twenty-four hours. I promise!"

"I hope so," Jack yelled, sounding not at all reassured. "I sure as shit hope so!"

Chapter Thirty-one
Traces of Red

The sky was overcast that morning, a dull, gunmetal gray when Polly left for work at ten o'clock. She was still hoping that she would find an opportunity to hit the road, so she hadn't bothered to take her suitcases out of the car trunk. This morning, though, convinced that the police had her under surveillance, she pushed aside any thoughts of leaving . . . for now.

No, she told herself, she had to act as if everything was one hundred percent normal . . . even considering that her boyfriend had been murdered less than a week ago, her husband was somewhere up on Mount Agiochook looking for his missing and presumed dead friend, a police search party was out there hunting for him, and her stepdaughter had moved out of the house last night.

You never saw this on "Ozzie and Harriet," she thought with bitter sarcasm.

No wonder she hadn't been sleeping well for the last several nights. The tension was definitely starting to get to her. Why, just last night, sometime around midnight, she had awoken, absolutely convinced that someone was in the house. She had sat up in bed and listened as footsteps moved stealthily around downstairs. Her first thought had been that whoever had killed Dennis had come back for her, but she had been too frightened to do anything, even to dial the police. Instead, she had cowered in her bed, shivering as she listened to the footsteps come slowly up the stairs. She had closed her eyes, feigning sleep, and waited with bated breath, absolutely convinced that the intruder had opened her bedroom door a crack and had looked in on her before leaving.

Her first thought—the one she wanted to believe—was that Mark had come home. But Mark would have turned on all the lights and made a lot of noise downstairs before coming upstairs to talk to her before getting into bed.

No, if it hadn't been a dream—and now, in the diffused light of the overcast morning, that seemed the most likely explanation—then someone had broken into the house last night.

Before breakfast, she had checked upstairs and down, but hadn't noticed anything valuable missing. Still, even now, she couldn't shake the feeling that she was being watched.

Maybe it was simply paranoia, thinking that the police still suspected her for Dennis's murder, but she couldn't stop thinking that it might be something more than that.

That someone was staying close by the house,

keeping an eye on her, watching her every move and waiting to strike.

After three cups of coffee that morning, her nerves were even more jangled. Her first customer this morning, Mrs. Alvord, was going to be damned lucky to get out of the hairdresser's shop without a Mohawk.

As she locked the house door and went down the steps to the garage, Polly was still unable to get rid of the feeling that she was being watched. She kept glancing around the yard as she walked over to the garage, turned the door handle, and ran up the door. The clatter of metal wheels and springs drilled her ears. When she looked over her shoulder, she was surprised not to see that a police car had pulled into the driveway. What she *did* see was a faint glint of metal in the grass beside the back steps.

"What the hell—?" she muttered as she walked over to it, bent down, and picked it up.

It was the spare house key, the one they kept underneath the steps.

She wiped it clean with her fingers and inspected it closely.

What was this doing out here on the lawn? she wondered as she turned it over several times in her hand.

Maybe it had simply fallen from its hiding place, but what if someone had used it . . . last night . . . to get into the house?

She knelt down and, leaning forward until her cheek pressed against the top step, felt around underneath the stairs for the nail to hang the key on. It was when the top step was level to her eye that she noticed something else—a small splotch of blood, no bigger than a quarter, on the edge of the landing.

Her heart skipped a beat as she stared at the blood, glistening in the dull morning light with an oily freshness—dark red, almost black. She felt almost compelled to reach out and touch it, to see if it was still wet, but instead she squealed with surprise and pushed herself away from the steps so hard she fell backward onto the wet grass. She barely noticed that her clothes got wet as she scrambled to her feet. Her pulse was racing hard and fast in her throat, and she was unable to tear her gaze away from the blackish red smear.

Was it Dennis's blood . . . still there from that horrible night?

She glanced fearfully to the spot beside the garage where she had found Dennis's mutilated body. A cold, clutching fear filled her.

Did Dennis's killer come back last night for me?

Did he break into the house and come right upstairs, but then decide to leave me alone, to let me live . . . for now?

Is he stalking me right now, taunting me by showing that he can get me whenever he damn well pleases?

She knew the sensible thing to do would be to notify the police immediately, but she decided not to do that. She didn't trust the police any more than they apparently trusted her.

Polly was so preoccupied with thinking about what she should do that she didn't even notice the car that had pulled into the driveway until the driver's door opened and slammed shut.

"Something the matter?" Guy LaBrea asked. His voice sounded oddly close in the still air. He looked at her with flat, expressionless eyes as he walked up to her.

Polly felt numb as she turned to the police chief, shook her head, and managed to say, "Uh . . . no."

As soon as she looked away from the spot of blood on the landing, it grew in size in her imagination until it was the size of a spilled gallon of bright red paint. She was surprised LaBrea didn't notice it and comment on it right away.

"No," Polly said again after drawing a deep breath and bending down to wipe the dampness on the backs of her legs. "I was just—I slipped on the walkway and fell. I'm okay. God, sometimes I'm so clumsy!"

LaBrea nodded, then glanced up at the house. "I stopped by the high school earlier this morning to speak with Sandy. Had a few things I wanted to talk over with her, but she wasn't there. Is she home sick or something?"

Biting her lower lip, Polly shook her head. "No. As far as I know, she spent last night over at Karen Bishop's."

LaBrea narrowed his gaze.

"We—umm, well, Sandy and I had kind of an argument last night," Polly added feebly.

"I see," LaBrea said, scratching his chin thoughtfully. "Well, I happened to bump into Karen Bishop at the school, and she told me that Sandy was over to her house last night, but she said she didn't stay the whole night, that she must have left sometime around midnight and didn't come back." He nodded toward the house. "You sure she's not up in her room?"

"Positive," Polly said, shrugging tightly.

She had checked Sandy's bedroom while searching the house to see if anything had been stolen last night.

She had to fight the impulse to turn and look back at the house, afraid that she would scream the instant she saw the blood on the back steps. In her imagination, it had spread out into a glistening puddle that was dripping in thick, shimmering red globs from the steps and gushing out over the lawn. A wave of dizziness gripped her, and she felt as though a surging bloody tide was swirling at her ankles, tugging at her, trying to pull her down.

"I know she and her father had picked a meeting point out at the base of the Round Top Trail," LaBrea said, stroking his chin thoughtfully. "Maybe she's gone out there."

Polly thought his voice sounded steady, completely normal, as if he hadn't even noticed the bloodstain on the steps.

"I wouldn't know," she said, fighting the tremor in her voice.

"Maybe I ought to take a drive on out there and have a look around."

"She—uh, she never told me anything about that," Polly replied, her voice still flat and emotionless.

"Well," LaBrea said, looking squarely at Polly, "you also might want to know that we're calling off the search for both Mark and Phil. The weather forecast is calling for some pretty rough weather later today and tonight. I can't risk any more men than I have to up there. A skeleton crew of forest rangers is going to make one last sweep today, and that'll be it, at least until the weather clears."

"I see," Polly said numbly. She was surprised that apparently LaBrea still hadn't noticed anything seriously wrong.

"I don't want to upset you," he said, "but chances

are something's happened up there. We—well, you ought to know that one of the search parties located what we think was your husband's campsite yesterday." LaBrea took a deep breath and waited for her response, but Polly was still feeling too disoriented to react.

"It looks as though something's gone wrong up there. The tent and camping gear were all torn up, thrown all over the place. I'm not saying he's hurt or anything, mind you, but . . . well, there's been some fairly well substantiated reports of some kind of animal up there in the mountains, maybe a bear or something that's on a rampage. You might have heard what happened out at Josh O'Connell's barn several nights ago."

"No. No, I didn't," Polly said.

"Well, I don't want you to worry, but—" LaBrea shrugged as though he were helpless. "What with the weather turning bad and all, I just hope to hell Mark gets down off that mountain today."

"Is there anything I can do?" Polly asked in a trembling voice. Her face felt numb, and her leg muscles were shaking so badly she thought she was going to lose control of them and collapse.

Again, LaBrea shrugged.

"I think all *you* can do is go to work, carry on as best you can, and hope for the best. I have the number at Marilyn's Beauty Shop, so I can call if I hear from either Mark or Sandy."

"I—I'd appreciate that," Polly said, not really feeling it.

"Okay, then," LaBrea said.

Polly felt only a marginal sense of relief as she watched LaBrea turn and walk back to his cruiser, get in, start it up, and drive away. Even before the sound of his car had faded away, she ran up to the house, got a bucket of soapy water and a scrub brush, and washed away the last trace of blood from the landing. She wasn't entirely convinced it was Dennis's blood, but any speculation as to whose it might be was blocked out of her mind by her single, most worrisome fear.

What if the police and the whole town of Hilton blame me for what happened to Dennis? I'll never get out of this mess!

Chapter Thirty-two
Three Down

"Holy *shit!* The light hurts like a *bitch!*" Phil said, blinking his eyes rapidly.

Mark grunted as he eased Phil down onto the ledge outside the cave mouth. The sky was overcast—a dull gray ripple of high clouds.

"What do you expect, after being in total darkness for nearly a week?" Mark said softly.

He glanced up at the overcast sky and guessed it was a little after noon. They had less than six hours of daylight to get down off the mountain. He was positive they wouldn't make it back to town before dark, but he decided not to tell Phil just how bad things looked.

Taking the rifle from his friend, he walked over to the edge of the cliff and looked down. More than eighty feet below, he could see the bright dots of color that were Phil's torn jacket and backpack. He carefully scanned the area but couldn't see any sign of the creatures. The body of the one he had killed had been removed. He knew from all too painful experience, though, how easily these things could hide themselves among the rocks—and how fast they could move to attack. He clicked the safety off his rifle and started pacing back and forth along the ledge like a soldier on guard duty as he considered the easiest way to get Phil down to the base of the cliff.

Once his eyes had adjusted to the brightness, Phil, wincing with the pain and effort, dragged himself over to the edge of the cliff and looked down. Whistling softly under his breath, he said, "Christ on a cross! That rope's not gonna be enough to get us down from here, is it, bud?"

"I shinnied up that chimney in the rock over there," Mark said, pointing to the shallow funnel that ran up the cliff side. "I don't suppose you could slide down that steep an incline by yourself."

Phil considered for a moment, then shook his head. "No way. Not without the use of my legs."

"I didn't think so. Okay, then, we'll have to do it the hard way."

He took the coil of vines from his shoulder and shook it out. Altogether, there were more than twenty short pieces tied together. He tossed one end over the cliff edge, but the makeshift rope didn't even reach halfway down.

Mark groaned his dissatisfaction, then shrugged off his jacket. Taking his Swiss Army knife from his pocket, he began to slice the nylon shell into long, thin strips.

"C'mon! Get busy tying those together," he said as he handed the first few strips to Phil. "These with the vines should give us enough to reach the bottom. We can at least get you most of the way down."

For the next several minutes, both men worked in silence as Mark cut his jacket into strips and Phil knotted them together, end to end. By the time every useful piece of Mark's jacket had been used up and they tied one end of it to the knotted vine rope, their makeshift rope still looked as if it wouldn't reach all the way to the ground.

"It's gonna have to do. Should we risk it now?" Mark asked as he pulled the rope back up and tugged at each knot to make sure none of them would slip.

Phil nodded. "I don't think it'd be very smart to sit here the rest of the day just waiting for those bastards to come back, now, do you?"

"They're probably out hunting for more victims," Mark said.

He shivered as the memory of what had happened to his daughter stirred in his mind, but he forced those thoughts away, choosing instead to concentrate only on getting himself and Phil to safety. He'd have plenty of time to deal with his grief later.

Mark handed Phil his knife, then quickly looped the nylon end of the rope around his friend's waist and tied it off securely in a sling. He dragged Phil over to the rock chimney and then, bracing his feet wide, gripped the rope and started lowering him after Phil pushed himself away from the ledge.

The first jolt of Phil's weight almost yanked Mark off balance, but then Phil scrambled around into the right position and braced himself against the rock with his arms and his useless legs in the narrow indentation. After that, the going was a little easier.

While he was lowering Phil, Mark kept a wary eye

out for the return of any of the creatures. If one showed up now, Phil would be in deep shit. Mark would have to drop him so he could use the rifle to fend it off.

Rivulets of sweat dripped from Mark's face and ran down his neck. His back and shoulder muscles were hurting so bad he wondered how he would ever find the strength to get himself down the steep incline.

I will because I have to, he vowed silently to himself.

He grunted softly as he fed out the rope, knot by knot. The transition from the thin nylon to the thicker vine made his hands and arms ache all the more, but he gritted his teeth and kept feeding out the rope, inch by inch. When he reached the end of the rope, he twisted a few loops around his wrist and held on tightly.

"That's all I've got!" he called down to Phil. His voice echoed from the rocks below. "How much further have you got to go?"

The vine was slippery in his hands, and he knew he wasn't going to be able to hold on much longer.

"Not far," Phil answered, his voice sounding faint and thin. "Can't be more than ten or fifteen feet."

"Can I let you drop?"

"Just a second—Yeah, okay. I think I'm—"

The tension on the rope suddenly released.

With a startled cry, Mark rushed to the edge of the cliff and looked down. He expected to see Phil lying crushed and broken at the base of the cliff—or else being torn to shreds by one of the creatures, so he laughed out loud when he realized that Phil had cut the nylon and was leaning back hard against the rock, bracing himself with his arms. Phil's face was bright red from the effort, but—unbelievably—he was able to control the rest of his descent.

As soon as Phil was safely on the ground, Mark slung his rifle over his shoulder, crawled out over the edge, braced himself against the rock, and started down in a fast, barely controlled slide. It was a lot easier with gravity working with him, and before long he was standing next to his friend, brushing himself off. Both men were panting heavily from the exertion as Phil wiggled his way free of the nylon rope.

"That was the hardest part, right?" Phil said, smiling grimly.

"Yeah . . . right," Mark replied just as grimly.

He wasted no time in getting Phil up onto his back again and starting down the slope. They had several miles to cover, and by the looks of the sky, the weather was going to get nasty before long. The only consolation was that, if it started raining, it might hamper their pursuers as much as it hampered them.

The descent from the mountaintop was arduous—a nightmare of physical endurance. Under normal conditions, the hike down to the tree line would take no more than an hour, but it consumed better than three hours because Mark had to stop so frequently to rest. Almost every step of the way, he regretted leaving his canteen behind with Jack as thirst and fatigue rose to nearly unbearable levels.

The Wheaton Trail was the shortest trail off the mountain, but it was also the steepest, so Mark decided to stick with the longer Round Top Trail, which crossed the west branch of Sawyer River a little more than halfway to the trail head. They could get fresh water at the river, but he also chose this route because it was in the same general direction as his base camp. What with both a police search party and the creatures after him, he doubted that his camp had remained undetected, but he hoped there would still be some ammunition and possibly some food still there.

It was late afternoon by the time they reached the tree line. Every muscle in Mark's body was crying for relief as he eased Phil onto the ground. It was a relief to have soft, springy soil beneath his feet instead of the hard, unyielding stone. Mark stood up straight, rotated his shoulders, and knuckled the small of his back, but that didn't come close to relieving the bone-deep pain.

"Sure am thirsty," he said, licking his dried lips as he stared down the trail into the cool, green forest. He had been expecting the creatures to attack before now, while they were still high up on the rocks, exposed and defenseless. Now that they were down into the trees, he was discouraged by the prospect of carrying Phil down a steep trail that was hemmed in on both sides by dense brush. The creatures could easily wait in ambush for them and attack before either one of them could blink an eye. If these creatures were intelligent, they no doubt would hunt him in unison. Mark started wondering if maybe he should have waited up above the tree line and tried to finish them off up there before starting down. Then again, maybe the remaining creatures were too smart to be lured into a trap like that.

"Make sure you keep that rifle cocked and ready," Mark said once he was rested and was helping Phil climb up onto his back again.

They were about to start moving when a shifting of motion up on the mountain drew their attention.

Standing up straight, its body darkly outlined against the gray sky, was a large, man-shaped creature. It was looking down the slope, straight at them.

For a frozen instant, Mark recalled the first time he had seen one of these things, shambling out of the blowing snow over to where Phil lay unconscious at the bottom of The Zipper. That terrible day now seemed like a lifetime away. Cold tension gripped his stomach as he watched the creature lean its head back and shake its fists wildly as though punching the sky as it bellowed its rage. The sound the creature made was lost in the distance, but as the men watched, the creature jumped down from the rock and disappeared.

"One of them's after us," Mark said as he lowered Phil to the ground again and took his rifle from him. He quickly scanned the area, looking for the best place to make a stand if the creature was heading down to attack them. Off to one side of the trail was a large boulder. Mark quickly carried Phil over to it, then crouched in front of the rock with his rifle at the ready.

The silence surrounding them was deep and unbroken except for the high whistling of the wind in the trees overhead and the distant sound of birds down in the valley. Coiled tension was a palpable presence in the air as Mark waited silently, straining to detect the slightest indication of the creature's approach. The soft forest floor would mask all but the loudest sounds, so Mark kept glancing around as the seconds slowly ticked off.

"Think it might've gone to find the others first?" Phil whispered.

"I have no idea," Mark said, shaking his head but not stopping his scan of the area. His pulse was beating such a high, fast rhythm in his ears it made it difficult for him to concentrate. The lack of sunlight cast the entire mountainside in a shadowless, dimensionless gray pall.

"Maybe we should just keep going," Phil said, sounding more agitated. "The further we get into the deep woods, the better off we'll be, don't you think? They won't follow us all the way down, will they?"

"Oh, they'll follow us all right," Mark replied, grinning tightly. "They can't let us get away, and they're certainly smart enough to know that. I suspect they'll follow us right into town if they have to."

"What makes you think—"

Before Phil could finish his question, a piercing howl shattered the silence.

"God damn!" Mark shouted as he jumped to his feet, spun around, and raised his rifle.

Two of the creatures attacked in unison.

They were nothing more than swift blurs of brown motion as they leapt off the rock behind the two men. Mark managed to fire a single shot. The bullet tore through one creature's chest, killing it instantly. Mark tried to dodge to one side, but the creature landed on his back. The impact knocked the rifle from his hand as hot, stifling darkness enfolded him, suffocating him as the creature's heavy carcass pressed him face-first into the humus of the forest floor.

Mark's mind went blank with terror. He expected to be torn to pieces at any instant as he struggled to get out from underneath the burden of the beast. Then, with a deafening roar, the other beast pulled aside the body of its companion and grabbed Mark. The creature enfolded him in a tight, deadly embrace that pinned his arms to his sides and squeezed the air from his lungs. Bright, white lights exploded across his vision as the unrelenting pressure crushed him.

Time lost all meaning in a flood of panic and pain.

He knew he was going to die.

Heated animal breath blew into his face as the creature leaned close to him and, snapping its jaws, exposed its large, flat teeth. Thick, yellowish foam flew from the creature's lips and splattered Mark's face. Mark nearly gagged at the stench of the creature's breath. His awareness was spinning so far down into a cushiony, throbbing darkness that he was barely aware of the explosion of the gun. He never felt the splash of hot blood onto his face or the crazy twitching of the animal's body as a bullet tore through the back of its head, killing it instantly.

Mark continued to spiral downward, lost in a dizzying darkness thicker than any darkness he had ever experienced before. His whole existence seemed to be reduced to one tiny, flickering pulse of pain and despair.

Time lost all meaning as the darkness sucked him down. . . .

And then, from far away, he heard a faint voice calling to him.

He thought he recognized the voice, but it was so faint, so far away, he was positive he was already dead and drifting further and further away.

"Hey! . . . You all right? . . . Are you all right, Mark? . . . Come on, man, talk to me!"

Mark tried to suck in a lungful of air, but the pressure on his crushed ribs made it impossible for him to take a deep breath. The small amount of air that did enter his lungs felt like hot, fetid water. The darkness surrounding him was complete, but then, only vaguely at first, he became aware that he was no longer being held by the arms that had pinned him. His body was free and floating, as if he were tumbling weightlessly down a long, dark river. A hot, sticky liquid was dripping from his face and running down his neck.

My blood, he thought.

With the faint spark of hope that he wasn't already dead, he struggled to open one eye. It took a great deal of effort, but he managed to look around. The first thing he saw was Phil, staring at him with the most idiotic grin he had ever seen.

"You're alive!" Phil shouted. "Jesus God! I can't believe I got him! One shot!"

You got him? Mark wanted to say but couldn't.

"I crawled over and picked up the rifle, and I shot him!"

He was leaning over Mark, looking at him like he wanted to give him a great big bear hug. "I can't believe I didn't hit you, too!"

Mark sucked in a shallow breath that wheezed in his throat.

"Yeah," he finally managed to say.

He was trembling violently as he pushed the carcass off him and stood up slowly. Every joint and muscle screamed with pain as he stared in utter disbelief at the two dead creatures lying on the ground. The top of one's head, obviously a female, had been blown away by Phil's lucky shot. The other one was face-down on the ground with a wide, bloody hole in its back.

Mark grimaced when he looked at his gore-streaked hands and then wiped his face. He rotated both of his shoulders and kicked both legs to make sure nothing was broken, then took a deep breath, wincing with the pain of his expanding ribs. He might have one or two cracked ribs, he thought, and absolutely every part of his body hurt; but nothing else seemed to be broken.

He looked numbly over at Phil, who was sitting back on the ground, whooping with joy as he shook the rifle above his head.

"All right!" he shouted. "We got two more of 'em! We fucking-A got 'em!"

Phil cut himself short and looked at Mark when he grabbed the rifle, bolted it, and, crouching, cautiously glanced all around.

"Hey, come on," Phil said, his voice still trembling with excitement. "There aren't any more around. Don't you think, if there were any more, they'd have attacked by now?"

"Maybe . . . maybe not," Mark said as he rolled his head back and forth and massaged the back of his neck. It felt as though several vertebrae had been broken.

"So that's three down!" Phil shouted. "Three down and two to go!"

"Yeah," Mark said. He leaned over, panting for breath as he wiped the creature's blood from his face with the flat of his hand. "Three down and two to go . . . as far as we know."

Chapter Thirty-three

Down to the River

The clouds turned to the color of soot, and rain was threatening by the time they reached what used to be Mark's campsite.

The place was a shambles.

What was left of his tent was flattened and torn to shreds. The aluminum support bars had been ripped from the ground and bent into pretzel shapes. Tatters of brightly colored nylon along with the torn remnants of Mark's extra clothing were strewn all around on the ground and hung from the branches overhead, flapping in the stiffening breeze like medieval war pennants. Every can and package of food had been squashed or ripped open and scattered about on the ground.

"Who do you think did this?" Phil asked after Mark had lowered him to the ground.

With his hands on his hips, Mark looked around dejectedly.

"I'll give you three guesses, and the first two don't count," he said as he kicked at the mess. He didn't find anything useful, not even enough scraps of a heavy shirt he could put on to cut the chill.

"You think it was—" Phil hitched his thumb in the direction of the mountaintop "—them?"

Mark considered a moment, then nodded.

"Who else? We know from what we saw last night that—"

His throat closed off, and he had to blink his eyes rapidly to stop the tears from forming before he could continue.

"—they can be damned calculating in their viciousness. It must have been them . . . or else one of the search parties found it and didn't like the idea that I was so well stocked. But I doubt that."

He shook his head and gritted his teeth with anger. He spent several minutes probing the rubble with the muzzle of his rifle, hoping to find some ammunition, but he didn't even find a crushed and empty box. Whoever had done this had certainly wanted to make damned sure he couldn't resupply himself.

"It's going to be dark soon," Phil said. "Think we ought to camp here for the night, or try to make it all the way down?"

"If I could find just—All right! Bingo!" Mark bent down and picked up a single bullet, which had been pressed point-first into the soft ground. He cleaned it off and slipped it into the rifle. "Now, if I could find just a couple more bullets so I have a full load, I'd say we should chance sleeping here, taking turns keeping watch, of course."

"Of course," Phil echoed.

Mark frowned as he looked up at the lowering gray sky.

"I don't know, though. Something tells me if we don't get down from here tonight—"

"Hmm . . . yeah," Phil said.

Once Mark was satisfied there was nothing else of use to find, and feeling as rested as he was going to feel, Mark heaved a heavy sigh and scooched down so Phil could climb up onto his back. After making sure Phil was comfortable, he handed him the rifle and started down the trail that would take them to the west branch of the Sawyer River and—eventually—home.

The trail was less steep, and in spite of the stitching pain in Mark's chest, the going was a little bit easier the closer they got to the river. Long before they saw it, they heard the distant rushing sound of the water.

Overhead, the sky had turned deep gray. The wind was picking up. Rain had begun to fall in plump, heavy drops by the time they broke out of the woods onto the boulder-strewn shore of the west branch.

Mark couldn't believe the relief he felt as he gently lowered Phil to the ground. Every inch of his body felt like it was on fire with exhaustion. His lungs ached as he took a deep breath and held it before staggering like a shipwreck victim down to the water's edge and bending down to fill his cupped hands with water and raise them to his mouth.

The water was numbingly cold, so he cautioned himself not to drink too much at first, but he couldn't stop himself from greedily gulping it down, letting the coolness flood down his throat and numb his belly. For the first time all day, he began to think that they might actually have a chance of making it out of the woods alive.

"Hey, save a little for me, will you?" Phil called out, laughing as he watched Mark slurping the water. Once his thirst was satiated, Mark filled his hands and started back to where Phil was resting on the shore. Phil drank the small swallow of water that was left, smacked his lips, and sighed.

"How far do wc have to go?" he asked.

He had to shout to be heard above the roar of the river as he looked at the opposite shore, where the lessening light cast the forest with an eerie, deep green gloom.

For the first time, Mark glanced upriver, in the direction of the rope bridge which had been placed and maintained by the A.M.C. for crossing the river. His heart thumped hard in his chest when he saw the shredded rope strands on both sides hanging down from their support stanchions into the raging river. The wooden slats had long since floated away in the surge of water.

"Shit, they got us here, too," Mark whispered. He turned to Phil and pointed. "The fucking bridge is gone."

Gripping his rifle tightly, he squinted as he scanned the forest behind them. Suddenly every shadow was alive with menace. He imagined dozens of pairs of hate-filled eyes staring back at him, hungry for revenge. At first, he thought the flicker of motion he detected was just his imagination, but after a moment, he made out first one, then two dark silhouettes moving stealthily toward them through the dense brush.

"Shit! Let's get moving!"

"Where to?" Phil asked as he climbed onto Mark's back and clung tightly to his neck.

"We're gonna have to get a little wet," Mark shouted.

He went straight toward the river and, without hesitation, plunged into the icy water. The first blast of the river's power almost knocked him off balance, but he struggled to regain his footing and then started moving forward. Progress was slow against the powerful current.

"There they are!" Phil shouted, his mouth close enough to Mark's ear to hurt.

Mark resisted the urge to look back, concentrating instead on not losing his footing on the submerged rocks as he went deeper. The freezing water rose past his waist, up to his armpits.

"Keep the rifle dry!" he shouted.

"Jesus! They're coming in after us!" Phil yelled, his voice raw with fear.

They were a little less than halfway across the river. If those creatures could swim, Mark knew they'd never reach the opposite shore before they were caught.

He had to act—fast.

"Give me the rifle," he said.

Once the rifle was in hand, he turned around carefully and braced his legs wide. The water tugged at him like hundreds of hands, pushing and pulling, trying to knock him over.

Two bullets . . . and two targets!

The creatures had entered the water and were wading toward him, keeping at least twenty feet away from each other. Mark raised the rifle to his shoulder and sighted on one of them, but the surge of the river and Phil's shifting weight kept knocking his aim off. He had to concentrate hard to bring the creature into his sights, but when it was about fifty feet away, he sucked in and held his breath, steadied his aim, and squeezed the trigger.

Several things happened the instant the rifle went off.

The creature in his gun sights roared with pain and doubled over, clutching both hands to its stomach. Bright red blood squirted from between its fingers. Phil involuntarily jerked back at the sound of the shot, moving just enough to knock Mark off balance. When Mark shifted for better footing, he stumbled on a rounded stone underwater and, with a helpless shout, fell backward, pitching Phil into the water. For a few frantic seconds he floundered underwater, then broke the surface just in time to see Phil being swept away by the swift current.

The wounded creature wasn't dead, though; Mark could see that. It had turned back and was crawling up onto the shore, leaving behind a wide, dark track of water and blood on the rocks. Halfway to the forest edge, it stopped, slumped over, and lay still.

Undeterred by the sudden blast from the rifle, the other creature kept coming toward him, steadily closing the gap.

Mark bolted the rifle, took careful aim at its face, and pulled the trigger. The hammer fell with a useless click onto the bullet casing. He bolted the rifle and tried again, but got the same result. Mark's teeth were chattering wildly as he glanced over his shoulder for Phil but didn't see him. He was lost in the raging white foam of the rapids. When Mark turned back to face the approaching creature, it was less than ten feet away and closing fast, snarling viciously as it glared at him. With a snorting roar, it raised its arms over its head and lunged forward.

"Come on! Come and get it, you son-of-a-bitch!" Mark wailed.

The creature, apparently sensing that the rifle was now useless, bellowed and snorted, but it was the creature's eyes that held Mark transfixed. He could see in those eyes a glimmer of intelligence and satisfaction that events had played out this way. It wanted nothing but cold, animal revenge.

But that was what Mark wanted too, for Sandy's brutal death. Shivering wildly from the cold, he flexed his knees and gripped the muzzle of the rifle, preparing to swing. The river's current was pushing him back and forth in tugging surges, but he was counting on it to keep the creature off balance as well.

The creature towered above Mark, and then, grunting loudly, it started to drop on him like an avalanche. Mark gritted his teeth and grunted as he swung the rifle around viciously to meet the attack. The rifle butt connected solidly with the side of the creature's face. The impact sent a jolt of pain shooting up Mark's arms to his shoulders.

"Take that!" Mark shouted, laughing hysterically as the creature, stunned, staggered backward, the side of its face seeping blood.

"Come on! Come and get it! I've got some more for you! You want it?"

Mark took a few steps forward, jiggling the rifle threateningly in his grip.

The creature, while hurt, was far from down and out. With a roar that completely masked the raging sound of the river, it lunged again at Mark, slashing at him with clawed hands.

Mark stepped back just in time, swung the rifle back behind him, and brought it up and over, like a frenzied woodsman trying to split a log. The butt of the rifle smashed down hard on the top of the beast's skull, caving it in like an eggshell. Blood, brains, and chips of bone exploded in a red shower into the river. The intelligent glow in the creature's eyes suddenly glazed over into a staring, vacant expression of dulled amazement. With a bubbling growl, it collapsed into the river and was swept away by the swift current.

"Fuckin'-A!" Mark wailed, waving his arms above his head.

Tears of relief poured from his eyes as he looked up at the sky and let the now heavy rainfall splatter his face and wash away the blood that had speckled him. Still jacked up on adrenalin, he cocked his shoulders back and looked around as though expecting to see a stadium full of cheering spectators. It took him a moment to realize where he was and what had happened.

"Phil!" he shouted, and then, with a long, trailing cry, he dove into the water and let the current carry him away.

Somewhere down the river, he hoped—he knew he had to find Phil. The only question was—would he be dead or alive?

Chapter Thirty-four

Lost and Found

The river swept Mark away, fast and far.

He rocketed between water-smoothed boulders, tossing and turning like a useless piece of driftwood in the raging foam. Sky, forest, and river all blended together into one gray-green smear. The roar of the water was the single dominant noise, sounding like a continuous explosion of rolling thunder. The water chilled Mark to the bone as it crashed over his head, filling his nose and mouth every time he gasped for breath. At some point he realized that he was no longer clutching his rifle, but it no longer mattered.

Nothing mattered.

All feeling in his body was lost, and all hope was gone. He couldn't even begin to struggle against the irresistible pull of the current.

And his thoughts were as chaotic as the river.

The first clear thought he had was his conviction

that the two creatures who had attacked him and Phil were dead.

They had to be!

So as long as there were no other survivors left to carry the bodies away, someone—sometime—was going to be in for one hell of a surprise when they found that dead beast on the riverbank or the other one, washed up somewhere downstream.

Downstream. That was where Mark also expected to find Phil, as long as he, himself, didn't end up a rotting corpse somewhere between here and the ocean.

But almost certainly Phil was dead.

He *must* be!

With two broken legs and weakened by a week of torment in the creatures' cave, there was no way he would be able to keep his head above water, much less swim to safety. Unable to struggle against the current, he would eventually be smashed against a rock and go under.

So the person he had gone through all this trouble for, had risked his life to save, was dead.

As was Sandy!

That was something else of which Mark was positive.

The gruesome memory of seeing his daughter torn apart in a feeding frenzy of those creatures still left him dazed, with a hollow pit in his stomach that was more numbing than the freezing river. It was impossible for him to believe that he had seen it happen and not done anything.

But she was dead—gone forever—and nothing was ever going to bring her back.

And Polly . . . Polly was as good as gone, too.

He had suspected she'd been sleeping around long before Sandy had told him about the affair she'd been having with Dennis. But he had already screwed up his first marriage, and he hadn't been able to figure out how to handle this situation other than by avoiding any overt confrontation.

That was chickenshit, and he knew it, but he had to accept it.

He had failed in everything he had set out to do, so what was the use even of struggling against the river?

Why not just say *fuck it!* and let it whisk him away?

Just give up.

Stop flailing his arms and legs, and float out of control until he dashed his brains out on a rock or his lungs filled with water and he went down—down—down for the third time.

Lost in the chaos of his thoughts and the careening ride downstream, Mark was only distantly aware when something snagged his left leg, pulling his legs backward while the water continued to push the top half of his body forward. Before he realized that he had hit the shallow river bottom, the current propelled him out of the water and onto a sandbar at a bend in the river.

Air—real air, not water or spray—filled his lungs with a roaring intake. His arms and legs moved without conscious command from his brain as he scrambled away from the water's edge and, shivering wildly, collapsed again, digging his fingers into wet sand as though he had to cling to it to avoid being swept away again.

I'm not dead! Jesus! I'm not dead!

He had no sense of how long he lay there, burrowing his face into the sand and making vague swimming motions that scooped deep furrows into the sand. Rain was falling heavily, hitting him like tiny pellets when he was finally aware enough to lurch to his feet and start walking. His sodden clothes dragged him back at every step, but he pushed himself forward, his only thought that he had to get into the woods—he had to hide deep in the forest before . . .

. . . Before . . .

. . . Before *what?*

He felt an overpowering sense of danger, of threat, but didn't know—or recall—the source of that threat.

Then it hit him

Phil! . . . and Sandy . . . and those creatures!

Looking back toward the river, he noticed for the first time a crumpled form on the water's edge, no more than twenty feet from where he had washed up. He instantly recognized who it was.

"Oh, shit! *Phil!*" he shouted, his voice booming like a single shot from a rifle.

His teeth were chattering from the cold, and his legs threatened to give out from underneath him as he ran over to his friend. Dull, aching sobs racked his chest when he reached the body and knelt down beside it.

"Oh, shit!—oh, Jesus!—oh, *shit!*" he sobbed as all of his pent-up emotions poured out of him.

He placed one hand lightly on Phil's shoulder, stunned by the cold, lifeless feel of the body, and made a feeble attempt to lift him. He knew he didn't have the strength to roll Phil over, much less pick him up, but it didn't matter.

Phil was dead, just as he was going to be dead—if not soon, then certainly by the time darkness fell and the weather turned colder . . . too cold for him to stand without either a heavy jacket or a match to light a fire.

"I'm so sorry, Phil . . . Jesus, so sorry," Mark whispered.

He clutched his friend's shoulders with both hands and, leaning forward, pressed his face against Phil's back. Agony like he had never known before, blacker and colder than the deepest river in hell, filled him as sobs ripped from his throat. His tears mingled with the rain that was streaming down his face. He was so lost in his misery that it took him several seconds to realize that he could feel Phil's back moving.

Yes!

Ever so slightly, he could feel a slow, steady expansion and contraction.

"Oh, my *God!*" Mark whispered.

He turned his head to one side and, pressing his ear against Phil's back, listened.

Yes!—beneath the steady hissing roar of the river, he could hear a faint, erratic *thud-thud-thud.*

Phil wasn't dead.

Not yet!

Mark had no idea how he found the strength, but he rolled Phil onto his back, slid his arms underneath him, and picked him up. Carrying him like a baby, he walked across the jumble of rocks at the river's edge toward the forest margin, intent only on making it to the woods. Beyond that, he had no clear idea what to do. Hopefully he could find enough dry wood to get a fire going, but without matches, he didn't know how he was going to manage that.

Step after agonizing step seemed to bring him no closer to the woods. Phil's unconscious body sagged in his arms like a useless feed sack. One of Phil's hands hung down and kept knocking against Mark's leg, threatening to trip him with every other step.

Exhaustion blazed in Mark's muscles, but it gave his soaked and shivering body no warmth against the cold air. A small voice in the back of his mind was whispering to him, telling him that they still weren't saved, that maybe he was insane with exhaustion and had imagined hearing Phil's heart beating. Even without any more of the creatures to attack them, the forest could just as easily extinguish both of them once night fell, and the cold and dampness settled down on them.

But Mark wasn't about to give up now.

He would fight defeat with whatever strength he had left, and he would not surrender until death pulled him down for that final time.

He made it to a small clearing under the trees. Rain still dripped from the branches overhead, but at least they were out of the steady, direct downpour. Mark cleared a small area with his foot and then gently lowered Phil to the ground.

"You know, maybe we'll make it out of this yet, pal," he said in a voice that sounded thick and strangely foreign to his own ears.

Mark looked around the thicket, wishing he had a blanket or tent drop cloth or something to cover his friend. He knew that the immediate danger—for both of them—was hypothermia. There was no other alternative but to dig into the ground and cover up his friend with whatever dead leaves and soil he could scrape over him.

He worked quickly, covering Phil right up to his neck in hopes that the mulch would provide enough insulation so his body heat would keep him alive. As he worked, though, Mark couldn't resist the horrifying thought that Phil was already dead, and he was simply burying him.

"I've got to go for help alone," he said, once the job was done. "I can't carry you anymore, but hang in there just one more night, okay, buddy?"

There was no response from Phil. He lay there with his eyes closed, looking like a corpse.

"That's all I'm gonna ask of you. You've got to do it for me. Just hang in there another couple of hours."

Mark was sobbing quietly as he rested his hand on Phil's unmoving face. The skin was waxy and white, cold and hard to the touch, like a cheap plaster mask, not at all like real flesh.

Mark stood up slowly, reluctant to leave his friend but positive that he had no other choice. Before leaving, he piled up some boulders at the edge of the woods in a rough arrow formation to mark the spot. Then, using his Swiss Army knife, he cut off a piece of his pant leg and hung a flag from a branch that would be easy to see, even from the riverbank. Night was only an hour away, so he turned and started walking.

"I'll be back," he shouted as soon as the grove was out of sight. "I found you once, buddy, and I'll find you again. I promise I'll get you out of here! You hear me, Phil? I promise you!"

Rain was falling steadily as Mark resumed his hike. The sky gradually darkened, or else his vision was fading; he couldn't tell the difference and didn't care. He staggered through the forest like an enraged drunk, careening off trees, walking around in circles, for all he knew.

Without a compass or trail map, he was unsure of which direction to head in. There certainly were no clearly marked trails within sight, and in the gathering darkness, he no doubt would have lost the trail had there been one.

But he kept hacking at tree trunks with his knife, marking his path, however meandering it might be, telling himself that someone had to find their way back to Phil in the morning.

As night descended, Mark sometimes imagined that he was still floating down the raging river, his body slamming against rocks as he struggled to keep his head above water. At other times, he was so distanced from his own physical pain that he could easily imagine he was flying high above the clouds, getting buffeted back and forth by angry blasts of wintry wind.

Time meant nothing to him.

He knew only cold and darkness as he fought through the night-stained underbrush, hoping to strike onto something familiar. He almost didn't realize where he was when he tripped on something and fell forward, skinning his hands and knees on something smooth and flat.

Asphalt!

Jesus! A road! I made it!

He stood up stiffly and staggered into the middle of the road, looking up at the sky as he spun around in a wide circle, his arms extended wide open as if to embrace the night. He couldn't expect to recognize where he was. All he cared about was knowing that this was a country road—a *paved* country road somewhere in the middle of nowhere. Eventually, someone was going to have to drive by. Rather than start walking, with a fifty-fifty chance of heading in the wrong direction, Mark decided that he needed rest. He saw nothing wrong with lying down on the roadside and closing his eyes as he waited.

He had no idea if he was dreaming, hallucinating, or if it was real when, some time later—minutes or hours, who could tell?—he awoke to see twin circles of bright yellow light bearing down on him like an angry demon's eyes. He tried to rouse himself but couldn't as he listened to a car or truck door open and slam shut.

Then footsteps slowly approached.

A voice, sounding amazingly like Police Chief LaBrea's, spoke from the stinging glare of light.

"Jesus Christ, Mark! I almost hit you! What the hell are you doing, sleeping in the middle of the goddamned road? Trying to get yourself killed?"

Mark looked up but was unable to say a word.

"Come on," LaBrea said, bending down and extending his hands to him. "Let me help you up. We've got to get you to the hospital."

Chapter Thirty-five

Recovering

"Well, you're looking a damn sight better," Guy said as he shouldered open the hospital room door and walked over to the bed where Mark lay.

"Compared to what?" Mark said, smiling weakly as he raised his head slightly from the pillow and squinted up at his visitor. His lips were cracked and dry, and his throat felt like chopped meat, but—fortunately—the medication the doctors were giving him blunted most of the pain.

"Well," LaBrea said, smiling tightly, "compared to what you looked like last night, 'round about ten o'clock, when I found you face-down in the middle of the road, looking half dead."

"I like to think of it as half alive," Mark said.

Even with the curtains drawn and the lights turned down low, it hurt too much to keep his eyes open for long, so he shut them and eased his head back down.

The loud crinkling of the pillow sounded like a string of firecrackers going off inside his head.

"What time is it, anyway?" he asked, smacking his lips.

Guy glanced at his wristwatch.

"Little before ten o'clock . . . Saturday morning, in case you're wondering."

Mark tried to focus on what he was saying, but Guy's voice seemed to be coming from far away. He slid his eyelids open just enough to see the watery blur of the hospital room so he'd know that he was safe, not back on the mountain and imagining all of this.

"Did you guys—have you found Phil yet?" he asked, trying his best to release the winding tension in his body.

"Oh yeah. We found him all right. No problem there," Guy said. "You left a pretty clear trail." He chuckled softly. "Although it did weave around a bit. But you can relax now. He's safe and sound—"

"How's he doing?"

Guy paused a moment before he spoke. To Mark, it seemed as though he took far too long to answer. It made him wonder if the policeman was trying to keep something from him.

"Well, the doctors say he's in pretty rough shape. Not as bad as that other fella, though."

"You mean Jack? You found him, too?"

"Uh-huh. His broken legs have healed all wrong, and he's smashed up pretty bad. It's going to be a while before either one of them's up and about. They've been through a hell of a lot, physically and mentally. Frankly, I think it's a goddamned miracle either one of them made it out of there alive. You ought to be damned proud that you—"

"I couldn't save Sandy, though," Mark said.

His voice broke, rasping like metal scraping against stone, and his eyes were burning with tears.

"No matter what else you can say, I couldn't . . . I didn't save *her*."

"You can't think like that, do you hear me?" Guy said, placing one hand firmly on Mark's shoulder and giving him a reassuring squeeze.

Mark looked up at him and took a shuddering breath.

"You did things not too many people could have done. You can't go blaming yourself for what they—for what those creatures did to her."

Mark's eyes fixed on the policeman.

"So you believe me," he said, fighting hard to control the waver in his voice. "You don't think I was making them up, or hallucinating them, then, huh?"

"Not at all," Guy said, shaking his head. "But to tell you the truth, it wasn't just what I saw in the cave that convinced me. Sandy convinced me long before that."

"Sandy—? What the hell did she know about them?" Mark's vision began to swim with tears. "At least before it was too late?"

Guy quickly told Mark about Sandy's accident on the road from the Round Top Trail, and how he had been skeptical about her report until he saw the damaged Jeep. He then told Mark how he had gotten worried when Sandy didn't show up at school the next day, and he decided to check out at the trail head for her in case she had tried to meet up with him.

"And as it turned out," Guy said, "it's a goddamned good thing I got hung up on some other business and didn't get out there until late last night. Otherwise, I might not have found you . . . until it was too late."

"So what the fuck is it up there, some kind of Bigfoot monster or something?"

"I have no idea, but I think you can say *used* to be up there . . . if—like you say—you killed them all. But, yeah—I believe you're telling the truth. Oh, and it's looking like the state investigators are convinced it was one of those monsters that killed Dennis Cross outside your house, too."

"You know, I think it was looking for me," Mark said, in a ragged whisper. He closed his eyes as a wave of chills raced through him. "They knew I had seen them, and all along they were hunting for me . . . ever since last weekend, when me and Phil were hiking up there."

"Well, I don't know about that. You might be giving them a tad more credit than—" Guy cut himself off when a light tapping sounded at the door. They both looked up, and Mark tensed when he saw Polly walk into the room.

"I guess I'll get going for now," Guy said, rubbing his hands together as he regarded Polly with a harsh stare. He walked past her toward the door, then stopped. "I'm sure you two have a lot to talk about," he added.

Polly nodded a stiff greeting to Guy, then approached the bedside with her head bowed and her hands folded in front of her. She stood there silently for a moment, waiting for Mark to say something.

Mark's pulse was racing high and fast in his ears as he closed his eyes and settled back onto the pillow. He realized right then just how horrible their marriage was, because his first thought upon seeing her was that she was the last—not the first—person he wanted to see right now.

"I—I'm so glad you're—you're all right," Polly said.

Her voice was faint and unnaturally flat. She took hold of the bed railing with both hands and held on to it tightly, as if it were all that kept her from falling over.

"Yeah. I'm okay . . . but Sandy isn't," Mark said, knowing—and not caring—how much that would hurt Polly. Right now, he felt as though he had more than enough pain to share.

"Yes, Chief LaBrea told me that she was . . . that she died up on the mountain," Polly said.

Even without looking at her, Mark knew that she was crying, but he couldn't help but wonder just how genuine her tears were.

"Do you have any idea what she was doing up there?" he asked, his voice trembling with emotion. He still had his eyes closed so he wouldn't have to look at her, because, he knew in his heart that, whatever else happened after this, any love or affection he had once felt for her had been permanently changed . . . and all for the worse.

"No—she was—I don't know," Polly said, "but there's . . . I don't know, maybe now's not the time to talk about it, but there's something—" She took a deep breath and let it out slowly. "There's something I have to tell you."

"You mean about Dennis?" Mark said, knowing—and hoping—even as he said it that his words would cut straight to her heart.

After a long, awkward silence, Polly said, "Uh-huh."

"Well, maybe I can make it easy for you," Mark said.

He opened his eyes and looked squarely at his wife, unable to deny the rush of emotion he still felt for her; but he also couldn't ignore how different, how distant she looked to him—like she was someone he had never even met before . . . or a person he had known in another lifetime. Everything he once felt for her was blunted if not obliterated by what he had seen and been through on the mountain.

"I know all about you and Dennis, all right?" Mark said. His throat was on fire, but he couldn't even bring himself to ask her to pass him the glass of water on the stand beside his bed. He didn't want to owe her anything.

For several seconds, Polly said nothing. Her mouth kept opening and closing, but the only sound that came out was a high, strangled whimper. Her eyes were glistening with moisture, and tears were streaming down her cheeks.

"And I suspect—" he said. "No, I'm *positive* that it wasn't the first time. Was it?"

He wanted to grasp her by the throat and strangle her as he screamed at her, hoping to break her down and make her cry, force her to admit it all; but he simply didn't have the strength. The medication made keeping his eyes open and speaking barely above a whisper more than enough of a challenge.

Polly cleared her throat but still couldn't speak.

"To tell you the truth," Mark went on, "I don't know what to make of it all. You know, I'm going to be in the hospital for a while, at least a week, and when I get out, I—I—"

He gave a feeble shrug of the shoulders and let his sentence hang, unfinished.

Polly tried to say something, but her voice choked off as she wiped her tears with the flats of her hands. It looked to Mark as if she were trying to claw her own eyes out.

"What can I say . . . except that I—that I'm . . . sorry, all right?"

Mark remained silent, finding the effort of speaking and the emotional strain just too much to bear.

"After what happened to Sandy and all, I know that what you've been through has been just terrible," Polly said. "But maybe we can—we can use this as a new beginning . . . for us. I—I promise you—I *swear* to you that I'm sorry for what I've done. You don't know how sorry I am. It was horrible of me to treat you like that, and from now on I—"

She reached down and lightly gripped his hand, resting limply on the bed.

"From now on I promise I'll never do anything like that again. Ever! I'll be faithful to you, Mark. I promise! You have to believe me!"

Although an explosion of thoughts filled his head, Mark said nothing. Medication and exhaustion were dragging him down so his body and mind could heal. He knew that his feelings and emotions would stay wounded much longer than his body ever would, but right now, the soft, enfolding darkness of sleep was pulling him irresistibly down . . . down. From far away, he heard Polly's voice, a faint, reverberating ruffle, speaking to him.

"I promise you, Mark . . . I swear to God, from now on I'll be the wife you've always wanted me to be. . . ."

Chapter Thirty-six

Change of Heart

"It's been horrible, Mom—really *horrible!*"

Polly was sitting in the living room with her feet up on the coffee table and the telephone base resting in her lap. The receiver was perched on her right shoulder, pressing hard against her ear. The sun had set over an hour ago, and for the past half hour she had been going over the events of the last week with her mother.

"I know that what you said—you know, that I should probably hang in there—is probably right. I know that's what I should do, but I just don't know, Mom. I'm just so . . . so confused."

"Listen to me, darling. I know you'll do what's best," her mother said for what seemed like the hundredth time. "I don't want to tell you how to live your own life, but I do wish you would stop drinking. How can you expect to think clearly?"

"I haven't had much to drink," Polly said as she eyed the nearly empty bottle of whiskey on the end table.

"Look, dear, I have to be going now, but give me a call tomorrow and let me know what you decide, okay? I'm sure you'll do the right thing, but if you need a place to stay, you can always come home."

"Thanks, Mom. I appreciate that," Polly said as a wave of disappointment swept through her. Her sense of loss, of absolute desertion, was as strong as it had ever been, even back before her father died. All her life, it seemed, she had been asking—begging—her mother for help and guidance that she simply had never provided. No wonder her life was so screwed up!

"I—uh, I'll talk to yah later then."

" 'Bye, honey. Remember, I love you."

"Love you too, Mom," Polly said. " 'Bye."

Polly hung up the phone but made no move to put it back on the bookcase. It slid off her lap and onto the couch cushion beside her as she reached for the whiskey bottle, unscrewed the cap, and poured what was left into her glass. The ice had long since melted, but she didn't care. The whiskey burned the back of her throat as she swallowed it, actually enjoying the fire it lit in her stomach and the dulling of thoughts in her brain. Ever since the phone call last night that had informed her Mark had been admitted to the hospital and was in serious—if not critical—condition, she had been lost in a morass of worry, guilt, and doubt.

At least the whiskey was helping blunt it all.

"And the cops aren't bugging me anymore," she said before taking another sip. As long as she was no longer under suspicion for the death of Dennis Cross, she was free and clear. She could even leave town if she wanted to.

If she *wanted* to!

That was the question uppermost in her mind.

What the hell did she want to do?

Did she still love Mark?

Even if the answer was a resounding *yes*, which it wasn't, what chance did they possibly have to pull their marriage back together after she had betrayed his trust so many times? He knew that Dennis wasn't the first one, so how could he ever trust her again?

But if she left, where would she go?

She could head down to Florida and stay with her mother, at least until something better came along; but that would create as many problems as it would solve.

So where should she go?

What could she do?

Polly shifted her feet to the floor and would have stood up except for the muffled pounding inside her head. The room seemed to slip to one side as she flopped back, took a deep breath, and leaned her head back against the couch.

Maybe she *had* had a little too much.

"But I've gotta do *something!*" she whispered. "I've gotta get the hell out of here. This damned town—everything about it—is driving me fucking *crazy!*"

Her voice was slurred as she raised her glass to her mouth and sipped. Whiskey sloshed out onto her chest, but she didn't care.

The car was still packed. All she had to do was grab a few more things and leave.

She stared at the glass as she rolled it back and forth in her hands, amazed at how all of a sudden the whiskey seemed to be hitting her, as if talking to her mother had been keeping her sober, but now . . .

"To freedom," she said, raising her glass like a reveling Shriner.

She opened her mouth, about to gulp some more whiskey, but then froze with the glass halfway to her lips.

She had seen something—the mere hint of a shadow—move past the living room window, rippling over the gauzy curtains.

Her eyes opened wide with surprise and fear, and a bone-deep chill raced up her back as she stared at the window. She desperately wanted to convince herself that it had been nothing more than a fleeting shadow cast by a passing car or something, but the longer she stared at the curtains, the more she became convinced there was someone standing right outside there, looking in at her.

Moving slowly, forcing herself to make every motion appear completely natural, she lowered her glass to the end table, all the while keeping her gaze fastened on the window. She glanced at the phone beside her, then quickly snatched up the receiver. Her hands were trembling as she pressed the speed button for the police station, then brought the receiver to her ear. The phone beeped the seven numbers, but before anyone answered at the station, the shadow—this time looking quite solid and large—moved up closer to the window. Polly let out a high-pitched scream when something—a fist or a foot—slammed against the glass, making it vibrate.

"Hilton Police. Officer Clark speaking."

Polly tried to say something, but her throat closed off. All she could think was, this had to be the person who had killed Dennis.

"Hello," said the voice over the phone. "This is the Hilton Police Station. May I help you?"

"Yes, this is Polly—Polly Newman calling."

Her voice sounded like she'd been gargling with Drano.

"I think there's a—"

Before she could say anything more, the living room window exploded inward. The window sheers bulged like full-bellied sails as shards of broken glass filled them like a blast of buckshot. One sweep of a huge hand yanked the curtains down off the curtain rod. They fell, covering the intruder, but Polly could see that he was huge. Broken wood and glass crunched underfoot, but every sound was masked by a loud animal roar.

Polly dropped the telephone. Her mind was paralyzed with fear. She didn't hear or understand the voice of the police dispatcher, shouting to her through the receiver.

After a moment of struggle, the figure shook itself free of the entangling curtain and stepped forward with its arms held out wide, as if to embrace her. Polly's mind went blank with terror when she saw what looked like an enormous, hairy ape. Flashing eyes sparked like lightning as the beast peeled back its thick lips, exposing its teeth, and roared again.

"Mrs. Newman . . . Can you hear me?" the tinny voice said over the phone. "I have a patrolman in the area right now. He'll be there in less than a minute."

Polly screamed once, loud and sharp as the creature charged at her. Somehow, she found the ability to move. With a quick kick, she propelled herself over the back of the couch, tumbled onto the floor, scrambled to her feet, and then started to run. The house filled with the enraged bellow of the beast.

Polly didn't dare look behind her, but she could *feel* the creature closing the gap between them as she hooked her hand on the doorjamb and pivoted herself around, into the kitchen. Her only thought was to get the hell out of the house!

As she turned the corner, though, her momentum carried her too far. Her feet slipped on the linoleum, and she went down hard, banging both knees on the floor.

Terrified, she looked behind her and ducked just in time as the animal swung its ham-sized paw at her head, missing by inches and punching a basketball-sized hole in the wall. The gigantic bulk of the beast loomed above her, filling her mind with blinding white terror as she scrambled on hands and knees across the kitchen floor toward the back door.

The beast's thundering roar filled the kitchen, vibrating the walls and rattling the windows as Polly stood up. She grabbed a chair as she ran past the kitchen table and flung it behind her, hoping to slow down her pursuer, but she knew with heart-stopping certainty that anything she tried to do to stop it would prove futile. Even if she made it outside, it wouldn't take long for the creature to run her down.

Where could she run?

Where could she hide?

She banged into the door and was fumbling to turn the doorknob and open the door when the creature swung its hand in a wide arc that caught her squarely on the side of the head. Bright lights and sounds exploded inside her head as she was swept to one side and slammed into the wall. Dazed from the impact, she slid to the floor and then scrunched up into as tight a ball as possible as she cowered back, pressing hard against the wall and wishing to heaven she could fall through it into safety.

But she knew she couldn't.

This was the end.

The creature stretched to its full height, its head almost bumping against the ceiling as it braced its feet wide, flung its arms back, and let loose another terrifying howl. Polly couldn't help but think it sounded more like a cry of pure joy.

Raising both hands high above its head, it swung down first one hand, then the other. There were two instances of blazing pain as the beast's thick-nailed claws ripped down both sides of Polly's face, removing large chunks of hair and flesh. The stinging pain was incredibly intense. Polly clapped her hands to her face and was sickened by the slick, bloody divots that had been her cheeks.

Dazed with pain, Polly turned and looked upward, aware only of the swelling darkness that seemed to be pulsating all around her as she began to drift away, high above the panic and pain. She wasn't feeling anything whatsoever when the beast grabbed her by the neck and straightened up with her limp body nestled under one arm. After positioning her head in the crook of its elbow, it twisted her head sharply to one side. She heard a sharp *crack* as her neck snapped. With one last, bubbly gasp in her throat, Polly died.

The creature grunted with satisfaction as it looked down at the dead woman. It was just shifting her body around so it could rip her belly open and feast on her entrails when the back-door window exploded as three shots rang out in rapid succession. The creature's face instantly dissolved into a bloody splash as bullets ripped through its head, blasting fur and fragments of skull against the kitchen wall. The creature staggered backward, clawing futilely at its ruined face, but it never made another sound before it dropped to the floor, twitched for a second, and then lay still.

Guy LaBrea kicked the door open, pushing Polly's broken body aside as he stared at the bloody havoc. He'd seen a lot in the line of duty, but never anything like this. His stomach did a quick flip. He turned and dropped to his knees on the back doorstep and vomited. After the initial rush of nausea had subsided, he stood up, wiped his mouth on his sleeve, and went back to the cruiser, which was parked at the foot of the driveway. He kept his service revolver cocked and ready as he sat down behind the steering wheel and thumbed the radio microphone button to call the station.

"This is LaBrea," he said in a ragged gasp. He couldn't stop his hands from shaking as he waited for the dispatcher to acknowledge his call.

"Roger, Chief. This is Elliott. What's up?"

"I was—"

He had to take a deep breath before he could continue.

"I was on my way to the Newmans' house when your call came in. I—umm, I'll be needing some backup out here right away. Also I'm gonna need the coroner and an ambulance pronto."

"What happened?"

For a moment, LaBrea considered telling him, but

then he smiled grimly, shook his head, and simply said, "I don't think you'd believe me if I told you right now." He took another deep breath and let it out in a shuddering rush. "Let's just say it's all over for now, okay?"

"Sure thing, Chief."

"Over and out," LaBrea said.

Sighing heavily, he eased back in the car seat and shook his head, desperately wishing that he could erase the memory of the bloody mayhem he had glimpsed inside the Newman house. He knew that eventually he was going to have to face it again, but he had decided to wait right here in the cruiser until more policemen showed up. Right now, there was no way he could deal with what he had seen—Polly Newman's severed head, lying on the tiled floor. Her eyes had been wide open and staring up at him, and he wished to God he wasn't positive he had seen her eyes blink . . . just once.

"Yeah—" he said in a trembling whisper as he hung up the radio microphone, leaned his head back against the car seat, and rubbed his eyes.

"Let's just hope to hell it's all over!"

The End

Introduction to "Chrysalis," "Deal with the Devils," and "The Birch Whistle"

It seems as though whenever I do a book-signing, someone will invariably tell me that *Little Brothers* is their favorite novel of mine. In fact, I've heard it so often that several years ago (more than I care to remember, actually) I wrote a handful of additional stories and "myths" involving the Untcigahunk, those creatures who appear from underground every five years, wreak a little mayhem, then disappear. Four of those stories (and three "myths") were published in *Night Visions 9*. A few more are lingering unpublished in old computer files, and I have ideas for a couple more. Maybe someday I'll pull them all together and publish them with the original novel as *The Complete Little Brothers.*

As it turned out, when Don D'Auria at Leisure wanted to publish *The Mountain King* in paperback, the manuscript came up a little short. The shorter-length novel—about half of what I usually write—worked well as a "limited edition" hardcover from CD Publications, but it didn't work economically as a mass market paperback.

The solution was simple.

Since I always regarded the creatures in *The Mountain King* as a sort of mirror image of the Untcigahunk—the "big" brothers to my "little" brothers—I suggested that we include a couple of the Untcigahunk stories with the novel.

Don't worry. You needn't have read the original novel to "get" what's going on in these stories (although I wouldn't stop you from going out and buying the book). But they stand alone and, I hope, all have a nice mixture of gruesome and freaky and fun.

Enjoy.

—Rick Hautala

Chrysalis
Chapter One

Fall, 1972

"You know, from this far away, if you squint your eyes, doesn't it sorta look like an anthill?" Stan Walters said.

He and his older brother, Chet, were lying back on their elbows on a grassy slope, watching the Maine State Highway construction crew at work. Both boys had heard plenty about the project to straighten out Route 25 south of their hometown of Thornton. Day after day, their father complained about how many extra miles he had to detour so he could make it to work on time in Portland. In the distance, bulldozers, dump trucks, and men moved through billowing clouds of yellow dust that rose like sulfurous smoke into the heat-hazed July sky. All sound was lost in the distance except for the blaring *beep-beep-beep* of the backup warning buzzers as the heavy equipment carved away the hillside.

Stan's eyes darted back and forth, trying desperately to keep track of all the activity. "Look at everything they're digging up. I'll bet I could find some really cool rocks for my collection."

"You know what I think?" Chet asked lazily as he slid a spear of grass between his two front teeth and smiled. "I think you've got rocks in your head!" He swatted Stan on the shoulder. "Naw—just kidding. But you know what pisses me off is how they're ruining Watchick Hill. Damn! There ain't gonna be nothin' left of it by the time they're through."

Stan smiled at his older brother's use of profanity. Chet had just turned thirteen, and he took every opportunity to swear like a pirate whenever there weren't any adults around. Chet's swearing in front of him made Stan feel older . . . accepted . . . well, at least a little bit.

"I know, but look up there. See all those holes in the hillside?" Stan said. "There's gotta be more than twenty holes up there where they've been blasting. I think they might have opened up into a whole bunch of tunnels or something. I can just imagine the different kinds of rocks they're turning up—"

"Yeah, and *I* can just imagine the reaming we're *both* gonna get if we're not home in time for supper," Chet said. He hoisted himself to his feet, brushed off his butt, and started down the grassy slope to the road where Stan had left his bicycle. "And if you don't get your sorry ass moving, I'm gonna take your bike and ride it home."

"Oh, yeah? The hell you are!" Stan yelled as he leapt up and started running.

The race was on.

Chet had a good head start, and even though Stan knew it was hopeless, he ran full tilt boogie down the hillside, his arms pumping madly as he chugged through tall summer grass that whipped at his legs, threatening to trip him up. He watched in frustration as his older brother easily outdistanced him. Once he was beside the bicycle, Chet turned and crossed his arms triumphantly over his chest while he waited a moment. When Stan was no more than ten feet from him, he picked the bike up by the handlebars, spun on his heel, and started running off with it. After a few quick steps, he vaulted onto the seat and started pedaling furiously. Derisive laughter curled like a scarf over his shoulder as he sped away.

"Come on, Chet!" Stan shouted. *"That's not fair!"*

His breath came into his lungs hot and hard as he cupped his hands on his knees and leaned forward, expecting at any second to puke his guts out. Sweat dripped down the sides of his face and stung his eyes. His lower lip was trembling as he watched his brother easily put distance between them. For several pounding heartbeats, he watched helplessly, waiting for Chet to turn around and come back; but without even a backward glance, his brother rounded the curve and disappeared out of sight.

"Fuck *you*, you *bastard!*" Stan wailed, shaking his clenched fist at the empty road. It was safe to swear now. Chet was too far away to hear him. But he wasn't about to start crying. No way! Crying was for babies!

Chapter Two

After a quick supper of a hamburger, French fries, and green beans—and a brief tussle with Chet for taking his bike—Stan went up to his bedroom. He grabbed his flashlight and the burlap bag he used to collect rock samples and ran back downstairs. As he raced out the front door, he shouted to his mother that he was going outside to play.

"Where are you off to?" she called after him.

"Just out," he replied, letting the screen door slam shut behind him. He was halfway down the walkway to where Chet had left his bike when she leaned out the front door and yelled to him, "Just make sure you're home before dark!"

Pretending he hadn't heard her, Stan slipped the flashlight into the hip pocket of his jeans, wrapped the burlap bag around his handlebars, and started pedaling furiously down Elm Street. He had only one goal in mind: he had to get out to the construction site and check it out now that the highway workers were gone. This was probably his best chance to find some cool new rocks for his collection.

His feet were a blur as he sped around the curves and up and down the slopes of Route 25. The closer he got, the more his excitement rose until it felt like a bubbling gush of cool water inside his chest. In spite of the cool evening air washing over his face, the exertion made him break out into a sweat. When he saw the flashing yellow warning lights up ahead, he squeezed the hand brakes and skidded to a stop where the road changed from asphalt to hard-packed dirt. He swung off his bike and walked it along the stretch of stripped highway, taking his time to look around.

The hillside was eerily quiet in the gathering gloom of evening. White barricades with flashing yellow warning lights lined the strip of gravel the construction workers had laid down for the road base. Along both edges of a long, deep trench were round, black metal balls. The wicks at the top flickered with fat orange flames that gave off thick, sooty smoke. The yellow dust had settled, skimming everything with a hazy coat that reminded Stan of the scum of pine pollen that floated on Little Sebago Lake when he went swimming in early summer.

But it was the scarred hillside towering up against the darkening sky that riveted Stan's attention. Deep gouges lined the steep side of the hill where the men had blasted away the red granite ledge. Huge blocks of rock jutted out from the dirt like the rotten, crooked teeth of a long-buried giant. In the dimming light, Stan could see high up on the hillside more than a dozen dark tunnel mouths, looking like black, sightless eyes. Mounds of rubble lay at the base of the hill, waiting for the workers to return in the morning to load them up and truck them off.

Did they even bother to check over these rocks to see if there was anything valuable? Stan wondered. Did anyone even bother to look inside those tunnels? Watchick Hill could be honeycombed with caves that could be loaded with Indian arrowheads or part of an old gold mine, for all anyone knew.

Stan stared up at the nearest cave opening, no more than forty feet up the hillside. It looked three, maybe four feet wide. He couldn't stop wondering what might be hidden in there.

"Only one way to find out," he answered himself aloud.

Unwrapping the burlap bag from the handlebars, he leaned his bike against one of the wooden barricades, jumped the trench, and started up the hillside. The slope was steeper than it had looked. He had to lean way forward and paddle his hands on the ground in front of him for balance as he made his way up. Loose soil and gravel kept slipping out from underfoot, and just about every step started a mini-landslide. He found that by cutting across the face of the hill first one way, then the other, he could zigzag back and forth. Before long, he arrived at the narrow slanting ledge in front of the open cave mouth. Another, stronger shiver rippled through him as he got onto his hands and knees and stuck his head into the dark hole. The air inside blew cold and dank from the tunnel into his face, carrying with it a hint of moisture that smelled like an old, stagnant pond.

"What the—?" Stan whispered.

His voice echoed from the dark recesses of the cave with an odd reverberation. He knew that if air was blowing *out* of the tunnel, there had to be another opening somewhere at the other end.

Stan's footing wasn't all that secure. His left foot kept skidding out from underneath him on the tilted, dirt-coated ledge. He knew that if he didn't find the courage to crawl into the mouth of the tunnel soon, he would have to climb back down . . . before he fell down. Glancing at the roadbed forty feet below, he tried not to imagine how much it would hurt if he slid all the way in the dirt and gravel. And what if he started a *big* landslide? One big enough to cover him beneath tons of dirt and debris?

He had to decide—soon! Night was coming on fast, and the workers would be back in the morning. Even if he left for home right now, he wouldn't be back before dark, so it was a safe bet that he was going to be grounded for a couple of days, at least. By the time he was un-grounded, the whole hillside would probably have been hauled off. If he didn't check out this cave—right now—he wasn't *ever* going to get to check it out!

But did he even dare to go in there?

After glancing over his shoulder at the blaze of sunset on the horizon, he took a deep breath, tucked the burlap bag into his hip pocket, took out his flashlight, and clicked it on. Holding his breath like he was diving under water, he got onto his hands and knees and edged into the doorway. The oval of light illuminated a hard-packed dirt floor. Cool—actually *cold* air raised goose bumps on his arms as he skittered forward. Because of the low ceiling, he had to feel blindly for a handhold to pull himself all the way inside.

Even with the feeble glow of the flashlight, Stan felt deep rushes of nervousness as he started crawling along the stone-lined tunnel. The walls seemed to narrow gradually, squeezing in on him from all directions. More than once, he considered backing out and was grateful, at least, that Chet wasn't here to tease him about being a sissy.

But maybe being a sissy wasn't such a bad idea, Stan thought as he inched his way deeper into the earth. After each lunge forward, he would look back over his shoulder almost longingly at the receding oval of burning orange sky and think how pitifully small his flashlight beam was against the darkness that pressed in on him from all sides.

"Damn it!" he muttered when his hand holding the flashlight hit hard against the ground and the beam flickered. His voice reverberated oddly in the narrow confines of the tunnel, but even before the echo died, he thought he heard something else—a soft, hissing, *scratching* sound—like ripping wet cloth. He froze, directing his light straight ahead and craning his neck forward as he listened tensely for the sound to be repeated. He was positive of only one thing: *he* hadn't made that noise!

Ripples of fear raced up his back. In spite of the coolness inside the tunnel, sweat trickled down the sides of his face.

"All right, all right now," he whispered, trying to reassure himself as his eyes darted around, following the dodging flashlight beam. "Just take it easy . . . take it—"

His throat closed off, choking off a scream that otherwise would have resounded throughout the entire mountain when his left hand, reaching forward, touched . . . something. He jerked back too quickly and bumped his head against the roof of the tunnel.

The impact stunned him, and the flashlight dropped from his hand. It winked out the instant it hit the stone floor. Dirt and grit showered down onto him like rain on a tin roof as he reached forward, furiously groping in the darkness for his light. His only fear was that he would touch that . . . that *thing* again before he found his flashlight. To his relief, his hand closed around the metal cylinder. His heart was pounding hard as he clicked the switch uselessly back and forth.

The light was dead.

For several seconds, Stan remained motionless, breathing heavily and listening to his racing heartbeat until it finally began to slow down. A thin sheen of sweat covered his forehead like dew. He couldn't stop thinking about whatever that was that he had touched. It had felt cold—almost dead cold, and clammy and sticky, like a dead animal or something. The tunnel was too narrow for him to turn around, so, still shaking, he started retreating backward, fighting the urge to scramble out of there as fast as he could.

But wait a second! he thought, suddenly halting his backward retreat. He hadn't found any rocks worth beans, but what if that thing was something . . . neat?

He crouched in the pressing darkness, feeling equally compelled to go forward to find out what that thing *was* and to get the hell out of there while he still could . . . at least until he got another flashlight. His pulse was thumping heavily in his ears as he debated what to do. In the end, his curiosity won out. Even though his whole body was trembling, he started forward again, reaching blindly ahead until his fingers once again grazed the squishy, cold, *dead*-feeling thing. He jerked his hand back, fully expecting the thing to move even though he knew, just by the touch, that whatever it was, it wasn't alive.

It may have been once, but it was stone cold now.

"Oh, *shit!*" Stan whispered when—once again—a soft, rustling noise echoed from deep inside the cave. It sounded like someone dragging something heavy across the stone floor of the cave. Although the sound had definitely come from up ahead, in the echoing darkness, Stan had the illusion that, like the rock walls, it was all around him, threatening to come crashing in on him any second. With steadily rising terror, he grabbed the burlap bag from his hip pocket, spread the mouth of the bag open wide, and, without touching the thing any more than he had to, rolled and pushed it into the bag. The mere touch of it made him feel queasy, and he was relieved once he had it bagged.

The cave was too narrow for him to turn around, so he started working his way backward, probing his path with one foot so he wouldn't lose his way or go screaming out off the ledge and down the rocky slope. As he dragged the bag along behind him, his fear-heightened state made the return trip seem infinitely longer. He tried to sort out his impressions of what the thing he had found might be. It had felt rubbery and cold, just about the size of a football, maybe a little bit narrower, and it felt like it was composed of thick, segmented rings like donuts that came to a blunt point at either end.

The sun had set by now, so even when he was near the cave entrance, Stan wouldn't have known it except for the strong draft of cool, fresh air that curled around him. He shivered, wondering what the hell this thing in the bag was. It made him feel woozy, almost sick to his stomach just remembering how squishy and cold—

And dead!

—it had felt. Try as he might, he couldn't get rid of the thought that he had discovered a dead man's rotting, severed arm.

Finally, over his shoulder, Stan could see the circle of starlit sky drawing ever closer. He sighed with relief when his foot kicked out free in the open air. Scrunching up his legs, he spun around and hung his feet out over the ledge. Just as he was about to push off down the slope, he heard again that hollow, rasping sound—much louder now, and coming closer. Its rippling echo filled the dark cave.

Whatever it is, it's coming this way! Stan thought as a white bolt of panic flashed through him.

Intense cold pressure squeezed his stomach as he leaned back, stuck his feet out in front of himself, and began a slow, controlled slide down the slope, clutching the burlap bag tightly against his chest. It may have been just his imagination—it *must* have been—but he was *positive* that the instant he pushed off the ledge, something rushed up to the cave mouth and either threw something at him or else made a quick grab at him. He had no idea what it was, but he felt *something* whisk by his head close to his ear like a bat, unseen in the dark. He didn't have any time to think, though, because just then his left foot snagged on a rock and catapulted him forward. Before he could recover, he was tumbling head over heels down the gravelly hillside. His long, trailing scream filled the night as he and a building wave of dirt and gravel rushed headlong toward the roadbed below.

Rolling over and over, Stan was knocked nearly

senseless until he came to rest flat on his back at the bottom of the hill. Loose dirt hissed around him like an angry snake as it slid down in his wake. He shook his head, trying to clear it, as he leapt to his feet and hurriedly brushed himself off. There didn't seem to be a square inch of his body that wasn't battered and bruised, but a quick inventory proved that he wasn't hurt except for a single stinging cut above his left eye. He sure as hell *felt* as though he had just been put through a high-speed meat grinder.

Unbelievably, he had managed to hold on to the burlap bag throughout his fall. He was desperate to see what was in it, but there wasn't enough light to see by. When the image of a dead man's severed arm rose again sharply in his mind, he felt all rubbery and sick.

Dazed from his fall, he kept rubbing his head to reassure himself that it was still attached. Lit only by the flames of the smudge pots and the blinking yellow warning lights, the night pressed close around him. For a panicked instant, he imagined he was still inside the cave. His head was throbbing with pain as he started toward the road, stopping every few steps to shake his head and hope that the waves of dizziness would pass soon. Once when he turned and looked back up the hillside at the cave mouth, he was sure he saw something moving around up there. He tried to convince himself it was just a trick of the darkness, but it sure as hell *looked* like something dark was shifting against the darker black of the cave opening.

Trembling, he was just turning to leave when a hand shot out of the darkness and grabbed him by the neck.

Chapter Three

"I *knew* I'd find you here!"

Chet's voice drilled into Stan's ears as he spun him around and gave him a solid push that sent him staggering backward. Stan's mouth opened, and his lips moved, but the only noise he managed to make sounded like air hissing out of a punctured bicycle tire.

"Mom's been hollerin' and hollerin' for you for the past half hour," Chet said. "I figured you'd be out here collecting rocks, right?" His face glowed eerily in the flickering strobe of the warning lights.

"God *damn* you, you scared the *shit* out of me, you motherf—"

"Ut-ut," Chet said, wagging a warning finger in front of Stan's face. "Better watch your language, or I'll tell Mom. You're in enough trouble as it is. Hey! What you got in the bag?"

Chet made a move to grab the bag from him, but Stan swung his body around protectively.

"None of your damned business," he shouted.

"Ohh . . . ohh, little mister foulmouth," Chet said, taunting. "Come on. Lemme see." He darted first one way then the other in an attempt to get at the bag, but he finally gave up. "Well, it better not be any more rocks. God knows your junk takes up enough space in the bedroom as it is. We'll just see what you have to say once you get home, wise guy. Mom is *really* pissed you weren't back when she said to be."

"Yeah, well, I just sorta lost track of the time," Stan replied weakly. He was still feeling a little dizzy from his fall, and his pulse hadn't slowed down from the surprise Chet had given him. He was trying his best to control himself, but he felt like he had to go to the bathroom *r-e-a-l* bad.

"Come on, then," Chet said.

He suddenly darted ahead of Stan, heading toward the open trench. At the very edge, he leapt up into the air. The flashing lights made his movements strobe like in an old-time movie as he hung suspended against the night sky for an instant. Then he landed with a grunt on the other side. One foot caught at the edge of the trench and knocked some dirt down into the darkness below. He looked back at Stan, his face horribly underlit by the flickering orange flame of the smudge pots.

"Hey, man—if you don't get a move on, I'll take your bike again!" Chet shouted. His mouth hung open; he looked like he was about to say something else, but he cut himself short when a faint noise from down inside the open trench drew his attention. Craning his head forward, he looked down.

"Hey! What's the matter?" Stan shouted, remembering the odd noises he had heard inside the cave. His hand clutched the closed mouth of the burlap bag as the image of a dead, severed arm rose up in his mind.

Maybe the rest of this dead guy is buried down there!

Chet didn't say anything as he stared down into the dark trench, waiting tensely to hear the sound repeated. When it didn't come again, he muttered a curse and kicked some loose gravel down into the darkness. When there still was no response, he straightened up, looked back at Stan, and started walking away. The instant Chet's back was turned, Stan thought he saw a shadow shift within the darkness of the trench.

"Hey, Chet!" he called out, his voice high with fear. "Wait up!"

"No way! You wouldn't show me what you've got in the bag, so I'm not gonna wait for you!"

The skin at the back of Stan's neck prickled as he eyed the opened trench and recalled the hissing, dragging sounds he had heard inside the cave.

"Come on! Wait for me!" he shouted. It took effort to control the wavering in his voice.

"Come on, yourself, then! Move your lard ass!" Chet shouted back, his voice receding into the darkness as he started running down the road.

Stan was about to yell again, but when he opened his mouth, a clump of dirt at the edge of the trench slid noisily down into the darkness below. One of the smudge pots teetered at the edge for a moment and then fell, sputtering as it rolled into the ditch. The flame blazed higher for a moment before it winked out, but in that same instant, Stan was positive he heard a short, barking yelp of pain. Slinging the burlap bag over his handlebars, he leapt on his bike and took off down the road like a shot, hoping like hell to catch up to his brother.

Chapter Four

"I was up in my tree house, Mom. Honest!" Stan said. Cringing inwardly, he glanced over at Chet, just waiting for his brother to tell her the truth. Even when Chet remained silent, Stan was convinced it was only so he could use this little white lie against him some other time when it would be more to his advantage.

"Is that how you got so dirty, and how you got that cut over your eye?"

Stan shook his head, trying to think of an excuse, but his mind was a blank.

"Well, you know what I think about that tree house of yours!" Lisa Walters said.

"I must've dozed off or something, 'cause I never even heard you calling for me. Honest, Mom!"

"I swear to God, I'm going to have your father tear that—that *monstrosity* down this weekend," Stan's mother said. The scowl on her face deepened as she placed her hands on her hips and glared at Stan. "I don't want you up there in the trees like that. Why, just this morning, Mrs. Emerson was telling me about the problem they're having out there in Cornish and Limington with rabid squirrels. She—"

Before she could say more, first Chet and then Stan started snickering with repressed laughter. One boy set the other off, and before long, they couldn't stop themselves. Both of them were snorting, fighting hard not to roar in hysterical laughter.

"Oh, so you think it's *funny*, do you?" their mother said, glaring back and forth between the two boys.

"Come on, Mom," Chet said, choking back his laughter. "You got to admit that the idea of . . . the idea of a . . ." He couldn't force himself to say any more when he looked at Stan, and another gale of laughter took hold of him. In an instant, Stan lost control and was howling, too. He lost control, imagining himself cornered in his tree house, held at bay by a rabid squirrel looming in the doorway. No, not one—a whole *pack* of little gray squirrels, foaming at the mouth as they moved slowly toward him. The image sent him into paroxysms of laughter.

"Well, you boys just go ahead and laugh," their mother said angrily. "You know, it isn't just dogs and foxes that get rabies. Squirrels—even field mice can get the disease." She let her voice trail away as her two sons continued to blubber hysterically. "But right now, I want the both of you to march yourselves up to your bedrooms. *Move it!* And you—Stanley Walters! You march yourself into the bathroom right now and take a shower!"

"Okay, Mom," Stan said, still unable to stop chuckling as he started up the stairs. It was almost enough to make him forget how much he still hurt from his roll down the hillside; but as funny as his mother's irrational fear was, the idea of being attacked by a rabid squirrel wasn't what occupied his mind as he hurriedly undressed and stepped into the shower. He felt at least a bit relieved that he hadn't lied to his mother. He *had* been in his tree house just before coming into the house. He had climbed up the rickety ladder into the darkness and deposited the cold, rubbery, football-shaped thing, burlap bag and all, in the safety of his tree house.

After his shower, as he settled down to sleep, he couldn't stop wondering what that thing was. He could hardly wait until morning when he would even risk the danger of encountering a rabid squirrel to go up to his tree house and find out what was in the bag!

Chapter Five

"I'm not hungry!" Stan said. "I'll eat something later!"

The screen door slammed shut behind him, cutting off his mother's shouted advice that breakfast was the most important meal of the day as he raced out across the back lawn, heading straight into the woods that fringed the yard. About a hundred yards along the narrow, winding path, he came to the towering oak tree that supported his tree house. Without a backward glance or any hesitation, he scampered like a monkey up the slats of wood he had nailed into the tree trunk as a makeshift ladder. He was panting heavily as he poked his head under the heavy canvas sheet he used for a door. It took his eyes a while to adjust to the gloom inside the tree house, but after a moment, he saw it over in the corner, right where he had left it.

After waiting in the entrance for a moment, he hooked the canvas onto the nail he used to hold the door open and entered. Shadow-dappled sunlight angled across the rough pine plank flooring, but it didn't quite reach the burlap bag in the far corner. A tightening tension gripped Stan's throat as he crawled over to it on his hands and knees.

"Now, let's just see what we've got here," he whispered, his voice rasping like sandpaper in the moist gloom. His hands were shaking as he picked up the end of the bag, sucked in a deep breath and held it before dumping the thing out. It hit the floor with a dull *thud* and rolled to a stop in the darkest corner of the tree house. Stan sat back on his heels and stared at the object long and hard. Just like last night, he was strongly and equally drawn and repelled by the thing, whatever it was.

In rough outline, it was indeed about the size of a football, but there the similarity ended. It had a thick, doughy look and was pinched at both ends into a blunt point. In the dim light, the thick, segmented rings were the color of sour milk, white blending into dull yellow. In the middle, where it was thickest, it was about half a foot thick, maybe a bit more. Although the diffused sunlight didn't quite reach it, it glistened moistly, almost as if it had its own internal light source.

"Damn, but don't that look like a maggot," Stan whispered. "A big, fat, bloated, dead *maggot!*"

Stan didn't quite dare to get any nearer to it. Just the thought that he had picked up and carried a monster *maggot* all the way home sickened him. And God Almighty! Even though it had *felt* dead, the thing sure as heck *looked* like it might still be—

"*Alive!*" Stan whispered, sitting back and prodding it with the toe of his sneaker.

The instant he touched it, the maggot-looking

thing twitched. The middle segments puffed up with a barely audible sucking sound, making both ends contract and point at each other like a fat crescent moon. Squealing in surprise, Stan jerked back and banged his head against the low ceiling of the tree house. Trailing curlicues of light wiggled across his vision as he rubbed the back of his head and stared in utter disbelief at the thing.

It *had* to be a maggot or worm or cocoon of some kind. He could tell that much—but what? What kind of worm or slug ever got as big as a football?

Tense seconds passed as Stan just sat there staring at the thing, waiting for it to move again. When it didn't, he tried to convince himself that it hadn't moved the first time; it must have just been his imagination . . . or a shifting shadow that had made it *look* like it moved. How could a worm that big even exist, much less be alive?

After a minute or two, when the thing still hadn't moved, Stan scrambled out of the tree house. Climbing up onto the pitched roof, he reached up and snapped off an oak branch about two feet long. After stripping off the leaves and twigs, he swung back down onto the platform and reentered the tree house. With the stick held out in front of him like a sword, he cautiously approached the giant maggot-thing again.

"Just what in the hell *are* you?" he whispered.

His hand trembled as he reached forward and gently prodded the thing. He expected the sharp stick to pierce it easily, but the milky white skin had a rubbery resistance that deflected it. No matter how hard Stan pressed the stick against the thing, even hard enough to make it shift across the rough floor, he couldn't puncture it.

"Well, then, maybe a knife will do it," he said aloud.

He leaned forward and reached into his front jeans pocket, then sighed out loud when he remembered that his mother had taken his jackknife away from him last week. Frustrated, he whacked the middle of the maggot-looking thing with his stick. In a flash, the worm twisted around and flipped over. Stan screamed so loud it hurt his throat when he saw the underside. It looked . . . weird, all puckered up and wrinkled like a dirty sock that was turned inside out. Inside the fat, folded wrinkles, it looked almost as though there were a face—a horribly twisted face, distorted and squashed flat against the thick, milky wrapping. Round, bulging eyes stared unblinkingly at him. Squashed up flat on each side and running halfway down the length of the thing were what looked like the faint outlines of two arms . . . arms that ended in small, flat, clawed hands.

Stan was barely aware of the whimpering sound he was making as he scurried toward the tree house door. He felt his way blindly with his hands and feet, unable to tear his eyes away from the distorted face that was gazing steadily at him. He tried desperately to convince himself that there couldn't really be a face—an almost *human*-looking face—on the underside of this thing. No matter *what* it was—a slug, a maggot, or whatever—there was no *way* in heaven it could have a *human* face! His whole body shook as though a powerful electric current was jolting him as he swung over to the ladder and scrambled down to the forest floor. Halfway to the ground, he let go of the steps and sprang out into the air. Landing on his feet, he caught his balance and started running as fast as he could back to the house.

Chapter Six

Throughout the morning, Stan was uncharacteristically silent—enough so that even Chet commented on it. After lunch, Stan went right out and mowed the front lawn without his father having to tell him more than once. When he was done with that job, he even offered to rake up the clippings—a job Chet usually did whenever Stan did the mowing. A couple of times during the day, Chet tried to talk to him, to draw out of him whatever was bothering him. Several times Stan was tempted to spill his guts and tell Chet all about the weird human-faced dead *maggot*-thing he had stashed up in the tree house, but he kept his peace, all the while wondering if he truly had seen what he thought he had seen . . . and if those bulging, round eyes had been looking back and had seen *him!*

Supper came, and although Stan was still withdrawn, he was also starting to feel nervous and anxious . . . curious. He continually bounced his legs up and down at the supper table until his father told him to stop. Although he was hungry, he had to leave his slice of lamb untouched because the light beige color of it reminded him of the thing up in his tree house. Once supper was over and the dishes were done, he was free to go do whatever he wanted to—at least until dark. Against his better judgment, he felt drawn, nearly compelled to go out to the tree house just to verify that what he had seen—what he *thought* he had seen—had just been his imagination. Anticipation gnawed at his nerves like a worm working its way to the core of an apple. Before long, he knew he *had* to go out there, only this time he'd be prepared. Although he knew his father kept a pistol in his desk drawer, Stan didn't dare go quite that far. But he did manage to sneak his jackknife out of his mother's top bureau drawer. With that, Chet's flashlight, and a length of rope in case he had to tie the thing up or whatever, he left by the back door and disappeared down the trail leading to the tree house.

When he got to the oak tree, he stood for a moment, looking up at the underside of the tree house. Never in all the years since he and some of his friends had built it had it ever seemed so scary, so ominous. The dark, jagged timbers of the roofline and flooring were black, dimensionless blocks against the paling evening sky. The sheet of canvas hanging down over the door looked like a sodden blanket, and Stan couldn't stop wondering what in the name of Sweet Jesus was behind that curtain.

"I'll take the dead human-faced giant-maggot-thing behind Door Number One," he whispered, chuckling softly to himself for courage as he started up the ladder to the platform. His breath caught, dry and scratchy in the back of his throat, as he pulled back the canvas door covering. Before entering, he folded the three-inch blade out of his jackknife and held it in out defensively in one hand as he snapped on the flashlight and, bending low, went inside.

The sun was setting behind his back. It angled across the tree house floor with a wash of bright orange that illuminated every detail of the rough planks of the floor and walls. The quiet of the evening seemed to magnify every sound around him—the harsh rasping of the canvas door, the creaking of rusty nails in weathered wood, the swishing of leaves as the branches supporting the tree house bent beneath his shifting weight. The oval of light from his flashlight darted like a laser beam over to the corner, his eyes desperately seeking the maggoty thing. As soon as he saw it, his heart started pounding hard in his chest, and tears started in his eyes.

"You *bastard!*" he hissed as he swept the beam of light back and forth over the tangled, white mess that littered the tree house floor. "You lousy, scumsucking, rotten *bastard!*"

He couldn't believe what he was seeing. The only thing his brain could register was: whatever that thing had been, it was gone now, smashed and ripped and torn into hundreds of tiny, fleshy shreds. The floor was saturated with a thick, gooey liquid that had dried into a black crust on the old wood.

Stan had no doubt who had done this; it *had* to have been Chet and his friends. Sometime in the afternoon, probably while he was mowing the lawn, they must have sneaked out here, found what Stan had stashed up here, and destroyed it. Why? Simply to piss him off, of course—just like Chet *always* did!

"I'm gonna get even with you for this," Stan whispered, his voice vibrating as he probed the remains with the tip of his knife. Even with a sharp blade, the outside covering resisted cutting or puncturing, as if it were some kind of thick, white rubber. He still couldn't quite bring himself to touch what was left of it, so he sat down and used his foot to push the remains of his prize into a pile over in the corner.

Once he had gathered most of it up, though, he realized that something was dreadfully wrong.

"There isn't enough stuff here," he whispered.

His eyes darted back and forth, following the beam of the flashlight around the interior of the tree house to see if he could have missed any.

As he was looking around, a faint scratching sound from overhead drew his attention. Cringing backward onto the floor, he was just swinging the flashlight around and up to see what it was when something dropped onto his back.

Stan realized instantly that whatever this was, it must have been clinging to the underside of the ceiling where he couldn't see it. He let loose a wild scream that almost completely masked the high-pitched chattering sound close to his ears as tiny, sharp claws punctured his neck and ripped into the back of his head. His mind went white with terror as his skin was ripped away. Blood began to flow, hot and sticky down his back. He swung out wildly with both hands, batting behind his head in a desperate attempt to dislodge the thing, but all to no avail. Whatever it was, it had wrapped its tiny arms around him like a clawed leech. Stan's jackknife slipped from his sweaty grip as he thrashed around on the pine wood floor. The flashlight beam swung wildly back and forth, sweeping the inside of the tree house like a searchlight as he repeatedly hammered at the slick, skinny body that had attached itself to him.

A rabid squirrel, he thought through a numbing flood of panic. *I'm being attacked by a goddamned rabid squirrel!*

As he rolled back and forth on the floor, he reached out blindly for the knife he had dropped. Several times he raised his head and slammed it back hard against the floor, hoping to kill the thing or at least knock it out. With each impact, the creature let out a sharp, high-pitched squeal, but it dug its claws into him all the deeper. Finally, knowing it was his only hope to get free of the thing, Stan started moving toward the door. He needed room to move. If he could just get outside, get down to the ground, he might be able to get rid of the thing by banging it against the tree trunk or something. He knew he didn't have much time. Tiny, razor-sharp teeth were burrowing deeply into his shoulder muscles, sending burning jolts of pain throughout his body.

But in his pain and panic, Stan overreacted. Doubling his legs up underneath himself, he pushed back as hard as he could. Too hard. He shot out through the doorway and started falling . . . falling. Branches whipped past him as he plummeted downward. For a frozen instant, he was sure that he was going to die as soon as he hit the ground, but then—miraculously—the underside of his left arm hooked over one of the lower branches. For an instant, his fall was halted, and in that split second, his other hand reflexively shot out and grabbed the branch. The impact jerked his body, slamming his teeth together so hard he bit off the tip of his tongue. The force also was sudden enough and strong enough to dislodge whatever the thing was off his back. Muscles straining, Stan struggled to hold on to the branch. From down below, he heard an ear-piercing squeal when the thing hit the ground with a sick, heavy *plop*. Then came the rustle of leaves as whatever it was scurried off into the deep brush.

"Jesus Christ! Stan! What the hell are you *doing?*"

The shout boomed like thunder through the woods. Frantic and wild-eyed, Stan looked down, trying to locate the source of the voice. Tears, sweat, and blood streamed down his face and neck. His whole body was throbbing with the effort of hanging on to the branch. Down below, he heard the heavy tread of footsteps coming closer. In the dense twilit brush, he finally made out his brother's face, glowing eerily like a pale moon as he stared up at him.

"How in the hell did you get yourself—"

Chet was cut off by a loud cracking sound as the branch suddenly snapped. Stan pictured himself as nothing more than a speck of dust being sucked into a vacuum cleaner as his body plummeted toward the night-stained ground. He landed with his left leg cocked behind his back; but he was unconscious by the time he hit the ground, and he never felt the painful snap that broke his leg in two places . . . at least not until several minutes later, once Chet had raced back to the house for help and returned with his mother and two guys from MedCu.

Chapter Seven

With its red warning lights flashing, the ambulance raced through the night, taking the curves of Route 25 perhaps a bit faster than it should have. Stan's leg was completely numb. He couldn't stop thinking that it had been cut off, and he kept checking to make sure it was still there. The physician's assistant had given him a shot for the pain, but his neck and shoulders still felt like they were burning. His eyes were narrowed to slits as he looked up at his mother from the ambulance stretcher. The physician's assistant, whose badge read *Cochran*, was also leaning over him.

"I *told* you I didn't want you going out there to that tree house," his mother said. Her voice was a perfect mix of anger and concern as she stared down at her boy. "I *never* liked you playing out there!"

Stan wanted to say something, but he knew if he opened his mouth, the only sound he'd be able to make would be a faint whimper . . . or else a scream. In spite of everything Cochran had done, cleaning and dressing the wounds, Stan still thought that giant, dead maggot-*thing* was clinging to his neck, digging its claws into his flesh.

"I'll just bet it was one of those squirrels I warned you about. It was, wasn't it?" his mother asked, unable to keep the edge of accusation out of her voice. "Just like I was telling you yesterday . . . it was one of those rabid squirrels."

Cochran raised one eyebrow and looked at her with a half smile as if he thought she might be kidding; then he looked at Stan, who shook his head in weak denial. Tears threatened to spill from his eyes, but he wasn't about to let himself cry; not in front of his mother and this guy he didn't even know. No way! Crying was for babies!

"Well, whatever it was, Mrs. Walters," Cochran said mildly, "it's too bad it got away." He looked down at Stan and gave him a light but bracing touch on the back of the hand. Turning to Stan's mother, he said softly, "We'll have to keep a watchful eye on those cuts to make sure they don't get infected."

Stan's mother bit down hard on her lower lip, sighed deeply, and shook her head. "If you had only listened to me, Stanley," she whispered. "If only you had listened."

Chapter Eight

"Look out!" the man riding up in front with the ambulance driver suddenly shouted.

They were approaching the construction site where the state highway workers had been blasting away at Watchick Hill. The asphalt abruptly ended and the road changed to hard-packed dirt, but that wasn't what had drawn the man's attention. Off to his right, in the flickering light of the yellow warning light, he had seen a dark blur of motion. Before the driver could respond to his warning, something small and moving fast had darted out of the woods, heading straight toward the trench on the opposite side of the road. The driver hit the brakes, but it was too late. The tires skidded on the gravel just as a heavy *thump* sounded from underneath the ambulance.

"Aww, shit! You hit him!"

"Hey! Watch your language up there!" Cochran said.

"What the hell—? Was that some kind of dog or

something?" the ambulance driver asked. His expression was tight as he played the steering wheel back and forth while stepping down hard on the brakes. The ambulance swerved to a stop as the siren died down with a warbling hoot.

"Come on, man," the passenger said. "You can't stop now. We have to get this kid down to Maine Med."

"Shouldn't we check it out? If that was a dog, we have to report it," the ambulance driver said.

"We have to get this kid to Maine Med. We can check whatever that was on our way back."

They delivered Stan and his mother to Maine Med in Portland and, once the paperwork was completed, headed back up Route 25 to the Thornton Fire Station. As they neared the construction site, the driver slowed down, scanning both sides of the road.

"I know it was around here someplace," he whispered. A second later, he saw a dark lump of . . . something on the road up ahead. He braked, jammed the shift into *park*, and opened his door. As he stepped out into the night, the other man got out and walked around to meet him at the front of the ambulance. Both men focused on the dark splotch lying in the middle of the road.

"What in the name of—?" the driver muttered.

Flattened onto the hard-packed dirt was a tangled piece of dark, scaly flesh. Blood and purple guts had spurted out of its open mouth. Huge, rounded eyes bulged out of the eye sockets, glistening like exposed bone in the bright headlight beams. Not quite daring to touch the thing, the driver knelt down and stared at the array of tiny, pointed teeth that lined the squashed lower jaw. The body—at least what was left of it—looked like a long, flattened tube with distorted hind legs and long, thin arms tipped with flat, clawed hands.

"What the fuck *is* that thing?" the driver said.

"Looks to me like somebody else ran over it after we did," the passenger replied. "Either that, or else you really creamed it. You *were* going kind of fast."

The driver wiped his forehead with the flat of his hand as he leaned closer, tensed, half expecting the thing to suddenly leap up at him.

"You ever see anything like this?" he asked, barely able to restrain the nervous quaver in his voice as he stood up and looked back and forth between his partner and the splattered roadkill.

"Nope," his partner replied coolly. "Can't say as I have. But I'll tell you this much: Whatever it is—or *was*—it sure as shit wasn't no dog!" He took a deep breath and let it out slowly. "Come on. Let the crows have it. Let's get our butts back to the station."

The driver didn't move. He just stood there for almost a full minute, his eyes glued to the strange mess of twisted flesh on the road. Then, heaving a deep sigh, he followed his partner back to the ambulance, got in, and drove away. In the morning, the passing dump trucks flattened the roadkill into the gravel before the crows could get at it.

Deal with the Devils
Chapter One

Summer, 1982

"Hey! You don't be doin' that!"

The gruff voice of Tyler Clay's grandfather, coming so suddenly from behind him in the dark barn, made both Tyler and Chuckie Harper, his best friend, nearly jump out of their skins.

What made Tyler's grandfather yell at them was not so much what they were *doing*, but what they were *thinking* of doing. It didn't take much for Old Man Clay, as everyone in the town of Thornton called him, to figure out what these two boys were up to. After all, although it might not seem like it was possible, he had been a rambunctious ten-year-old kid once upon a time, and on a hot summer afternoon, what is any ten-year-old boy up to after his chores are done if it isn't a bit of trouble? If Old Man Clay had been ten years old right then, he most likely would have been there with them, trying to lift the iron grate and see what was down in that tunnel under the barn.

"Jeez, Grampa, you scared the be-jeez—scared the heck out of us," Tyler said, looking at his grandfather with fear-widened eyes.

"Meant ta," Old Man Clay said. His scowl deepened as he made his way across the barn to where the two boys were standing. His bad left foot dragged behind him, leaving scalloped curlicue marks on the hard-packed dirt floor.

"Let's get outta here," Chuckie whispered, leaning close to Tyler. Twin lines of sweat ran from his armpits and down his sides, tickling his ribs. As much as Chuckie liked Tyler, he disliked Tyler's grandfather. The old man gave him a serious case of the heebie-jeebies. Besides that horrible limp of his, which reminded Chuckie of Long John Silver, the old man's left hand was missing two fingers at the knuckle joints. His pinkie and ring fingers ended in little knobs of white scar tissue that made his hand look more like a claw than a real hand. If he had lost much more of his hand, he might have had a hook like Captain Hook.

"We was just . . . just checking this out," Tyler said, trying his best to sound all innocence. He slipped his hands into his jeans pockets and bounced up and down on his sneakered toes.

"Well, I don't know how many times I have to tell yah, but I want you stayin' away from there," Old Man Clay said. He tilted his head toward the grate that covered the three-foot-square hole in the far corner of the barn, over behind the cow stalls. Thick iron bars were set in a heavy metal frame that was held in place by a large rusted padlock with a hasp on one side and twin heavy-duty hinges on the other.

Tyler had discovered this curiosity while playing in his grandfather's cow barn shortly after he and his folks first moved to the old family homestead about four years ago, back when Tyler's father lost his job at the National Paper Products mill in Hilton. Tyler remembered asking back then what the iron grate was for and where the stone-lined tunnel led. The answer his grandfather had given him hadn't quite convinced him, and like many childhood questions that go unanswered, this one had festered until it was close to the most pressing question on his mind. So now, after weeks of talking and planning, he and Chuckie had decided—today—to try to lift up the iron grate so they could get inside the tunnel and see exactly what was down there.

"We were just checking it out. What is this thing, anyway?" Tyler asked. He stared at his grandfather, who was still eyeing the heavily barred grill.

"If I tole yah once, I tole you a dozen times," Old Man Clay said. "That there's the poop chute. Used to be used for cleanin' out the stalls. Easier to shovel cow shit down there 'n' clean it out from the bottom, I guess."

"But it doesn't really look like it would drain out all that good," Tyler said, staring at the grate with narrow-eyed suspicion. He and Chuckie had also checked out where the tunnel came out behind the barn. It, too, was closed off with a similarly constructed iron grate.

"I mean, if this tunnel goes straight down here, wouldn't it have to be—"

" 'N' what d'yah be needin' that length of rope

for?" Tyler's grandfather asked as if he hadn't even been listening to him. "I hope to Key-rist you wasn't thinkin' about tryin' to go down there!"

He squinted as he looked from one boy to the other. Chuckie didn't like the way the old man's gaze lingered on him, as though he were sizing him up or something.

"We—uh, well, you remember that ring with the red stone I used to have?" Tyler asked with sudden inspiration. "I—uh, I dropped it down in there just now when me and Chuckie were looking in."

"Consider it gone, then," Old Man Clay snapped. "Your loss."

"Come on," Chuckie said, taking a pinch of Tyler's shirtsleeve and jiggling it. "Let's get outta here."

"And *you*, boy," Old Man Clay said, pointing a shaky finger at Chuckie. The white nubs of his amputated fingers curled into the palm of his hand. "You don't be egging my grandson on to do nothin' stupid, you understand?"

"I—I didn't," was all Chuckie could say before sputtering into silence.

"You boys may not've known it, but I was out here in the barn 'n' I overheard everythin' you was sayin'," Old Man Clay growled.

Flustered and unable to recall exactly what either of them had said, Chuckie took a few quick steps backward. He stumbled and almost fell when the back of his foot caught on the edge of the iron grate. The dirt he kicked up rained down into the dark hole with a soft, hissing sound. It might have been his imagination, but Tyler thought he heard a long, rasping echo from deep inside the tunnel.

"You think you're so damned curious to go down

inta that tunnel there, huh?" Old Man Clay asked. His usual dark scowl deepened. "Well, maybe I've got a mind to open 'er up and lower you on in. Would'cha like that?"

"No—no, honestly, Mr. Clay," Chuckie stammered. "We didn't mean nothing by it. Honest! I'm sorry if I—"

"Well, then, you just stay away from my barn, understand? Both of yah! Stay the hell out of my barn!"

With that, Old Man Clay turned and stalked toward the barn door, dragging his gimpy leg behind him. The boys waited until he was gone before either one of them dared to move.

Chapter Two

"When we eatin'?" John Clay, Jr., Tyler's father, asked. It was late in the afternoon when he got home from the lumberyard, entered the house, and dropped his black metal lunchbox on the counter.

Katie Clay looked up from the vegetables she was peeling, let her gaze shift past her husband, then looked back to her work. She hated the way her husband always stormed into the house like that without a single word of greeting, as if she were as much a fixture in the kitchen as the stove or refrigerator.

"Have you heard 'bout what happened?" she asked with a tight tremor in her voice. Using her paring knife as a pointer, she indicated the copy of the *Portland Evening Express* on the kitchen table.

" 'Nother kid's gone missing, huh?" Junior asked after scanning the headline. He hooked the rung of a chair with his foot, pulled the chair out, and sat down heavily.

"That's right," Katie said as she wiped her hands

on a faded dishtowel. She turned around and leaned back against the edge of the counter, fighting the impulse to go straight to the refrigerator and get her husband a beer. Let him fend for himself once in a while, she thought bitterly.

"This one disappeared outside of town, somewheres up near Highland Pond."

"Don't see where that's any concern of ours," Junior said.

"That's three kids," Katie said, holding up three parboiled fingers. "All boys between the ages of nine and twelve from 'round here—all gone missing within the space of a few weeks! I'd say it's our concern, 'specially considering what happened just north of here in Holland a few years back."

"What's that supposed to mean?" Junior snapped. He was starting to feel edgy, wondering where in the hell his beer was. Maybe Katie had forgotten to buy a twelve-pack the last time she was at the store. He sure didn't feel like hauling ass down to Nicely's just for a cold one.

"Well, there was that fella—what's his name? I can't recall. Anyway, he was pickin' up kids from around town and killing them, sinkin' their bodies into the Bog up there." Katie's worried eyes shifted past her husband when she saw Junior's father limping up the walkway. "If we got some kind of loony like that on the loose, I think you better talk to Tyler and make sure he doesn't talk to any strangers 'round town."

"Sure, sure," Junior said. He finally decided that Katie wasn't about to get him his beer, so he heaved himself out of the chair and went over to the refrigerator himself. He grabbed a bottle of Budweiser and popped the top on the counter edge. "Hell, Tyler's smart enough to take care of hisself."

"What's this 'bout Tyler?" Old Man Clay asked as he slammed the screen door open. He dragged his bum leg over to the kitchen table and sat down heavily. Sweat-streaked dirt and hay chaff covered his weathered face, hands, and clothes.

"Oh, nothin' . . . nothin' a'tall," Junior replied. He grabbed another bottle of beer without asking if his father wanted it and handed it to him. Old Man Clay opened it with his pocketknife and took a long, noisy gulp. Wiping his mouth with the back of his hand, he glanced at the headline in front of him. Dropping his fist down hard on the table, he flattened the folded newspaper.

"Kids!" he snarled, his voice no more than a low rumble. "Goddamned! Gotta be careful as hell 'round about this time o'year!"

Chapter Three

"He only told us to stay out of the *barn*," Chuckie said, leaning close to Tyler's ear. They were both crouching on the ground out behind the barn where the back bordered the woods. "He never said nothing about us having to stay out of the *tunnel*."

Built against the slope of a steep hill, the foundation of Old Man Clay's barn was constructed of huge blocks of granite. Out back, from ground level it was nearly ten feet straight up to the ground floor. Several tall oak trees cast thick green shadows over the boys. Sunlight flickered through the leaves, making the foundation look alive with electrical energy.

Tyler shivered as he studied the iron grating that filled the dark tunnel entrance at ground level on the back corner of the foundation. It was almost identical to the one on the barn floor, but the heavy iron bars of this one were embedded no more than four inches apart in a thick layer of cement that collared the top of the tunnel's mouth. The bottom half of the bars were sunk deeply into the ground. How deeply, no one knew; but Tyler and Chuckie were trying to find out. They had dug down more than two feet and still not found the bottom.

"Come on, Chuckie," Tyler said, frowning seriously. "You know darn right well he meant he didn't want us snooping around in there." He indicated the tunnel mouth with a tight nod of his head.

"Yeah," Chuckie said, laughing softly, "but you've gotta find that precious little ring of yours, remember?"

"You know I was lying about that!"

"Yeah, but were you lying about wanting to see where this tunnel goes?" Chuckie asked. His voice was sharp and taunting as he sat back on his heels and smugly placed his hands on his hips. His face and clothes were caked with smudges of dirt.

"Well," Tyler said, looking from his friend to the dark tunnel mouth. "We know there's some kind of tunnel inside there 'cause we've seen it."

"And as far as you 'n' me know, this opening here and the opening in the floor up there in the barn are the only two ways to get in there, right?"

Tyler gnawed at his lower lip and nodded. "Yeah . . . unless they ain't even connected."

" 'N' who knows what might be in there, huh? I mean, what if there's a whole room inside there just around where the tunnel curves out of sight? What if there's a whole cellar under the entire barn, filled with all sorts of neat stuff?" Chuckie lowered his voice with mock awe and added, "This is a wicked old barn. What if there's like treasure or something buried under here?"

"My grandpa told me the whole inside of the foundation is filled up solid with dirt and rocks," Tyler said.

"That's what he told you," Chuckie said, leering.

Tyler snorted with laughter. "And anyways, why would anyone want to bury treasure under my grandfather's barn?"

Chuckie shrugged and said, "Who knows? But don't you think we ought to get inside there and see for ourselves?"

Bringing his hand up to cover his mouth, Tyler shook his head. "I dunno . . . I think maybe we ought to leave well enough alone. I don't want to get in troub—"

"You ain't chickenshit, are you?"

"No! No way!" Tyler said, shaking his head with determination.

"Well, then—let's get digging. These bars sure as shit can't go all the way down to China."

Chapter Four

The sun was close to setting by the time Tyler and Chuckie got the hole dug down to the bottom of the frame that held the iron bars. Both boys were covered with dirt and dripping with sweat as they sat back and admired their work.

"We've either gotta get this thing out of the cement or else dig down far enough so we can get up underneath it," Chuckie said.

Tyler sighed with exasperation and shrugged, thinking either prospect seemed like more work than he cared for.

"My mom's gonna kill me for tearing this shirt," he said, displaying the rip he'd gotten while leaning against the rough stones of the foundation and trying to get leverage to loosen the grate.

"Yeah, well, just don't tell her how you did it, okay?" Chuckie said. He looked from his friend back down to the hole they had dug. Nodding with satisfaction, he asked, "Think we ought to wait till tomorrow, or do you want to give it a try now?"

"I think we ought to wait," Tyler said, his frown deepening. Wiping the sweat from his forehead with the back of his arm left a thick streak of mud above his eyes that looked like Indian war paint. "It's gonna be dark soon, anyway."

Tyler didn't want to mention it, but several times while they had been digging, he had heard—or thought he had heard—a faint scuffing sound echo from deep within the tunnel. He only mentioned it to Chuckie the first time he heard it. After Chuckie teased him about "going pussy," he decided it must just be the echoes of their work . . . if not his imagination.

"And anyway, it don't matter how dark it is," Chuckie said. "It's gonna be dark as West Hell in there, no matter when we go in. 'Sides, we've got flashlights with us. What do you say we do it right now?"

Tyler was ready to tell his friend *no* again, but just then he heard the harsh clanging of a cowbell—his mother's signal to let him know it was time to come home for supper. Trying hard not to show the relief he felt, he got up, hastily brushed off his knees, and shouted that he was on his way.

"Gotta go. Catch you later," he called over his shoulder as he started up the steep slope toward the house. Before Chuckie could say anything, Tyler was around the corner and out of sight.

For a long while, Chuckie remained where he was, staring at where Tyler had disappeared. Then his gaze shifted back to the iron grate, the stone-lined tunnel, and the digging they had done so far. It was all well and good that they had gotten a start on this, he thought, but why wait until tomorrow to get in there?

What if Tyler's grandfather came out behind the barn and saw what they had done?

He'd know in an instant who had done it, and Chuckie knew that gimpy old pirate wouldn't hesitate a second to blame him for instigating the whole thing.

"What the hell!" Chuckie muttered.

Sucking in a deep breath, he gripped the shovel with both hands, leaned forward, and started digging again, throwing scoop after scoop of dark earth over his shoulder. With the lessening of light, he found it increasingly difficult to see what he was doing. He considered using one of the flashlights but decided that he didn't want to chance drawing any undue attention to himself.

Darkness seeped in all around him, spreading like an ink stain from the woods behind the barn. Crickets trilled in the field, and the sudden squawk of a night bird sent shivers up his spine, but Chuckie kept working furiously. He wasn't about to quit now—not until he got that damned iron grating out of the way and he could see for himself what was inside that tunnel. He didn't realize there was someone standing behind him until a hand clamped down hard on his shoulder. For an instant, he thought it was Tyler, now finished with supper and come back to give him a scare. When he glanced to the side and saw that the hand was missing two fingers, a feeble little squeak escaped the back of his throat. Tears filled his eyes as the white nubs of scar tissue dug painfully into the meat of his shoulder.

Chapter Five

"So you think you're some smart guy, huh?" Old Man Clay asked.

Before Chuckie could answer, the old man clamped his other hand over Chuckie's mouth. He leered close to him from out of the darkness, letting his hot, beer-sour breath wash over Chuckie. A cold prickling filled the boy's stomach.

"So you want to see what's down in this here tunnel, huh? Well, mista' smart guy, looks like you're gonna get your wish after all."

Chuckie's eyes were wide open with a fear so strong he wasn't even able to blink as he looked up at Tyler's grandfather. He tried to shake his head in vigorous denial, but the pain in his shoulder spread like fire up his neck. He wanted to speak, wanted to beg the man to let him go, wanted to tell him that he hadn't meant any harm, but the old man's other hand cupped his lower face like a vise, squeezing anything he might have said back into his chest.

"So now—" Old Man Clay said, his voice lowering to a growl. "Why don't you come along with me, 'n' I'll show you something you won't *ever* forget!"

With a quick motion that caught Chuckie completely by surprise, the old man spun him around and gripped him tightly in a hammerlock with one arm. For an instant, he removed his hand from Chuckie's mouth, but as soon as Chuckie opened his mouth and sucked in a breath to try to scream, the old man stuffed a crusty handkerchief into his mouth. It tasted horrible. Something sickly and sour bubbled up from Chuckie's stomach into his throat, but the handkerchief forced it back down. Clasping both of Chuckie's arms behind him at the wrists, Old Man Clay pulled his hands up hard, as if he were working a pump handle that was frozen stuck. A bright bolt of pain shot up Chuckie's spine, exploding in his brain like a firecracker.

"Come along, then," the old man wheezed as he pushed and dragged the boy up the hill and around the side of the barn. With his arms pinned behind his back, his mouth gagged, and his vision blurred by tears of pain and terror, the boy stumbled several times, but the old man wrenched his arms back and forced him to keep on moving. They went around the side of the barn and in through the front door. The rich smell of fresh manure and hay chaff stung Chuckie's eyes, making it even harder for him to see in the lessening light.

"You know right where it is, don't 'cha, boy?" Old Man Clay hissed as they walked down the row of stalls. Several cows turned and looked at them, their sad, dumb eyes glistening brightly in the evening gloom as their tails flicked at the flies swarming around their haunches.

Chuckie worked his tongue against the cloth blocking his mouth, but so much was stuffed inside he couldn't apply enough pressure to expel it. He thought he was going to suffocate. Inside his mind, he was screaming, begging Old Man Clay to let him go, but no sounds escaped. When at last they reached the corner of the barn where Chuckie could see the dark square that was the iron grating, his knees went all rubbery. He stumbled and almost fell.

"You're gonna learn something not too many people alive today even know about," Old Man Clay said. Chuckling deeply in his chest, he hawked and spit off into the darkness. He released his grip on Chuckie's arm, but before the boy could make his body respond to his mental command to run, Old Man Clay shoved him into the corner of the barn, where he blocked any possible retreat. There was a clinking of metal as the old man fished about in the pocket of his bib coveralls. Finally, he produced a ring of keys, which he held up to the fading light while he searched for the correct one.

Kneeling down, all the while keeping his eyes fixed on the terrified boy, he felt blindly for the lock. Chuckie cowered in the corner. He was on the verge of bawling like a baby. After a bit, Old Man Clay fitted a key into the lock, twisted it, and released the shackle. The sound of metal clanging against metal was magnified in the darkness as it echoed in the stone-lined tunnel; but even as the old man pulled the lock away, Chuckie heard something else—a faint rasping sound from down inside the tunnel.

"That might be them comin' already," Old Man

Clay said. "Gotta hurry." He sniffed softly with laughter.

Chuckie's entire body went numb as he stared in utter horror at the iron grating on the floor. Whatever was down there making that noise sure as hell sounded like it was getting closer!

"You see, boy, these here iron bars are necessary to make sure what's down there stays down there. Catch my drift?" Old Man Clay said. "But you know—I don't think that's the only thing that keeps 'em down there."

Paralyzed with terror and too stunned to cry out for help, Chuckie slowly raised his hand to his mouth and started to pull the cloth from his mouth. The insides of his cheeks were desert dry, so he had to lick his lips before he could speak. His voice was tight and high, but he managed to say, "What—? What's down there?"

Old Man Clay looked sharply at him, his eyes gleaming with a kind of madness, but he continued talking as if he hadn't even heard him.

"For the longest damned time, you know, I was losing cows up here in the barn. Oh, not often, but every couple of years, some mornin' I'd come out here 'n' find one of 'em all ripped open and half et. It took me quite a while to realize there was a pattern to it all. Finally I noticed that things like that was happening just about every five years. Usually in the summer, but sometimes in the spring or fall. 'N' then one night, must've been, oh, twenty years or more back, I heard one helluva commotion out here. I came a'runnin' out 'n' got here just in time to see—well, I ain't 'xactly sure what I seen, but I sure as hell saw *somethin'*! Looked sorta like a dwarf, all gnarly and brown-like. It went scurryin' back down into that hole there. First thing next morning, I made myself a couple of grates out of iron. Fixed one into place here 'n' put the other one out back where you was just digging. This one, though, is a bit different, you see. It's got hinges."

Saying that, he stood up and stepped forward, being careful to keep his weight on the grate . . . almost as if, Chuckie thought, he was making sure to keep it down. A warm pressure was building up in Chuckie's bladder as he stared at the old man, all the while listening to the faint scratching sound that was definitely getting louder.

"What's down there?" he managed to say, his voice raw and broken as he watched the old man slowly approach him.

"I ain't got the faintest goddamned clue," Old Man Clay said, smiling broadly. Without warning, his hand darted out like a striking rattlesnake and snagged Chuckie's arm. "This tunnel or whatever the hell it is must've been here since back when my father built this here barn," he said as he started to drag Chuckie forward. "But you know what? I have a theory. Wanna hear it?"

Feeling faint with terror, Chuckie couldn't even nod as the old man hauled him over toward the grate.

"I think this here tunnel goes straight down to hell," Old Man Clay said in a voice tinged with reverence. "That's what I think. 'N' what I saw out here that night—what's been comin' up into my barn every now and then to kill my cows—is a horde of devils! Demons! You hear me, boy?" His eyes widened and rolled ceilingward with excitement. "I said *demons*!"

A strangled squeak escaped Chuckie's mouth as he

looked from the old man down to the iron grate and the gaping black hole at his feet. He was barely aware of it when his bladder released, spreading a warm wash of urine down his legs. The old man's grip on his arm tightened painfully and pulled him relentless toward the opening. When the old man got to the edge, he placed his toe under the lip of the grate and raised it. Reaching down with one hand, he took the edge of the grate and flung it wide open. The rusty hinges squeaked in protest as the door fell open and hit the dirt floor with a loud *clang*.

"You see," Old Man Clay said. "I made a sorta deal with these particular devils. Once I realized they only come around every five years or so, I figured when I know they're comin' 'round again, I could give 'em a little something so's they'd leave my cows alone. Seemed reasonable, and I reckon they're satisfied, 'cause I don't believe for a minute they couldn't rip this open if they really wanted to. Actually, one time one of 'em did come at me, but—fortunately—I had the grate closed 'n' he only got a couple of fingers off me."

He raised his palm out and wiggled the stumps of his amputated fingers under Chuckie's nose.

"But ever since then, they've been pretty much leavin' me be," Old Man Clay went on. "That's 'cause every five years I send 'em down a little treat. One year it was a sick calf that I didn't 'spect to live. Usually, though, I try to get 'em a person. I find someone who's been givin' me some trouble 'n' I bring him on out to the barn here."

Without warning, the old man gave a quick kick to the back of Chuckie's knees. The impact knocked him to the floor. All resistance drained out of the boy as he felt himself being pushed relentlessly face-first toward the narrow, dark opening. He spread his arms and legs out wide, trying to grab on to anything to keep himself out of there, but it was no use. His hands and feet left deep furrows in the dirt floor. Then, in an instant, he felt himself pitching forward into the bottomless hole. He reached out and grabbed the far edge of the opening, clinging on to the grate as if it were a life raft as his legs dropped down into the black maw below him.

"Please, Mr. Clay!" he pleaded as he looked up at the old man. "You can't put me down there!"

He was hoping to see a small trace of pity in the old man's face, but there was none. His lower lip trembled, and his eyes filled with tears.

"This is just a joke, right?" he whimpered. "You're just trying to scare me 'cause of what I was doing. Pull me up now . . . please?"

"Please, nothin'!" Old Man Clay snarled. "You were the one eggin' on my grandson to go down there 'n' see what's in there, right? So now—"

He cut himself short when they both heard a loud scraping sound echo from inside the tunnel. Chuckie's grip on the grate held, but his fingers were going numb, and he could feel himself starting to slip. His feet scrambled against the unyielding stone of the tunnel mouth, trying to find something to stand on. The effort was futile. Chuckie made an almost animal-like sound when the old man placed his foot on his head and stepped down, applying steady pressure.

"Yup," Old Man Clay said, smiling broadly. "I'd say they're definitely on their way."

Standing back, he cocked his foot up and then

brought it down hard onto Chuckie's hand. Yelping with pain, the boy reflexively let go and, with a short, ragged shout, he dropped out of sight. His cry echoed as it faded away to nothing.

Old Man Clay moved quickly. Bending down stiffly, he grabbed the hinged grate and swung it back over the opening. It clanged shut just as another faint scream echoed from down below. A loud scrambling sound was followed by a burst of angry chattering noise. The distant sound of Chuckie's scream rose shrilly for a moment and then cut off abruptly. As Old Man Clay held the grate down with his full weight and fumbled the lock back into place, the only sound that came from down below was a smacking, wet, chewing sound.

Once the grate was locked shut, Old Man Clay stood up slowly and brushed his hands on the seat of his pants. A smile creased the corners of his mouth as he stared for a moment at the iron grate. Then, nodding with satisfaction, he quickly scuffed out the marks Chuckie had made in the dirt floor before heading back up to the house.

"Well, then," he said softly to himself, "he was a bit skinny, but I reckon that ought to keep them little devils satisfied for another five years." He snorted and wiped his mouth. "Leastways, I hope so."

The Birch Whistle
Chapter One

Spring, 1987

As Eric and Patty Strasser guided their bright yellow Old Town canoe into Cooking Pot Cove on the Saco River, Eric, who was sitting in the prow, noticed something swirling in the water ahead of them. At first he thought it might just be mud, stirred up from the riverbed by the current, but the closer they got to it, the reddish-brown tint looked more and more like blood in the water.

"Jesus Christ, will you look at that?" he said, glancing over his shoulder at his wife.

"What?" Patty asked.

The wide straw hat she was wearing shadowed her pale face. She cocked an eyebrow and regarded him with a sad, sour expression. Eric instantly read her frustration and, not wanting to bother or worry her, indicated the shore with a wide sweep of his hand.

"Why, at . . . at how beautiful this place is," he said grandly. "It's even nicer than Carmine described it, don't you think?"

"Umm—yeah. I suppose so," Patty said, forcing herself to smile as she stopped paddling and wiped the sweat from her forehead with the back of her arm.

Straight ahead was a short expanse of clean, nearly white sand, no more than fifty or seventy-five feet long. Bordering both ends of the beach like bookends on an empty shelf were large piles of boulders. Some of the stones looked as big and round as Volkswagens. Beyond the beach, the brooding forest, deep and green, rose up a steep embankment. Inside the sheltering cove, the water was calm, flat and black. It reflected the trees and cloudless blue sky like a dark, polished mirror. Birdsong filled the clear, late afternoon air.

"I just want to stop *paddling*," Patty said, her voice nearly breaking from exhaustion. She sighed deeply and let her paddle drag in the water behind her. "I have blisters the size of silver dollars on both palms, my shoulders are sunburned, and my back and shoulder muscles feel like hamburger."

Eric smiled sympathetically, then dipped his paddle into the water and gave it a solid stroke. The canoe glided smoothly toward the shore. As they passed through the swirling stain in the water, his eyes darted downward, but he kept his thoughts to himself—even when he lifted his paddle and saw it dripping with a thin, red wash.

"Full speed ahead," he called out as he leaned hard into the next stroke.

He could tell by the drag at the stern that Patty wasn't with him on it. Now that they were so close to where they were going to camp for the night, she was just too damned tired to do anything else. His paddle blade flashed golden in the lowering sun as he increased his pace, trying to gain more speed.

When the bottom of the canoe hissed up onto the sand, Eric shouted, "All right! We made it!" and shipped his paddle. Standing up, he braced himself with both hands on the gunwales. Before Patty could even lift her paddle out of the water, he leapt onto the shore and pulled the canoe further up onto the beach. The sand was warm, almost hot beneath his bare feet.

"There's still enough daylight left," he said. "I think we can take a bit of a break before we pitch the tent."

He held out his hand to assist Patty onto dry land. Once her feet were under her, he pulled her close and engulfed her with a tight, passionate embrace. His mouth sought hers, and they kissed on the beach, their tongues darting playfully into each other's mouth. When Eric's hand started to slide down her back to the curve of her hips, she broke the kiss off and quickly pulled away.

"Let's not get anything started, all right?" she said with a tight chuckle. She clasped her arms against herself and scanned the surrounding woods. A slight shiver shook her shoulders.

Eric shrugged and slapped his thighs with the flats of his hands. "Hey, who's going to notice?" he asked, all innocence. His spirits dropped when he saw the cloud descend behind his wife's eyes. "Come on, Patty," he said softly. "You can't let it get you down so much. It's been—how long?—over four months now. And the doctor said we can always try again. Real soon." He craned his neck back and rubbed his shoulder as he looked up at the clear vault of sky. "What better place to make a baby than right here, in good ole Mother Nature?"

"Speaking of Mother Nature, I think I hear her calling my name," Patty said.

Just a hint of a smile crossed her lips, and Eric smiled back at her, telling himself—at least for now—that was enough.

"Ladies' room's to the left, I believe, over by those rocks," he said, hitching his thumb in that direction. Keeping her eyes averted, Patty walked away slowly. Eric watched her until she disappeared behind one of the large boulders.

"No fair peeking," Patty shouted once she was out of sight.

"Ahh, come on!" he called out, laughing perhaps a bit too loudly at her joke. But he felt good, knowing that, although she wasn't exactly swinging from the trees, this weekend away—just the two of them—was definitely what she needed to help her finally get over losing the baby. It might have been easier, he told himself, if the miscarriage had happened sooner, during the first trimester, but with only a month to go . . . *Christ!* It was almost like losing a real person. Even though they had never gotten to know him, they had given the baby a name before the funeral.

While Patty was occupied, Eric figured he'd get busy unloading their camping gear from the canoe and choosing a tent site. He went back to the beached canoe, but just as he was reaching for the canvas bags that held their weekend supplies, a shrill scream echoed in the hollow of the cove.

Eric kicked up fans of sand as he dashed across the beach and around behind the boulder. He felt an immediate rush of relief when he saw Patty standing there, apparently unharmed; but as soon as he saw what she had found, cold terror tightened around his heart. He wanted to go over and hug her, reassure her, but for some reason, he didn't dare take his eyes off the twisted, black . . . *thing* lying on the ground in front of her. He knew it was dead—that much was obvious—but something about it gave him a queasy feeling of danger.

"You know what that looks like!" Patty shrieked, her hands covering the bottom half of her face. "You know what that looks like almost *exactly?*"

She was trembling, nearly hysterical, and looked almost pathetic standing there with her pants unsnapped and halfway down her legs, the Call of Nature all but forgotten. Her face was chalk white, and her eyes were near-perfect circles as she stared at the dark object lying facedown on the sand at the river's edge.

"I don't know what the hell it is," Eric said as a tight dryness gripped the back of his throat. "It looks to me like some kind of . . . of animal or something. It's dead, whatever it is."

Walking quickly to the fringe of woods, he picked up a long stick and, crouching low, cautiously approached the dead thing. Patty cowered back against the rock. As soon as he touched it, blackened skin flaked off and dropped like sprinkled pepper onto the sand.

"Looks to me like it's been burned or something," Eric said.

Patty's breath came in sharp, loud sips. Tears filled her eyes, blurring her vision as she watched Eric prod the dead thing. But even as she forced herself to look at it and tried to figure out with him what it was, she couldn't stop seeing it as anything other than the shriveled, purple, *dead* thing her own body had expelled a little over four months ago.

"That's no *animal!*" she said. Her voice rasped like metal against metal. "Look at the arms . . . and those *hands!*"

Eric tried to wedge the stick under one of the arms so he could lift it, but it kept sliding off the stick and hitting against the sand with a soft crinkling sound, like tissue paper being crumpled into a ball. At last he got the right angle, lifted the arm, and held it suspended in the air for a moment while he studied it. The arm was surprisingly heavy for its size. Lean, almost sticklike, it ended in a hand that was broad and flat, like a shovel tipped with curved, black claws. Eric's first impression was of a mole's forelegs, but this thing was the size of no mole *he* had ever heard of. Its entire body was caked with cracked, leathery, black skin that looked like the charred remains of a burned log. If it was any kind of animal, it looked like a mutated monkey or something.

Sighing deeply and shaking his head, Eric let the arm drop back onto the sand. Then, bracing his foot in the sand, he wiggled the stick under the creature's neck. After a bit of effort, he managed to prop it up and then roll it over onto its back. The thin arm flopped onto the sand, exposing a thin, compact chest, narrow hips, and long, knobby-jointed legs that ended in wide, flat feet that looked almost froglike.

But it was the thing's head—its head and face—that riveted Eric's attention. He had never seen anything like it anywhere. It was narrow and pointed at the snout, conical like a rat's with a sloping forehead and flared, pointed ears. Its eyes were closed, but Eric could tell by the bulges under both crisped eyelids that they were large orbs—certainly not the narrow slits of an overgrown mole or shrew that he had been expecting. Beneath the wide, lipless mouth, a row of long, narrow, pointed white teeth protruded, again reinforcing the impression of a rat's face. All in all, the creature looked to be about three feet tall. Eric knew damned well there were no rats *that* big in Maine or anywhere else!

"Beats the shit out of me," he said as he backed away from the creature. When he looked over at Patty and saw how close she was to breaking down completely, he tossed the stick aside and went to her. With a low whimper, she collapsed into his arms, her whole body stiffening.

"*It looks like my baby!*" she wailed, shaking violently as she buried her face in his chest and poured out her grief. "*It looks just like my little boy . . . my little baby who didn't live!*"

Chapter Two

"I think we should do something about it," Eric said. "We *have* to!"

He and Patty had worked for nearly an hour, unloading the canoe, setting up the tent, spreading out their sleeping bags, and establishing a fireplace between the tent and the water's edge. They were both too exhausted to start preparing supper right away, so they were sitting side by side in front of the tent. Eric was sipping a beer, and Patty was nursing a wine cooler as they held hands and watched the sun touch the lowering clouds on the horizon with an edge of vermilion fire.

From time to time, Patty's grip on Eric's hand tightened painfully, and he could tell what she was thinking, but she remained silent as she kept her gaze fixed straight ahead out across the rippling river. Her breathing shuddered, making her lungs sound like faulty bellows. As much as she tried not to let it happen, tears stung her eyes.

"I mean, we can't just leave it out here," Eric went on, pressing his point. "We don't even know what it is! We've got to do something about it! At least bring it back so someone can try to identify what the hell it is."

"I told you what I want you to do," Patty said, her voice low, no more than a whisper. "I want you to bury it. I never want to see it again because of what it . . . what it reminds me—"

Her voice choked off before she could finish, and she fell silent as she sniffed back her tears.

"But it's not like anything I've ever seen," Eric said.

He was trying to be sensitive to Patty's feeling, knowing that in some twisted way the dead thing *did* look a bit like an aborted or miscarried fetus, but whatever that creature was, it intrigued him.

"It's clearly some type of animal. As impossible as it may seem, I think it might be something scientists may not even know exists. What if it's never even been discovered . . . until now?"

When Patty eased her head around and looked at him, there was a cold, flat distance in her gaze that disturbed him. He knew that as much as she might be sitting here talking to him, a good part of her mind was dwelling on when she lost her baby four months ago.

"And anyway, what difference is it going to make?" Eric asked, suddenly rankled with anger. "I mean, for Christ's sake—I'll wrap the damned thing up in a blanket or something. You won't even have to look at it ever again, I promise!"

Patty's mouth opened, but no sound came out.

"I just think someone ought to take a look at it, is all," Eric went on. "I know it's all burned and deformed and all. It probably is just some dog or something—but . . . what if it's, like, a U.F.O. alien or something? Maybe one of their flying saucers crashed nearby."

Patty looked at him, her eyes betraying not even a trace of humor. "I said it before and I'll say it again," she said, her voice steady and measured. "I want you to take the spade and bury that . . . that thing." She shivered before wrapping her arms around herself. "God! I never want to see that thing—I don't even want to think about it! I just know it's going to give me nightmares!"

"Well—" Eric said, stiffening his shoulders. "I'm sorry, honey, but I'm not going to do that." He heaved himself to his feet, pausing to brush the sand off the seat of his pants. "I'm not about to leave something like this behind. It's too unusual." Looking down at her, he was stunned by the cold distance in her eyes. He turned and went down to the canoe to get the square of canvas ground cloth he hadn't bothered to put under the tent when he pitched it. "I'll wrap it up and stow it in the bow of the canoe. You can forget all about it. You won't even know it's there."

Chapter Three

Firelight flickered bright orange against the pressing night and underlit the draping branches of the nearby pine trees. A half-moon rode low in a sky dusted with diamond points of starlight. Blue light rippled on the water. The sheltered cove resounded with the snap and crackle of the campfire while, far off, the sounds of night birds, frogs, and crickets filled the darkness. Huddled in a sweater against the chill, Patty sat on the sand with her arms wrapped tightly around her legs.

"The trick of this," Eric said, "is to get the bark to slide easily."

He was sitting cross-legged in the sand, a nearly empty bottle of beer between his legs. He had a thin birch twig pressed between the palms of his hands and was rolling it vigorously back and forth. He paused repeatedly to check it and then, once he was satisfied, took his jackknife, cut a circle around one end of the twig, and slid the thin coat of bark down. After cutting an angled notch at one end of the twig, he held it between his thumb and forefinger and placed it on the edge of his lower lip.

"The other trick is that you have to blow *very* gently," he said.

After taking a shallow breath, he blew into the notched end. At first, there was just the hissing sound of his breath through his pursed lips, but as he worked the bark collar up and down, he eventually found the correct position and produced a high-pitched whistle. As he adjusted the bark collar slightly up, the sound rose up the register until it disappeared. Smiling with satisfaction, he held out the birch whistle and inspected it by the firelight.

"God damn, I haven't made one of these in years," he said. "Not one that actually worked, anyway."

"That hurt my ears," Patty said, rubbing the sides of her head with the flats of her hands.

"Yeah, that was the thing about these birch whistles," Eric said with a laugh. "When I was a kid, I always thought—you know, like those silent dog whistles they sell, that I could use one to call my dog, Bullet. But with every damned one of these I ever made, whenever I'd blow into it, my dog would start whining and yipping, and then he'd run away from me." He sighed softly as he took a swig of beer and stared into the flames of the campfire. Shaking his head sadly with the memory, he said, "Good old Bullet. I'll tell you, he was one hell of a dog."

Leaning forward, Eric held the birch whistle out to Patty. "Come on. Give it a try."

Patty took the whistle from him and raised it to her mouth. With Eric coaching her, she positioned the notched tip on the edge of her lower lip and slid the bark collar up and down. After several tries, she was still unable to produce any sound.

"It's making me dizzy," she said, shaking her head.

"I think you're blowing too hard into it. Just the tiniest little breath will make the sound. You must've whistled using a blade of grass or piece of paper between your thumbs, right? It's just like that, only you have to control your breath."

Patty tried it a few more times but still couldn't get any sound out of the birch whistle. Eric watched her as she worked at it, her face bright orange in the firelight. She seemed actually to be concentrating on it, giving it her best, but there was still a distant darkness, like a glazing of deep ice, in the depths of her brown eyes—a darkness he had never seen there before . . . at least not until four months ago. He also hadn't missed how, when they sat down around the campfire, she had positioned herself so she was looking away from the river and the beached canoe, as though just knowing that burned, shriveled, dead thing wrapped up in the canoe was too much of a reminder of other things—things she'd just as soon forget but couldn't.

Finally, in frustration, she handed the birch whistle back to Eric. He slipped it into his shirt pocket before leaning his head back and draining his beer. Glancing at his watch, he sighed and said, "Well, it's almost nine-thirty. What do you say we tuck in for the night?"

"Isn't it funny how it seems so much later?" Patty said. She twisted around where she sat, letting her gaze shift past the dark silhouette of the canoe to the silvery river beyond. The flowing water made a soft whispering sound in the night.

"That's how it is when you get back to a more natural sense of time. And speaking of time, we've got nothing but time, so maybe we could—you know, fool around a little." Eric arched his eyebrows in a wicked Jack Nicholson leer.

Patty scowled. Biting her lower lip, she shook her head and said, "Not tonight," hugged her shoulders, and shivered. "I dunno . . . I just don't feel—"

Her voice faded away as she looked back at her husband and saw the depth of genuine concern in his eyes. She stood up, went over to him, and, bending down, kissed him firmly on the mouth. His hands reached up for her, grasping her by the waist and pulling her down on top of him as he keeled backward onto the sand. They undressed each other slowly and made love on the sand with the campfire warming their skin with its soft orange glow. Half an hour later, satisfied, they slipped into their sleeping bags contented and drifted off to sleep.

Chapter Four

"What was that?"

Patty's voice hissed like tearing cloth in the dark confines of the tent as she reached out blindly and jiggled Eric's shoulder.

"What was what?"

"I think I heard something," she whispered as she kicked aside her sleeping bag and, on hands and knees, leaned over the dark lump that was her husband. "I think there's something down by the river, near the canoe."

Eric groaned and tried to sit up as his wife crawled over him toward the tent door. As quietly as possible, she started unzipping the fly screen.

"That zipper sounds like a mosquito farting," Eric said, snorting with suppressed laughter as he rolled onto his belly and army-crawled up to the tent opening beside his wife.

"Shush! Look . . . down by the river."

Side by side, they lay on their stomachs, staring out

at the night. The moon had set hours ago, and the campfire was nothing more than a small pile of glowing red coals. Above the jagged black line of the trees, the sky practically vibrated with dusty blue starlight. The beach sand glowed with an eerie phosphorescence. A light breeze and the faint murmur of the river were all they could hear.

"Maybe you were having a dream," Eric said, but then he cut himself off when he caught a shifting of motion beside the black hulk of the canoe. At first, he thought it was nothing more than a moving shadow, but his mind instantly asked him what could make a shadow shift in pitch darkness. A shiver danced lightly up his back between his shoulder blades as he peered toward the river. After a few seconds, he noticed more dark shapes moving around the canoe. Then he heard something scratch lightly against the metal side of the canoe.

"What the—"

"I told you," Patty whispered. Her breath was hot against his ear. "Something's trying to get into the canoe."

"Probably just a couple of raccoons or something," Eric whispered as he pulled himself up into a crouch. "They can smell the body of that thing we found and must think it's some kind of food."

He looked at Patty but in the darkness couldn't make out the expression on her face. When he looked back out at the canoe, though, he saw another one of the visitors move from the fringe of woods over to the canoe. As he tracked it, Eric could have sworn it looked like a small, deformed person. The chill tingling up his back got stronger.

"Wait a sec," he whispered. "I've got an idea." He

crawled to the back of the tent, rustled about in the darkness for a moment, and then, grunting with satisfaction, rejoined Patty at the front tent flap. Lying flat on his belly, he propped himself on his elbows and raised his hands to his mouth.

"You might want to block your ears," he said, and then, very gently, he started to blow into the birch whistle.

When the first, high-pitched note sounded, the effect was instantaneous and surprising. The canoe seemed to explode with activity as loud, squealing sounds filled the night. Several animals leapt out of the canoe, hit the beach sand running, and disappeared into the shadows under the trees and behind the boulders. They moved too fast for Eric to see clearly what they were, but within seconds the night was silent, and the beach was deserted as if they had never been there.

"You see? I told you this thing was good for scaring away animals."

"Yeah, sure," Patty said, her voice a trembling whisper, "but what *were* they? They didn't look like raccoons to me."

"Me either," Eric said, shrugging even though he knew the motion was wasted in the darkness of the tent. "But I can't see squat in the dark. They must have been raccoons, but they sounded more like foxes, judging by the way they yelped." He decided not to mention the one fleeting impression he'd had that at least one of the creatures had looked—well, almost like a monkey or a dwarf as it shambled across the beach. "I'd better check out the canoe, though, just to make sure they didn't—you know, ruin anything." He didn't specifically mention the twisted black thing they had found, knowing how much it might upset her.

He handed the slim whistle to her and then felt around in the darkness until he found the flashlight. Without bothering to put on his jeans, he ran the fly screen zipper all the way up and crawled out of the tent. The night air was cool on his skin, almost cold. He shivered but clenched his teeth so they wouldn't chatter. His breath made tiny puffs of steam that instantly dissolved into the darkness as he swung the light around the perimeter of the beach.

"What the fuck?" he muttered as he started slowly toward the canoe. In the circled beam of light, he could see dozens—hundreds—of tiny footprints crisscrossing the sand. Even to his untrained eye, they didn't look anything like raccoon or fox tracks. Hell! They looked almost like human footprints . . . tiny human footprints, as if a whole pack of kids had been out here playing after dark.

"Wha—what is it?" Patty called, her voice sounding even higher, tighter.

"Oh—nothing. Nothing at all," Eric replied. "Everything's cool."

He directed his flashlight into the bow of the canoe, shining it full on the canvas-wrapped body of whatever the hell that thing was. To his relief, he saw that the animals hadn't gotten to it. The canvas was still intact. When he trained the flashlight downward, he grunted with surprise to see dozens of fresh scratches on the side of the canoe. And these weren't little digs and dings from paddling too close to the shore. Some of the marks were a foot long and longer—deep furrows that had removed the yellow paint right down to the shiny metal surface.

"What the shit is this?" Eric whispered.

He was concentrating so intently on the damage to his canoe that he didn't hear the creatures approaching him from behind. In an instant of blinding panic, once it was too late, he sensed something—many somethings—rushing at him from the surrounding darkness. Patty's shrill scream ripped the night as he grabbed a canoe paddle and, crouching low, spun around just as more than a dozen small, compact bodies slammed into him from several directions at once. Low-throated, chattering noises mingled with the sound of clicking claws. The sounds reminded Eric crazily of swarming insects. With a strangled cry, he swung the paddle once, smiling grimly when he felt it crack solidly against one of the creature's heads. Before he could swing again, though, he fell to the ground, crushed beneath their massed weight. Within seconds, long, curved talons sank into him and tore him to bloody shreds. The last sound he made was a long, wavering, bubbly howl.

Chapter Four

Patty was too frightened to scream again as she crouched inside the tent, trembling with terror. She watched in horror as the seething dark mass of creatures overwhelmed her husband. A small corner of her mind was trying to convince her that this wasn't happening—that this couldn't be happening! It had to be all in her imagination! A dream or something. But she couldn't ignore for long the testimony of her own eyes and ears. After Eric's scream cut off, she heard raw, wet, ripping sounds and a stomach-churning crunching that could only be—

"Oh, God! No!"

—teeth crushing bone.

She tried not to think it, but she knew that those creatures out there were *eating* Eric. She didn't realize she was making a low, whimpering sound in the back of her throat until she saw first one, then several of the creatures turn their attention toward the tent.

They know I'm here! she thought as her blood turned to ice water. *And I'm next!*

She backed out of the doorway, her eyes flicking back and forth in the darkness, wondering frantically if there was something—anything—she could use as a weapon. Eric always brought along an axe and mallet on camping trips, but he had stored them away in the canoe after they had set up their campsite and chopped their firewood for the night. Suddenly she was aware that she was still holding on to the birch whistle, gripping it so tightly that the palm of her hand ached.

It was her only hope.

If she could just make a sound with it—enough to scare those things away—she might be able to keep them at bay long enough for her to get to the canoe and out onto the river.

She had to try.

Tears stung her eyes, blurring her vision as she crawled to the front of the tent. Her heart stopped beating for a frozen instant when, through the fly screen, she saw that the beach was deserted. Her hands were shaking wildly as she raised the whistle to her mouth, placed the notched end on the edge of her lower lip, and gripped the sliding birch bark collar with her thumb and forefinger. She was just inhaling to blow into it when both sides of the tent bulged inward. Loud, frenzied squeals filled the night as razor-sharp claws ripped down through the fabric, splitting the tent wide open. Howling crazily, the creatures poured into the tent, slashing and scrambling wildly. Before they could snag her and press her down, though, Patty kicked free of the tangles and propelled herself out into the night.

Still clutching the birch whistle, she ran down the beach toward the canoe. The sand dragged at her feet.

With every other step, she stumbled and almost fell, but she forced herself to keep going, knowing that the canoe was her only hope—as long as those damned creatures couldn't swim!

Her ears filled with the frenzied sounds of the creatures shredding the tent. She knew it was a matter of seconds before they came after her, caught her, dragged her down, and ate her, too. She ran, lurching toward the canoe, her eyes fixed on the dark, motionless lump lying in the sand next to the broken canoe paddle. Through her terror, she tried to convince herself that this wasn't Eric.

It couldn't be!

It looked as though large pieces of him were . . . missing. She wanted to scream, but the night air filled her lungs like flames, searing off any sound she might have made.

She reached the canoe, stumbled, and banged her knees hard against the side. The impact made a resounding gong. She shouted as pain lanced like a bolt of electricity up to her hips. When she glanced down and saw the twisted tangle of black, glistening meat that seconds before had been her husband, she nearly fainted. Then the sudden barking yelp of one of the creatures behind her snapped her back to attention.

They were coming after her.

Digging her feet into the sand, she grunted loudly as she leaned against the bow of the canoe and frantically pushed to get it off the shore. For a terrifying instant, the canoe felt like it was stuck there. Then, grating loudly on the sand, it started to slide into the water. Her teeth chattered wildly as she waded into the cold river, guiding the boat away from the shore. Once she was knee-deep, she glanced back and saw that the creatures had drawn to an abrupt halt at the water's edge. She almost laughed out loud as she dove face-first into the canoe and grabbed the one remaining paddle.

"There, you bastards!" she shrieked.

Nearly hysterical, she tossed her head back and let loose a wild burst of shrill laughter.

"You won't get me!"

She got down onto one knee and began furiously chopping the water with the flat side of the paddle. Fans of silvery spray flew high into the night sky, but she was so lost in her fear that she didn't realize what little distance she was actually putting between herself and the shore. The full impact of what had happened still hadn't hit her. All she knew, all she could admit at this point was, Eric was dead! Killed by those things!

Massing on the shore, the creatures barked and gibbered in a frenzied pack as Patty's wild paddling gradually brought her further away from the shore. One or two of the creatures approached the water's edge, but as soon as they touched it, they howled and pulled back onto the beach. With only the faint glow of starlight to see by, it was impossible for Patty to see clearly what these creatures were as they howled their anger.

"Yeah, well, *fuck* you!" she cried. *"Fuck you all!"*

Tears coursed down her face, and violent tremors rippled through her body. She kept slapping the water, unmindful of her progress as the canoe darted wildly back and forth until it finally drifted out of the cove and into the open river. Realizing she was safe, she allowed a measure of relief to flood through her, but she didn't dare to stop paddling. Once she was floating along with the sluggish current close to shore, she noticed that, in spite of everything, she was still holding on to Eric's birch whistle. She sat forward and slid it into her jeans pocket, then continued paddling wildly. She didn't notice the drifting log in the darkness until she slammed it with the paddle. The sudden shock sent the paddle flying from her grip. It landed with a loud smack far out in the water, where it was caught up and swept away by the faster current.

"No! No!" Patty screamed, wanting to cry as she watched the paddle float away from her. Fear, cold and bright, gripped her when she looked around and saw that she was now drifting toward the shore. Cupping her hands, she leaned forward from the stern and started paddling furiously. The water was so cold it numbed her arms up to the shoulders. She realized the true extent of her danger when she saw several dark, slouched forms moving silently through the woods, tracking her agonizingly slow progress along the shore as she drifted closer and closer to land.

This can't be happening! her mind screamed as the canoe glided closer and closer to the wooded riverbank. She couldn't hear the creatures above the splashing sounds she was making, but her eyes were riveted on the woods where their black shadows mingled with the twisted shadows of low-hanging branches. Even redoubling her paddling efforts didn't seem to help. The canoe was gliding steadily closer to the shore as if in the grip of a powerful, relentless magnet.

Before long, the dark shoreline was seething with the creatures that were following along beside her. Patty wasn't even aware that she was crying hysterically as she leaned forward and slapped the water with both hands. She expected at any moment to hear the canoe grind against the river bottom and knew that, when that happened, it wouldn't be long before she felt the stinging slash of their claws and teeth.

Barely realizing what she was doing, she sat up and fished the birch whistle out of her jeans pocket. She brought it up to her mouth, took a deep breath, and blew hard into it. The only sound she produced was the shrill hissing of her own breath. Eric's words echoed in her mind—

You're blowing too hard into it . . . Just the tiniest little breath will make the sound.

But Patty was so panicked now she was close to fainting. There was no way she could stop the raw panting of her breath or the trembling that shook her body. No matter how hard she tried, she couldn't blow gently enough to produce the sound that she knew would keep these creatures at bay.

"Please . . . *please*," she whimpered, fighting hard to control her shaking hands.

"Just one little note . . . please . . . just one little note!"

But the canoe was drifting steadily closer to the wooded shore, and she could see the creatures waiting for her there. When she was no more than six feet from the shore, a sudden inspiration hit her. The sudden motion almost flipped the canoe over as she lurched to the bow of the canoe and grabbed the canvas-wrapped figure. Struggling to stand up and not lose her balance, she faced the creatures that were massed on the shore.

"Is this what you want?" she shouted.

Nausea and fear filled her stomach with sour acid as she wondered how in the hell she could ever have thought that her baby—*her poor, lost baby boy*—had looked even a tiny bit like this—this monstrosity. Spreading her feet for balance, she began to swing the canvas-wrapped body back and forth to gain momentum.

"One . . . two . . . three!" she counted in cadence.

On three, she let go. Tumbling end over end, the package and its terrible contents sailed through the air. She didn't see where it landed in the woods, but she heard it hit the ground with a sickening thump.

"Take it!" she shrieked. *"There! Are you satisfied?"*

In answer, she heard a rising chorus of ghastly shrieks and squeals that made her think of a pack of rabid dogs. But she knew that these things weren't even close to dogs. Even if the one she and Eric had found washed up on the shore had been damaged or burned somehow, these creatures were what Eric had said they were—some horrible mutation, a terrible abomination of nature.

As the canoe drifted under the overhanging branches of a large pine tree, Patty was satisfied that her plan had worked. Maybe all they had wanted was the body of their dead companion. But a rustling sound in the trees overhead quickly drew her attention, and she looked up into the night-black network of branches just in time to see several dark shapes moving above her. With low, terrifying growls, they dropped down onto her and within seconds their claws sliced her to bloody tatters. Moments later, her lifeless body was thrown on to the shore, where dozens more of the hideous creatures piled down on top of her and began to feed.

While this was happening, an Old Town canoe with blood streaking its sleek yellow sides was caught up in the swift current and swept downstream under the moonless, star-filled sky. Trailing behind it, spinning around in the swirling, bloodstained water, was a tiny slip of a birch branch with a small notch cut into one end.

THE BEAST THAT WAS MAX

Gerard Houarner

Max walks in the borderland between the world of shadowy government conspiracy and the world of vengeful ghosts and evil gods, between living flesh and supernatural. For Max is the ultimate killer, an assassin powered by the Beast, an inner demon that enables him to kill—and to do it incredibly well. But the Beast inside Max is very real and very much alive. He is all of Max's dark desires, his murderous impulses, and he won't ever let Max forget that he exists. The Beast *is* Max. So it won't be easy for Max to silence the Beast, though he knows that is what he must do to reclaim his humanity. But without the protection of the Beast, Max the assassin will soon find himself the prey, the target of the spirits of his past victims.

___4881-7 $5.99 US/$6.99 CAN

Dorchester Publishing Co., Inc.
P.O. Box 6640
Wayne, PA 19087-8640

Please add $2.50 for shipping and handling for the first book and $.75 for each book thereafter. NY, NYC, and PA residents, please add appropriate sales tax. No cash, stamps, or C.O.D.s. All orders shipped within 6 weeks via postal service book rate.
Canadian orders require $2.50 extra postage and must be paid in U.S. dollars through a U.S. banking facility.

Name____
Address____
City_______________________State_______Zip__________
I have enclosed $ ___________ in payment for the checked book(s).
Payment <u>must</u> accompany all orders. ☐ Please send a free catalog.
CHECK OUT OUR WEBSITE! www.dorchesterpub.com